RĀMĀYANA UNRAVELLED

RĀMĀYANA UNRAVELLED

Lesser-Known Facets of Rishi Vālmiki's Epic

AMI GANATRA

BLOOMSBURY

NEW DELHI • LONDON • OXFORD • NEW YORK • SYDNEY

BLOOMSBURY INDIA
Bloomsbury Publishing India Pvt. Ltd
Second Floor, LSC Building No. 4, DDA Complex, Pocket C – 6 & 7,
Vasant Kunj, New Delhi, 110070

BLOOMSBURY, BLOOMSBURY INDIA and the Diana logo
are trademarks of Bloomsbury Publishing Plc

First published in India 2022
This edition published 2022

ISBN: PB: 978-93-54353-32-1; eBook: 978-93-54356-57-5

15 14 13 12 11

Typeset in Adobe Caslon Pro by Manipal Technologies Limited
Printed and bound in India Gopsons Papers Pvt. Ltd.

ॐ

श्रीरामचन्द्रचरणौ मनसा स्मरामि ।
श्रीरामचन्द्रचरणौ वचसा गृणामि ।
श्रीरामचन्द्रचरणौ शिरसा नमामि ।
श्रीरामचन्द्रचरणौ शरणं प्रपद्ये ॥

CONTENTS

Acknowledgements ix
Introduction xi
Summary Storyline xxv

PART 1: CONTEXT AND SETTINGS

1 The Divine Inspiration 3
2 Bloodlines 10
3 Cities and City Life in the Rāmāyana 23

PART 2: PERSONALITIES, EVENTS AND EVENTUALITIES

4 Vishvāmitra's Quest 33
5 The Making of Vishvāmitra 47
6 Ahalyā 58
7 The Descent of Gangā 63
8 A Twist of Fate 69
9 Sahadharmachārini 105
10 Kinship in Kishkindhā 149
11 Vāyuputra 185

12 The Trap of Lust 218
13 The Difficulty of Being Good 243
14 Soumitri 259
15 Rāmo Vigrahavān Dharma 275
16 Rāma's Rājya 294

PART 3: EPILOGUE

17 A Short Note on the Approach to Understanding Itihāsa 305
18 Shambuka Vadha 307
19 Forsaken 311

Notes 323
Also from the Author 339

ACKNOWLEDGEMENTS

I bow to Rishi Vālmiki and all Rāma bhaktas who have kept the flame of Rāma nāma burning in the Indian consciousness.

I express my heartfelt gratitude to my weekend reading group for giving me the opportunity to dive deep into the Rāmāyana swādhyāya and for the churn of thoughts the group discussions helped create.

I will remain ever grateful to Ajay Dave and Vikram Abhishek Mall for taking the time to go through the drafts and providing valuable inputs; to the team at Bloomsbury—Nitin Valecha, Sanjiv Sarin and Syed Dilshad Ali—for bringing the book to life; to Hitharth Bhatt for the beautiful sketch of Shri Rāma; to J.Sai Deepak (JSD) and my brother Sagar Ganatra for being a constant source of encouragement and motivation.

I also extend my gratitude to all the readers who wholeheartedly accepted and appreciated my first book *Mahābhārata Unravelled: Lesser-Known Facets of a Well-Known History*, thus motivating me to attempt *Rāmāyana Unravelled: Lesser-Known Facets of Rishi Vālmiki's Epic.*

To Praveen Tiwari, I can never offer enough thanks. I owe my foray into book writing to him.

What to say of Maa, Kavita Ganatra; I am what I am because she is what she is.

And lastly, I owe it all to my Kanha. He wills, He makes it happen!

श्रीकृष्णार्पणमस्तु!

Introduction

No epic has moved the consciousness of a billion people like the Rāmāyana has. No person has invoked the kind of emotions in a billion people like Rāma has. Ushering in Rāma Rājya has been a romantic ideal cherished by us Bhāratiyas since times immemorial. In the times of Mughal atrocities, when no cloud seemed to have a silver lining, the story of Rāma narrated by our saints kept us going. It was the promise of Rāma Rājya that rallied people behind Mahātmā Gāndhi in the struggle against the British for independence. When Yudhishthira was in vanvās, he was upset about destiny dealing him a raw hand. Rishi Mārkandeya narrated to him the story of Rāma, giving him hope that courage and perseverance will see him through the tough times.

Rāma is an ideal son, a great friend, a king like no other, who, like most of us, had to undergo numerous trials and tribulations in life. But unlike most of us, he doesn't crib or complain; he toils through the challenges thrown at him by life and emerges victorious due to his valour, skill and resilience. The story of Rāma's life has found resonance with people across the length and breadth of Bhāratavarsha. So much so that wherever the people of this land went, they took Rāma with them—be it to Southeast Asia more than a thousand years ago, or to the Caribbean, around two hundred years ago.

In Thailand, the kings are referred to as Rāma to this day. One of the provinces of Thailand is Ayutthayā, in memory of Ayodhyā. In Jāvā and Bāli, folk culture and folk art have been significantly influenced by stories from the Rāmāyana. Performances based on the Rāmāyana continue to enthral Indonesians even today. In the islands of the Caribbean, people chanting Rāmcharitmānas and Hanumāna Chalisā are a common sight.

The appeal of the Rāmāyana is such that from the North to the South and from the East to the West, it has caught the imagination of innumerable poets and authors, and this is by no means a recent phenomenon. From Jain scholars to Bhavabhuti and Kamban to Goswāmi Tulsidās, many more have retold the story of the Rāmāyana in their own language, infusing their own unique flavour.

In fact, this prolificity has led to confusion about the 'original' Rāmāyana. A.K. Rāmanujan's essay 'Three Hundred Rāmāyanas' sparked a debate about whether there was an original Rāmāyana at all. While most of the versions have a similar core storyline, differing only in some incidents and details, some retellings deviate significantly in their depiction of the characters and the relationships between them.

Some scholars wedded to particular ideologies argue that every version and retelling is equally valid. This stance is illogical because the Rāmāyana is not just another story. It is our itihāsa, the history of our ancestors. Saying that anything goes and everything is acceptable suggests that anyone can make any story out of the characters of the Rāmāyana and present it as their version of history, a trend that has been on the rise in recent times.

While itihāsa literally translates to history, it has a much broader and deeper significance. By way of narrating the life of our ancestors to us, the objective of our rishis was to instruct us in the purushārthas of dharma, artha, kāma and moksha—the building blocks of Sanātana Dharma—which are the key to living a worthwhile and fruitful life. Thus, for us to imbibe the intended lessons, knowing the itihāsa for what it is becomes extremely important.

The question then is—how do we decide which rendering is the original Rāmāyana?

The noted Sanskrit scholar Shatāvdhani Dr R. Ganesh has written an excellent rebuttal to this controversy of multiple Rāmāyanas in his Kannadā essay 'Behind the Mask of the Three Hundred Rāmāyanas' translated into English by Sandeep Bālakrishnan. He categorically states, giving references:

> There has been widespread and intense debate over A.K. Rāmanujan's essay titled 300 Rāmāyanas in the media. These debates are nothing new for the Rāmāyana scholars. The Shatakotipravistara—that is, the long, uncountable list of various Rāmāyanas have been subject to extensive discussions and debates in our Itihāsa and Puranas over thousands of years. However, what was indisputably upheld was the fact that all Indian traditions traced their Rāmāyana retelling, studies, interpretations, and scholarship to Vālmiki, and not to any other source.

Among other things, Dr Ganesh also shows that most latter-day poets, both of Sanskrit and of regional languages, have expressed their reverence for Rishi Vālmiki, leaving no doubt about the 'original version', which is Rishi Vālmiki's Rāmāyana. Hence, for *Rāmāyana Unravelled*, I have used the Sanskrit–Hindi Vālmiki Rāmāyana published by Gita Press, Gorakhpur, as the key reference text along with translations available at https://www.valmikiramayan.net/ and https://www.valmiki.iitk.ac.in/. In addition, I have also referred to the Oriental Institute, Baroda's critical edition of the Vālmiki Rāmāyana, as needed.

But when there is so much written on the Rāmāyana, why add to the crowd with one more book?

During discussions related to the Rāmāyana, it is not rare to hear comments like:

> Rāma's ideals are not for this day and age. One must rather follow Krishna.
>
> I find it very difficult to relate to Rāma; he seems too rigid.
>
> I can't come to terms with what Rāma did with Seetā; it just wasn't fair.

These comments are often made by well-meaning people who are otherwise very rooted in Hindu culture. Such sentiments are increasingly common among youngsters today.

I have also seen many prominent kathāvāchakas speak about the dichotomy of Rāma and Krishna, usually in the context of 'end doesn't justify means' for Rāma and 'end justifies means' for Krishna. Often, the conclusion of such discourses is that Krishna is ready to break a rule at the first available opportunity but Rāma will not budge, come what may, almost bordering on obstinacy. Such conclusions are not only overly simplistic and unfair to both the Vishnu avatārs, but they are also completely wrong. Both Rāma and Krishna strove to establish and live by dharma. They did what was needed to ensure adharma was destroyed and dharma prevailed by setting the right examples for the sustenance of the society. Their personalities were different, but not their value systems and, least of all, their understanding of dharma.

I started my previous book, *Mahābhārata Unravelled: Lesser-Known Facets of a Well-Known History*, with the chapter 'What Is Dharma?' Hence, I will refrain from repeating it here. But in short, dharma refers to the overarching principle that leads to the sustainability of society. In practice, it is a broad term that could mean duty, responsibility, virtue, righteousness, probity and/or religion, as per the context. Adharma is the exact opposite—that which leads to unsustainability and destruction.

I must confess I too was culpable and carried such inferences before I decided to read the itihāsa for myself, inspired by the lectures of Professor B. Mahadevan of the Indian Institute of Management, Bengaluru. I realised that just like the Mahābhārata, a lot of what we think we know about the Rāmāyana is based on writings/interpretations/retellings rather than what Rishi Vālmiki, a contemporary of Shri Rāma, has narrated to us.

Moreover, many contemporary writings on the Rāmāyana have not been written to understand the itihāsa and learn from it. Rather, these works seem inclined to impose their own narratives on society, making it all about class, gender and race conflicts. According to these stories, Rāma killed Rāvana not because of the latter's terrible deeds but because of the differences in their races. Shurpanakhā was punished by Lakshmana not because she tried to harm Seetā, but because of Lakshmana's misogynist tendencies.

While anyone is free to take creative liberties in writing fiction (and may that genre grow), it becomes important to remind ourselves of what the actual itihāsa is, time and again, especially when fiction starts setting the tone of the social narrative for a civilisation as ancient as ours.

There are also other retellings seeped in the Bhakti rasa. Here, Rāma is the ishta, the beloved lord of the poet. Every word that the poet writes is so full of bhāva and shraddhā that it enraptures the readers and listeners, drawing them into a sea of emotions of love and longing, becoming sad in Rāma's sorrow, happy in his joy. In such retellings, Rāma is an epitome of stoicism, love, empathy and magnanimity, unmoved and unaffected even by the most challenging of situations. Goswāmi Tulsidās's Rāmacharitmānas is one such beautiful rendering. No wonder it continues to be one of the most popular renditions of the Rāmāyana in Hindu households.

In Rishi Vālmiki's Rāmāyana too, Rāma is undoubtedly of divine birth, an avatār of Vishnu himself. But his personality is more human, undergoing the full range of human emotions including despair, disappointment and anger. What makes him special is his mental strength, clarity of thought, strength of character, resilience in the face of challenges and, most important, his understanding of dharma and swadharma. While he feels all emotions and deeply so, his decision-making is not sullied by personal emotions, biases or short-term gratifications, even when experiencing extreme despair.

What appeals to me the most in Vālmiki Rāmāyana is the insight into Shri Rāma's decision-making, be it about accepting vanvās, taking a call not to return when Bharata comes calling, punishing Vāli, inducting Vibhishana and even provoking Seetā to perform agni parikshā. If we can cultivate even a small fraction of his clarity and objectivity in thought, we are bound to make better decisions. This aspect of Rāma needs more focus and discussion. I hope I have been able to bring that out in the book. That, at least, has been my intention.

And beyond the key events of Rāma's life, there is so much to learn from the Rāmāyana—Vishvāmitra's penance, Hanumāna's wit, Seetā's grit, Lakshmana's unfailing support, Vibhishana's sense of right, Shurpanakhā's deceit, Rāvana's call for his own downfall and much more—that I firmly believe it is necessary to revisit the Rāmāyana as narrated to us by Rishi Vālmiki to develop a better perspective towards our own lives.

Some questions that I aim to clarify through the book are:

- What lessons from his growing-up years shaped Rāma's values as a king? Why did Rāma agree to go to vanvās—was it only to obey his father or was there more to it?
- Was Lakshmana an angry young man as he is thought to be usually, or is there more depth to his character?
- How was the relationship between Rāma and Seetā? Was Seetā a pitiable, oppressed woman or an assertive woman with a mind of her own?
- What led to the downfall of Rāvana? Did he refrain from forcing himself on Seetā because he cared for her consent? Did he abduct Seetā to avenge his sister?
- How was the Nala Setu built? Was it a miracle of floating stones as it is thought to be or was it an engineering marvel?
- What is the real story of Ahalyā? Was she really a stone—what is her story in the Rāmāyana?
- Is the Rāmāyana inherently misogynist or quite the opposite, considering the characters of Seetā, Shurpanakhā, Kaikeyi, Tārā?
- Why does Krishna say in the Srimad Bhagavad Geetā that 'among the warriors, I am Rāma'?

... and many such questions.

In this book, to convey the right pronunciation of names while keeping the text simple to read, I have used only the diacritic ā in Sanskrit nouns and names that have an 'aa' (आ) sound. The names ending in 'a' without the diacritic must be read as अ.

The book is structured in three parts. The first part sets the context of the story, describing the lineages and kingdoms mentioned in the Rāmāyana. It begins with the events that led to the composition of the Rāmāyana by Rishi Vālmiki. The second part has chapters narrating either the key events that shaped the course of Rāma and Seetā's lives or stories bringing out the personalities and relationship dynamics of the different characters.

In these stories, more than the events per se, which are commonly known, my focus has been on the details of how and why certain people acted in a certain way or made certain decisions. For example, it is not news to anyone that Hanumāna located Seetā in Lankā. But what was of more interest to me were the thoughts going on in Hanumāna's mind while he was searching for her: what made him approach Seetā the way he did, or what were the reasons Seetā gave for choosing to wait for Rāma to come to Lankā rather than escape with Hanumāna? Or take another instance—that Rāma accepted vanvās is a well-known fact, but rarely discussed are the reasons he gives to Lakshmana for his decision. In such details lie the essence of the Rāmāyana and the brilliance of Rishi Vālmiki.

The chapters are not in chronological order and hence there is some repetition of events. My attempt has been to keep it to a minimum. Where repetition was necessary for completing the individual story, I have tried to summarise the events briefly, except in the chapters 'Soumitri' and 'Rāmo Vigrahavān Dharma' in the second section. These chapters are meant to bring together all the aspects of Lakshmana's and

Rāma's personalities, glimpses of which the readers get in the preceding chapters. The repetition in these chapters is intended.

The third section is Epilogue. It contains write-ups on two events that occur in Uttara Kānda of Vālmiki Rāmāyana, which are often cited to dismiss the entire Rāmāyana as a casteist and misogynist text. Until the third section, my attempt has been to bring out events from Vālmiki Rāmāyana as is, without adding my own perceptions and opinions, while taking the liberty to summarise dialogues and contextualise events as necessary. In the third section, however, I narrate the events and also share my views about them. My own understanding is evolving; hence I do not claim that this is the only way to understand the events. Rather, the idea is to trigger further thought than settle for a simplistic interpretation.

This brings up another important question—is Uttara Kānda an integral part of the original Rāmāyana at all?

There are seven sections in Vālmiki Rāmāyana namely, Bāla Kānda, Ayodhyā Kānda, Aranya Kānda, Kishkindhā Kānda, Sundara Kānda, Yuddha Kānda and Uttara Kānda. From Bāla Kānda to Yuddha Kānda is the main plot of the Rāmāyana, right from the birth of the four brothers to Rāma's coronation after killing Rāvana and returning from fourteen years of vanvās.

Uttara Kānda has incidents that happened after Rāma's coronation. It has the two most controversial events of the Rāmāyana—the abandonment of pregnant Seetā and the killing of Shambuka. Rāma's actions in both these situations seem uncharacteristic of him and, on the face of it, even unfair.

However, this kānda also has many interesting stories which were alluded to in the previous kāndas but not narrated in any detail. For example, the particulars of birth and lineage of Rāvana, the boons given to him and his brothers, as well as the various curses pronounced on Rāvana, while mentioned briefly in the previous kāndas, find better enumeration in Uttara Kānda. The story of Dashagreeva becoming Rāvana is also present in this kānda. In a way, Uttara Kānda reads like an addendum to the previous sections.

Scholars of the Rāmāyana are split over the question of the authenticity of Uttara Kānda. There are very pertinent arguments both in favour and against. While the verdict is yet to be pronounced, both the Baroda critical edition and the Gita Press edition of Vālmiki Rāmāyana have Uttara Kānda included in them. Hence, for this book, I have taken interesting stories from Uttara Kānda as relevant and mentioned them in the notes. And the two controversial events—I have added them separately in the Epilogue.

Once we read the itihāsa for what it is, how we analyse and take learnings from it eventually boils down to our own worldview and shraddhā. But to judge a scripture of such prominence and a personality as tall as Rāma based on an incident or two, driven by the limitation of our own contextual understanding, is incorrect. An honest analysis should take into account the overall context, including the past and present behaviour, not just a single event in isolation.

That is not to say that anyone or anything is beyond questioning. Societies are defined by the heroes they look up to. Hence, heroes cannot be and should not be beyond critical enquiry. As society evolves, heroes have to be put through a critical gaze to examine their relevance. This also helps society redefine and recalibrate its value systems. But let the critical enquiry happen with genuine curiosity to learn and evolve rather than out of an urge to dismiss. Not for the sake of Rāma—his tale has survived the scrutiny of thousands of years—but to expand our own frontiers of perception and put the right paradigms in place for ourselves and our society.

Studying Vālmiki Rāmāyana has been an emotionally enriching journey for me. It is nothing but देवानुग्रह to get this opportunity to write a book on the Rāmāyana. Now I know and fully understand why a citizen of Ayodhyā calls Rāma 'रामो लोकाभिरामो'—'Rāma enchants the world'. Once we know Rāma deeply, we cannot but be enchanted by him, and by his story in the Rāmāyana. This story of one of our greatest ancestors will continue to evoke interest and our deepest emotions for centuries to come. Such was also Brahma deva's pronouncement regarding the Rāmāyana as he inspired Rishi Vālmiki to compose it. Brahma deva had said:

यावत् स्थास्यन्ति गिरयस्सरितश्च महीतले ।
तावद्रामायणकथा लोकेषु प्रचरिष्यति ॥

> As long as the mountains stand and rivers flow on earth, this story of Rāma will flourish in the world.[1]

My own wish and hope for the book are that it inspires readers to read the Vālmiki Rāmāyana in the original.

An appeal to the readers—please bring to my notice any typos or errors that may have been overlooked. They will be corrected in the subsequent editions.

Siyāvar Rāmchandra ki jai!
Pavansuta Hanumāna ki jai!

Summary Storyline

The Birth (Bāla Kānda)

- King Dasharatha, a scion of the Ikshvāku dynasty, was a popular monarch of Kosala. From the capital city of Ayodhyā, he held sway over the entire Bhāratavarsha.
- His subjects loved him. His contemporary kings swore allegiance to him.
- He had three wives—Kaushalyā, Kaikeyi and Sumitrā, but no progeny who could carry forward the Ikshvāku lineage.
- To beget a successor Dasharatha called upon Rishi Rishyashringa to conduct the Ashwamedha and Putreshti yajnas.
- The ritual bore fruit and four sons were born to the queens—Rāma to Kaushalyā, Bharata to Kaikeyi and twins Lakshmana and Shatrughna to Sumitrā.
- Under the able guidance of Rishi Vashishtha, who was also the royal priest, the boys were educated in scriptures and warfare.
- Dasharatha loved all his sons but his ātmā resided in Rāma. This eldest son of Dasharatha was exceptionally mature and virtuous.

The Marriage (Bāla Kānda)

- One day, when Rāma was just a little under sixteen years of age, Rishi Vishvāmitra came to

Dasharatha's court. Two rākshasas—Subāhu and Māreecha—were obstructing his yajna sankalpa.[1] He wished to take Rāma to his āshram to guard his rituals and keep the rākshasas at bay.

- After initial reluctance, Dasharatha sent both Rāma and Lakshmana with Rishi Vishvāmitra.
- Guarded by the young princes, Vishvāmitra completed his yajna successfully.
- Then, along with Rāma and Lakshmana, Vishvāmitra went to Mithilā, the capital of Videha, to participate in the grand yajna organised by King Janaka.
- Janaka had in his possession a precious heirloom, the bow of Shiva—the Shiva Dhanush. He had resolved to marry his daughter Seetā only to the prince who could string the Shiva Dhanush successfully.
- Many kings, desirous of Seetā's hand in marriage, tried to string the bow but failed. Rāma succeeded in stringing Shiva's bow, but he also managed to break it.
- Janaka arranged the wedding of Seetā and Rāma. He also married his younger daughter Urmilā to Lakshmana and the daughters of his younger brother Kushadhwaja—Māndavi and Shrutakirti—to Bharata and Shatrughna respectively.
- The newly-weds returned to Ayodhyā.
- Rāma–Seetā and Lakshmana–Urmilā spent a few blissful years in Ayodhyā.
- Bharata and Shatrughna went to the Kekaya kingdom to spend time with Bharata's maternal side of the family.

The Banishment (Ayodhyā Kānda)

- A few years later, in consultation with his ministers and citizens, Dasharatha announced Rāma as the successor to the throne of Ayodhyā. Coronation was scheduled immediately, on the next day itself.
- The news ruffled Mantharā, an old and loyal handmaiden of Kaikeyi. She misled Kaikeyi into believing that the coronation of Rāma would spell doom for her only son, Bharata. Mantharā's provocations rattled Kaikeyi.
- Dasharatha had granted Kaikeyi two boons in the past for saving his life on a battlefield. She decided to put them to use to seek Bharata's coronation and Rāma's vanvās—banishment to the forest—for fourteen years.
- Dasharatha was left aghast at Kaikeyi's demands but was helpless and gave in.
- On learning about Kaikeyi's wishes and his father's situation, Rāma accepted the fourteen years of forest stay and prepared to leave immediately. Seetā and Lakshmana accompanied him.
- As directed by Rishi Bharadwāja, the three of them spent the first year of their vanvās in Chitrakoot.

Death of Dasharatha (Ayodhyā Kānda)

- Rāma's departure took a huge toll on Dasharatha. He died soon after.
- Bharata and Shatrughna were called back to Ayodhyā to perform the last rites of their deceased father.
- Bharata was extremely embarrassed and angry on learning about the havoc caused by his mother in

the royal household. He rebuked his mother and refused the throne of Ayodhyā.

- After performing the last rites of his father, Bharata headed to Chitrakoot to bring Rāma back and get him crowned the king. Bharata also informed Rāma about Dasharatha's death.
- Rāma remained firm in his resolve to live in vanvās for fourteen years as he had promised his father.
- Finally, Bharata declared that he would manage the affairs of the kingdom for the next fourteen years, not as the king but as a custodian of Rāma. He took Rāma's pādukā (sandals) and carried them on his head to show the intention and intensity of his resolve.
- Once back in Ayodhyā, Bharata gave up the palace and its luxuries and went to live in an āshram in Nandigrām, outside the city. He managed the affairs of the kingdom from Nandigrām in the name of Rāma.
- After spending a year in Chitrakoot, Rāma, Lakshmana and Seetā headed further south to Dandakāranya.

Dandakāranya Days (Aranya Kānda)

- Learning about their arrival in Dandakāranya, some rishis approached Rāma to seek his protection from the menace of the rākshasas in the forest. The rākshasas, under the patronage of Rāvana, would interrupt the rituals of the rishis, destroy their āshrams and even eat them up.
- Rāma, Lakshmana and Seetā spent the next ten years travelling in the forest. They stayed in the

āshrams of different rishis and protected them from the rākshasas.

- In the eleventh year, on Rishi Agastya's advice, they went to Panchavati in Janasthāna to spend the remaining days of the vanvās. En route to Panchavati, they met Jatāyu, who introduced himself as Dasharatha's friend.
- One day Shurpanakhā, Rāvana's sister, set her eyes on the handsome princes of Ayodhyā. She approached them for marriage, but Rāma and Lakshmana rejected her advances.
- Blaming Seetā for her rejection, Shurpanakhā attempted to kill her. To punish this audacity, Lakshmana cut her nose and ears with his sword.
- Shurpanakhā complained to her cousins Khara and Dushana and sought revenge by killing the two princes. Khara and Dushana had been appointed by Rāvana as custodians of the Dandakāranya region.
- With an army of fourteen thousand rākshasas, Khara and Dushana attacked Rāma and Lakshmana. Lakshmana took Seetā to a safe place while Rāma single-handedly defeated their entire army, killing all the fourteen thousand rākshasas.

The Abduction (Aranya Kānda)

- Shocked at the unexpected result of the fight, Shurpanakhā fled to Lankā and instigated Rāvana to get Seetā for himself.
- Rāvana planned to abduct Seetā with Māreecha's help. Māreecha took the form of an exquisite multi-hued deer to lure Seetā.

- Seetā, desiring the deer, requested Rāma to get it for her. Rāma agreed and went after it.
- The deer took Rāma far away from the āshram. Rāma managed to kill it, only to learn that it was a trap by Māreecha. Before dying, imitating Rāma's voice, Māreecha called out Lakshmana's name, seeking help. Sensing danger, Rāma rushed back to the āshram.
- Meanwhile, in the āshram, Lakshmana and Seetā heard the cry for help in Rāma's voice. Lakshmana suspected foul play. Seetā panicked. She pressurised Lakshmana to go and look for Rāma.
- Seeing Seetā alone in the āshram, Rāvana came dressed like a rishi, asking for food. As Seetā came closer to give the food, he lifted her in his arms and escaped in his flying chariot.
- Jatāyu saw Rāvana flying away with Seetā and intervened with all his might. But Rāvana was way too strong. He fatally injured Jatāyu and carried Seetā away.
- Rāma and Lakshmana returned to the āshram only to find Seetā missing.
- While searching for Seetā, they met the injured Jatāyu, who informed them about her abduction by Rāvana. But he died without giving any clue of Rāvana's location.
- Their search for Seetā continued.
- One day, the brothers encountered a ferocious-looking rākshasa, Kabandha. Kabandha tried to capture the two brothers and gobble them up for his food. Rāma and Lakshmana humbled

him with their prowess, after which the rākshasa directed them to go to Rishyamukha mountain near Kishkindhā and seek help from Sugreeva. Rāma and Lakshmana headed to Kishkindhā.

- On the way, they met Shabari in the āshram of Rishi Mātanga.

Kishkindhā Arrival (Kishkindhā Kānda)

- Sugreeva was the prince of a vānara tribe residing in Kishkindhā. His elder brother Vāli was the king of the tribe.
- A misunderstanding made the people of Kishkindhā believe Vāli was dead. They crowned Sugreeva as their king. But Vāli was alive. He returned and was furious to see Sugreeva on his throne.
- Determined to kill, Vāli chased Sugreeva around the globe. He also forcibly took away Sugreeva's dear wife, Rumā.
- Sugreeva and his five trusted ministers, one of whom was Hanumāna, found shelter in the precincts of Rishyamukha as Vāli had been forbidden to enter the area by Rishi Mātanga.
- One day, one of Sugreeva's ministers spotted two young, handsome and strong warrior-like youths with mighty bows coming towards Rishyamukha.
- Dressed as an old hermit, Hanumāna approached Rāma and Lakshmana. Convinced that they were not Vāli's men, Hanumāna led them to Sugreeva.
- On hearing about Seetā's abduction, Sugreeva showed Rāma some ornaments that were thrown at them by an obviously unwilling woman being

carried away by a rākshasa. Rāma instantly recognised them as Seetā's.

- Rāma and Sugreeva agreed to help each other—Rāma promised to kill Vāli and help Sugreeva get back his wife and kingdom. Sugreeva promised to do all he could to find Seetā and help bring her back safely.
- Rāma killed Vāli and crowned Sugreeva the king of Kishkindhā.
- After the rainy season, Sugreeva divided his vānaras into four teams and sent them in each direction to look for Seetā.
- As Rāvana and his Lankā were known to be in the south, Rāma and Sugreeva were most hopeful of finding Seetā there. Hence, Rāma gave Hanumāna his ring to prove his credentials to Seetā, if and when he found her.
- After a month, troops from the north, east and west returned without any success.
- The team that went south continued their search and met Sampāti, an old and disabled garuda, who was Jatāyu's elder brother.
- Sampāti was distressed to hear about his brother's death. He had also seen Seetā being carried away by Rāvana. Sampāti informed the vānaras about the location of Lankā.
- The question facing the vānaras now was—who could jump across a hundred yojanas to confirm Seetā's location in Lankā?

Seetā in Lankā (Sundara Kānda)

- Overcoming the challenges including his own doubts, Hanumāna arrived in Lankā, jumping over a distance of a hundred yojanas, and began his search.

- Not finding Seetā anywhere in the city, Hanumāna entered a huge forest nearby. Here he finally spotted Seetā sitting underneath an Ashoka tree surrounded by fierce-looking rākshasa women.
- Seeing Rāvana enter the premises, Hanumāna hid among the branches of an adjacent tree.
- Rāvana pleaded with Seetā to accept him. When she refused, he threatened her. Seetā firmly rejected every overture of his.
- After Rāvana left, Hanumāna approached Seetā and introduced himself, handing her Rāma's ring.
- Hanumāna offered to rescue Seetā and take her to Kishkindhā right then. But Seetā refused. She chose to wait for Rāma to come, kill Rāvana and take her back.
- To assess Rāvana's military prowess, Hanumāna had to catch the attention of the rākshasas. He did that by ravaging the Ashoka forest.
- Furious, Rāvana sent his chieftains to catch Hanumāna. Hanumāna fought them single-handedly, eventually letting Indrajeet, Rāvana's formidable son, capture him.
- Rāvana ordered Hanumāna to be killed. But on Vibhishana's intervention, he changed the punishment to burning the vānara's tail and parading him in Lankā.
- Using this as an opportunity to free himself, Hanumāna ran around with a burning tail, jumping over different edifices, homes and

gardens of Lankā and setting them on fire before returning to Kishkindhā.

Destination Lankā (Yuddha Kānda)

- With Seetā's location confirmed, Rāma, Lakshmana, Sugreeva and the vānara army headed to the coast to find a way to reach Lankā.
- In Lankā, Hanumāna's exploits startled Rāvana and his ministers. Rāvana called his ministers to discuss the plan concerning Seetā.
- Except for Kumbhakarna and Vibhishana, most ministers backed Rāvana's decision to keep Seetā in captivity.
- Vibhishana tried his best to convince Rāvana to not bring about the destruction of Lankā due to his desire for Seetā.
- Rāvana, however, insulted Vibhishana so much that the latter decided to leave Lankā and take refuge with Rāma.
- At the coast, Varun deva's intransigence to show them the way angered Rāma. Finally, afraid of Rāma's ire, Varun appeared and instructed Nala to construct a bridge over the ocean.
- The vānaras constructed a bridge in five days, using boulders, stones, trees and barks, and crossed over to Lankā.

The War (Yuddha Kānda)

- The news of the vānaras reaching the Lankān shores unnerved many rākshasas. Rāvana's mother, maternal grandfather and some of his wise ministers advised him to let go of Seetā, but all in vain.

- Before formally kicking off the war, Rāma sent Angada as a messenger to Rāvana's court to give him one last chance to return Seetā and save Lankā.
- Rāvana ordered the capture of Angada, but Angada managed to escape through the ceiling of the palace. War conches were then sounded.
- The vānaras and the rākshasas fought, causing immense damage to each other.
- After the first set of commanders sent by Rāvana were killed, Indrajeet came to fight.
- Resorting to his powers of creating illusions, Indrajeet inflicted severe injuries on the vānaras as well as on Rāma and Lakshmana. With his nāgapāsh, Rāma and Lakshmana collapsed on the ground, unconscious.
- But help came to them in the form of a garuda, who freed them from the grip of the nāgas and helped them regain their strength.
- After some more rākshasa commanders were killed, Rāvana himself entered the battlefield. Rāma rendered him weaponless and chariot-less but spared his life at that time.
- Kumbhakarna entered the battle next and began his carnage. No vānara could withstand his brute force. The field became gory with the blood and flesh of the vānaras and the rākshasas alike.
- Kumbhakarna eventually met his death at the hands of Rāma.

- Other sons, brothers, nephews and ministers of Rāvana came to the combat zone and met the same fate as those before them.
- Indrajeet re-entered the battlefield and invoked the Brahmāstra. To maintain the sanctity of the Brahmāstra, Rāma and Lakshmana surrendered to the impact of the divine weapon and fell unconscious.
- To revive the brothers, Hanumāna brought mrita-sanjeevani and three other herbs from the Himālayas.
- Yuddha resumed. More rākshasa commanders were killed.
- This time, resorting to his tricks of illusion, Indrajeet conjured an image of Seetā and pretended to kill her to demotivate Sugreeva's army.
- Rāma became distressed on hearing about Seetā's death. Vibhishana lifted everyone's spirits by puncturing Indrajeet's claim of killing Seetā and informed them of Indrajeet's strategy to buy time to conduct a yajna at the Nikumbhilā temple and become invincible. To defeat him, disrupting the yajna before its completion was now paramount. Lakshmana was handed the task to kill Indrajeet.
- Lakshmana and Indrajeet duelled over three days and three nights, both putting up a magnificent fight. Finally, killing Indrajeet, Lakshmana emerged victorious.
- With all the commanders dead, Rāvana entered the battle once again to fight Rāma.
- The battle between Rāma and Rāvana was one of its kind. Even gods in heaven came out to witness this clash of the titans.

- During the battle, Rāma severed Rāvana's head but another one popped up. This happened over a hundred times.
- Then Rāma summoned his divine astra and shot at Rāvana, aiming for Rāvana's chest. Rāvana's chest was ripped asunder. The mighty rākshasa collapsed dead.

Agni Parikshā (Yuddha Kānda)

- After Rāvana's cremation and Vibhishana's coronation, Rāma sent Vibhishana to bring Seetā, if she so wished.
- Rāma had gone through immense pain on separation from Seetā. But when Seetā finally came to him in Lankā, Rāma refused to accept her, casting doubts on her chastity.
- Aghast and determined to prove her virtue, Seetā ordered Lakshmana to light a pyre. 'If my intention and my actions have been chaste, the fire will protect me,' she declared before stepping into the flames.
- Agni deva vouched for Seetā's purity of thoughts and actions. Seetā emerged out of the flames, untarnished. Rāma was pleased. He explained that he never had an iota of doubt about Seetā. But he wanted society to be a witness to Seetā's purity and never question her character.

The Homecoming (Yuddha Kānda)

- Fourteen years of their vanvās had ended. Bharata was waiting for their return. Rāma expressed his desire to Vibhishana to return to Ayodhyā as soon as possible.

- Vibhishana arranged for the Pushpak vimān to fly the entire contingent of the vānaras, along with Rāma, Lakshmana, Seetā and him, to Ayodhyā.
- Making a stop at Kishkindhā to take the wives of the vānara commanders along with them as desired by Seetā, the entourage landed at Prayāg at the āshram of Rishi Bharadwāja.
- Rāma sent Hanumāna to Nandigrām to inform Bharata of their arrival.
- Bharata was genuinely overjoyed. He got Ayodhyā ready to welcome Rāma home.
- Rāma returned to Ayodhyā and took over its reign.
- He ruled the kingdom for many years. The kingdom of Rāma was the epitome of happiness and prosperity, thanks to his just and compassionate administration, forever engaged in the welfare of all citizens—this is what Rāma Rājya signifies till today.

Summary of Uttara Kānda

In Rāma's court, rishis came and narrated the stories of the emergence of rākshasas, the birth of Rāvana and his siblings and his exploits and misadventures.

Rāma heard of the gossip widespread in the kingdom which questioned Seetā's character after her abduction and confinement by Rāvana.

Rāma was extremely pained, but to honour public opinion, he banished a pregnant Seetā to the forest, where she was given shelter by Rishi Vālmiki in his āshram. Her twin sons Lava and Kusha were born there. The boys grew up in the āshram, receiving education in the scriptures and training in warfare under the guidance of Rishi Vālmiki.

On advice from his brothers and ministers, Rāma undertook the Ashwamedha Yajna. Lava–Kusha were young boys at that time, just twelve years old.

By then Rishi Vālmiki had composed the Rāmāyana and taught it to the boys. The rishi went to participate in the yajna along with Lava–Kusha and his students.

One day, the boys sang the Rāmāyana in Rāma's court, during which the identity of the two boys as the sons of Rāma and Seetā was revealed.

Rāma called for Seetā and requested her to prove herself once and for all and return to him.

Seetā did swear by her virtue but did not return to Rāma. Instead, she called for mother earth to take her in her womb.

Granting her wish and proving her purity, the earth split open, taking Seetā in.

Rāma eventually departed to his heavenly abode along with Bharata and Sugreeva. Lakshmana had moved on some time earlier. In keeping with Rāma's wish, Hanumāna stayed on to narrate the story of the Rāmāyana to future generations.

Part 1

Context and Settings

I

The Divine Inspiration

In an āshram by the banks of the Tamasā river lived Rishi Vālmiki with his students. One day, Devarishi Nārada came visiting and the two got talking. Rishi Vālmiki listed sixteen virtues desirable in a man, especially a king. He wanted to know if there was such a man who lived in their times. He asked:[1]

> Who in contemporary times is endowed with virtues, valour, dharma, gratitude, fortitude and firm determination?
>
> Who has impeccable character and is forever devoted to the welfare of all beings, and who is erudite, capable and very handsome?
>
> Who maintains composure in all kinds of situations, has won over his anger, emanates resplendence, and has no jealousy; and who, when angry, is feared even by the gods?

Nārada replied promptly: 'There is one person that we know in the present times who is indeed like you describe. He is the king of Ayodhyā, born in the dynasty of Ikshvāku—Rāma.'

Devarishi Nārada went on to recount the story of Rāma—his unexpected vanvās, life in the forest, Seetā's abduction by Rāvana, Rāma's sorrow, friendship with the vānaras, construction of the bridge over the sea, victory in Lankā and coronation to the throne of Ayodhyā.

The Composition

After Nārada had left, the rishi went to the banks of Tamasā for his bath. He spotted a couple of kraunch birds fluttering happily around in each other's company.

Suddenly, a hunter shot dead the male kraunch. The female kraunch began screeching in shock and sorrow. Rishi Vālmiki was deeply pained witnessing this cruel act of the hunter that separated two birds in love. Instinctively, he uttered a curse condemning the hunter for causing such pain to the birds.

'Oh hunter, since you have killed one bird of the couple when it was infatuated by passion, you will be deprived of your pratishthā, your peace.'

Having uttered the words, Vālmiki became thoughtful. He was struck by the structure of the verse that he had spoken. He narrated the verse once again to a disciple nearby and said, 'Overcome by grief, the words I uttered seemed to have come out arranged in a poetic metre of four parts. Like a shloka, it can be rendered as a song when set in rhythm on a stringed musical instrument.' The disciple happily committed the words to his memory.

The shloka uttered by Rishi Vālmiki was:

मा निषाद प्रतिष्ठां त्वमगमश्शाश्वतीस्समा: ।
यत्क्रौञ्चमिथुनादेकमवधी: काममोहितम् ।।[2]

The chhanda (metre) of this shloka is Anustup which is very easy to set into rhythm for musical rendition. Anustup metre is made up of thirty-two syllables divided into four parts, called padas. Each pada has eight syllables. In addition, there are rules about what kind of syllable—guru (hard) or laghu (soft)—is to be used in which position. The fifth syllable of each pada is laghu and the sixth is guru. The seventh syllable of the second and fourth padas is laghu and of the first and third padas, is guru.

Both the Rāmāyana and the Mahābhārata, including the Srimad Bhagavad Geetā, have been composed in the Anupstup chhanda.

Rishi Vālmiki returned to his āshram, his mind preoccupied with the sorrowful incident he had witnessed and the verse he had uttered. That day, he had a divine vision. Brahma deva manifested before him. The Pitāmaha smiled for he was aware of the thought nagging the rishi and said, 'What you composed is a shloka indeed. Do not think otherwise. The words were uttered in that manner due to my will. I want you to narrate the life of Rāma.'

Brahma deva said, 'I want you to talk to the world about the virtuous, steadfast and courageous Rāma, about whom you heard from Nārada. All the details of the events in the life of Rāma, Lakshmana, Seetā and the rākshasas will be revealed to you. Not a word you write in the epic will be untrue. *As long as the mountains stand and rivers flow on earth, this story of Rāma will flourish in the world.*'

A strong belief took shape in Rishi Vālmiki's mind. 'I must compose Rāmāyana in its entirety,' he resolved.

The rishi sat down in deep meditation to learn the details of Rāma's life. By the strength of his yogic powers, he could see the events in Rāma's life play out before his eyes, as they had happened. He could see things as clearly as one sees a fruit held in the palm. Not only did he see what had happened, but also what was yet to happen.

Thus was composed the Rāmāyana, one of the most important itihāsa of Bhāratavarsha, replete with nava rasas—the aesthetics for romance, wonderment, pathos, comic, fury, fright, valour, disgust and peace.

The Rendition

Having compiled the itihāsa, the task before Rishi Vālmiki was to identify the right disciple who could render the epic to a larger audience. As he was contemplating this, two of his students, Lava and Kusha, came to meet him. These young boys were smart, virtuous, well-versed in the Vedas and adept in music. Rāma looked like the reflection of Vishnu on earth. Lava and Kusha looked like a reflection of Rāma.

Rishi Vālmiki made the boys memorise the Rāmāyana. The boys imbibed the epic in its entire profundity and rendered it wherever they went, singing perfect notes and moving the audience to its core.

They sang about the glory of Ayodhyā, the birth of Rāma and his brothers, their marriages and the sudden twist of fate in Rāma's life. They narrated the lives of Rāma, Seetā and Lakshmana in vanvās, Seetā's abduction by Rāvana, the glory of Lankā and the falling out of Vibhishana and Rāvana. They sang about the pangs of the longing of Rāma and Seetā, the ferocity of the war in Lankā, the heart-wrenching moment of Seetā's agni parikshā, the eventual happy union of Rāma and Seetā and Rāma's grand coronation in Ayodhyā.

As the boys sang, the audience identified themselves with Rāma and Seetā, ebbing and flowing with the emotions they had lived through, savouring the rhythm of Lava and Kusha's recitation recounting the life of their beloved king.

One day, Rishi Vālmiki heard of the grand Ashwamedha yajna being performed by Rāma. Guests from all over thronged Ayodhyā to participate in the yajna and the celebrations. Rishi Vālmiki went too, along with his students. Lava and Kusha were among them. One day, the boys were singing the Rāmāyana on the streets and by-lanes of Ayodhyā when Rāma saw them. He invited them to his palace to sing before his brothers, courtiers and the public.

Lava and Kusha began to sing the story of Rāma before the great man himself!

As the Rāmāyana was rendered then in the royal court of Ayodhyā, so it is rendered to this day. As it moved people then, so it moves people even now. The rishi says that merely hearing the epic confers punya on the listeners because the Rāmāyana is not just an epic documenting the life of Rāma, Lakshmana, Seetā and others, but it is a work that brings to life, through their life and lessons, the wisdom of the Vedas.[3]

About the Rāmāyana, it is said:

कामार्थगुणसंयुक्तं धर्मार्थगुणविस्तरम् ।
समुद्रमिव रत्नाढ्यं सर्वश्रुतिमनोहरम् ॥

(It) abounds in qualities of pleasure (काम) as well as nuances of dharma;
it is like an ocean of beautiful gem-like thoughts and is as pleasing to the mind as the gist of all shrutis.[4]

May the life and actions of Rāma continue to inspire us all!

Who Was Rishi Vālmiki?

In the Rāmāyana, there is very little information about Rishi Vālmiki. All we are told is that he is a celebrated rishi and yogi, who lives in an āshram by the banks of River Tamasā. During their vanvās, Rāma, Seetā and Lakshmana pay him a visit before heading to Chitrakoot.

There is one instance in Uttara Kānda of the Rāmāyana where Rishi Vālmiki introduces himself. He says he is the tenth son of Prachetā and has done intense tapasyā for many years.[5]

However, another popular tale about Rishi Vālmiki has a lot more detail. The source of the story is *Skanda Purāna*. According to the Purāna, Rishi Vālmiki was a hunter in his previous birth. An encounter with Rishi Shankha changed his life. Rishi Shankha gave him the Rāma nāma mantra. Due to the regular chanting of the Rāma mantra, he was born as the son of Rishi Valmiki in his subsequent birth. Being the son of Valmiki, he was also known as Vālmiki and is credited with the composition of the Rāmāyana.[6]

In another version of the story, the hunter is born as Agni Sharmā (variably, Ratnākar) and is again engaged in hunting. After a chance meeting with Saptarishis, he began chanting 'marā, marā'. When chanted continuously, 'marā, marā' sounds the same as 'rāma, rāma'. Agni Sharmā became so engrossed in chanting the Rāma mantra that he lost all sense of the present. An anthill—valmik—developed on his body but he continued to chant. Because of the valmika, he got the name Vālmiki and went on to compose the Rāmāyana.[7]

कूजन्तं रामरामेति मधुरं मधुराक्षरम् ।
आरुह्य कविताशाखां वन्दे वाल्मीकिकोकिलम् ॥

ॐ ψ ॐ

2

Bloodlines

The Lineage of Rāma

> From the ancient era of Prajāpati till the present day, this earth has been reigned by kings of the Ikshvāku dynasty. In this very lineage was born the great king Sagar who reigned the earth with pride, surrounded by his sons. He was the one who got the mighty ocean dug up. It is in this family of illustrious monarchs that the great epic called the Rāmāyana is set. This Rāmāyana is endowed with dharma, artha, kāma,[1] and we will sing it today in its entirety. May you all listen to it with a pure heart and mind.

This was how Lava and Kusha began their recital of the Rāmāyana in the court of Rāma.[2]

While the main story of the Rāmāyana revolves around the life of Rāma, Rishi Vālmiki has preserved his entire ancestry in the epic. He has also narrated a few stories related to Rāma's forefathers. Ikshvāku was the progenitor of this dynasty which ruled from Ayodhyā; hence the name Ikshvāku vamsha—the lineage of Ikshvāku. The dynasty is also called Raghu vamsha from Raghu, another great king in the Ikshvāku dynasty. Other renowned descendants of Ikshvāku and ancestors of Rāma were Anaranya, Trishanku, Sagar, Dilip, Bhageeratha, Kakustha, Pravruddha and

Dasharatha. The descent of river Gangā on earth is credited to Rājā Bhageeratha of this dynasty.

Rāma, Bharata and the twins Lakshmana and Shatrughna were sons of Dasharatha born to Kaushalyā, Kaikeyi and Sumitrā, respectively. Being descendants of Kakustha and Raghu, Rāma and his brothers are addressed as Kākustha and Rāghava multiple times in the Rāmāyana. Being sons of Dasharatha, they are also called Dāsharathi. Lakshmana and Shatrughna are often called Soumitri, sons of Sumitrā, Dasharatha's third wife.

In the Rāmāyana, Rāma's lineage is recounted twice by Rishi Vashishtha—first at the wedding of Rāma and Seetā and then again in Chitrakoot, when Bharata was trying to convince Rāma to return to Ayodhyā.[3]

Surya Vamsha and Chandra Vamsha

Ikshvāku was the son of Manu and the grandson of Vivasvān. Vivasvān being the name of Surya or the Sun, Ikshvāku's vamsha is also called the Surya vamsha—the lineage of the Sun or the 'Solar dynasty'.

The story of the Mahābhārata is of the kings of Chandra vamsha, the lineage of the Moon, also called the 'Lunar dynasty'. The original ancestor of Chandra vamsha is also Vivasvān, but on the maternal side. Manu married his daughter Ilā to Budha, the son of Soma, Soma being another name for the Moon. Through the union of Ilā and Budha, Pururavā was born. Pururavā was the progenitor of the Yādavas, Kurus and Pānchālas, among others. Manu is considered the progenitor of all human beings.

Brihadbala, one of the descendants of Rāma, fought on the side of Kauravas in the Mahābhārata war and was killed by Abhimanyu. It is believed that Gautama Buddha was a Suryavamshi, a descendant of Rāma.

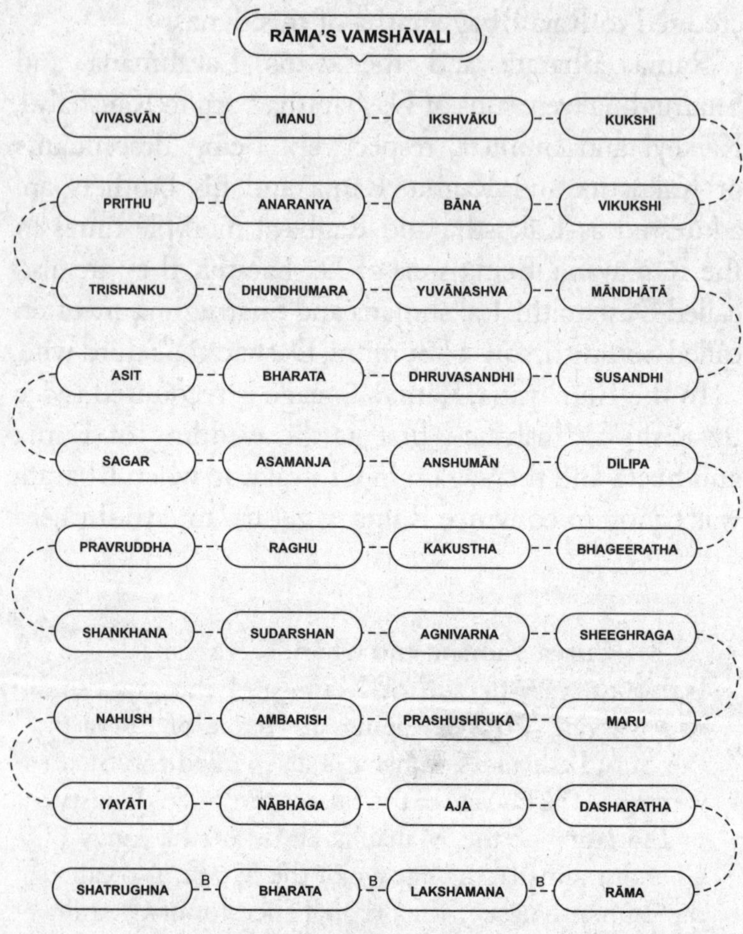

Fig. 1 Rāma's vamshāvali

The Lineage of Seetā

Seetā was the daughter of Rājā Janaka and his wife Sunainā, but she was not born to them. Janaka found her in the womb of the earth while clearing the land for a yajna. The baby was lifted by the blade of his plough. Janaka and Sunainā adopted the baby and called her Seetā, meaning a furrow. The couple brought up the child with a lot of love and care. They had one more daughter of their own after that, Urmilā. But Seetā had a special place in Janaka's heart. Janaka had a brother by the name Kushadhwaja, the custodian of janapada of Sānkāshya. He had two daughters, Māndavi and Shrutakirti.

Janaka was the king of Videha. Mithilā was his capital. He was born in the lineage of the great ancient king Nimi, who founded this kingdom. Nimi's son was Mithi from whom the city of Mithilā got its name. Mithi's son was Janaka (not Seetā's father). He was the first one to be called by that appellation. From then on, the kings of Videha were addressed reverentially as Janaka or father. Seetā's father, Janaka, was twenty-third in this lineage of Nimi. Devarāta was another distinguished king in the dynasty, sixth from Nimi, seventh overall.

King Devarāta had been entrusted by the devās with the Shiva Dhanush—the bow of Shiva. Since then, this had become a family heirloom for the kings of Nimi's lineage. Janaka had decided that he would marry Seetā only to the mighty warrior who could string this bow of Shiva.[4]

After Rishi Vashishtha informed the assembly of the lineage of Ikshvākus before Seetā–Rāma vivāha, Janaka recounted his own.[5] The four daughters of Janaka's household were then married to the four sons of Dasharatha. Seetā with Rāma, Urmilā with Lakshmana, Māndavi with Bharata and Shrutakirti with Shatrughna.

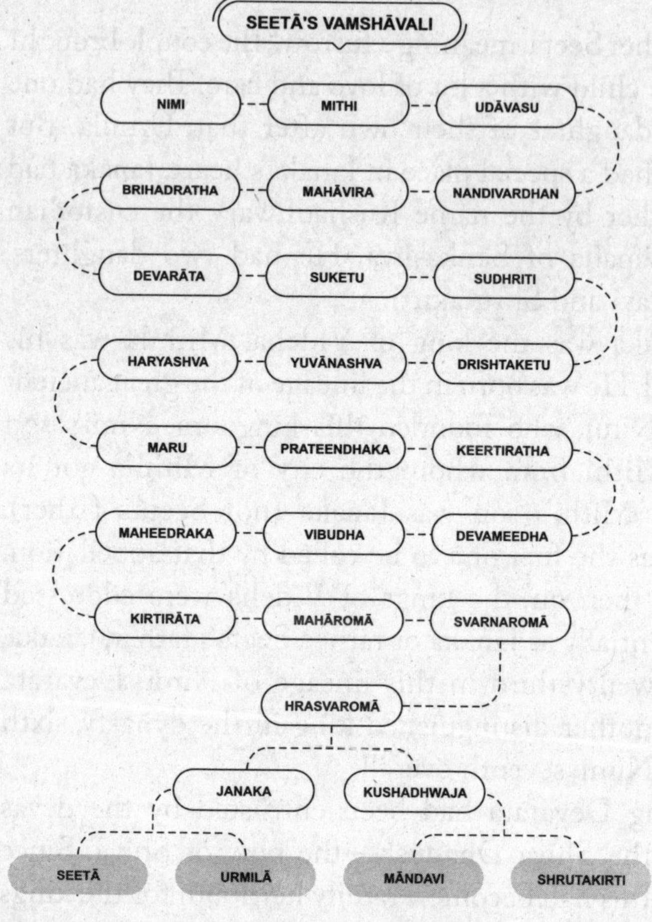

Fig. 2 Seetā's vamshāvali

The Lineage of Rāvana

Once there lived a famous rishi by the name Pulastya. He was the son of Brahma deva. His wife was Mahātejasvi. They had a son as erudite as his father. His name was Vishrava. Rishi Bharadwāja married his daughter to Rishi Vishrava. Through their union, a noble son, Vaishravan, was born. He came to be known all over the world as Kuber. Happy with Kuber's tapasyā,[6] Brahma deva gave him the Pushpak vimān as his vāhan. On Vishrava's suggestion, Kuber went to Lankā, then a deserted island, and established a flourishing kingdom there.

Before Kuber came there, Lankā had been inhabited by a rākshasa tribe, which had abandoned the place and moved on. Seeing prosperity return to the place, many people of the rākshasa tribe returned and settled there happily.[7]

One of the kings of rākshasas was Sukesh. He had three powerful sons, namely, Mālyavān, Sumāli and Māli. Sumāli had a daughter named Kaikasi. Kaikasi was an extremely resplendent lady, as splendid as Goddess Lakshmi. Like every father, Sumāli was eagerly waiting to find a worthy husband for his exceptional daughter. However, a good match was hard to come by. Fearing rejection, most suitors were hesitant to even approach her.

One day Sumāli saw Kuber in his Pushpak vimān, going to meet his father. He was extremely impressed by this radiant, young king of Lankā. An idea struck him—one that could help his daughter get a worthy husband and help restore the lost glory of his tribe at the same time. He convinced his daughter to approach Rishi Vishrava and choose him as her husband. A husband like Vishrava would ensure Kaikasi had distinguished children just like Kuber, he thought.

When Kaikasi reached Rishi Vishrava's āshram, he was in deep tapasyā. She waited patiently before him. When the rishi finished his rituals and looked up, he saw a beautiful damsel waiting for him. 'Who are you and what brings you here?' he asked. 'May the respected Sir, by the strength of his tapasyā, himself figure out the reason for my coming,' she replied coyly and added, 'but let me assure you that I come here with my father's approval. My name is Kaikasi.'

The rishi meditated for a few minutes and said, 'Hmm, so you come here with the desire of having children with me. Thus, it will be. But the time when my eyes fell on you was not the most auspicious. Hence, the children born to you will be violent and cruel.' Kaikasi was shocked. 'You are a distinguished rishi and very revered. I do not expect cruel children from you. Please be kind to me,' she implored. Vishrava comforted her. 'Our youngest son will undoubtedly be virtuous and kind.'

Thus it came to be as Vishrava had foreseen. He and Kaikasi had four children, three sons—Dashagreeva, Kumbhakarna and Vibhishana, and a daughter, Shurpanakhā. Vibhishana was the youngest of the four. Dashagreeva came to be popularly known as Rāvana—the one who made the world cry.

Kaikasi was fond of Kuber and would often tell Dashagreeva to strive to be like his elder stepbrother. One day when jealousy and anger got the better of him, Rāvana declared, 'Do not lose heart, Mother. I promise that I will become equal to or even better than Kuber.' He headed to Gokarna, along with his brothers, to undertake severe tapasyā and please Brahma deva.[8]

After years of intense effort, they succeeded. Brahma deva came to fulfil his wish. 'What do you desire, sons?' asked he. Rāvana desired immortality, but Brahma deva refused. 'No being can live forever. Ask for something else,' he said. Rāvana gave it some thought and requested, 'Grant me immortality from devas, asuras, dānavas, daityas, gandharvas, yakshas, garuda and nāgas. Other beings I have no fear of, especially humans. Human beings are like strands of straw before me, so you may exclude them.' 'So will it be,' declared the Pitāmaha.[9] Kumbhakarna, Kaikasi's second son, was born with immense strength and excessive hunger. Not able to control his hunger, he would eat anyone who came his way, more so the ascetics and innocent people. Hence, when Brahma deva sought to fulfil his desire, all devas protested. To protect the world from becoming devoid of humans and animals, Brahma deva put Kumbhakarna in a state of perpetual sleep. This upset Rāvana. He pleaded for making some concessions for Kumbhakarna. Brahma deva agreed and said, 'Kumbhakarna will wake up once in a few months and then go back to sleep again.'

Vibhishana desired only one boon—to remain steadfast in dharma even in the most adverse of situations. 'Your intellect will never deviate from the path of dharma,' blessed Brahma deva and left.[10]

Rāvana had many wives. Mandodari, the daughter of Maya dānava was his chief queen. Maya was aware of the cruel nature of Rāvana, but taking into account his birth in the noble lineage of Rishi Pulastya, Maya married his extremely beautiful and gracious daughter Mandodari to Rāvana. Mandodari was the mother of Rāvana's sons Meghanād and Aksh. Meghanād was better known as Indrajeet for having defeated the king of devas, Indra himself. Kumbhakarna was married to Vajrajvālā, the granddaughter of King Bali. Kumbha and Nikumbha were his better-known sons. Vibhishana was married to Saramā, the daughter of the king of Gandharvas, Shailush. Rāvana got his sister Shurpanakhā married to the powerful commander of the Kālkeya tribe, Vidyutjihvā.[11] A few years later, following a tussle with the Kālkeyas, in the heat of the moment, Rāvana killed Vidyutjihvā, making his own sister a widow.[12] Shurpanakhā was distraught. To make her feel better, Rāvana asked her to go and live in Janasthāna in the Dandaka forests with his cousins Khara and Dushana.

The Kumbhakarna Syndrome

The syndrome exhibited by Kumbhakarna, as described in the Rāmāyana, is similar to what modern medicine calls a hypothalamic disorder. This disorder, also known as Klein–Levin syndrome or hypothalamic obesity, is characterised by periodic episodes of somnolence (excessive sleep), hyperphagia (excessive hunger) and hypersexuality, along with other behavioural and cognitive difficulties.[13]

Research papers have been written theorising that Kumbhakarna may have been suffering from this disorder.

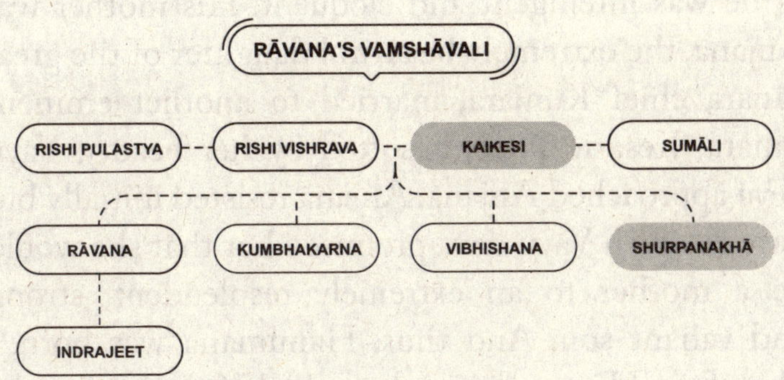

Fig. 3 Rāvana's vamshāvali

Vanchāri or Vānaras

Forest-dwelling tribes living in various parts of Jambudwipa were called vanchāri or vānaras[14] who subsisted on fruits and food found in the jungles. They owed allegiance to a mighty king named Riksharāja who ruled from Kishkindhā,[15] a city in the Dandakāranya region.[16]

Riksharāja had two sons, Vāli and Sugreeva. Vāli being the elder became the king after Riksharāja. He was extremely powerful but short-tempered. That he had once humbled Rāvana, who had come looking for Vāli for a duel, was a testimony to his strength. Vāli had an equally worthy son Angada through his wife Tārā. Tārā was a very intelligent and learned lady. After Vāli was killed by Rāma, Sugreeva was crowned the king of the vānaras. His wife was Rumā.

Other prominent vānaras aligned with Sugreeva who came to support Rāma against Rāvana included Jāmbavana, Neela, Nala, Sushena and Hanumāna.

Hanumāna was especially gifted. He was as strong as he was intelligent and eloquent. His mother was Anjanā, the extremely beautiful daughter of the great vānara chief Kunjara, married to another eminent vānara, Kesari. Once, besotted by her beauty, Vāyu deva approached Anjanā. Anjanā resisted initially but gave in when Vāyu deva promised her that she would be a mother to an extremely resplendent, strong and valiant son. And thus, Hanumāna was born.[17] Therefore, Hanumāna is also called Vāyu putra—the son of Vāyu.

In other texts like *Skanda Purāna*, Anjanā is said to have undertaken tapasyā to beget a son. Her tapasyā involved mediation on the vital breath (prāna vāyu). Pleased with her tapasyā, Vāyu deva granted her wish and Hanumāna was born.[18]

Ārya Unārya

There is a popular theory that the word Ārya denoted a race of fair-complexioned people who came from grasslands in Europe to the Indian peninsula. They brought with them Sanskrit and the Vedic culture and displaced the original inhabitants of Saraswati–Sindhu civilisation—the Dravidians. The Dravidians, or Unāryas, were then pushed South due to the influx of the Āryans. This is known as the Āryan migration theory (previously Āryan invasion theory). Many recent storytellers have retold the story of the Rāmāyana, imposing on it this Āryan–Dravidian framework, inferring that the story of Rāma and Rāvana has more to do with a racial conflict between the Aryans and the Dravidians than dharma and adharma.

A lot of work is being done to prove and disprove the Āryan migration theory by different groups. The scope of this book does not permit any critical examination of this theory. However, given the imposition of Āryan–Dravidian conflict on the Rāmāyana, it is worth noting how the words Ārya and Unārya are used in the epic.

Both these words occur multiple times in the Rāmāyana. The usage, very categorically, is *not racial* in nature. The word Ārya has been consistently used to denote a quality—a 'gentlemanly' quality, a behaviour expected of civilised people who can differentiate right from wrong.

One may argue that these Āryans thought of only themselves as civilised and hence considered the quality synonymous with their own race. If we were to accept this line of argument, then the textual inference from the Rāmāyana would be—everyone in the Rāmāyana times, from the north to the south of the Indian peninsula, including the Ikshvākus, the rākshasa tribes of Rāvana as well as the vānaras affirmatively belonged to the same race.

This proposition is based on the following:

- Dasharatha calls Kaikeyi Unārya for seeking Rāma's exile.
- Seetā calls Lakshmana Unārya for not rushing out to help his brother in Janasthāna.
- Rāvana and Indrajeet call Vibhishana Unārya for going over to Rāma's side.
- Rāvana calls his charioteer Unārya for taking him away from the battlefield.
- Angada tells his vānaras who were running away from the battlefield not to behave like Unāryas.

- Seetā exhorts Hanumāna to not kill the rākshasis because they were only following Rāvana's orders. Such behaviour (that is, not killing them), she says, is expected of one who is Ārya.
- Mandodari and other wives of Rāvana, as well as the commanders of the rākshasa army, refer to Rāvana as Ārya and Āryaputra (son of an Arya—son of a decent man, hence a decent man himself).
- Tārā refers to Vāli as Ārya.

These are only a handful of examples. Ārya and Unārya have been generously used throughout the epic. Arya is used as a term to imply a gentleman or woman and Unārya is used to imply an uncivilised, deceitful, cowardly person—man or woman.

The race theory of fair-complexioned Aryas doesn't seem to hold either because Rāma is himself called Shyām, one who had a dusky complexion. Krishna, Draupadi, and Veda Vyāsa are other examples of dark-skinned heroes and heroines in Indian epics.

Another point worth mentioning is that Rāvana and the people of Lankā are shown to perform yajnas and chant Vedic mantras just like Rāma and the people of Ayodhyā. Rāvana, after his death, is cremated according to Hindu rites. In fact, Rāvana is praised by Vibhishana as one who would regularly perform grand yajnas as prescribed in the scriptures.

ॐ ψ ॐ

3

Cities and City Life in the Rāmāyana

Ayodhyā

On the banks of river Sarayu stood the great janapada of Kosala, flourishing and abundant. Its capital was the famous city of Ayodhyā. It was said that the great Manu had himself established Ayodhyā. When Dasharatha ruled, Ayodhyā was a sprawling megapolis[1]—12 yojanas[2] in length and 3 yojanas in breadth. The city had well-laid pathways and royal highways that were routinely sprinkled with water and strewn with flowers. Tall, multistorey edifices, huge arched gateways, gem-studded mansions, beautiful gardens and neatly-lined markets adorned the town. There was no space that was left unutilised. Houses were close to each other and constructed on levelled land. Farms had plenty of grains and the stables had the best breeds of horses from Kāmbhoja, Bāhlika and Vanāyu regions, and elephants from Vindhyas and Himālayas. Even the water in Ayodhyā was sweet like sugarcane juice. The deep moats and weaponised fortifications surrounding the city made access impossible for trespassers and insurmountable for enemies, thus living up to its name—Ayodhyā, that against which one cannot fight a war.

Size of Ayodhyā

To get a sense of the size of city, consider this comparison:

City	*Area*
Ayodhyā in the Rāmāyana times	6,000 sq km
Mumbai	600 sq km
New Delhi (city)	1,484 sq km
New York City	1,213 sq km
London	1,572 sq km
Shanghai Municipal Area	6,340 sq km
Mumbai Metropolitan Area (including Thane, Vasai, Panvel, Navi Mumbai, etc.)	6,328 sq km

The city was bustling with activity. People from different communities, professions and walks of life called Ayodhyā their home, be it sculptors, architects, groups of male and female actors, all kinds of artists, bards, rishis and ascetics, pandits well-versed in Vedas, and many others. Citizens and merchants from numerous countries adorned the city with their presence. Feudatory chiefs and kings of other janapadas would come to pay their taxes to Dasharatha.

The people of Ayodhyā, men as well as women of all communities, were virtuous, of strong character, well mannered, with self-restraint and content—almost saint-like. There were no thieves in the city, nor anyone living in poverty. There was no one, neither man nor woman, who was unclean, without wealth, without elegance or embellishments and fragrances on their bodies. There was no one who was famished, or uncharitable, or imprudent. Subjects of Ayodhyā were pious and loyal to their king. They were great hosts and took good care of their guests. The people lived long and healthy lives.

The peace and prosperity of the state were ensured by Dasharatha and his team of eight ministers through their able administration. Wise counsel and guidance from their royal gurus—Rishi Vashishtha and Rishi Vāmdeva—helped the king to stay on the virtuous path. Dasharatha was powerful enough to subjugate his enemies and generous enough to keep his friends and allies in good stead. He ensured the treasury was full and weaponry well-stocked to provide stability and peace to his people. It was said of Dasharatha that he was a 'Rājarshi'—a saintly king.

Dasharatha had chosen his ministers well. They were of sharp intellect and capable of comprehending minute nuances of issues. They were experts in policy, economics and administration. Always soft-spoken, they knew how to manage treasury, maintain the army in good form and keep secrets. They also understood the nature of alliances and war. They kept a close eye on all happenings inside and outside the state by way of a strong network of spies. The ministers were objective and unbiased and would not shy away from punishing even their own sons if found guilty. Nor would they inflict punishment on innocent people.

A fair process was followed to determine guilt. Only after considering all aspects of a case was an appropriate punishment determined.

Such was the splendour of Ayodhyā and its people.[3]

Kishkindhā

Ayodhyā was in the plains, by the Sarayu river; Lankā was perched on a mountaintop. Kishkindhā was situated inside the dense forest of Dandakāranya. The city seemed like a colossal cave. It had ornate, gem-studded mansions—none having just a single storey—surrounded by beautiful and bountiful orchards, wide pathways and flowing springs of crystal-clear water. Sweet fragrances of sandalwood, lotuses, flower-liquor and fruit wines permeated its air. Many vānaras, dressed in rich garments, wearing garlands and ornaments, strutted about the streets of Kishkindhā, highlighting the city's grandeur.[4]

In the Rāmāyana, we get a glimpse of Kishkindhā through Lakshmana's eyes.

Lankā

Vishvakarmā had himself designed the city of Lankā, ensconced between Trikuta and Suvel mountains on the southern coast. He built this city for the rākshasa tribe led by Heti. The grace of Brahma had made the rākshasas powerful and prosperous. But with time, this power also made them arrogant and oppressive. Eventually, Vishnu intervened and defeated the rākshasas. Following this defeat, the rākshasas abandoned Lankā and retreated to the interiors. After many years, the city was re-established by Kuber. In his reign, Lankā became a place of luxury and affluence, surpassing its past glory.

After Rāvana acquired the boon of near-immortality from Brahma deva, his maternal relatives provoked him to stake his claim on Lankā. Rāvana rejected the idea at first—Kuber was his elder brother after all. Kuber had always been very affectionate towards his siblings, including Rāvana. But the instigations continued, making Rāvana believe that the rākashasas had been wronged and Lankā belonged to them. The maternal relatives also told Rāvana that if they gained control of Lankā, he would become the ruler.

Convinced, or rather tempted, Rāvana sent a messenger to Kuber with the message that said, 'This city of Lankā previously belonged to rākshasas led by my maternal grandfather Sumāli. It is only fair that you return to the rākshasas what is truly theirs.' Kuber replied with poise to his younger brother, 'Our father had instructed me to come and live here. When I came, Lankā was devoid of rākshasas and other inhabitants. It is through my effort that Lankā is what it is today. But you are my brother. Whatever is mine, is for you to enjoy too. I have never kept you away from it.'

Kuber sought advice from his father, Rishi Vishrava, on the future course of action. Rishi Vishrava advised Kuber to let Rāvana have Lankā. 'Rāvana had previously made this demand to me. I admonished him that trying to capture Lankā in this manner will lead to his downfall. But Brahma deva's boon has made him arrogant and wicked. Hence, I urge you to give Lankā to your brother. Move to Kailāsh and live happily over there.' Kuber took the advice and Rāvana became the king of the affluent city of Lankā.[5]

It was this Lankā that awed Hanumāna when he first arrived on the island. The city, located atop the Trikuta mountains, was surrounded by beautiful forests, gardens in full bloom with all kinds of fruits and flowers, lakes with ducks and swans, and deep moats filled with lotuses. Impregnable golden walls enclosed the city. Dreadful looking rākshasas manning the outer wall further strengthened its fortifications. The city, bedecked with mountain-like white mansions and tall towers, appeared to be floating in the sky.

Ensconced within the golden walls were multistorey houses, storehouses and workshops. The houses, some seven- and eight-storeyed, were constructed in auspicious shapes of lotuses and swastikas. They exuded opulence with gem-studded floors, pillars of gold and diamond-studded window lattices. The buildings were neatly lined up, close to each other. Huge golden arches decorated the pathways. The city dazzled with numerous lamps illuminating the houses. Sounds of laughter, musical instruments and loud chatter resounded through them. Hanumāna could hear the tinkle of ornaments of well-dressed maidens and the sounds of footfalls on the stairs from the houses. From some, he also heard chanting of Vedic mantras and from some others, drunken revelry. The inside of the city was also well guarded, with spies in various disguises and armed soldiers patrolling.

The Lankā that Hanumāna saw was hustling and bustling with activity. The splendour of the city was no less than Indra's Amrāvati![6]

Other Prominent Cities and Places

- Mithilā—capital of Videha, ruled by Janaka
- Kekaya—city of Kaikeyi's parents
- Siddhāshram—Rishi Vishvāmitra's āshram
- Shringaverpur—Rāma's good friend Nishādarāj Guha's city
- Chitrakoot—Rāma, Seetā, Lakshmana's first abode during their vanvās
- Panchavati—place from where Rāvana abducted Seetā

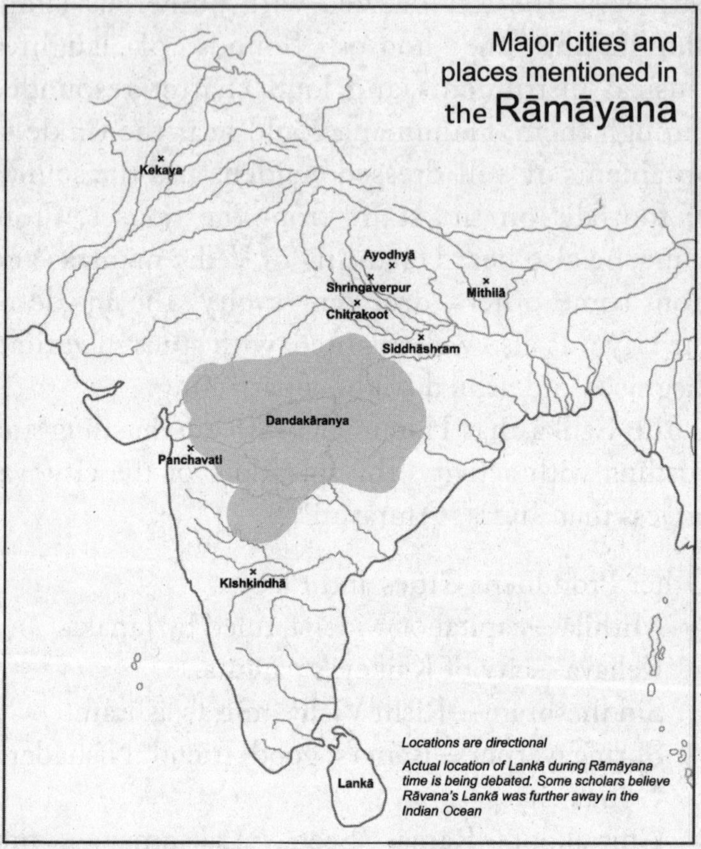

Major cities and places mentioned in the Rāmāyana

Kekaya

Ayodhyā

Shringaverpur

Chitrakoot

Mithilā

Siddhāshram

Dandakāranya

Panchavati

Kishkindhā

Lankā

Locations are directional

Actual location of Lankā during Rāmāyana time is being debated. Some scholars believe Rāvana's Lankā was further away in the Indian Ocean

Map 1 Prominent places mentioned in the Rāmāyana

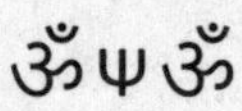

Part 2

Personalities, Events and Eventualities

4

Vishvāmitra's Quest

Dasharatha was pondering about the wedding of his sons when a royal guard rushed in. 'Mahārāja, Rishi Vishvāmitra seeks your audience,' he announced. Dasharatha was elated. He went to the door and escorted the rishi to his royal court. After the customary courtesies, when everyone was seated, Dasharatha expressed his joy at seeing Rishi Vishvāmitra. 'Your arrival here is as gratifying as the pouring of rain during a famine, as the news of begetting a child through a deserving wife. What can I do for you? It will be a matter of great fortune for me to be able to fulfil your wishes. Your wish is my command. Let me know and I will get it done.'

Vishvāmitra was pleased with Dasharatha's warm welcome. 'I will tell you what my desire is, may your words of fulfilling it be true. I have undertaken a sankalpa of completing a major yajna. But I am not able to do that because of two powerful rākshasas, Māreecha and Subāhu. They throw pieces of raw flesh in my yajna vedi[1] and disrupt the rituals. This has happened many times, rendering all my efforts futile. Even though capable, I am not inclined to punish them myself, as the act of retribution will impact my sankalpa. To help guard my yajna, let your eldest son Rāma accompany me for ten days. Under my protection, I am certain that

Rāma is competent enough to destroy the mischief mongers. For that, I will confer upon him skills and strengths that will bring him fame in this world. I assure you of Rāma's safety, fret not. Do not let your fatherly love colour your decision. In consultation with your ministers and the esteemed sages such as Rishi Vashishtha, let me know your decision.'

Dasharatha was taken aback. Rāma was everything to him. His ātmā resided in Rāma. For a few moments, he was dumbfounded. Then slowly gathering his thoughts, he spoke, 'But Rāma is only a child, not even sixteen yet. He may not be ready to face the deadly rākshasas. It may not be right to put Rāma in such a dangerous situation. I have a huge and capable army. You may have that. I can come with you, too. I promise to fight the two demons till my last breath. Who are these rākshasas that are causing grief to you?'

'Māreecha and Subāhu work under the protection of Rāvana and take commands from him. Rāvana is born in the lineage of Rishi Pulastya. His father is the great Rishi Vishrava. A boon from Brahma deva has made him ruthless and arrogant. Where he doesn't go, he sends his minions to cause terror,' informed Vishvāmitra.

Dasharatha was unnerved hearing the name of Rāvana, 'Rāvana is way too strong to be contained even by me. Not even devas can fight him. Please have mercy on me and my son. I cannot send Rāma to fight these rākshasas who are like the Lord of Death himself. I will come with you. I promise to fight one of them with my army,' pleaded Dasharatha.

Vishvāmitra was not pleased at all. He said rather sarcastically, 'Did you not promise that you will do as

I wish? Now you are backtracking on your words. This is quite unbecoming of the scion of Raghu's vamsha. But if you believe what you are doing is right, then so be it. I will leave as I had come. May you be happy with your false oath.'

Sensing the fury of Rishi Vishvāmitra, Rishi Vashishtha intervened: 'Dasharatha, you are known for your probity, truthfulness and honouring your word. Call not infamy upon yourself by going back on your words. Nobody knows Vishvāmitra the way I do. His tapasyā is immense. His prowess is unfathomable. There is no weapon that he doesn't have knowledge of. Under his care, no harm can come to Rāma. He is very capable of reining in the rākshasas himself. Yet, he seeks Rāma, not for himself but for your son's benefit out of his affection for him. Let Rāma go.'

Vashistha's words served as a balm to Dasharatha's agitated mind. He agreed to send both Rāma and Lakshmana with Rishi Vishvāmitra.[2]

Thus began a stint that was to prepare Rāma for the times to come.

The Journey to Siddhāshram

Vishvāmitra walked ahead and the boys followed him, carrying their bows on their shoulders and a quiver of arrows on their backs. Resplendent swords hung by their waist. There were no chariots waiting to drive them or inviting soft beds for their rest. The journey to Siddhāshram, Vishvāmitra's āshram, involved a four-day trek, crossing many forests. But the boys did not complain.

Rāma and Lakshmana were princes who had grown up amidst all comforts and luxuries at their disposal. But now, as they accompanied Vishvāmitra, they left behind all the comforts to live by his instructions. Rāma and Lakshmana did not need to be told this; they were well trained by Rishi Vashishtha in following the decorum and protocol of living with a guru.

About a yojana-and-a-half outside of Ayodhyā, by the southern bank of the Sarayu river, Vishvāmitra halted. He asked Rāma to sip some water from the holy river and get ready to imbibe the knowledge of Balā and Atibalā vidyā. These were powerful mantras by whose potency Rāma would not feel any physical pain or mental fatigue when engaged in his ordained tasks. The mantras would ensure Rāma would never be overpowered by his enemies even when asleep or unaware. 'There will be no one on this earth comparable to you in strength or in wisdom. Neither hunger nor thirst will ever cause trouble to you. O Rāma! Partake from me this Balā–Atibalā vidyā, which is considered the mother of all knowledge,' said Vishvāmitra as he proceeded to give this rare knowledge to the princes.

Balā–Atibalā Vidyā

Rishi Vishvāmitra imparted the Balā–Atibalā vidyā to Rāma and Lakshmana. The vidyā was meant to make them immune to hunger, thirst, sleep and fatigue while giving them immense strength and wisdom.

Rishi Vālmiki mentions the name of this potent knowledge in the Rāmāyana but gives no details. More information about Balā–Atibalā vidyā is found in an Upanishad related to *Sāmaveda*, the *Savitri Upanishad*. The vidyā is essentially a mantra anushthān, which must be undertaken only under the guidance of a capable guru.

The three of them spent that night by the banks of Sarayu. The princes of Ayodhyā slept on the grass under the vast, open sky. Vishvāmitra treated them with a lot of affection and the boys reciprocated with respect and obedience.[3]

The rishi woke them up at dawn the next morning. The three of them continued their journey. On the second evening, they halted in an āshram in Angadesh[4] by the confluence of the Sarayu and Gangā rivers. Vishvāmitra narrated to them the legend about the name of the place and some other stories before retiring for the day.

Venkatesh Suprabhatam

The shloka uttered by Rishi Vishvāmitra, as Rishi Vālmiki tells us, for waking up Rāma is sung every morning in many Hindu households even today. The shloka is:

कौसल्या सुप्रजा राम पूर्वा संध्या प्रवर्तते ।
उत्तिष्ठ नरशार्दूल कर्तव्यं दैवमाह्निकम् ॥

O Rāma, obtaining a son like you, Kaushalyā is considered the fortunate one. Wake up, O lion among men, it is the break of dawn. May you get your morning prayers and rituals done.[5]

A famous hymn 'Venkatesh Suprabhatam Strotam', has this shloka. The strotam is prominently sung to wake up Bhagvān Venkateshwara (Vishnu) in Tirumala Tirupati Devasthānam.

Their journey on the third morning began from the banks of the Gangā. Using a boat, they navigated the mighty river to reach its southern banks. On the way, Rāma wanted to know why the water there created such loud noises. His curiosity pleased the rishi who explained that they were at the confluence of the two rivers Gangā and Sarayu and the turbulent noise was created by the waters of the two rivers surging into each other with force.

On the other side of the Gangā, a dense and dangerous-looking forest awaited them. It seemed bereft of any human settlement. Sounds of wild animals, birds and insects reverberated through the forest. Vishvāmitra recounted to the boys how the forest came to be.

> Once upon a time, this place was home to two bustling and prosperous cities, Maladā and Karushā. One fateful day, a cannibal rākshasi named Tātakā cast her eyes on this place. She possessed the strength of a thousand elephants, thanks to a boon of Brahma deva. Māreecha, one of the rākshasas interrupting my yajna, is her son. She wreaked havoc on the cities. She killed the citizens for food, destroyed their homes and laid waste to this entire region which eventually turned into a dense forest.

Then with some authority, Vishvāmitra said, 'Rāma, Tātakā has devastated this place and continues to do so till date. For making headway in the forest, this wretched rākshasi deserves to be killed; slay her.' Rāma was not sure how he could kill Tātakā. She was a woman after all. Didn't the scriptures prohibit the killing of women and brāhmins? Vishvāmitra, as if reading Rāma's mind, exhorted him and said categorically:

> You must harbour neither disgust nor doubt about killing a woman like Tātakā. Being a prince, you must do what is in the interest of all your subjects.[6] For a king, the protection and welfare of his citizens must be paramount. For the sake of his people, a king should be willing to undertake any kind of action, be it harsh or gentle, virtuous or apparently sinful. This is indeed the dharma ordained for all those entrusted with the responsibility of ruling kingdoms. So, hesitate not. Eliminate adharma by killing this rākshasi. There is not an iota of dharma in her.

Rāma readied his bow to follow the rishi's command and plucked its string hard. The thunderous twang of the bow echoed through the forest startling its inhabitants. Tātakā heard the sound too. Furious, she rushed in the direction of the princes. Rāma saw Tātakā charging towards him and quickly aimed his arrow at her. A gruesome duel followed. Tātakā was strong and ferocious. She showered huge boulders and tree trunks on the princes. Rāma hit her with his sharp arrows which hurt her no doubt but fell short of killing her. Despite Vishvāmitra's initial encouragement, Rāma couldn't get himself to slay Tātakā immediately. 'This rākshasi is a woman and I am not enthused to kill her. Instead, I will make her disabled, cutting her limbs, nose and ears,' said Rāma to Lakshmana. But Tātakā showed no mercy on the princes. She brutally attacked them, resorting to her powers of creating illusions.

Discerning that Rāma still had qualms about killing Tātakā, Vishvāmitra encouraged him again. 'Stop having mercy on this treacherous rākshasi. Take her down before the sun sets. Else she will become invincible once it starts becoming dark,'[7] he told Rāma. Having got a taste of Tātakā's strength and brutality, Rāma firmed up his mind and wasted no more time. He rained a volley of arrows on her. Injured and angry, the rākshasi rushed towards the princes. Rāma then aimed at her chest and shot a deadly arrow. The aim was perfect. The arrow tore apart Tātakā's chest. She collapsed on the ground, dead.

Vishvāmitra was pleased with Rāma's achievement, more so with the display of his valour and skills. They spent the night in the forest that seemed to come alive after Tātakā's death. The next morning, Vishvāmitra bestowed upon Rāma many celestial weapons and the methods to summon them. Having witnessed the duel between Rāma and Tātakā, the rishi felt confident that Rāma was well-deserving and ready to handle these divine but lethal weapons.[8]

The menace of Tātaka was removed. But the task for which Rāma and Lakshmana had been brought was pending. The boys followed Vishvāmitra onwards to Siddhāshram. This was their fourth day since leaving Ayodhyā. On the way, Rāma wanted to know the history and significance of the place.

'In the ancient past, Vishnu in his Vāmana avatār[9] resided in Siddhāshram for many years. I chose this place for my sankalpa due to my bhakti for Vāmana,' explained the rishi.

That evening they reached Siddhāshram. After a brief rest, Rāma and Lakshmana politely conveyed to Vishvāmitra that he could consecrate the yajna soon as they were geared up for the task of protecting it. Vishvāmitra initiated the yajna. The yajna also involved maun vrata—vow of silence—by the rishi for the duration of the ritual, that is, for six days and nights, Vishvāmitra would not speak a single word and focus only on the yajna. Rāma and Lakshmana had to safeguard the yajna from being disrupted and ensure its completion.

Five days and nights went by peacefully. The sixth day dawned and the chants of the Vedic mantras filled the air. Rāma cautioned Lakshmana about the possibility of Subāhu and Māreecha attacking the yajna that day. As Rāma was speaking, a deafening sound of thunder reverberated in the sky. The princes became alert. Rāma spotted the two rākshasas and their minions rushing towards the āshram, splashing streams of blood around. 'Look Lakshmana, the man-eating rākshasas are here. I am going to chase these cowards away just like a gush of wind dispels the clouds,' exclaimed Rāma.

He shot the powerful Mānavāstra[10] at Māreecha. The power of the weapon and the momentum of

Rāma's shot was such that Māreecha was thrown into the sea a hundred yojanas away. The force of the blow rendered him unconscious. For Subāhu, Rāma pulled out the fatal Agneyāstra and shot at his chest. Subāhu collapsed dead, in an instant. Then, using the Vayavyāstra, Rāma killed the remaining rākshasas who had accompanied Subāhu and Māreecha.

With all the obstacles gone, Vishvāmitra completed his yajna.[11]

Destination Mithilā

Vishvāmitra's sankalpa had been fulfilled. In return, Rāma had acquired several valuable weapons and the techniques for operating them. But the rishi wasn't done yet. He had one more task to accomplish. His next destination was Mithilā, to participate in a grand yajna being conducted by Rājā Janaka of Videha. He asked the princes to accompany him. He told them, 'Janaka has a precious heirloom, a bow of Shiva. The bow is so massive and heavy that even gods have not been able to string it, what to say of men. Many kings have made attempts to lift it, in vain. You boys should come along with me to Mithilā to see that bow and participate in the yajna ceremony.' They obeyed. On the way, Vishvāmitra kept the boys and the rest of his entourage consisting of other disciples entertained with stories and anecdotes. Before entering Mithilā, they made a brief stop at a secluded āshram to get the darshan of Ahalyā Devi.

When Janaka heard of Vishvāmitra's arrival in Mithilā, he, accompanied by his purohit[12] Rishi Shatānanda, rushed to welcome the celebrated rishi. Janaka was curious to know more about the two handsome and strong young men with the rishi. Vishvāmitra introduced the two princes of Ayodhyā and narrated the happenings of the last few days. Shatānanda was especially delighted to hear about Rāma and Lakshmana's visit to his mother, Ahalyā. He was the first-born child of Ahalyā and Rishi Gautama.

One day Vishvāmitra suggested to Janaka to let the princes have a look at his heirloom—the Shiva Dhanush. Janaka sent for the bow to be brought there. Meanwhile, Janaka told them about his dear daughter Seetā. He had found Seetā in the womb of the earth while tilling the land for a religious ritual. Overjoyed to get this gift from Mother Earth, Janaka decided then that he would marry his precious daughter only to the person who could string the divine bow of Shiva. That was his virya shulka for Seetā. 'Since Seetā has come of age,' continued Janaka, 'many kings desirous of marrying her have attempted to string the bow but none have been able to even move it. Some kings considered it an insult to their prowess and besieged Mithilā. This siege lasted for over a year. Eventually, my army chased them away. That bow which has been inaccessible to even the devas and gandharvas, I will show to Rāma and Lakshmana now. If Rāma lifts the bow and strings it, I will marry Seetā to him.'[13]

The Shiva Dhanush was brought in an eight-wheeled iron case. That it took 5,000 well-built young men to pull the case gives an inkling of how huge and heavy the bow was. With Vishvāmitra's and Janaka's consent, Rāma opened the case and had a keen look at that most splendid bow. Then, to everyone's utter astonishment, Rāma held the bow from its centre, lifted it and strung it, as if it was a child's play. With the bow firmly in his hands, Rāma, very simply, pulled the string towards his ears, as if shooting an arrow. But his force was such that the mighty Shiva Dhanush broke into two with a loud bang. The assembly was stunned! Janaka was euphoric. He had found the most worthy match for his daughter by the blessings of Shiva. He wasted no time in sending a messenger to Dasharatha to inform him of the marriage and seek his permission as well as presence at the wedding.

Thus, Seetā and Rāma were married, so were Urmilā–Lakshmana, Māndavi–Bharata and Shrutakirti–Shatrughna.

Virya Shulka

Virya shulka literally means 'valour or heroism as price'.

In ancient times, there were several types of marriages. In royal kshatriya families, swayamvara was common. Here the girl chose the man she liked from a group of assembled suitors. Another prevalent practice was of virya shulka, in which potential bridegrooms had to take a challenge designed to test their strength and valour. Sometimes the test of strength was undertaken in a swayamvara setting. The suitors would compete and the winner would take the bride home.

In the Mahābhārata, Drupad had a swayamvara organised for Draupadi, but he had devised a challenge as well—a machine with a target was suspended in the air. There was a small hole in the machine. The suitors had to shoot five arrows through that hole and hit the target. In that sense, Drupad had also set a virya shulka for his daughter.

Other kinds of shulkas were rājya shulka and dhana shulka. In rājya shulka, the suitor had to make a commitment that only the girl's son would be the heir to the suitor's kingdom. This was the condition laid down by Dāsharāj for marrying his daughter Satyawati to Shāntanu, Bhishma's father.

It appears that Dasharatha may have made such a commitment to Kaikeyi's father at the time of their marriage. However, this is mentioned only once in the Rāmāyana (Ayodhyā Kānda 2.107.3) by Rāma to Bharata while convincing him to forgive his mother. There is no other reference of either Kaikeyi or Mantharā or Bharata's maternal family speaking about it anywhere else in the epic.

Dhana shulka, also often referred to only as shulka, literally means money or wealth as price. In some families, there was a tradition to take money from the suitor before marrying the girl. This type of wedding is also called 'asura vivah'. Pandu was married to Mādri in this manner according to the tradition in Madra.

In Rāmacharitmānas and Kamba Rāmāyana, we find an elaborate description of Seetā's grand swayamvara ceremony where many princes came but failed in their attempt to gain her hand. There is also a beautiful narration of Rāma and Seetā falling in love on seeing each other in a garden before the swayamvara takes place. This part is not in Vālmiki's Rāmāyana.

Rishi Vashishtha was correct when he said Rishi Vishvāmitra did not seek Rāma for any personal gain but had come for Rāma's benefit. Through Vishvāmitra, Dasharatha's eldest son got acquainted with life in the forest, was enriched with weapons and newer arts of warfare, and found a worthy wife in Seetā. Most importantly, he received a practical lesson in Rāja Dharma. These lessons would shape his future course of action.

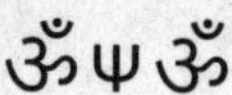

5

The Making of Vishvāmitra

Rishi Vishvāmitra wasn't born as Vishvāmitra. In his past life, he was Kaushika, an illustrious king of the Kusha dynasty. As the son of Gādhi, he was also called Gādhiputra. Kaushika's prowess and valour were known far and wide. It is said the entire Bhāratavarsha was under his sway either directly or through feudatory kings. Kaushika's transformation into Vishvāmitra is the stuff of legends, no less.

The story of Vishvāmitra was narrated to Rāma and Lakshmana in Mithilā by Rishi Shatānanda, Janaka's purohit. 'There is nobody on earth more fortunate than you Rāma, that this scion of Kusha is your benefactor. His deeds are extraordinary and his brilliance unbounded. By his intense tapasyā he has achieved the highest stature of Brahmarshi,' Shatānanda had lauded before proceeding to recount the extraordinary tale.

Brahmarshi

A rishi is one who attains realisation through knowledge and wisdom, as prescribed in the Vedas and Upanishads.[1] Typically, rishis lived an austere life, having gained control over their senses (indriya-nigraha), involving themselves in the study and teaching of shāstras, doing meditation, conducting yajnas, chanting Vedic mantras and performing other activities as prescribed in the scriptures, with the intent of the well-being and happiness of all.[2]

Most rishis received royal patronage as they served as guides and teachers to the king and presided over the rituals he performed. Depending on the level of indriya-nigraha and corresponding siddhis (supra-normal physical and mental abilities) attained by them, certain appellations were used. In the increasing order of realisation and accomplishment, these appellations were Rājarshi, Rishi, Mahārshi and Brahmarshi.

Rājarshi was a king with the attributes of a sage, one who was solely concerned with the well-being of his people and those who sought his refuge and had himself risen above worldly material desires. A Brahmarshi was at the top in the order. He was one who had realised Brahma, the ultimate truth.[3] He operated from the highest level of consciousness and transcended the dualities of sorrow and joy, love and hate, as well as impulses of lust, anger, greed, pride, delusions and jealousy.

A Rude Awakening

Many years ago, King Kaushika reigned over a sprawling kingdom. He was a noble and just king, liked by his subjects. Once he undertook a journey across vast regions of the earth, taking along one akshauhini army.[4] They travelled for many days through forests, mountains, janapadas and āshrams, crossing several rivers along the way. One day, he and his army reached the āshram of Rishi Vashishtha.

Seeing the celebrated rishi, Kaushika prostrated at his feet. Vashishtha welcomed the king with delight. After he was seated, Vashishtha enquired of Kaushika, 'Are you doing fine, O king? Are you ruling your kingdom in a just manner and keeping your subjects satisfied? Are you taking good care of your employees? Do they obey your orders? Have you vanquished your enemies? Are your treasury, army and family in good health?'

Kaushika responded in the affirmative. Both of them had a pleasant discussion for quite a while. Later, Rishi Vashishtha offered to host the entire army of Kaushika. Kaushika was reluctant. He was aware that feeding his huge army would be a difficult task for the rishi. But he gave in to Vashishtha's affectionate insistence.

Vashishtha called his mottled cow, Shabalā. Shabalā was Kāmdhenu, the wish-fulfilling cow. The rishi respectfully requested, 'I have offered to host the king and his army. Please arrange a feast for the royal entourage. Shower us with the most delectable of foods.' Instantly, Shabalā started presenting every kind of drink and delicacy that the guests could possibly wish for. The army feasted to its heart's content. Kaushika looked on in amazement.[5]

Soon it was time to leave. Kaushika approached Vashishtha with a proposition. 'My army and I are extremely grateful for your generous hospitality. I have an offer to make to you. I will give you a hundred thousand cows in lieu of Shabalā. Let me have her. In a way, she rightfully belongs to me.' Rishi Vashishtha was a little taken aback. He politely refused. 'Shabalā cannot be separated from me. Not for a hundred thousand cows nor a hundred crore or any other form of wealth can I give her to you. The fulfilment of my sacred rituals is dependent on her. She is everything to me.'

Kaushika thought Vashishtha was looking for a bargain, so he upped his offer, adding fully decked elephants, golden chariots, horses of the best breeds and lavish amounts of gems and gold. But the rishi was not open to any negotiation. 'Shabalā is my wealth; she is my life; I will not part with her,' he asserted.[6]

Not used to hearing a 'no', Kaushika decided to take the cow by force. He began to drag the visibly unwilling and upset Shabalā away. The cow, using all her strength, pulled herself free from him and ran towards the helpless rishi. The king's soldiers began pulling her again. This time, she made a loud sound of 'moo'. From that sound emerged a group of fierce warriors. The warriors began to slay Kaushika's soldiers. They even killed his sons. His army was no match for these warriors. Kaushika returned to his kingdom, embarrassed and shocked. He lost his will to rule. Handing over the kingdom to his only surviving son, Kaushika headed to the Himālayas, determined to serve and please Shiva.

His tapasyā bore fruit. Shiva manifested to grant him a boon. 'What do you seek, Kaushika?' Shiva asked. 'Let all the best techniques of warfare and all the weapons in the universe come to me,' requested Kaushika. 'So be it,' blessed Shiva and disappeared. Kaushika was beaming. He thought he was now invincible. No army could defeat him. Armed with his newfound strength and hubris, he attacked Vashishtha's āshram and began razing it to the ground. The disciples and the animals ran helter-skelter, trying to save their lives.

Vashishtha was now furious. 'You have destroyed this āshram which was so lovingly built by me. Your stupidity and wickedness will surely destroy you,' thundered the rishi as he lifted his danda which was as powerful as the Yama-danda—the baton of the lord of death. With the strength of his tapasyā, he not only repelled Kaushika's attack but also destroyed all his weapons.

Kaushika was humiliated once again. That he, the king who was feared by one and all, was no match for an unarmed rishi came as a rude shock to him. 'Darned be all my kshatriya-balam, my warrior prowess. The real strength is what Vashishtha has, his brahma-balam. I will also undertake intense penance and achieve the power that comes with becoming Brahmarshi,' declared Kaushika and went away.

Brahma-Balam

The out-of-ordinary physical and mental vigour of a Brahmarshi due to complete control over all senses, mind and intellect is referred to as 'brahma-balam'. The strongest of warriors and the best of weapons can do no harm to such a person. A Brahmarshi can burn an opponent to ashes with the heat of his own innate strength. A Brahmarshi is also intuitively discerning of when to use his powers and when not to. Even his anger has a larger purpose.

Trishanku's Desire

The loss at the hands of Vashishtha had left Kaushika agitated. Determined to take his revenge after acquiring equivalent prowess, he headed southwards with his queen and plunged himself into deep tapasyā, subsisting only on fruits and roots. His effort succeeded and Brahma deva appeared to him. 'You have achieved the stature of Rājarshi. Hereby I proclaim you as one,' he said and left. Kaushika was embarrassed and dejected. 'All this effort and all I could gain is Rājarshi-hood,' he thought, but he was not the one to give up. He doubled down on his tapasyā.

At the time when Kaushika was deep in tapasyā, there lived another king named Trishanku. He desired to go to heaven before his death. He wanted to enter heaven with his earthly body. Trishanku approached Rishi Vashishtha to sanctify a yajna that could make it happen. Vashishtha refused, saying such a feat was not possible. Trishanku took his request to Vashishtha's sons. They too declined to oblige Trishanku and even berated him for seeking other rishis when Rishi Vashishtha had discouraged him from the deed.

Trishanku reached out to Kaushika and told him of his desire as well as the rejection by Vashishtha and his sons. Kaushika recognised this as a great opportunity to use his newfound powers and position himself as a more accomplished rishi than Vashishtha. He agreed to conduct a grand yajna for Trishanku and sent invitations to many other rishis, including Vashishtha's sons, to participate in the yajna.

Vashishtha's sons scoffed at the invitation. Kaushika was infuriated by the insult. Using the power accrued through his penance, he cursed them with death.

Scared of his wrath, the other rishis obeyed him and sanctified Trishanku's yajna. But that didn't seem to work. The devas refused to be complicit in something that violated the law of nature. This made Kaushika even more furious and determined to send Trishanku to heaven in his earthly body. As this deed wasn't welcome in the existing heaven, Kaushika decided he would create a new heaven for Trishanku. He did that. Kaushika created an artificial heaven for Trishanku and established him there with his earthly body.[7]

This entire incident, however, had disrupted Kaushika's tapasyā. He headed to Pushkar to start again.

The Lure of Lust

Once again, Kaushika began practising intense austerities. After a few years, Brahma deva came once again to bless him. 'You have achieved Rishi-hood,' he said. Brahmarshi-hood still appeared out of reach. Kaushika stayed in Pushkar, continuing his tapasyā. Then one day, a woman of unmatched beauty, the celestial nymph Menakā, arrived in Pushkar for a bath. Kaushika's eyes fell on her. A shiver of excitement ran through his body. Overcome with lust, he approached the lady. Attracted by the resplendent Rishi Kaushika, she acquiesced.

Both spent over ten years in each other's company, till one day it dawned upon Kaushika that he had lost both time and merit accrued through years of tapasyā. In spite of all the strengths he had attained through his tapasyā, he had failed to achieve control over his lust. The realisation made him sorrowful and repentant. His heavy sighs scared Menakā. Kaushika looked at her affectionately and asked her to take leave. Menakā was disappointed but she knew this day would come. She too wasn't meant to stay forever. Menakā left.

With a firm resolve to overcome the hold of lust, Kaushika went to the north, settled by the banks of the River Kaushiki and took up even more intense meditation and penance. Many years went by. Kaushika resolutely continued his penance. Finally, Brahma deva came and said, 'I am very pleased with your unfailing commitment. I bestow upon you Mahārshi-hood. You have now achieved prominence among rishis.' Kaushika bowed down to the deva with folded hands: 'Pitāmaha, through the merits I have accrued, if you confer upon me the stature of Brahmarshi, I will consider that I have achieved control over my senses.' Brahma deva smiled. 'You haven't achieved that completely yet, son. Continue with your efforts,' he said.[8]

The Anger Impulse

Kaushika resumed his penance, making it even more intense. This time he meditated standing up, with his hands raised over his head. He gave up all kinds of food and survived only on air. Come rain, come heat, come cold, Kaushika persisted. The devas were disturbed by the fervour of Kaushika's tapasyā. Indra, asked Rambhā, a celestial nymph of immaculate beauty, to go near the rishi and distract him. Rambhā did as told. Seeing Rambhā, Kaushika smelled mischief. He understood that it was an attempt to hinder his efforts. Mad with anger, he pronounced a curse on Rambhā.

As soon as he had uttered the curse, the words of Brahma deva flashed in his mind. You haven't achieved control over your senses completely, he had said. His angry utterance made Kaushika realise that he was still far away from gaining control over his anger. All his hard work in the past had amounted to zilch because of his failure to restrain his anger. He was flustered. But he was not going to give up. He resolved to never give in to anger or speak any untoward words out of anger. He also resolved to conquer every single impulse of his—be it emotions or bodily needs like hunger, thirst and even breathing. 'Come what may, I will not give up till I have achieved complete self-restraint,' Kaushika proclaimed.[9]

He went eastwards and began his tapasyā again. His tapasyā went on for many years and throughout he maintained a vow of silence. Many obstacles and challenges came his way, but Kaushika remained steadfast. The stipulated time ended. Kaushika had accomplished the impossible. A sankalpa of such proportion had not been undertaken before, nor would it be repeated ever again by anyone else. There was not an iota of anger left in him.

At the end of his tapasyā, after many years of fasting, he finally prepared some food and was about to eat his first morsel, when Indra came seeking food, disguised as a brāhmin to test Kaushika's resolve. Kaushika did not flinch nor resist. Very calmly he handed over his food to the guest and stood silently as the guest ate. Kaushika was resplendent, exuding a divine aura. The world seemed to have dulled before his radiance.

All the devas conceded that Kaushika had transcended lust, anger and other such impulses, and had achieved complete control over his senses. There was no trace of impurity or ill-will in him. He had truly transformed into a Brahmarshi. The resplendence was the splendour of his brahma-balam. Brahma deva arrived and bestowed upon him Brahmarshi-hood. He also proclaimed that from then on, Kaushika would be known in the world as Vishvāmitra, the friend of the world.

Kaushika was happy, but he had one final request. 'May the best of the sages, Brahmarshi Vashishtha himself, acknowledge that I have become a Brahmarshi.' Vashishtha came and was delighted to see the transformed Kaushika. 'There is not a doubt that you indeed have become a Brahmarshi; all the wisdom will come to you in accordance with your status,' said Vashishtha. Vishvāmitra bowed down to Vashishtha reverentially.

Kaushika had embarked on a journey to seek revenge on Vashishtha but now, as Vishvāmitra, no jealousy, no anger, no sense of revenge remained in his heart.[10]

When Vashishtha had assured Dasharatha in the court the day he came to seek Rāma that he knew Vishvāmitra well, he had spoken the truth. No one knew Vishvāmitra as Vashishtha did—Vashishtha was the cause of Vishvāmitra's transformation!

Real strength lies in conquering our base instincts of lust, anger, greed, attachment, pride and jealousy. Real power lies not in doing as we desire but in making our senses and desires subservient to our wisdom, in acting as we should rather than as we like. Real freedom lies in unshackling ourselves from the bondage of likes and dislikes.

The *Rigvedic* Gāyatri Mantra, one of the most sacred Vedic mantras for Hindus, is attributed to Rishi Vishvāmitra. He is considered as drashtā—the seer of the Gāyatri mantra.

ॐ ψ ॐ

6

Ahalyā

The journey of the princes of Ayodhyā with Vishvāmitra and his disciples from Siddhāshram to Mithilā was a lesson in history and geography. Vishvāmitra instructed the young boys using stories of Samudra Manthan—the churning of the ocean—the origin of various rivers and the establishment of different cities on their shores. Along the way, they stopped at several places—one night by the banks of Sona, another by the banks of the Gangā. They spent the third night in the city of Vishālā. On the fourth day, they reached Mithilā. But before entering the city, in a grove that they were crossing, Rāma saw an āshram, old and abandoned. He wanted to know more about it.

'Let me tell you all about how this āshram came to be accursed,' said the rishi and proceeded to tell him the story of Ahalyā—a story of a momentary lapse of judgement, of the subsequent catharsis and the eventual transformation, no less fascinating than the story of the making of Vishvāmitra himself!

Janaka's purohit, Rishi Shatānanda, was the eldest son of this lady Ahalyā and her husband Rishi Gautama.

Once upon a time, said Vishvāmitra, this was the celebrated āshram of Rishi Gautama and his wife Ahalyā. The rishi undertook many great austerities here. Ahalyā was a very attractive lady, true to her name, which means 'without any deformity',[1] that is, one of immaculate beauty. Her elegance was known far and wide. Even Indra couldn't help but desire her youthful charms. He was waiting for a chance to lure Ahalyā.

The opportunity came when Rishi Gautama was away from the āshram one day. Indra, disguised as Gautama, entered Ahalyā's room. 'O lady endowed with such fine limbs, I desire your indulgence,' he said directly, without mincing any words. Ahalyā recognised Indra even in his disguise. Ahalyā was excited and even curious that Indra himself desired her—how could she refuse? The excitement impulse caused a lapse of judgement. Ahalyā willingly gave in to Indra's desire.

Then, feeling content and realising that Gautama could be back soon, she said, 'Surashrestha,[2] I am gratified by consenting to your wish. Now please leave as soon as possible and protect me from Gautama's wrath.' Indra smiled: 'I am extremely satisfied and will go away as quickly as I came.' Indra tried to rush out, but Gautama had arrived and spotted him by then. It didn't take Gautama long to put two and two together. He realised what had transpired in his absence. Indra had desired a lady who was someone else's wife and his wife had been unfaithful.

Gautama looked at Indra, burning with anger. Indra was already shivering with fear. Gautama pronounced a curse on Indra: 'You took my form and did what shouldn't have been done. That is why you will become impotent from now on.' As soon as the words were spoken by Gautama, Indra's testicles fell off.

From his wife, Gautama sought atonement.[3] 'May you live here in seclusion, unseen by the world, engaged in intense tapasyā, fasting and surviving only on air. One day Rāma, the son of Dasharatha, will arrive in this āshram. When that happens and when you have welcomed him, cleansed of your greed and delusions, you will unite back with me.' Saying so, Gautama walked out of the āshram to live in the Himālayas.[4]

Indra had to eventually get new testicles. Testicles of a ram were implanted on him.

Vishvāmitra continued, 'Come along to this āshram of Gautama and redeem Ahalyā, who resides here in the form of the goddess[5] herself.' Rāma and Lakshmana followed Vishvāmitra into the āshram. There they saw her, shining bright, illumined by the radiance of her tapasyā. It was impossible to look at her—just like we cannot stare at the intense light of the sun reflected from a pool of water. Her aura was like that of a full moon shining from behind a cloak of fog.

The arrival of Rāma marked the success of Ahalyā's tapasyā. Rāma and Lakshmana bowed down and touched her feet reverentially. Ahalyā welcomed them. While Rāma and Lakshmana were in the āshram accepting Ahalyā's hospitality, they heard some steps approaching them and then Gautama appeared at the door. He had kept his word. So had Ahalyā. They were both united once again in their nuptial bond.

Unless we consciously make an effort, it is only human to be vulnerable to the lures of the senses. But to become aware of the vulnerability and strive to overcome it is what makes a person inspire reverence. Who knew this better than Vishvāmitra? No wonder, he had such high regard for Ahalyā. He addressed her as Devarupini—goddess-like—and encouraged the boys to touch her feet as a mark of respect. When Shatānanda was informed about Rāma meeting his mother, he was joyous. He referred to his mother with utmost piety, calling her Mahātejā—superbly radiant—and Yashasvini—the glorious one.

It is only apt that Ahalyā is celebrated as one of the five illustrious women of Indian epics—the Panchakanyā.[6]

Ahalyā in Popular Depiction

Popular retellings of the Rāmāyana depict Ahalyā as being tricked by Indra into submitting to his desires. She is also shown as becoming a stone from Gautama's curse and is liberated only when Rāma touches the stone with his foot.

As we see from the story here, the depiction in Vālmiki Rāmāyana is different and much more reverential to Ahalyā. She gave in to Indra willingly. And willingly lived through her atonement and tapasyā, mastering her senses, just like Vishvāmitra had.

Some narrations also depict Indra escaping scot-free and only Ahalyā being punished by Gautama. But as we see in Vālmiki Rāmāyana, Indra is not let off without punishment. He is rendered impotent for this transgression.

ॐ ψ ॐ

7

The Descent of Gangā

En route to Mithilā, among many stories Rishi Vishvāmitra narrated to the princes of Ayodhyā was one that traced the descent of the mighty Gangā on earth. He recounted this story one evening on the banks of the Gangā. This story was important because of the multi-generational effort put in by Rāma's ancestors in making this grand phenomenon take place.

Bhāratavarsha will remain forever indebted to the kings of the Ikshvāku lineage for Rāma and for Gangā. To this day we reap the benefits of their enterprise.

How was a task of such gigantic magnitude achieved?

The Search for a Horse

Sagar was a renowned king of the Ikshvāku dynasty who ruled around twenty generations before Rāma. He had two wives. Through one, he had a son called Asamanja. Sagar banished him from the kingdom due to his cruel ways. Through his other wife, he had 60,000 sons, thanks to the boon of an esteemed rishi.

Once Sagar initiated a grand Ashwamedha Yajna in which a horse of a good breed was allowed to traverse whatever path it wished. The horse was followed by an army of the king. In whichever kingdom the horse set its foot in, the host had to either fight the army or accept the sovereignty of the king.

This Ashwamedha Yajna of Sagar made Indra uncomfortable. Sagar was already a very powerful king. The successful completion of the yajna would make him almost invincible. Hence, afraid of losing his status, Indra stole the horse. Sagar sent his sons to search for the horse and get the yajna completed to avoid demerit. The sons looked everywhere, but couldn't find it.

They began digging the earth, hoping to unearth the horse from underneath. Finally, they found the horse loitering around in a place where an accomplished sage named Kapil was seated in deep meditation. The sons, believing Rishi Kapil was the culprit, tried to capture him. Enraged, the rishi burnt them down with the power of his tapasyā. The sons were reduced to ashes instantly.

When Sagar received the news, he was shaken. He sent his grandson Anshumān, Asamanja's son, to confirm the news, bring the horse back and do jaladāna—a ritual offering of water to the dead done to ensure the safe journey of the ātmā beyond the earthly abode—for his dead uncles. Anshumān got the horse back but couldn't do the jaladāna as there was no water around the place where the ashes were lying.

The only way jaladāna could be performed for his sons, Sagar was told, was by getting Gangā to descend on earth and flow into the region dug by his sons, where they now lay dead. The task wasn't a trivial one.

The Effort

Deliberating on the idea of making Gangā descend to the earth, Sagar ruled for many years. Then handing over his throne to his grandson Anshumān, he went to the Himālayas and undertook an intense tapasyā for Gangā. After his death, Anshumān followed suit. Dilip, Anshumān's son, also did tapasyā for many years, but the goal was very far away. Bhageeratha, Dilip's son, did not wait to retire and then undertake the tapasyā for Gangā. He went to the Himālayas soon after ascending the throne and started his efforts. After many years of intense penance, Brahma deva appeared and said, 'Appease Shiva, my boy. The momentum of Gangā is such that the earth will not be able to hold it. To avoid deluge, request Shiva to hold her in his locks and allow a smooth landing.'

Bhageeratha did as he was told. Shiva was pleased with Bhageeratha's dedication. He allowed Gangā to descend on his head. The matted locks of Shiva were so dense that Gangā got lost in them. Bhageeratha had to appease Shiva once again to convince him to provide Gangā with a way out. Shiva consented and Gangā came out of his matted hair, jumping and gurgling like a happy young girl. The impossible had been achieved. But the objective was yet to be attained. Gangā had to reach where the ashes of Sagar's sons were lying.

Bhageeratha made the way and Gangā followed. Somewhere along the way, her flow was obstructed by a king named Jahnu who was conducting a yajna. On Bhageeratha's pleadings, Jahnu made way for her, and Gangā began to flow once again, tracing Bhageeratha's path. Eventually, she arrived at the place of the ashes of Sagar's sons. Gangā rushed in, filling the entire area with her sacred waters. Bhageeratha performed jaladāna for his ancestors and completed the enterprise initiated by Sagar.

Because Bhageeratha brought her down from the Himālayas, Gangā got the name Bhageerathi. Because Jahnu eventually cleared her obstructed flow, making her emerge once again, Gangā is also called Jāhnavi.

Because the large expanse of land dug by Sagar's sons was filled by the waters of Gangā, turning the expanse into a sea, a sea in Sanskrit is also called sāgar, that is, one that came to be due to Sagar.

The place from where Gangā emerges from the Himālayas and reaches the earth is a sacred teertha, a place of religious importance, for Hindus. This is situated around 18 km uphill from Gangotri and is called Gomukh. Gomukh literally means 'the mouth of the earth'. It is a small opening underneath a mountain of snow-capped peaks from where the Gangā comes rushing out, as you can see in the picture.

Img. 1 Gomukh

Img. 2 Bhageerathi peaks

The peaks of the Himālayan range underneath which the Gangā emerges have been named Bhageerathi peaks, visible in the second picture. The author had the good fortune to see Gomukh for herself in 2019.

Decoding the Imagery

Many people have explained the story of Gangā's descent as an imagery of a real phenomenon. The interpretation is as follows:

During Sagar's reign, a widespread drought affected the kingdom. The only way to address the calamity was by finding a new source of water. Hence, the search for Gangā began. The project was started by Sagar and was carried forward by his successors. Immense efforts went into carrying out the geological and topological study of the region around the Himālayas to identify a possible source of water. This search led them to glacier lakes in the upper regions of the Himalāyas.

Once the source was located, the challenge was getting the water from the upper regions down to the lower regions in a way that it did not come crashing down. This feat was achieved by Bhageeratha by identifying an opening at the foothill of the Himālayas. He found a way to ensure a smooth landing of Gangā from such heights and made a way for her to eventually enter the sea after travelling a long distance through the plains.

The task undertaken by the ancestors of Rāma was a multi-generational infrastructure and engineering project taken to its completion by Bhageeratha. Bhageeratha's feat is an engineering marvel, no less.[1]

'A Herculean task' is a phrase used to describe something extremely difficult to achieve. The equivalent phrase in Indic literature is 'Bhageerathi prayāsa'.

ॐ ψ ॐ

8

A Twist of Fate

With the marriages of the four princes—Rāma, Lakshmana, Bharata and Shatrughna—Dasharatha had fulfilled his role as a father, but an important duty as the king of Kosala was yet to be discharged. Age was fast catching up with him and the successor to Ayodhyā's throne had to be announced. One day, a few years after the marriage of the princes, he began thinking about his heir.

Dasharatha loved all his sons equally. They were virtuous and wise. Rāma, however, held a special place in the king's heart. Rāma was a warrior par excellence; he was equally well-read in scriptures. He understood the nuances of finances as much as those of arts and modes of entertainment. In fact, he was adept in music and art. He was often referred to as Gāndharva shreshtha.[1]

Unperturbed in any situation, Rāma had a complete grip on his emotions. No one could make out the thoughts in his head from his face. It was difficult to not like Rāma. The people of Ayodhyā loved him. He was as approachable as he was discerning. But that didn't mean he was always soft. He was aware of the value of anger in public life and knew how to use it. Rāma was very perceptive about his own self and of others. An eloquent speaker and a master strategist, he was also an expert negotiator. He understood the importance of time and place in policy and behaviour.[2]

Dasharatha wished to see Rāma as the king of Kosala after him. But as a king he was accountable to his subjects, so he had to get the approval of his people before handing over their fate to a new king.

The Deliberations

Dasharatha called for a meeting of his ministers, officers, feudatory kings and prominent citizens dwelling in the cities as well as villages, to deliberate on the succession to the throne of Ayodhyā. As he was in a hurry to decide, he did not invite the kings of Kekaya and Mithilā. Once decided, they would know the good news soon, he thought. Kekaya was the maternal kingdom of his queen Kaikeyi, and Mithilā was the home of the in-laws of his sons. Dasharatha possibly wanted to avoid any interference from family that could have a conflict of interest while making such an important decision for his state.[3] At that time, Bharata and Shatrughna were in Kekaya.

In the meeting, once everyone was seated, Dasharatha addressed them, 'Just like the previous kings of the Ikshvāku dynasty, I have endeavoured, to the best of my abilities, to nurture this kingdom of my ancestors, like a father sustains and nourishes his children. Engaged earnestly in the welfare of my kingdom, this body of mine has now become old. I wish to rest now. Hence, with your permission, I am eager to hand over the reign of Ayodhyā to my eldest son Rāma and retire. Rāma, I believe, has all the qualities that will make him a capable administrator. But this is just my preference. If you believe that there are other people who are more capable, please make your thoughts known. Consider all the pros and cons of the situation at hand and then decide.'

As soon as the king had said these words, a wave of joy spread through the assembly. Everyone unanimously welcomed Dasharatha's decision to appoint Rāma as his heir. But Dasharatha wanted to be doubly sure of the will of his citizens. 'This unanimous agreement makes me suspicious. Are you agreeing just because I proposed it or do you genuinely believe Rāma is the most suitable person to reign over this kingdom that I have governed so righteously? Please elaborate why you think he is an apt choice,' he said. Many people responded with their views:

'Rāma is intelligent and virtuous. In wisdom, he is as good as Brihaspati, the guru of devas; in valour, he compares to Indra; he is forgiving like the earth and cool like the sweet rays of the moon; by his actions and engagements, Rāma strives for the happiness of the people of the kingdom.'

'He has a strong character and a stable intellect. Always polite, he is compassionate towards one and all. He inspires trust due to his commitment to truth. He never acts out of impulse.'

'He respects the learned and the elders. He keeps the company of the wise and reveres them as a prince should.'

'Rāma is an expert in warfare. There is no weapon that he doesn't excel in. His proficiency in music is also unmatched. He is generous and has profound intellect. He knows when to punish and when to forgive.'

'There hasn't been an operation that he hasn't successfully accomplished. When he returns to Ayodhyā after having protected the borders and warding off enemies, he inquires of the citizens as he would of his own family. In that, he doesn't forget to ask about the welfare of the women, children and house-helps. In need, he stands by his people. On joyous occasions, he heartily celebrates with them.'

'His anger and favour are not without a reason or purpose. He rightfully kills those who deserve to be killed. But he never targets those who are innocent and not worthy of being killed.'

'Because of his virtues and his personality, Rāma is loved by one and all. Even the women of this kingdom, young and old, pray for his well-being every day. Your coronating Rāma will fulfil the wish of all the citizens of Kosala.'

One by one, the people present in the court put forth their reasons for supporting Dasharatha's proposal. Thus, it was agreed that Rāma, indeed, would be the next king of Ayodhyā.[4]

Dasharatha requested Rishi Vashishtha and Rishi Vāmadeva to begin preparations for the coronation. Vashishtha and Vāmadeva got to the task immediately, giving instructions for the things to be done and people to be invited to the ceremony. Dasharatha then called Rāma and informed him of the coronation. 'Dear son, given your virtues, you are fit to become the next king of Ayodhyā. Hence, we have decided to coronate you as the crown prince of this kingdom on the auspicious day of pushya nakshtra.[5] You are naturally inclined to dharma, but I wish to share a few thoughts with you so that you always remain humble and alert,' said Dasharatha and then went on to give valuable lessons to Rāma.[6]

1. Never let anger and lust drive your actions.
2. Always be aware of minute details of your kingdom directly by talking to people and indirectly through your spies.
3. Ensure your treasury is always full. Use your wealth to nourish your ministers, officers, allies and citizens.
4. Always put up your best behaviour, keeping your impulses in check.

Rāma bowed to the king and went to see his mother Kaushalyā to inform her about Dasharatha's decision. The news had already reached Kaushalyā. Her heart was filled with unadulterated joy.

When all the citizens and allies had left, Dasharatha got his council of ministers together once again to discuss the plan of action for the coronation. He was informed that pushya nakshatra was the next day itself. Dasharatha was in a hurry to formally appoint Rāma as the crown prince. His intuition seemed to suggest an ominous event in the future. He wanted to complete the ceremony before any calamity struck. He decided to hold the coronation the next day itself instead of waiting for the next auspicious day and called for Rāma once again.

On seeing his eldest son, Dasharatha was overcome with affection. He hugged Rāma tenderly and, as if confiding his fears in him, said, 'I have lived a very fulfilling life till now. I have only one task left to complete and that is crowning you as the king of this kingdom according to the wishes of the people. For the past few days, I have been seeing bad dreams and observing inauspicious omens. Our jyotishis tell me that my birth nakshatra has been afflicted of late. Hence, I want to perform the coronation immediately before my mind is deluded, and you should support me in getting it done. Today the moon is in punarvasu nakshatra and tomorrow it will be in pushya. Therefore, we'll get the ceremony done tomorrow itself. Spend the night today undertaking a fast, along with Seetā as prescribed for the ritual, and get ready for tomorrow.'

'I believe it would be appropriate to get over with this function before Bharata returns from Kekaya. Not that I doubt Bharata's intentions. Your brother is a man of virtue, and he idolises you. But sometimes the mind can be very fickle and can beguile even otherwise noble people,' added Dasharatha, his heart ill at ease. He had a premonition of something untoward happening. What 'untoward' would look like, he knew not—not then, at least.[7]

The Connivance

Rāma and Seetā got busy with the preparations as did everyone else in the city. The entire city of Ayodhyā had come alive and all the temples, palaces, homes and public spaces were being decorated for the ceremony the next day.

The news of Rāma's coronation reached Mantharā, an elderly handmaid of Kaikeyi. She had been with Kaikeyi since she was a small child and had accompanied her to Ayodhyā after her marriage to Dasharatha. The news rattled Mantharā. She rushed to Kaikeyi's palace and found her resting on her bed. 'Wake up, you naïve woman. Calamity befalls you and here you are happily lying down, unaware and unconcerned. You behave as if you are the beloved of your husband and boast of your good fortune. But you are like a river who is about to go dry in summer. Your husband comes to you and talks sweet words to amuse you but does only that which is to Kaushalyā's liking. If Rāma becomes the king, can you imagine what will happen to Bharata and his future? He will become a non-entity in this dynasty,' exclaimed Mantharā angrily as she informed Kaikeyi of the intended crowning of Kaushalyā's son.

To Mantharā's utter surprise, Kaikeyi was delighted with the news. Kaikeyi loved Rāma as much as she loved Bharata. Rāma too loved and respected her as he loved Kaushalyā. Kaikeyi jumped with joy, 'Mantharā, you couldn't have given me better news. Rāma is as much my son as Bharata is. Rāma has all the qualities of being an able king. He is the eldest son, and I am certain he will look after his brothers as a father would. I am so happy to learn about the king's decision. Ask me for a gift you like, and I will give it to you.'[8]

Kaikeyi's composed response flustered Mantharā even more. Letting out an exasperated sigh, she said, 'Out of your stupidity, you can't see the catastrophe brewing. Once Rāma gets the throne, his progeny will succeed him. Bharata and his children will get nothing and will be deprived of the wealth and prosperity of the Ikshvākus. Rāma may banish him from the kingdom, or possibly even get him killed. Bharata is the only one from whom Rāma has any fear of losing the kingdom. Lakshmana and Shatrughna are too young to make a claim anyway. Don't we have to be careful of those who consider us a threat? There is only one way to secure your well-being—seek the throne for Bharata and get Rāma banished to the forest.'

Kaikeyi's expressions had begun to change. Observing that her words were having an impact, Mantharā continued, 'Forget not, a stepbrother is as good as an enemy. Since Bharata was a child, he has spent more time in Kekaya than here, so there is little chance that Rāma has any affection towards him, unlike Lakshmana, who has always been close and loyal to Rāma. Hence Rāma will not harm Lakshmana but there is no such bonding with Bharata. Don't you remember, in the hubris of being the beloved of the king, how you have often mocked Kaushalyā? Now Kaushalyā is all set to become the mother of the future king. Will she not avenge her insults? Kaushalyā is going to have the last laugh while you rue over your and Bharata's misfortune.'[9]

Now Mantharā had struck a raw spot. She had instigated Kaikeyi's motherly insecurities and a co-wife's jealousies. These emotions got the better of

Kaikeyi. She couldn't possibly let Kaushalyā win. She couldn't let Bharata be deprived of royal privileges. Dasharatha had indeed deceived her. She was his favourite. Wasn't she who he spent the most time with? And here he was favouring Kaushalyā over her when it mattered the most. Kaikeyi started burning with anger. She was determined to get what she thought was rightfully hers.

But how could she convince Dasharatha to do her bidding? Mantharā reminded Kaikeyi of the two boons conferred upon her by the king once when she had saved his life in a battle when he was severely injured. The king had asked Kaikeyi to seek whatever she wished for, and he would make it happen. Kaikeyi hadn't asked for anything then. There couldn't be a better time to put those boons to use!

'You had told me about these boons. I have cherished them in my thoughts because of my love for you, even though you have forgotten them. Now make the best of those boons. Use one to get the kingdom for Bharata and the other to banish Rāma to the forest,' Mantharā coaxed.

'Once Bharata gets the throne my job is done. Why send Rāma to the forest?' asked Kaikeyi.

'The people of Ayodhyā love Rāma. If he stays before their eyes, they will not be able to accept Bharata. With Rāma out of sight, Bharata will be able to carve out a place for himself in their hearts and consolidate his power,' reasoned Mantharā. 'Now remove your ornaments, rub out your make-up and wait for the king in the krodhāgār[10] and when he comes, do not look at him. Do not speak to him. But let your eyes and expressions convey your anger and your grief. The king is crazy about you. He cannot be angry at you, nor can he see you upset. For you, he can give up his life. Use that power of yours and remind him of the boons. There is no way the king will refuse,' she added.[11]

The idea appealed to Kaikeyi. She entered the krodhāgār. As was his routine, having wrapped up the affairs for the day, Dasharatha came to spend the night with his favourite queen. Kaikeyi was young and pretty. Dasharatha loved her more than his own life.[12] He was surprised to find she was not in her room. The maids informed him that Kaikeyi was waiting for him in the krodhāgār. Dasharatha got worried and hurried towards the room. There he saw Kaikeyi lying on the floor, unadorned, distraught and angry. Dasharatha was panic-stricken. He rushed to comfort her and understand the reason for her wrath. Kaikeyi refused to speak, as tutored by Mantharā.

Dasharatha became more and more desperate with every passing moment. 'What is it? Just tell me—what is it that you seek? If any ailment pains you, I will get the best of the vaidyas to serve you. Or do you want me to do a favour for someone you like? Or is it that you want someone punished? Don't cry, my lady. Do you want me to kill someone not worthy of being killed or release someone who deserves to be punished by death? I and all my staff are your servants. Your wish is my command. Tell me and it will be done,' pleaded Dasharatha, unsuspecting of the consequences of the offer he was making.[13]

Finally, Kaikeyi turned to look at him, softening her expression. She could see that Dasharatha was concerned and was also driven by his desire for her. 'I will tell you only if you promise that you will do as I wish,' she said. Dasharatha was more than eager to do her bidding and please her. 'There is only one person dearer to me than you, and that is Rāma. I pledge on Rāma to fulfil your desire.' Satisfied, Kaikeyi reminded him of the two boons he had bestowed on her and put forth her demands, loud and clear:

रामस्यारण्यगमनं भरतस्याभिषेचनम्

'Rāma's exile to the forest and Bharata's coronation,' she demanded.[14]

'And please arrange it as soon as possible. I wish to see Rāma leave for the forest today itself.'[15]

Kaikeyi's words resounded in Dasharatha's ears. He couldn't believe what he had just heard. He was devastated. He reproached her angrily at first, calling her heartless, destroyer of the family and a poisonous snake. He then beseeched her to reconsider her demands. 'What has Rāma done to you to deserve this? He has always treated you like his own mother. There is no one like him in this world and you want me to abandon my son for no fault of his? I can let go of Kaushalyā and Sumitrā. I can relinquish my royal wealth, but I cannot give up an obedient son like Rāma. If you insist and want to test my love for Bharata, I accept your demand of coronating Bharata. But let Rāma stay. I will not survive if Rāma leaves.

I prostrate before you, please desist from making this demand' he begged pitiably.[16]

Kaikeyi was unmoved. She angrily brushed aside the king's pleadings. 'Why commit to give boons and then repent? Why did you make the promises if you had no intention of keeping them? You may wish to go back on your word and tarnish the reputation of your ancestors. But I will not let you get away like that. I know your plan. You wish to give the kingdom to Rāma and have fun with Kaushalyā. Be it right or wrong or good or bad, there can be no breaking of the word given to me. Or else I will consume poison and kill myself right here before you. I'd rather die before seeing Kaushalyā become the Queen Mother and get people to bow down to her,' declared Kaikeyi adamantly.[17]

Dasharatha cried. He begged her to change her mind, to no avail. Suddenly, he felt a strong sense of guilt over his indulgent behaviour towards Kaikeyi and his neglect of his other wives. He was worried about how the decision to banish Rāma would impact them and, more so, how Seetā would take it. Dasharatha couldn't stand straight for he was feeling faint and losing consciousness. As a desperate measure, he even threatened to forbid Bharata from conducting his final rites if Bharata agreed with Kaikeyi's demands.

Kaikeyi had assured herself that despite all the protests, the king would not refuse what she wanted. She asked for Rāma to be called. Dasharatha sent a messenger to do so. Rāma came immediately. Lakshmana was with him. The brothers were startled at seeing their father looking extremely miserable. Rāma enquired after him. When the king could not speak a word in response, Rāma turned pale. He asked Kaikeyi about what the matter was.

'You are very dear to your father, hence he hesitates in breaking the news to you. He has made a promise to me, and you should strive to keep your father's word,' answered Kaikeyi, quite unabashedly. She then told him about the boons and her demand for his exile and Bharata's coronation.[18]

Rāma heard Kaikeyi's words patiently. His expression was as unperturbed as ever. 'Evam astu, so be it,' he said, finally. 'I give my word to you that I will go to the forest according to my father's commitment to you, dressed like a tapasvi, wearing tree barks for clothes. Had this come from you directly, I would have happily honoured your order too. Please assure my father that I can do anything for him. He should never harbour any apprehension about that and I never go back on my words.'

Kaikeyi was happy to see Rāma showing no resistance. She became even more brazen: 'You seem quite eager to go to the forest already. Hence, I think we shouldn't waste any more time. You must leave as soon as possible. Till you are here, your father won't eat nor will he bathe.' The words pierced Dasharatha's heart, and he fainted once again.[19]

'I will let my mother Kaushalyā know and plan to leave today itself,' said Rāma, taking leave of his father and stepmother. He left the way he had come, with a pleasant countenance. Rāma didn't want to alarm his well-wishers and cause them grief.

Lakshmana followed him. Unlike Rāma, Lakshmana was agitated.[20]

To Go or Not to Go

Life as the queen of Ayodhyā had been a mixed bag for Kaushalyā. She was the eldest and the chief queen. Dasharatha hadn't taken that away from her. The people of Ayodhyā looked up to her and respected her as a mother figure. But after Dasharatha's marriage to the princess of Kekaya, Kaushalyā's equation with the king had never been the same. Kaikeyi was young, very attractive and charming. In her presence, the king desired no one else. He was lust-stricken and the young queen indulged him ever so happily.

Since the birth of Rāma, Kaushalyā's life had found a new meaning. Rāma had imbibed her devoutness, kindness and humility. Whatever be her situation with Kaikeyi, Kaushalyā ensured Rāma would treat all his father's wives alike and with equal respect. Kaikeyi reciprocated wholeheartedly. Rāma's qualities were such that no one could remain unimpressed. The king too loved him more than his own life.

When the news of Rāma's coronation had reached Kaushalyā, she had run to the temple and sat down with eyes closed before her Vishnu murti, her heart full of emotion and gratitude. It was the culmination of all her efforts and her dreams for Rāma. Her son was capable and was being recognised for it.

Leaving Kaikeyi's chambers, when Rāma entered her palace, she was surrounded by many people, including brāhmins, and was busy getting some rituals conducted for Rāma's well-being. When she saw Rāma, she got up to embrace him and held him close. She then offered him food to eat. Rāma just touched the food and left it. He had to break the news of his exile to her. He said slowly, but calmly, 'Maa, you may not have heard, but a situation has developed which is likely to cause grief to you, Seetā and Lakshmana. I will be going to the forest for fourteen years and will be living like a tapasvi, eating fruits and food found in the forest. Father has given the throne to Bharata and fourteen years of exile to me. I must leave today according to his instructions.'

To Kaushalyā, it felt as if all that she had ever lived for had come crashing down in a moment. The emotions she had buried deep within couldn't stay hidden anymore. 'If this is how it was meant to be, then I would have been happier if you weren't born. I could have lived being childless but at least I wouldn't have had to bear this pain of separation. Your father has not given me any happiness befitting the eldest queen. The king treats the maids of Kaikeyi better than me. You were my only joy. Even with you here, I have been at the receiving end of the insults of the women in the palace because of his neglect. With you gone, these insults will only get more bitter and aggravating. There is no way I will survive without you,' Kaushalyā's lamentations wouldn't stop.[21]

Rāma had managed to keep his composure despite his mother's sorrowful wails. But Lakshmana couldn't keep quiet anymore. 'I don't agree with your acceptance of exile. You have done no wrong to be banished like this to the forest, deprived of this prosperous kingdom. The king's mind has become deluded due to old age and sensual desires. He is influenced by Kaikeyi's words. Otherwise, who in his right mind will take an honest and virtuous son like you to the altar for sacrifice?'

'We cannot take this injustice lying down,' he continued. 'We should take over the kingdom with our strength before the word spreads. The king's mind, instigated by Kaikeyi, has degenerated. How can he hand over the kingdom to Bharata just like that when it has been promised to you according to the wishes of the people? If need be, for behaving like our enemy, I will imprison our father or even kill him. Haven't we been taught that even if it is a guru who goes rogue and harms the interest of the state, he must be punished?' Lakshmana made no attempt to hide the contempt in his voice for his father's decision.[22]

Encouraged by Lakshmana's protestations, Kaushalyā too weighed in again, 'Son, you've heard your brother's views. Now do what is right. You shouldn't obey the unjust orders of my co-wife. Also, you are as much my son as your father's. I order you not to go. You must honour my words, too. And if you must go, take me with you or you will see me die here.'[23]

Rāma comforted both Lakshmana and his mother. He understood and appreciated their emotions, but he was sure that he had to go. His mind was made up, justice or injustice was not important at that moment. He made an honest attempt to explain the reason to his mother and Lakshmana. Not disobeying his father was certainly a very important reason, but there were other factors at work too.

'Many great men have achieved greatness by obeying their father's words unconditionally, even if they were seemingly unrighteous. I am only following their example. I also honestly believe that father's order is aligned with dharma. Kaikeyi might have conveyed the decision to me, but the decision was our father's. Right now, you are agitated and hence cannot see this. But I am convinced that following my father's order and accepting exile is the right thing to do for any son who is not given to impropriety. He is not just our father, but the king of Ayodhyā and our guru as well. I cannot disobey him for the lure of this kingdom. These joys are only temporary. Hence, do not grieve, Maa. Trust my decision, send me off smiling and wait for my return after successfully living through the exile of fourteen years.'[24]

Addressing Lakshmana, Rāma exhorted, 'Give up your anger, Lakshmana, and give this situation a patient thought. I can't do anything that will emotionally or mentally disturb our father. He has always striven to be on the side of truth. He is anxious about the consequences that he may have to bear due to any kind of falsehood being attributed to him in this world or beyond. If my coronation is not stopped and I stay back, he will never find peace, knowing that he has gone back on his promise to Kaikeyi. That awareness will always eat into his conscience. I can never be happy seeing him suffer like that.'

Rāma added, 'And there is one more point. I don't remember doing anything, knowingly or unknowingly, to our father or any mother, that can be faulted. I have always treated all our mothers equally. Kaikeyi too has always loved me like her own son. It is unthinkable that she would want to hurt me. But something has inspired such a thought in her mind. Our father, too, who otherwise loves me so much, has accepted her wish. I was so close to being crowned the yuvarāja of Ayodhyā, and suddenly it has been taken away from me, just like that, without any fault of mine. There is no rational explanation for the way things are turning out, on their own accord without I having done anything to trigger them. Hence, I am of the firm belief that this must be the work of destiny.'

Rāma continued, 'It is indeed fate that has planted this thought in Kaikeyi's mind. The influence of fate is unfathomable and cannot be averted. It is evident that adversity has befallen me and Kaikeyi. The words she used to instigate the king were also not what one could have ever expected from her. What, if not fate, made Kaikeyi, the illustrious princess of Kekaya and queen of Ayodhyā, behave like an uncultured woman? It is nothing but fate that is pulling me in this uncertain, unknown direction. The only way to know what fate has in store is by flowing along and letting the events unfold. This is also why I am accepting exile. It is futile fighting destiny.'[25]

Rāma had thought this through. When one can't make any sense of why a situation unfolds the way it does against every expectation, despite having done nothing to deserve it, it is best to surrender. It might be a sign of destiny having other plans for us.

Lakshmana was not convinced. 'To give in to destiny is cowardice,' he objected. But Rāma was firm on his decision. Lakshmana deferred to his elder brother's discernment but then insisted on accompanying him. Rāma dissuaded him, concerned about the well-being of Kaushalyā and Sumitrā. 'Who will take care of our mothers if both of us are gone? What if Kaikeyi mistreats them? One of us must stay back for them,' he urged.[26]

'Bharata will take care of them. I will come back and kill him if he doesn't. Besides, Mātā Kaushalyā is capable of fending for herself. She will take care of Mātā Sumitrā as well. She has in her possession over a thousand villages. She is capable of providing shelter to thousands of people like me,' reminded Lakshmana and insisted on accompanying Rāma.[27] Rāma was aware that his mother was not financially dependent on anybody. He consented to Lakshmana joining him in exile.

Kaushalyā, too, stopped resisting. She knew her son would not do anything which was not appropriate. She let him go.

Rāma now had to break the news to Seetā. When he spoke to Seetā, her concern was not the exile at all. All she wanted was to go along with her husband. Rāma tried to scare her, explaining how dangerous forest life could be. But Seetā was determined to go anyway. Finally, Rāma agreed.

Role of Destiny

Rāma explains his reasons to Lakshmana for accepting his father's decision. He says the situation is fated and hence one should not fight it. Does that mean people should accept whatever fate they are dealt with, and not even fight a just fight? Is Rāma being fatalistic?

Not at all. That would be an erroneous reading of Rāma's pragmatic approach to life.

When Rāvana abducts Seetā, Rāma doesn't leave it to destiny to find her and get her back. He does it himself. Then when does this approach to let destiny have its way work?

Rāma has categorically said that when a situation develops suddenly and unexpectedly, throwing all our plans out of the window, *despite our best efforts* (Rāma had done his best to be a good son to Kaikeyi and Dasharatha) and nothing we know at that time can explain the situation (Kaikeyi's behaviour wasn't normal, nor was Dasharatha's agreement to her demands), then such a situation could be attributed to fate.

When events happen which are beyond our control, notwithstanding our best efforts, rather than crib and complain, it is better to accept the situation and let it unfold. It might just usher in a whole new phase of life. We have seen such turns of events in the lives of many great people—events that seemed devastating at that time but eventually turned out for the better.

In adhyāya 18, shloka 13–14 of the Srimad Bhagavad Geetā, Krishna explains five factors that determine the success or failure of an undertaking. These are:

1. कर्ता—the doer
2. करणम्—the instruments being used

3. अधिष्ठानम्—place, time and approach
4. चेष्टा— different activities and processes undertaken
5. दैवम्—destiny

Destiny is a factor, says Krishna, but it is only one of the five factors. The first four factors are under our control. Attribution to destiny can happen only after the first four are performed to the best of our abilities. That is what we can control.

This approach is to help us navigate through life pragmatically, without losing hope. It doesn't mean escapism or lethargy. These two will always result in failure.

One other aspect to be considered is who is it that we are dealing with. Here, Dasharatha is Rāma's father and the king. Rāma's claim to the kingdom was because of Dasharatha. Sometimes, preserving the sanctity of a relationship, especially that of a parent and child, is of greater importance than fighting for an assumed 'right'. We must pick and choose worthy battles to fight.

The Departure

Rāma, Seetā and Lakshmana wrapped up all pending work and proceeded to leave Ayodhyā. By then, the news of Rāma's exile had spread like wildfire. Dasharatha's ministers, his wives, Rishi Vashishtha and other sages had assembled in Kaikeyi's palace by the time the three of them came to bid farewell to Dasharatha.

Dasharatha was as if torn apart. He was shackled by the need to abide by the 'truth'—honouring his promises by agreeing to give Kaikeyi what she wished. At the same time, Kaikeyi was pushing him to expedite Rāma's departure. Finally, he spoke, his eyes bloodshot and body frail, 'I have been duped by the boons I had given to Kaikeyi. Whatever is happening is not to my liking. This vile woman has tricked me. Rāma, imprison me and become the king of Ayodhyā.' In that way, he hoped he wouldn't have to see Rāma go away, nor would there be any stigma of reneging on his promises.

Rāma wasn't going to do anything like that. 'Father, may you live a thousand years and rule this kingdom. I have no desire for it. I look forward to returning after fourteen years and holding your feet. I relinquish any claim to this prosperous country. May you give it to Bharata,' he said, with immense concern for Dasharatha.[28]

Dasharatha offered to send the army as well as money along with them so that his sons and daughter-in-law may have a comfortable life in the forest. Kaikeyi opposed that. 'How can Bharata rule without an army or wealth if you send everything to Rāma?' she asked. She had started to become impatient. Not only did she want her way, but she also wanted it to happen immediately. She wanted to see Rāma leave as soon as possible. 'Why do you behave as if you are the only one to banish your son? This has happened before in the family of Ikshvākus. Your ancestor Sagar had thrown out his son Asamanja from the kingdom earlier,' she commented slyly.

The comparison was outrageous. It came as whiplash to the people assembled there. They were already shattered by the news of Rāma's exile. Sumantra and Siddhāratha, two of Dasharatha's ministers, rebuked Kaikeyi for making such preposterous demands. Siddhārtha even pointed out the false equivalence in her comparison of Rāma and Asamanja. Kaikeyi did not care. Instead, she got valkal, that is, dresses made of tree bark that tapasvis living in forests wore, and handed them to Rāma, Lakshmana and Seetā.

Rāma and Lakshmana accepted valkals and wore them. Seetā was shocked for she had never worn a valkal before. She tried to don it but couldn't and stood there embarrassed, tears welling up in her eyes. Rāma quickly came to her rescue. He helped her tie the valkal over her silk garment. Everybody was stunned at the utter shamelessness of Kaikeyi.

Sagar and Asamanja

In the Ikshvāku dynasty, there was a renowned king Sagar. His eldest son was Asamanja. Asamanja had turned out to be a brat. He would harass the citizens of Ayodhyā for fun. Throwing babies of common people in the River Sarayu was his favourite pastime.

Troubled and tired of his misdeeds, the people complained to Sagar. As a punishment, Sagar banished Asamanja, removed his royal privileges and exiled him from Ayodhyā forever.

Siddhāratha, Dasharatha's minister, was quick to point out to Kaikeyi that her comparison of the two incidents was flawed. Asamanja was guilty of committing heinous crimes. Rāma had done no wrong whatsoever.

The women in the palace were crying uncontrollably. They requested Rāma to let Seetā stay in Ayodhyā.[29] Rishi Vashishtha had been observing everything quietly till then. But Kaikeyi's audacity made him speak up. 'You have crossed all the limits, Kaikeyi,' he said. 'Haven't you tortured the king enough already? No way will Seetā go to the forest. Not only will she reside here in the palace, but she will also reign Ayodhyā till Rāma returns. A wife is considered the ātmā of her husband. By that identification, Seetā will rule the kingdom while Rāma is away.'[30]

However, Seetā did not want the throne. She wanted to be with Rāma; it didn't matter where he lived. She politely informed everyone about her desire to accompany her husband.

Dasharatha, too, tried to put his foot down regarding Seetā's departure. He reproached Kaikeyi for making Seetā wear the valkal. He had never made any commitment to sending Seetā to the forest anyway. Her wish to accompany Rāma was her own and hence there was no obligation for her to wear valkal. He ordered for a supply of good clothes and ornaments to be sent over for Seetā.

It was time to leave. Before leaving, Rāma made just one request of Dasharatha. 'Please take care of my mother. She is already old and pale. Now my going away is going to make her very upset. She has always wished for your well-being. Please ensure her welfare while I am gone,' he said.

Then the three of them bid their final goodbyes and started walking towards the forest.

Rāma's Dutifulness

Before leaving, Rāma and Seetā took a few actions which demonstrate their sense of empathy and accountability towards those who worked for them and were under their patronage to ensure they weren't rendered helpless once Rāma and Seetā were gone.[31] A sample is as follows:

1. They collected all their ornaments, items of use including vessels, mattresses, clothes and so on, which were not going to be of any use to them for the next fourteen years and distributed them among the people who worked for them.
2. They gave huge donations comprising foodgrains and animals such as cows and bulls to brāhmins, officiating priests and students under their patronage, and also to those who were under the patronage of Kaushalyā. Rāma wanted to ensure that the people of Ayodhyā took care of his mother even if Kaikeyi and Bharata did not.
3. To his charioteer and handyman Chitrarath, Rāma gave one thousand cows and other animals.
4. In addition, to all their employees, Rāma paid fourteen years' salary in advance so that they wouldn't have to suffer in their absence and could continue to work in the palace. Rāma didn't want to leave them dependent on Bharata for their subsistence. 'Please maintain Lakshmana's and my homes till we are back,' Rāma requested them. The employees were overwhelmed by their master's generosity.
5. Rāma distributed whatever wealth that remained among the less fortunate sections of the society.

Leaving the weeping and mourning Ayodhyā behind, the chariot driven by Sumantra moved on, carrying Rāma, Lakshmana and Seetā. Some people followed them till the banks of Tamasā where they halted on the first night. The next day, Rāma, Lakshmana, Seetā and Sumantra left the place extremely quietly, before dawn, leaving behind the people of Ayodhyā who had followed them all the way.

Sumantra accompanied them till Shringaverpur, a city just outside the boundary of Kosala, by the Gangā river. They crossed many villages of Kosala along the way. The news of Rāma's vanvās had spread far and wide by then. People were heard lamenting the misfortune of Ayodhyā brought about by the lust of their king Dasharatha and the cunningness of his young queen Kaikeyi.

On hearing about Rāma's arrival at the outskirts of his city, Guha, the king of Shringaverpur, of the kingdom of Nishādas, came to see him. Rāma and Guha were old friends. They were meeting after a long time. Rāma hugged him tightly. Guha insisted that they spend the next fourteen years in his kingdom. But Rāma was firm about living in the forest. That was the condition imposed on him.

The next morning, Guha arranged boats to take Rāma, Lakshmana and Seetā across the Gangā from where they were to enter a dense forest. Their first task was to find a place in the forest where they could build their dwelling. Walking through the forest adjoining Vatsadesh (present-day Prayāg), Rāma, Lakshmana and Seetā reached the āshram of Rishi Bharadwāja by the confluence of Gangā, Yamunā and Saraswati.

Rishi Bharadwāja suggested them to go to Chitrakoot to set up their hut. Chitrakoot was a beautiful hill a few kilometres away, by the River Mandākini.

In Chitrakoot, Rāma decided on the place where a hut could be built, a place close to the river and surrounded by delightful flora and fauna. Lakshmana made the hut with his own hands, using wood, stems, straws and leaves. This was their first abode outside Ayodhyā. The life of exile had begun.

Dasharatha's Death

Sumantra had tried to convince Rāma one last time at Shringaverpur to reconsider his decision and return to Ayodhyā. When Rāma didn't budge, he insisted on staying with them through the fourteen years. But Rāma convinced him to return. 'Kaikeyi will find peace only when she is assured of my going to the forest. Unless you go back and confirm it, she won't let my father live in peace. Hence, you must return.'[32] Sumantra was left with little choice. He drove the empty chariot back to the city.

Dasharatha's weak heart couldn't bear the separation from Rāma. The speed at which the events had moved had broken him. He couldn't gather the strength to tell Kaikeyi that Rāma's exile was not acceptable, even if it meant going back on his words. Given that the people of Ayodhyā had wholeheartedly given their consent to Rāma as their future king, Dasharatha owed it to them, too, to refuse Kaikeyi's demands. He could have given the desire of the people of Ayodhyā to see Rāma as their king as the reason. But he didn't. And once Rāma was gone, Dasharatha couldn't bear the sight of the queen who was his favourite until then. He had been deceived by the woman he loved—and how!

Dasharatha told Kaikeyi, 'I have nothing to do with you or people who are with you from now on. I renounce the vows I took with you before agni at the time of our wedding. If Bharata accepts this kingdom as per your desire then he is prohibited from performing my last rites.' Dasharatha then asked to be taken to Kaushalyā's chambers.

It was the sixth night since Rāma had left for the forest. Dasharatha's health had been failing fast. That night, an incident from his past came back to him. He narrated the story to Kaushalyā, about the death of a young tapasvi, Shravan, at his hands.

It was an unfortunate night, many years ago, when Dasharatha was the crown prince of Ayodhyā. He had gone hunting in the forest. Dasharatha was proud of his skills of hitting a target just based on its sound. That night, however, he accidentally shot a young rishi named Shravan, mistaking the sound he made while taking water from the river to be of a wild elephant.

Shravan lived in the forest with his old, blind parents. He was their sole caregiver, a responsibility he fulfilled with a lot of dedication. Even while fatally injured by Dasharatha's arrow, he was concerned not about his own life but the well-being of his parents. He requested Dasharatha to inform his father of his death. In that way, he said, Dasharatha could also avoid being cursed by his father, whose sorrow would know no bounds on learning about his son's death.

Dasharatha was feeling guilty about what had happened due to him, even if unintentionally. He went to Shravan's old parents and conveyed to them the heartbreaking news. Their reaction was on expected lines. They were shattered. But Shravan's father was very dignified. Even though he was extremely angry, he acknowledged the prince's honesty. 'Had you not come yourself and confessed, trust me, your head would have exploded. When a warrior kills an innocent rishi intentionally, his head explodes into seven pieces, it is said. You have been honest about this; hence you are still alive.'

But unable to handle his grief, Shravan's father cursed Dasharatha that he would die a painful death separated from his sons.

The memory came to Dasharatha as a harbinger of his own end. He passed away soon afterwards. None of his sons was by his side at the time of his death.

> *The destiny of Rāma was being shaped much before he was even born.*

Bharata's Pledge

Ayodhyā drowned in grief. Their favourite prince was gone, and now their king was dead. To avoid the kingdom from falling into anarchy, Rishi Vashishtha sent for Bharata and Shatrughna to come back quickly.

The brothers came and were devastated to find their father dead and brothers exiled.

Kaikeyi was unrepentant even then. When Bharata came to see her on returning from Kekaya, still unaware of the tragedy that had befallen the family, she smugly described to him how she had secured the kingdom for him despite Dasharatha wishing to give it away to Rāma alone. She expected Bharata to be pleased. She thought he would be grateful for what she had done for him. To her utter shock, Bharata was angry and embarrassed. Not only did he refuse the throne of Ayodhyā, pledging instead to bring Rāma back, but he also held her responsible for his father's death.

'Because of you my father passed away. Because of you today Rāma has been exiled. And how unfortunate I am that you, my mother, made me a party to these sinful acts. In the form of a mother, you are truly my enemy. I do not wish to talk to you ever. I cannot carry the weight of the tears of the people of Ayodhyā who may consider me responsible for the tragedy that has befallen this kingdom because of you,' snapped Bharata.[33] His words pierced Kaikeyi's heart. But now there was no undoing her actions.

After completing the final rites of his dead father, Bharata declared before the ministers and rishis that he did not desire the throne of Ayodhyā and that he was determined to get Rāma back. He ordered an entire contingent, including the rishis, ministers and the three mothers as well as an army battalion, to get ready to go to the forest and request Rāma to return. The contingent left on an auspicious day to do that.

When Guha learnt of Bharata's expedition heading to Shringaverpur, he was alarmed. He assumed that Bharata, instigated by his mother, was coming to kill Rāma. Guha put his forces on alert, determined to stop Bharata in his tracks before he could reach Rāma. However, after meeting Bharata, his fears were allayed. Guha told Bharata of the direction in which Rāma, Lakshmana and Seetā had gone. He also arranged for five hundred boats to take the contingent across the Gangā. Then Rishi Bharadwāja directed them to Chitrakoot.

The brothers met. Rāma was overwhelmed seeing Bharata. But the news of Dasharatha's death made him sorrowful. He offered jaladāna to his departed father as a son should. As per the rituals, he also made an offering of wild fruit to his father. Kaushalyā was sad seeing her son, who had grown up in luxuries and who, not so long ago, had the best of delicacies for his consumption and offering, was now reduced to making an offering only of wild fruit. 'Such an offering doesn't befit a prince,' she choked as she spoke. Rāma had no such regret. 'What a man eats, his devas eat the same. O king, may you partake of this food,' he said simply while making the offering.[34]

Bharata requested Rāma to return to Ayodhyā. 'You have satisfied my mother by offering the kingdom to me. Now I give it back to you, please accept it. No one apart from you can effectively reign Ayodhyā. The sinful act committed by my mother is not to my liking. Only because I am bound by dharma, I have not already punished her with death. Please accept my request and shower your grace on me,' Bharata urged.

Bharata continued his appeal, 'Our father is now dead, and I shouldn't criticise him. But which person who understands dharma will act as our father did just to please a woman? Or maybe it is indeed true that a man loses his discretion when death is near. His act was a deviation from dharma. It behoves a good son like you not to toe the line of such a deviation. It is the duty of a warrior prince to get himself crowned the king so that he can protect his subjects. Do your duty Rāma, rule this kingdom of our ancestors without any distraction or hindrance.'[35]

Everyone supported Bharata's request. Rishi Vashishtha and Rishi Jābāli also made a case for Rāma's return. Rishi Jābāli made some interesting comments to further the request. 'A man is born alone, and a man dies alone. Hence, becoming too invested in all these relations of father, mother and brother are futile. No one belongs to anyone here. Like a traveller who rests a night in a village and moves on the next day, these relations are mere resting places in the larger journey of life. One need not get too attached to them. Dasharatha is now gone, as is expected of every being who is born. The relation of yours with him doesn't stand anymore, nor does the promise you made to him. It will be unfortunate to give up the wealth and kingdom which you have right in front of you, in expectation of a world beyond which you have no knowledge. Come back and take the throne, as it is the wish of everyone here.'[36]

It was a fair argument. But Rāma wasn't impressed. There was a basic flaw in the logic—if all the relations are assumed to end with one's death, there would be no sanctity of any relationships or contracts in society. How could a person ever trust anyone else if promises were nullified using such specious arguments? Accepting Jābāli's proposition would make people reckless because nothing they said or did would be binding on their successors once they were dead. For maintaining social systems, honouring promises and contractual agreements is important. For a system to sustain, there must be certain non-negotiables that every stakeholder in the system must sincerely adhere to; in that truth, accountability and trust are necessary.

Rāma understood this well. Being a prince and someone who people looked up to, it was even more important for him to maintain the sanctity of the word given to his father because citizens tend to follow the precedents laid down by their leaders. Besides, there was no huge leadership crisis threatening to push Ayodhyā into disorder that called for reneging on his words. The able ministers and gurus continued to manage the kingdom's affairs as they did in Dasharatha's time. Bharata himself was very capable. Therefore, Rāma remained firm in his resolve to spend the next fourteen years in exile.

He did not hold back from showing his displeasure at Rishi Jābāli's words as he explained the importance of being established in truth. As a rishi, Jābāli should have been more responsible with his words, Rāma believed. Rishi Vashishtha intervened to console Rāma and explain Rishi Jābāli's position. 'What he said is not because he believes in it. He understands the importance of truth. Rishi Jābāli only said what he did to convince you to return.' Rishi Jābāli too explained his position.[37]

Rāma made one commitment to the heartbroken Bharata. He promised to return after fourteen years and take over the kingdom. Bharata found solace in these words of Rāma. He made a pledge to govern Ayodhyā in Rāma's name until Rāma completed his exile and returned. He also declared that, like Rāma, he would also live in an āshram, wear valkal and give up the luxuries of the palace for the next fourteen years. Bharata held Rāma's pādukā on his head to underscore his pledge. 'Your pādukā will serve me as your guidance in taking care of the kingdom till you return. And if I do not see you on the first day of the new year after your fourteen years of exile, I assure you I will enter the funeral pyre,'[38] he asserted.

The contingent returned to Ayodhyā without Rāma. True to his pledge, Bharata gave up the palace, dressed like a tapasvi in valkal and moved to Nandigrām outside Ayodhyā to live in an āshram. He looked after the administration of the kingdom as a custodian of Rāma from there.

When Mantharā advised Kaikeyi to seek the kingdom for Bharata, she probably had Kaikeyi's best interest in her heart. She was not far-sighted enough to foresee how things would play out and where it would take Kaikeyi. Her interest was limited only to her mistress, forgetting that Kaikeyi was not just any woman, she was the queen of Ayodhyā, an important family member of the royal household. Mantharā acted according to her limited understanding of swadharma. What about Kaikeyi? Did she not know her swadharma? She should have known better than falling for Mantharā's short-sighted advice.

Kaikeyi's position of privilege entrusted her with the responsibility of taking care of the interest of the entire royal household and of Ayodhyā. Unfortunately for her and Ayodhyā, she considered none of her responsibilities when jealousy over Kaushalyā's good fortune gripped her. The shackles of greed, jealousy and insecurity were too strong to be loosened by Dasharatha's pleadings or Vashishtha's reprimands. At that moment, she had lost all sense of discrimination.

Kaikeyi's retribution was quick. Within days, she had lost it all—a doting husband, loving sons and the respect of the people of Ayodhyā. As for Rāma, Lakshmana and Seetā, the will of destiny was yet unknown. It would remain so for some more years. When it did unfold, it changed the course of the history of Bhāratavarsha, immortalising the story of Rāma for generations to come.

The Road to Gangā

When Bharata said in the royal court of Ayodhyā that he intended to find and bring Rāma, Lakshmana and Seetā back, his idea was to do it in style by coronating Rāma in the forest itself and then come back in a triumphant procession. The who's who of Ayodhyā, including his three mothers, were to accompany him on the expedition. To protect all these people and take care of their needs, Bharata decided to take an entire army battalion with him.

Rāma, Lakshmana and Seetā had travelled from Ayodhyā to Chitrakoot partly on a chariot and partly by walking through the forests. But for the size of the contingent that Bharata was planning to take along, walking through the forests was not possible. Hence, before undertaking the journey, Bharata got a levelled road built to allow everyone to travel on horses and chariots comfortably.

Sarga 80 of Ayodhyā Kānda talks exclusively of the process of road construction. Artisans of all kinds—excavators, mechanics, engineers and architects, road menders, carpenters, tree cutters, well-diggers, tanners, whitewashers and plasterers—were set to the task of making a road leading from Ayodhyā to the banks of the Gangā. The work involved clearing bushes, levelling surfaces, cutting trees that came in the way, planting flowering trees by the pathways, filling holes and pits along the way, digging wells and freshwater ponds for the travellers at regular intervals, bridging streams, breaking rocks and boulders, building platforms by the water bodies for the travellers to rest, pitching tents along the route, among others.

It was a huge civil engineering project undertaken by Bharata.

Such descriptions of construction activities documented in the itihāsa itself help us to imagine the lives and living conditions of our ancestors—no way can they be considered primitive people in any way. There were proper urban settlements, as we can gauge from the descriptions of the cities mentioned in the epic.

ॐ ψ ॐ

9

Sahadharmachārini

Rāma had no clue who Seetā was when he lifted, strung and broke the Shiva Dhanush. He had picked up the dhanush out of sheer curiosity, as would be natural for a kshatriya prince. The curiosity was natural, but not the parākram.[1] Rāma had accomplished a feat that no other kshatriya of the day had been able to. Seetā had probably never heard of Rāma till three days before her marriage. Janaka had vowed to marry his elder daughter to the man who was powerful enough to perform the feat of stringing the bow. Even though many princes had desired Seetā and had asked for her hand in marriage, no one had been able to meet Janaka's condition.

Rāma and Seetā met directly only at the time of their wedding ceremony. Putting Seetā's hand in Rāma's, Janaka had said, 'I offer you this daughter of mine. She will be your sahadharmachārini, your equal partner in dharma.' With every passing day after their marriage, Rāma and Seetā fell deeper and deeper in love with each other. Rāma's heart was fixed on Seetā. For Seetā, there was never a moment when Rāma was not in her thoughts.

Rishi Vālmiki tells us that the two were so deeply in love that between them there was no emotion and no thought that was hidden. They didn't even need words to communicate. They spoke through their hearts. Their life in the palace immediately after their marriage was like a dream. But the thing about dreams is that they don't last. Rāma and Seetā soon found themselves in throes of dreams, destiny and dharma.

The Exile

Seetā was busy preparing for the big day. Rāma would be back any time—he had been called by his father in the early hours of the morning. There was so much to be done, she fretted. But she couldn't stop smiling. Soon, her Rāma was going to be crowned as the successor of Dasharatha.

Seetā saw Rāma come in. She blushed. It was funny, she thought, how even after so many years, the sight of Rāma sent a wave of warm, fuzzy feeling through her heart. But as he came closer, her heart skipped a beat. Something was amiss. Rāma's face had lost its colour. He looked visibly ill at ease.

Rāma hadn't flinched when Kaikeyi told him that an exile awaited him instead of the throne of Ayodhyā. His face had retained its composure when he broke the news to his mother. He was perfectly calm while explaining to Lakshmana the reason for accepting vanvās. Yet, when he went to his chambers to inform Seetā about the drastic twist in their lives, he couldn't hold back his emotions. Beads of sweat broke on his forehead and a look of despondency spread across his face.

'What happened? Why do you look so pale?' asked Seetā anxiously.[2]

'Seetā, I have been banished to the forest by father and I must leave today,' said Rāma, narrating to her all that had transpired in Kaikeyi's chambers. 'While I am gone, please continue to serve both my mother and father respectfully, as you always have. My mother will need your care even more as she deals with my separation. Continue to treat Bharata and Shatrughna with love, like your brothers and sons. Bharata will now be the king, so do not do anything that is against his interest,' he said, regaining his composure.[3]

Seetā was shocked, not at Rāma's banishment but his indication that he was going without her. 'Why do you speak to me like some woman who does not know her role? Mother, father, siblings—they all live their individual destinies. Only the wife follows the fate of her husband. So, if you are exiled, I am exiled with you. If you must walk on the paths of thorns in the jungles, I will walk ahead of you, pulling out the thorns to make your journey smooth. And I don't need any instructions from you about how to deal with people; my parents have taught me well. Hence, I know what I must do. I will go with you. There is no way anyone, even you, can stop me from accompanying you. You need not worry. I will eat whatever is available in the forest and tend to your needs. Travelling through forests with you, I will admire the beautiful lakes full of lotuses and swans, and the tall mountains. All I care about is being with you. I don't even desire heaven without you,' declared Seetā, unable to control her tears.[4]

Rāma was not sure Seetā really understood what she wished to get into. Comforting her, he said, 'You have never shirked your responsibilities, I am aware. I urge you to live by them right here in Ayodhyā till I return after fourteen years. Life in the forest is full of hardships, which I do not wish for you. Unaccustomed to seeing humans, the wild animals are ever ready to pounce when they see one. The place is filled with roars of lions who are always on the prowl. The streams of rivers that flow through the forests are home to dangerous crocodiles. There are swamps all around, making walking extremely difficult. There are no beds. The forest dwellers have to sleep on dry grass. There are no delectable foods. One has to survive on wild fruits and roots and sometimes even these are difficult to procure. There could be bouts of wild storms and intense darkness. Poisonous snakes, spiders, scorpions and mosquitoes thrive in the jungle. Life in a forest is full of mental and physical struggles. Hence, it is better for you not to come to the forest.'[5]

Seetā was undaunted. 'Sure, there will be hardships. But with you alongside, these would matter little. I am certain the wild animals will run away when they see you. Everyone who has challenged you has run away scared, what to say of these animals. When I was still a young girl in my parents' home, an astrologer had predicted that I will have to live in the forest. Since then, I have been yearning to live in the jungles. This turn of events is therefore destined for me. You must take me along. I have been a devoted and loyal wife to you. I promise, whatever the situation, I will live through it without complaining. If you leave me and go, then trust me, you will see me dead.'

Rāma continued to dissuade Seetā by enumerating the dangers of jungle life. With every argument that Rāma presented, Seetā became more upset and annoyed. 'Did my father know that he had found a son-in-law who was a man only in physique but was otherwise more like a woman? If you go without taking me because you are afraid of the dangers, the world will surely think you lack courage and valour. Such insult of yours will be unbearable for me.[6] Or is there any other reason that you wish to forsake me? I will cause you no harm. I will follow you, ask for nothing, demand nothing,' Seetā pleaded and hugged Rāma tightly, tears rolling down her eyes uncontrollably.

Rāma steadied her and covered her in a warm embrace. 'Seetā, at the cost of making you unhappy, I do not desire even heaven. Nor am I scared of anyone or anything. I am very capable of protecting you myself. But I couldn't have forced you to come to the forest with me without fully knowing your desire. If you have been destined to go with me to the forest, you will.'

Everyone dissuaded Seetā from going to the forest. 'She doesn't deserve the hardships,' said some. 'Seeing her, we will miss Rāma less,' said others. Rishi Vashishtha even suggested that Seetā be given the throne in place of Rāma. But Seetā's mind was made up. Her firm decision was to go. She wished to be with Rāma, in thick and thin. Even the throne had no meaning for her without Rāma. Rāma didn't want to impose an exile on her. But when he was convinced of her desire, he was more than happy to take her along. Living without Seetā was not to his liking either.

The Charms of Chitrakoot

Seetā was at home in the forest right from the first day they arrived there after crossing the Gangā at Shringaverpur. With Rāma and the ever-vigilant Lakshmana by her side, she had nothing to fear. Lakshmana walked ahead of her, leading the way and Rāma behind her, protecting her from any unforeseen dangers. Lakshmana retained some angst against Dasharatha and Kaikeyi for sending Rāma away. Seetā, on the other hand, was joyous. Her dream of living in the forest with her beloved was being realised.

When Kaushalyā asked Sumantra, who had just returned from Shringaverpur, about the well-being of Seetā, Sumantra had told her to not worry about her daughter-in-law at all. 'There is not even a tinge of sorrow in Seetā's mind about the stay in the forest. She looks as happy and cheerful in Rāma's company as she was here. She roams about happily in the desolate forest, admiring the flora as if she is in some garden of Ayodhyā. Seetā is living her life in the jungle like a happy young girl. She asked Rāma about the janapadas and forests we crossed out of innocent curiosity and Rāma answered earnestly. She is blissful in Rāma's company. The physical hardship is of no concern to her. Looking at her, one would think she is on a leisure trip.'[7]

Rāma and Seetā's days in Chitrakoot were blissful. The place was beautiful. Both were immersed in each other, with no outside distractions. They would roam around the precincts of Chitrakoot. They would bathe in the Mandākini together. Often, Rāma would enthral her with information about the jungle, its trees and animals. Rāma would do his daily rituals and Seetā would ensure he had all the items he needed for his nityakarma.[8]

Their happiness was evident in Rāma's voice when, one day, he confided in Seetā: 'The sight of this mountain of Chitrakoot, these pretty birds flying free in the open blue sky, the branches of the trees bending under the weight of juicy fruits, the cool refreshing mountain breeze spreading the fragrance of the multitude of flowers growing here, the gurgling of the streams of crystal clear water running down the slopes, just the overall ambience of this place, all these make me so joyous that even the thought of the loss of kingdom or separation from my loved ones gives me no pain. With you and Lakshmana by my side, I can live here for the next fourteen years with joy.'[9]

Another time, bathing in the sacred waters of Mandākini with Seetā, Rāma was ecstatic. Holding Seetā's hands lovingly he said, 'Dearest, living like this with you here, partaking of the sweet, fresh fruit, I have no wish to return to Ayodhyā or conquer any kingdom.' Seetā blushed. Rāma had given words to her emotions.

After spending a delightful year in Chitrakoot, the three of them left for Dandakāranya, taking a cue from other tapasvis who were leaving the place because of the harassment by Khara, a commander of Rāvana, who had made their survival difficult. There was one more reason for leaving. Bharata and his mothers had come to Chitrakoot to plead with Rāma to return, but Rāma had persisted with the exile. The memory of his loved ones was etched in the place, making Rāma miss them. Going to another place would help avoid the painful reminders, he thought.

Anusuyā

En route to Dandakāranya, Rāma, Lakshmana and Seetā stopped briefly at the āshram of Rishi Atri and his illustrious wife Anusuyā.

Once upon a time, many years ago, the place around Chitrakoot faced a drought. Trees died, rivers dried and animals and birds were rendered helpless. To bring succour to the scorched earth, Anusuyā undertook an intense tapasyā. The power of her tapasyā diverted the course of river Mandākini to the area, ending the drought and famine of many years and making greenery flourish once again.

Rishi Atri asked Seetā to seek the blessings of Anusuyā, and he requested Anusuyā to bless her.

Anusuyā lovingly embraced Seetā. She was aware of the happenings in Ayodhyā. She also knew it was Seetā's decision to follow her husband in exile, the perils of the forest life notwithstanding. 'It is commendable that you have chosen to accompany your husband even in the jungle, giving up the luxuries and privileges of a royal life. No ordinary woman would have done this. May you always remain a sahadharmachārini to Rāma and gain immense merit and fame through your actions,' blessed Anusuyā, and gifted Seetā her own invaluable garments, ornaments and ointments. The garments and ornaments were such that they would never wither or fade.

After spending the night at the āshram, the three made their way to the Dandaka forest.

Days in Dandakāranya

Their entry into Dandakāranya was quite eventful. A rākshasa named Virādh saw the beautiful Seetā with two young men dressed as tapasvis. 'What is such a beautiful woman doing with these tapasvis? She deserves to be my wife,' he thought and stealthily lifted her away. The initial shock of Seetā's abduction was such that Rāma couldn't help but blame Kaikeyi for endangering Seetā's life. 'It was to put us through this pain that Kaikeyi had wanted us to be exiled,' Rāma agonised.[10] Lakshmana motivated him to fight instead. Rāma and Lakshmana attacked Virādh. After some struggle, they freed Seetā and killed the giant rākshasa. Having spent peaceful days in Chitrakoot, this was the first time the three of them came face-to-face with the real dangers of forest life.

After this incident, they went to the āshram of Rishi Sharbhanga. Many rishis came there to seek Rāma's help. The man-eating rākshasas in the region had been harassing them for quite some time. These rākshasas would disrupt their yajnas, ravage their āshrams and even kill the rishis living peacefully in the forest. Harassing the forest dwellers had become a source of entertainment for the rākshasas led by Khara and Dushana, Rāvana's commanders.

The rishis pleaded with Rāma to protect them, 'A king who collects one-sixth of the produce as tax and yet does not protect his subjects commits an act of grave adharma. Rishis and munis like us may not pay tax but a fourth of the merit we earn by leading an austere life undertaking tapasyā accrues to the king. Hence, it is the king's responsibility to protect all of us. A king who always takes care of his subjects like his own children, protecting them with his own life, attains fame and prosperity in this world and next. You are the prince of Ayodhyā. This whole area has been governed by the kings of the Ikshvāku dynasty. Therefore, you must protect us.'[11]

Rāma readily agreed and assured protection to the rishis.

Rāma's alacrity in accepting their request surprised Seetā. She expressed her uneasiness to Rāma. 'By accepting the request, I hope you aren't aligning yourself with adharma,' she said. 'As I understand, there are three actions that arise out of intense desire—speaking falsehood, lusting after women of other men and violence against those who have done us no harm. You have a lot of self-control and discipline. The first two vices can't come near you. I am worried because I believe you may be indulging in the third vice by accepting the request of the sages and arming yourself with weapons. The rākshasas have done us no harm. But by keeping arms, you may be tempted to use them on the rākshasas for no fault of theirs. We have been exiled to lead a peaceful life practising austerities, non-violence and forgiveness. Why should you want to engage in any kind of violence, then? You may engage in your kshatriya dharma once you are back in Ayodhyā,' she remarked rather anxiously.[12]

But Rāma had learned Vishvāmitra's lessons on Rāja Dharma well. He was not the one to ever deviate from his swadharma, be it in Ayodhyā or Dandakāranya. He explained this to Seetā. 'The sages are very unhappy about being troubled by the rākshasas. Every day they live in fear, uncertain who the rākshasas will harm that day and how. These forest-dwelling rishis are innocent and are being subjected to great harassment for no justifiable reason. As you know, Seetā, it behoves a kshatriya prince to ensure no innocent is harmed. How could I have refused the sages who came to seek my help? It is my dharma to protect the innocent and punish the criminals, and that I must do,' he said assertively, and added, 'Having said that, I appreciate your concern as well. I am aware you have spoken out of your care and love for me. I love you too, more than my own life.'[13]

Rāma, Lakshmana and Seetā spent the next ten years travelling around Dandakāranya, living in the āshrams of various rishis, providing them protection from the rākshasas.[14] Then one day, they went further south to Rishi Agastya's āshram. Rishi Agastya not only offered them warm hospitality but also blessed Rāma with knowledge of advanced weapons. He advised them to go to Panchavati, a place in Janasthāna to spend the rest of their days in exile. Before seeing them off, he had one more piece of advice for Rāma. 'Always do what Seetā likes. She has accepted this life of hardship because of her love for you. It is rare to find a woman like her who gives up everything for her husband.'[15]

Taking leave from Rishi Agastya, the three headed to Panchavati, a beautiful place by the river Godāvari. On the way, they met Jatāyu, who introduced himself as Dasharatha's friend. In Panchavati, they set up a humble but comfortable parnakuti—a thatched hut. Ayodhyā was only a couple of years away now.

Just when they had settled down, hoping to spend the last few years in peace, like the first year in Chitrakoot, destiny began to unfold itself, one day at a time!

Shurpanakhā's Deceit

Rāvana had appointed Khara and Dushana, his cousin brothers, as custodians of the Dandakāranya region. The two had set up their base in Janasthāna. In those days, Rāvana's sister Shurpanakhā was also in Janasthāna. One day, loitering around the jungle, Shurpanakhā saw Rāma in his hut. Shurpanakhā was Cupid struck. She was much older than Rāma. Still, she came to the hut to enquire from him and seek his indulgence.

'Who are you, young man, dressed as a tapasvi? What are you doing here in this forest frequented by rākshasas?' she asked. Rāma politely gave her his introduction and asked for hers. 'I am Shurpanakhā. The mighty Rāvana, Kumbhakarna and Vibhishana are my brothers. In prowess and valour, I am even better than them. Since my eyes fell on you, my heart has started yearning for you. I have come here to seek you as my husband.'

Rāma was amused. 'I am already married. My wife is right here. How can someone like you tolerate a co-wife?' he asked with a smile.

Shurpanakhā took a good look at Seetā. 'This wife of yours is ugly. She is not worthy of you. I will eat her. You and I can then live happily here in Dandakāranya, roaming around the beautiful forests and mountains,' she said.[16]

'Let me suggest you another option. Why don't you consider my brother? He has no wife here,'[17] Rāma asked in jest.

Shurpanakhā observed Lakshmana. He was as good looking and attractive as Rāma, just a little younger. She made the same offer to Lakshmana—to become her husband. 'But I am just a servant of Rāma. Why do you want to become a servant by marrying me? My brother here is a man of many virtues. You should marry him,' Lakshmana retorted with a grin.[18]

Shurpanakhā was angry. She thought the men were rejecting her overtures because of Seetā. 'You are rejecting me because of this ugly lady who is no match to me. See how I eat her up right here, right now,' she yelled and attacked Seetā, attempting to kill her.

Rāma's quick reflexes saved Seetā from Shurpanakhā. He was now very angry. 'This woman deserves to be punished for her crime,' he announced. Lakshmana took the cue and cut off Shurpanakhā's nose and ears with his sword.[19]

Shurpanakhā fled from their hut and stormed into the room where her cousins Khara and Dushana were sitting, insisting they kill Seetā as well as the two princes of Ayodhyā. Khara and Dushana assembled a force of 14,000 rākshasas and attacked the brothers. Rāma single-handedly killed all of them, along with both Khara and Dushana. Shurpanakhā was in shock. She escaped to Lankā to get help from her brother Rāvana, the king of Lankā.

In Lankā, Shurpanakhā was appalled to see Rāvana unaware of the happenings of Janasthāna. His cousin brothers and 14,000 of his men were killed but Rāvana did not even have an inkling of the carnage unleashed by Rāma. She rebuked Rāvana for the negligence of his kingly duties and went on to give a discourse on the importance of vigilance, before telling him about Seetā.

Embarrassed, Rāvana asked her to tell him in detail about the happenings at Janasthāna. He was curious to know about Rāma. Shurpanakhā told him about the fight between Khara's forces and Rāma, and how Rāma eliminated the entire rākshasa army all by himself. 'Rāma holds a huge bow, as big as a rainbow, using which he shoots a volley of sharp arrows at his opponents. He is so quick that all I could see were the arrows he shot but not his actions. He would pull out an arrow from his quiver, stretch the string of the bow, take aim and shoot even before the previous arrow had left his bow,' she said, admiration evident in her voice.

Shurpanakhā informed Rāvana about Janasthāna to incite him to take revenge. But she knew what would get Rāvana on his feet right away and make him go to Janasthāna. Her cut nose and ears were not going to do that, she was sure.

'This Rāma has a wife with large, beautiful eyes,' said Shurpanakhā, carefully measuring every word and observing Rāvana's expressions. 'Her hair, her breasts, her nose—every part of her body is elegant. She lives in the forest as if she is Goddess Lakshmi herself. This lady with a golden complexion and a thin, beautiful waistline, is the daughter of the king of Videha, Janaka. Her name is Seetā. I haven't seen another woman on earth who is as exquisite and comely as her. Fortunate is he who has her as his wife and enjoys her warm embraces. She has no parallel in virtue or beauty. A precious gem like her is worthy of being your wife. You are the best husband she can possibly get.'

Shurpanakhā's words had their effect. An intense desire for Seetā rose in Ravana's heart. 'I was hoping to get her here for you. But when I got close to Seetā to pick her up, Lakshmana, the vile younger brother of Rāma, attacked and disfigured me,' she lied. 'I have no doubt that you will be struck by desire the moment you see Seetā. If you want to experience that bliss, you must strive to make her your wife. Do remember, a direct confrontation with Rāma may not be wise, he is too skilled a warrior. Think through properly how you will make it happen,' she added slyly.[20] Rāvana's entire body was now craving Seetā. He was angry at Lakshmana, not so much for disfiguring his sister, but for not allowing her to get Seetā for him, as Shurpanakhā had claimed. Rāvana decided that he would have Seetā by hook or by crook. His crooked brain was at work already. He had a plan.

Shurpanakhā's Rebuke to Rāvana

When Shurpanakhā came to Lankā to find Rāvana revelling in the luxuries of his prosperity, she was furious. Lakshmana's disfiguring her had enraged her and the loss of the rākshasa army at the hands of Rāma had added insult to injury. And here was Rāvana, who had become so negligent and indulgent that he didn't even know that two ordinary humans were challenging his authority. She reproached Rāvana for his laid-back attitude. Shurpanakhā had an agenda, no doubt, but her words of caution to Rāvana make for interesting reading. A summary of what she said is given here:[21]

A king who, having given in to sensual indulgences, becomes negligent towards the affairs of his state, doesn't get any respect from his people.

A king who doesn't establish and maintain a network of spies to remain informed about the affairs the state, allies and enemies, is eventually betrayed by his own people.

A king who wishes to succeed must have a well-established spy network, a full treasury and a strong policy framework.

A king with following traits doesn't get respect or loyalty from his subjects—one with an angry and bitter disposition, one who doesn't pay his soldiers and employees timely and aptly, one who is deceitful and one who is extremely arrogant and haughty. His subjects and allies abandon him at the first sign of danger.

On the other hand, a king who is cautious, engaged in activities that lead to betterment of his people, controls his senses and cultivates a sense of gratitude and dispenses both favour and punishment as appropriate, is well-respected and rules his kingdom for a long time.

The Lure of the Exquisite Deer

Since the conversation with Shurpanakhā, Rāvana had no peace. His body was in pain. Seetā was his antidote. He soon left Lankā to seek help from Māreecha. In those days, Māreecha lived in Dandakāranya.

Rāvana told Māreecha about the killing of Khara and Dushana, and the disfiguring of Shurpanakhā at the hands of Rāma and Lakshmana. He then revealed to Māreecha his intention of kidnapping Seetā. 'The prince of Ayodhyā is a vile and unrighteous man. That is why his father, King Dasharatha of Ayodhyā, banished him from his kingdom along with his brother and wife. He is bitter, stupid and has no control over his senses. He is only interested in harming others. What he did to Khara, Dushana and Shurpanakhā, I will avenge by kidnapping his beautiful wife. You have to help to make it happen,' said Rāvana with an air of confidence.

When Māreecha heard the name of Rāma, he was startled. Surely, Rāvana didn't have a clue who Rāma was. Rāma was no ordinary human, he believed. Māreecha had barely survived Rāma's onslaught in Siddhāshram when the prince of Ayodhyā was just sixteen. After that, Māreecha found shelter in the forests of Dandaka. Here too, he had experienced the taste of Rāma's arrows when he and other rākshasas were on a mission to harass the innocent forest dwellers.

'O king of the rākshasas, it is easy to find people who will always speak what you would like to hear. But only a few genuine ones will say what is right even if it is not to your liking, and there are fewer who will hear such honest feedback,' Māreecha spoke, giving context to what he was going to say next.

'Rāma has not been discarded by his father, nor is he unrighteous or cruel. He is not bitter, and he is committed to protecting the innocent. You are certainly not aware of who Rāma is. Rāma is an embodiment of dharma. Rāma is as radiant as fire, with his mighty bow as its blazing flame.

'Seetā herself has the resplendence of a smouldering fire. Rāma loves her more than his own life. I wish the rākshasas well and hence I believe it is in our interest not to infuriate Rāma. Let your coveting of Seetā not herald the destruction of the rākshasas. I suggest you consult your ministers such as Vibhishana before you take any undesirable step. Deliberate the pros and cons of your action before making any reckless move,' he advised.[22]

Rāvana was furious at Māreecha's speech and the high praise he bestowed on Rāma. Hoping to dissuade Rāvana from committing hara-kiri, Māreecha shared his own past encounters with Rāma. But Rāvana was adamant. 'If you refuse to help me, I will kill you,' he threatened. Māreecha was left with no choice. He could advise and object, but he could not disobey his king. He agreed to be an accomplice in Rāvana's abduction plan.

Rāmo Vigrahavān Dharma

An oft-quoted statement in praise of Rāma is रामो विग्रहवान् धर्मः—Rāma is the embodiment of dharma.

This quote comes from Aranya Kānda Sarga 37 and is said by Māreecha to Rāvana. The full shloka is:

रामो विग्रहवान् धर्मः साधुः सत्य पराक्रमः |
राजा सर्वस्य लोकस्य देवानाम् इव वासवः ||

Rāma is the embodiment of dharma. He is saintly, established in truth and valiant. He is the king of all earthly beings just like Indra is the king of gods.[23]

As planned, Māreecha took the form of a uniquely resplendent, multi-hued deer with sapphire-blue tipped horns, spotted red face, blue ears, bluish stomach and rainbow coloured tail, hooves and limbs that appeared to be studded with pearls and gemstones, and began sauntering near Rāma's āshram, endeavouring to catch Seetā's attention.[24] Seetā's eyes fell on this deer. She was enraptured seeing such an exquisite deer. She hadn't seen anything like this before. She pointed out the deer to Rāma and requested him to get it for her. 'If you capture it alive, I will foster it like a pet and take it back with me to Ayodhyā,' she said excitedly. 'If not, I can use its skin as a mat to sit with you on.'

Lakshmana sounded a word of caution, 'No one has ever seen a deer like this before. It doesn't seem normal. I sense a conspiracy. This forest is filled with rākshasas capable of assuming any disguise they desire. One such rākshasa is Māreecha. We should not fall for this deer.'

'But it's only a deer, what can it do? I really want it,' Seetā pleaded. Rāma readily agreed. 'It is indeed a unique deer. We haven't seen any animal of this type in the forest,' he remarked, looking lovingly at Seetā. Addressing Lakshmana, he said, 'Just look at Seetā. How her face has lit up seeing the deer! Therefore, I must get it for her. If it is a rare deer then we would have procured a valuable item, and if it is the rākshasa Māreecha, as you suspect, I must kill him anyway. He has killed so many innocent people.'

Lakshmana found no reason to object. Picking up his bow, Rāma proceeded to go after the deer. 'Do not leave Seetā alone. Protect her. Be watchful of the rākshasas. They can come from any direction,' he instructed Lakshmana before leaving.[25]

The deer was very agile. It kept escaping Rāma's clutches, taking him far away from his āshram. Finally, Rāma managed to shoot it. He went near the injured deer to capture it. To his shock, the deer was no longer there. Instead, there was Māreecha, the rākshasa. He had given up his disguise and was breathing his last. Just before dying, Māreecha pulled a trick, which was a part of the plan with Rāvana. He imitated the voice of Rāma and screamed for help, 'Ha Seetā! Ha Lakshmana!' Rāma was spooked. The trickery was now clear to him. He ran back towards the āshram as fast as he could.

Meanwhile, Seetā and Lakshmana had also heard the voice. Seetā was terrified. She urged Lakshmana to go and save Rāma. Lakshmana was unperturbed. He was sure there was something fishy in the scream. He didn't move at all. Seetā was rattled by Lakshmana's indifference. 'Did you not hear that, Lakshmana? Your brother is in danger. Are you his brother or enemy? Ah, I see, you want him dead because you covet me,' she taunted bitterly.[26]

Lakshmana understood her concern. He responded calmly, 'Please do not fear. Have faith. Even if all nāgas, gandharvas, asuras and devas were to combine, and all kings were to come together with their armies, they would not be capable of defeating your husband. He is indomitable in any kind of war. Worry not. The sound we heard is most definitely not his. Someone has imitated him to mislead us. After Rāma killed Khara and his army, many other rākshasas have become our enemies too. It must be one such rākshasa creating this illusion. Rāma has entrusted your safety to me. There is no way I can leave you here alone and go.'

Seetā turned red with anger, 'You are a cruel man. Now I know why you followed us to the jungle. You thought Rāma and I would be alone so you will get Rāma out of the way and then lure me. Or has Bharata sent you? Let me tell you this outright—having Rāma as my husband, there is no other man who I would ever desire. If something happens to Rāma, I will give up my life.'

The allegations were too acerbic for Lakshmana to withstand. 'Your words are falling into my ears like molten iron and burning me. May the nature around here be witness to what I am going to say now. I have only said what I believe is true. But you have said unworthy words to me. Surely, you have lost your mind and are calling for your own destruction. You accuse me of wrong intentions just because you are a woman. I have always obeyed every word of my brother. But now I will go where Rāma is. May the devatās of the forest protect you.' Lakshmana left the āshram, leaving Seetā alone.[27]

Rāvana was waiting for this opportunity—to find Seetā alone. He wasted no time. Disguised as a rishi, he approached Seetā and requested for some food. Seetā was an honourable hostess. She couldn't refuse to feed a rishi. She brushed away the tears welling up in her eyes and got some food for Rāvana. Initially, Rāvana tried some small talk, elaborately praising Seetā's beauty. Having initiated a conversation, he gave his own introduction and began to woo Seetā.

'I am Rāvana, the king of Lankā, the one whose name itself sends shivers down the spine of all beings. Seetā, having seen you, I find no attraction in my wives. Come with me and become my chief queen. I have brought a lot of women from every part of the earth into my harem. You will rule over all of them. There will be no dearth of ornaments for you. Five thousand maids will serve you always,' he tempted.

'Do you not know my husband, Rāma?' Seetā snapped. 'He is unflinching like the mountain and as valiant as Indra himself. With my heart, mind and body, I am committed to him. I have no desire for any other man. I am a proud lioness and you are a wily fox. You can never get me. Just like no one can touch the aura of the sun, you cannot even touch me. Wanting to put your hands on Rāma's wife is like trying to swim with a heavy stone tied to your neck. It is as futile as believing one is going to remain hale and hearty after consuming some deadly poison.'[28]

Rāvana tried to convince her by trumpeting his own greatness. Seetā kept threatening him with dire consequences if he resorted to any misadventure. Rāvana realised Seetā was not going to go with him willingly. He had enough verbal confrontation. Giving up the sage's disguise, he assumed his original form. With his left hand, he pulled Seetā's hair, with the right he lifted her from the thighs and carried her along to his flying chariot.[29]

Seetā struggled to get out of his grip. She cried and screamed for help. Jatāyu heard her cries and came quickly, only to see Rāvana trying to fly away with Seetā. He attacked the king of rākshasas, mustering all his strength. Rāvana was surprised at the ferocity of his attack. But Rāvana, the rākshasa, was way more powerful. He cut the aged Jatāyu's wings and inflicted a fatal blow on him. There was nothing stopping him now. He had captured Rāma's wife. He had presumed it was but a matter of time before Seetā would consent and come happily to him.

Lakshmana Rekhā

A popular tale related to this episode is that before leaving, Lakshmana drew a rekhā or a line on the ground which he asked Seetā not to cross. Staying within the Lakshmana rekhā would keep her safe, Lakshmana had instructed. Rāvana could capture her only because she stepped out of that line drawn by her brother-in-law.

However, there is no mention of Lakshmana rekhā in Vālmiki Rāmāyana. The text simply says that Lakshmana left the āshram praying to the forest devatās to protect Seetā.

Seetā kept screaming and crying all the way to Lankā. When flying over Rishyamukha mountain, she saw some vānaras on the peak. As if wanting to leave a clue behind for Rāma and Lakshmana, she dropped her ornaments and a piece of the yellow silk garment that she was wearing for them to pick up.

On reaching Lankā, Rāvana tempted Seetā with his riches and luxuries. He pleaded for acceptance. But Seetā rejected his overtures and praised Rāma all the while. She minced no words in expressing her disgust for Rāvana. Seetā had no dearth of luxuries in Ayodhyā. She had given them all up for the sake of her husband. Luxuries of Lankā meant nothing to her.

Rāvana even threatened to kill her. Seetā was unmoved. Finally, Rāvana gave her an ultimatum. She had twelve months to make up her mind. 'If you do not come to me of your own volition after twelve months, I will have you chopped and eaten for breakfast,' he warned while dispatching her to Ashokavātikā, a forest of Ashoka trees within the boundaries of Lankā, under the supervision of ferocious-looking rākshasa women.[30] These women were to guard Seetā and get her to accept Rāvana by persuasion or fear, whatever worked.

Rāma's Agony

In Dandakāranya, when Rāma was rushing back towards the āshram, he met a very unhappy looking Lakshmana sans Seetā. Rāma was worried. He rebuked Lakshmana for leaving Seetā alone in the jungle amidst the rākshasas. 'Where is Seetā? Seetā left behind everything to be with me here. Why have you come leaving her all alone in the āshram? Without her, I do not wish to live even for a moment. Without her, I wish no kingdom, not even the lordship over the gods. If I don't see Seetā's smiling face on reaching the āshram, I will surely die. Please tell me what has happened to her. Has your negligence put her in danger? I left Seetā trusting you will take care of her. Why, then, have you come here alone?' he asked, distraught.[31]

Lakshmana told him about what had transpired in the āshram in his absence and how Seetā had been ruthless in casting aspersions on his intentions. 'But Lakshmana, Seetā was worried and angry. Why did you let her words, which were spoken in anger, affect you? Are you not aware that I can tackle the rākshasas myself? I am not happy with your action,' said Rāma.[32]

The situation was serious. There was no time to waste. The brothers ran towards the āshram, as fast as they could. As they feared, Seetā was missing and there were signs of struggle. Rāma was worried. He ran out of the āshram to look for his wife. In the isolated forest, there was no one around. He began to prod the trees, the rivers and the mountains of Seetā's whereabouts, like a mad man. 'Where is my Seetā?' he enquired of everything that came his way.[33]

Lakshmana tried to encourage him to give up sorrow and focus on the task at hand. 'Do not grieve like this. Come with me, let us keep looking for Seetā. She'll surely be somewhere around.' Rāma was in a state of shock. He continued to lament to Lakshmana, 'How will I go back to Ayodhyā without Seetā? Even heaven will be a lonely place for me without her. You return to Ayodhyā. I won't come. I cannot live without Seetā. I must have committed some terrible sin in my past life which has come back to haunt me. The events causing grief don't seem to end. I was banished from the kingdom and separated from my mother, then my father passed away. Because Seetā was with me, I could endure that sorrow. Now she is also gone.'[34] Lakshmana somehow got him to hold himself together and they began to look for Seetā.

Their initial efforts were in vain. They had no idea where to look. They checked all the places where Seetā could possibly have gone, but with no success. Rāma started becoming increasingly impatient. His sorrow had given way to fury. 'I will destroy this entire world and all the beings in it with my arrows if I do not see Seetā soon,' he shouted.[35] Lakshmana tried to calm him down. 'You are known for your composure, brother,' he said. 'Don't let anger and sorrow overwhelm you. A king is entitled to punish, no doubt, but the punishment must be given to the perpetrator and must be commensurate with the crime. We don't even know yet what has happened and who is guilty. If even after all our efforts we don't find Seetā, you may do as you please,'[36] he advised and thus tried to channelise Rāma's emotions positively. Massaging Rāma's feet to help him relax, he added, 'If you, of all people, are not able to contain your agony, how can ordinary people be expected to handle their sorrows with maturity?' Lakshmana went on to give examples of people who had suffered a lot more and had still dealt with their problems with utmost patience and fortitude.[37] His words had the desired impact. Rāma took a grip on his emotions and started thinking systematically. They began the search again.

It was then that they saw an injured Jatāyu covered in blood, fallen on the ground. Initially, Rāma thought it was some rākshasa who was soaked in Seetā's blood, after having eaten her. But as they went closer, they recognised Jatāyu. Jatāyu told them about Rāvana abducting Seetā. He was fatally wounded and died soon after. The brothers cremated him with respect. Jatāyu had given Rāma and Lakshmana a critical piece of information—now they knew who the perpetrator was. But they had no idea about where he had taken Seetā.

They continued their search. On the way, they had brief encounters with Ayo Mukhi and then Kabandha before finally reaching Kishkindhā. In Kishkindhā, they met Sugreeva, Hanumāna, Jāmbavana and others who joined them in their efforts. After months of searching without success, Hanumāna finally found Seetā in Lankā's Ashokavātikā.

Imprisonment in Ashokavātikā

When Hanumāna saw Seetā in Ashokavātikā, she was still clad in the same yellow garment whose piece she had dropped at Rishyamukha, along with her jewellery. That gave Hanumāna some hope that the lady in the vātikā could be her. Her silken garment was dirty, caked in mud. She looked visibly weak. She had been fasting for months, waiting for Rāma. The grief of separation from her husband and the rigours of captivity in Lankā were evident in her eyes. She was sitting underneath a huge Ashoka tree, surrounded by rākshasa women, looking lost and out of place, just like a female deer who has drifted away from her pack and is surrounded by wild dogs. But even in her sorrow, her beauty and resplendence shone through like a flame covered in smoke.[38]

The Beauty of Rishi Vālmiki's Poetry

Rishi Vālmiki is called Ādi Kavi, the foremost of the poets. He is venerated for his language and use of similes and analogies, among other skills. Here is an example of his eminence. While describing Seetā in Ashokavātikā, Rishi Vālmiki writes:[39]

Enveloped in a veil of grief, Seetā looked like:
A memory befuddled
A destroyed wealth
A lost hope
An achievement saddled with hurdles
An abandoned faith
An unjustified, blemish-tainted fame
A troubled intellect

As Hanumāna was observing Seetā, he noticed that she was bereft of ornaments. He was now confident that the lady was indeed Seetā. She had thrown her ornaments at him and other vānaras at Rishyamukha. 'This lady with a radiant and golden complexion is surely Seetā, the beloved wife of Rāma, who has been out of his sight but not out of his mind even for a moment. This is Seetā for whom Rāma's heart pines, for whom he is overcome with love, pain, worry and sympathy, all at once—love for his beloved, pain at her separation, worry for her well-being and sympathy for her grief. It appears to me that her heart is in Rāma and Rāma's in her and that is what is keeping both of them alive,' Hanumāna thought to himself.[40]

As dawn broke over the horizon, Lankā came alive with the sounds of the chanting of Vedic mantras. Suddenly Rāvana, surrounded by his women and bodyguards, walked in. His eyes were still groggy from the revelry of the night before, but they couldn't hide the lewd desire for Seetā. Seetā cringed as he came closer, gathering herself close as if trying to hide her body from his sight. Rāvana aggravated her unease with his shameless proposal. 'Why are you trying to hide from me, Seetā? Why are you afraid? I love you, O charming lady. Accept me. Come to me. You have nothing to fear because no one else can come here and harm you. It is not uncommon for rākshasas to force themselves on unwilling women. It is their trait. But I will not touch you unless you consent, even if Cupid burns my entire body,' he said as he tempted her with ornaments, soft mattresses, beautiful clothes and all material comforts.

'The Creator who has made you, I believe, stopped his work after you, as I see no other woman like you in the universe. But this youth of yours will also pass by one day, like the flow of a river. Do not waste it. Become my wife. What will you achieve by being loyal to Rāma? He is no match for me, neither in strength, nor valour, nor wealth, not even in fame. Come to me instead, and drink as you please, roam as you wish, enjoy all the luxuries that exist—I surrender everything I have to you,' he said, trying to convince her.[41]

Seetā had weakened physically, but her grit, her devotion to Rāma and her self-respect were as strong as ever. She rejected Rāvana's proposal once again. She held a straw of grass to keep Rāvana from coming too close. 'Take your mind off me and indulge in your own wives. Like a vicious man can never aspire to achieve spiritual growth, I cannot be aspired by you. I am married and not worthy of being your wife. A man who is not satisfied with his wives and covets the wives of others is destroyed by his own wavering senses. Don't the wise people in Lankā advise you well? Why are you so determined to destroy the rākshasas by your sins? I am inseparable from Rāma. No luxuries can tempt me to leave him. If you care about protecting your people and kingdom, let me go and try to befriend Rāma. Otherwise, your destruction is guaranteed, for you will not be able to withstand the force of Rāma and Lakshmana. Has a dog ever survived a fight with two tigers?' Seetā spoke politely but firmly.[42]

Rāvana was furious. The unsatisfied lust and the assault on his ego due to Seetā's rejection were too much for him. 'Two months—you have two more months left from the twelve months I had given you,' he said. 'If you do not climb into my bed after that, I will have you chopped and eaten for breakfast,' he threatened once again.[43] He was visibly shaking with anger. To calm him down, one of his wives, Dhānyamālini, came and hugged him. She said lovingly, 'Come, indulge me O king. Why should you amuse this unfortunate and miserable woman? There is no happiness in her destiny.' Other women also came and stood around Rāvana pleading with him to return to his palace. Rāvana left, still fuming.

After Rāvana left, the rākshasa women guarding Seetā took it upon themselves to persuade her, threatening to eat her if she didn't acquiesce. Seetā remained firm but she couldn't control the tears rolling down her cheeks. An old rākshasi, Trijatā, came to Seetā's rescue and asked the others to back off. She reassured Seetā that soon Rāma would come and liberate her from her miseries.

Hanumāna watched all this. Seetā's strength of character left him amazed. The challenge before him was to get to Seetā to tell her about Rāma's efforts for her and console her. This had to be done without alarming Seetā's guards. He shrank his body so that he was small enough to hide among the branches of the tree under which Seetā was sitting and began singing the glory of Rāma, narrating the story of his exile, abduction of Seetā and the eventual search operation undertaken by Rāma. Seetā was astounded. She thought she was hallucinating and looked around. Then her eyes fell on Hanumāna. She wasn't sure what to make of him. A little scared, she looked away, only to see him come close.

Hanumāna bowed to her and initiated the conversation. Seetā did not speak. Then Hanumāna asked, 'Devi, are you Seetā, the one whom Rāvana forcefully abducted from Janasthāna? Please tell me more about yourself.' His words helped Seetā to relax a little. She had heard about Rāma after months. She began telling Hanumāna about herself and Rāma. She also told him about Rāvana's ultimatum. 'Rāvana has given me two months to accept his proposal. But I will not be able to survive till then. I will give up my life if Rāma doesn't come for me,' she said with a sigh.

'Devi, I have come here as a messenger of Rāma. He has sent me to find you,' said Hanumāna. Seetā's face lit up. 'I am reminded of a wise saying—if a man remains alive, there is a chance happiness will come to him even after a hundred years,' she said smiling.[44] Seeing her relax a little, Hanumāna got closer. Suddenly, Seetā became suspicious of this vānara.

She remembered how Rāvana had deceived her, disguised as a sage. She felt the knot in her stomach tighten, 'Darn, this one is indeed Rāvana, how did I get myself to confide in him? He has come again to deceive me,' she fretted in her mind. Then she wondered, 'But, I am getting good vibes from this one. I feel pleased seeing him, probably he is not Rāvana.' Still, she wanted to test Hanumāna before completely trusting him. 'If you are indeed the messenger of Rāma, then describe him and narrate his virtues to me,' she said.[45]

Hanumāna happily complied and described the features of Rāma and Lakshmana in detail and recounted their virtues. He also narrated to her the agony of Rāma at her loss. 'Not being able to see you agitates Rāma's mind just like how an earthquake shakes a mountain. Not even the beauty of the rivers and forests gives any peace to his mind. Anxiety and anguish due to separation from you don't let him sleep at night. But now, you need not worry. He will soon come here, kill Rāvana and his men and meet you.'[46]

Hanumāna then presented Seetā Rāma's ring with his insignia.

Seetā was now fully convinced of Hanumāna's identity. She was elated. She became eager to meet Rāma and urged Hanumāna to request him to come as soon as possible to take her back. Hanumāna had an idea. 'Why don't you come with me right away and liberate yourself of this agony? You may climb on my back, and I will carry you to Kishkindhā. In this way, you can meet Rāma immediately.' But Seetā refused to go with him. She gave four reasons for her refusal:[47]

- Not being able to withstand Hanumāna's speed of flight, there was a chance she may topple into the sea.
- Fear of falling or being captured again due to retaliation of the rākshasas if they got to know of her attempt to escape. If recaptured, they could hide her elsewhere.
- Her belief that touching another man should be avoided as far as possible by married women devoted to their husbands. She regretted Rāvana's touch when he abducted her. But at that time, she was helpless as he had forcibly lifted her. It wasn't her choice.
- Her concern for Rāma's reputation. If Hanumāna saved her, people would question Rāma's valour thinking he was incapable of bringing his wife back himself and had to rely on someone else to make it happen.

'Hence, it will be appropriate for Rāma to come here, kill Rāvana and take me back. That will be worthy of him,' Seetā asserted.

Hanumāna accepted her decision and asked for a token or a sign to confirm her identity to Rāma. Seetā narrated an intimate memory, an incident that had happened in Chitrakoot that only she and Rāma were witness to.

An Intimate Memory from Chitrakoot

This is the story that Seetā narrated to Hanumāna, from their days in Chitrakoot, as a message for Rāma:

One day a crow, desirous of eating flesh flew into our āshram and kept poking me. I tried to shoo it away, but it would hide and then return to poke me again. I was frustrated. While trying to shoo it away again, my lower garment slipped a little. I tried to hold and tighten it. You saw that and laughed at me, amused. I was angry, shy and embarrassed. The crow began to torment me again, hoping for food. In that state, I came to you for protection.

You took me in your lap and consoled me. I was very tired and fell asleep in your lap for quite some time. After that, I woke up and you slept on my lap. The crow came again, pinching me and biting me between my breasts. My warm blood from the wound fell on your face, and you woke up. The wound between my breasts made you very angry. Your eyes fell on the crow who had hurt me. You decided to teach him a lesson. You shot a Brahmāstra at the crow, which followed the crow wherever it flew, trying to escape. Trying to save its life, the crow fell at your feet.

You were kind enough to not kill it. But some punishment had to be given because the Brahmāstra couldn't go waste. 'Let it hit my right eye,' implored the crow. Thus, the crow saved its life in lieu of an eye.

For my sake, you shot a Brahmāstra at a mere crow. Why would you then forgive the one who has abducted me this way? Have mercy on me and come to get me, Rāma.[48]

Seetā also praised Lakshmana profusely and requested Hanumāna to plead with him to come along with Rāma and rescue her. She then gave a jewel she was wearing in her hair—a chudāmani—to Hanumāna to give it to Rāma as a token of her identity. Hanumāna consoled her, promising to come back soon with Rāma, Lakshmana and the entire vānara army under the leadership of Sugreeva.

Agni Parikshā—the Test by Fire

Hanumāna returned and informed everyone of Seetā's imprisonment in Lankā. 'I will remain alive for just one more month. If I don't see Rāma by then, I will give up my life,' Seetā had conveyed through Hanumāna.[49] Hanumāna narrated his observations of Seetā, gave her message and handed her chudāmani to Rāma. Rāma was ecstatic and emotional, all at once, upon seeing the chudāmani. 'If Seetā can hold her life for another month, then I believe she is very strong—because having learnt about her, I don't think I can survive another moment without seeing her now. Please take me to the place where you saw my beloved. I cannot wait anymore.'[50]

Rāma, Lakshmana, Sugreeva and all the vānaras got to work immediately. They left no stone unturned to get to Lankā. A bridge was constructed over the ocean by Nala, another vānara, leading to Lankā. They reached Rāvana's capital. The war conches were blown.

Even while the war was on, Rāvana tried a couple of times to convince Seetā that Rāma had been killed and she had no protector left. He believed Seetā would acquiesce if Rāma was out of the way. Once, when Indrajeet, through his power of illusion, had made Rāma and Lakshmana unconscious, he even arranged to take her around the battlefield on his Pushpak so that she could see them lying dead. But his efforts were futile. Seetā's devotion wasn't based on any consideration of protection or luxury for herself. For her, there was no redemption but Rāma, a fact that Rāvana just couldn't understand. That there are emotions of love and commitment deeper and more profound than material and sensual pleasures, for which a person is willing to forgo every comfort, nay even her life, and endure every pain, was beyond his comprehension. Seetā never gave in.

Finally, the war ended. Rāvana was dead. So were most of the rākshasa warriors. Vibhishana was crowned the king. The only task left now for Rāma was to get Seetā back. Every second of their separation had been torture for both Rāma and Seetā. This was the moment both had been waiting for. Until now Rāma had a singular concern—to eliminate Seetā's tormentors. But now he was gripped by another apprehension—how would his people, the people of Ayodhyā and others, who were to learn about Seetā's stay in Lankā, perceive her? Wouldn't they cast aspersions on her character for spending so many months in Rāvana's captivity? Seetā was more than Rāma's wife. She was going to be the queen of Ayodhyā.

As the future king and Seetā's husband, Rāma had to ensure his wife was beyond suspicion. It wasn't going to be easy, but Rāma was going to do it anyway.

After Vibhishana's coronation, while everyone celebrated, Rāma's joy was visibly subdued. He did not hurry to call Seetā. Instead, he sent Hanumāna to Ashokavātikā with a message. 'Inform Seetā about our victory and well-being. Also, tell her about Rāvana's death. And ask her if she has any message for me.'[51]

Hanumāna conveyed Rāma's message to Seetā and assured her that she was no longer a captive. Seetā choked up out of happiness. Words failed her and she stood still, absorbing the news. After some time, she spoke, 'The news that you have given me Hanumāna is so precious that I don't even know how to felicitate you for this. I have nothing to give you to express my gratitude.' Hanumāna desired nothing. He was just happy to see the sense of contentment on her face. His eyes fell on the rākshasa women who were still around Seetā. 'These women have given you a lot of pain. If you allow me, I will kill them right away,' he said. Seetā being Seetā, stopped Hanumāna from harming the women. 'They were not harming me out of their volition. They were only following their master's orders. Possibly, what I had to live through was destiny ordained. They are not at fault. Or even if they are, I forgive them. Let them be,' she said.[52]

Hanumāna asked if she had any message for Rāma. 'I wish to see him,' she replied simply.[53] Hanumāna returned and informed Rāma of Seetā's wish. Hearing Hanumāna's words, Rāma was a little overwhelmed. His eyes moistened. He appeared lost in thoughts. Then, looking down at the floor, letting out a warm, deep sigh, he addressed Vibhishana, 'Get Seetā here without delay. Ask her to take a head bath, apply ointments and perfumes and dress up well, adorning herself with beautiful ornaments.'[54]

When Vibhishana informed Seetā of Rāma's instructions, she wondered why he wished to see her in that way. 'I wish to meet him right away, like this, without a bath,' she insisted. Vibhishana persuaded her to obey Rāma. She agreed, took a bath, dressed in a red silk garment and decked herself in gold ornaments. Vibhishana arranged for a palanquin to take her to Rāma. He then informed Rāma of Seetā's arrival to meet him. The rākshasa soldiers began pushing the vānaras away to make way for Seetā's palanquin. Rāma was a little irked and stopped the soldiers. He wanted everyone, the vānaras and the rākshasas, to see her, more so the vānaras. They had staked their lives on his victory. 'Ask her to get down and walk towards me,' he ordered.[55]

Lakshmana, Vibhishana, Hanumāna and others present there were puzzled by the grimness in Rāma's voice. They couldn't understand why Rāma was suddenly behaving so coldly. Seetā alighted and walked towards Rāma. All eyes were on her. She was a little shy, a little embarrassed but the light expectant smile of meeting her beloved danced on her face. She came and stood beside Rāma. To her surprise, there was no emotion in Rāma's eyes. He looked lost and distant.

Slowly but firmly, Rāma spoke to her. His manner seemed to suggest his words were for everyone to hear. 'Rāvana abducted you when I was not around. By that act, he challenged my valour. Your abduction was a stigma on the fame of the Ikshvākus. With my effort and the support of all my friends, I have punished Rāvana for his audacity. You must know, this entire exercise of coming all the way to Lankā and defeating Rāvana and his men was not meant to get you. It was meant to wash off that stigma from my family's name.'

Seetā looked on as if paralysed as Rāma continued, 'There is a suspicion about your character. You have lived with another man for so long. Given your beauty and charm, it would have been impossible for Rāvana to resist you. Which man in his right mind would accept his wife after she has been indulged by another man? Therefore, having successfully risen to the challenge that Rāvana had set for me, my job is done. You are free to go wherever you want and with whomever you like. I will have no objection if you want to live in the shelter of Bharata or Lakshmana or Sugreeva or even if you wish to live here in Lankā. You are free to do whatever you wish.'[56]

Everyone was dumbstruck and even disturbed. The coldness in Rāma's voice was palpable. But no one could muster the courage to speak up. Seetā could no longer hold her tears. She felt as if many sharp thorns were piercing her body simultaneously. Trying to push her tears away, she tried to speak but choked. She took control of herself and spoke nevertheless, slowly to begin with, 'Why do you speak to me such bitter and harsh words that hurt my ears? Why are you talking to me like an uncultured man talking to an uncultured woman? I am not what you are making me out to be. I swear on my own character. Trust me.'

Seetā continued, 'Just because some women are unchaste, how is it fair to doubt every woman of unwarranted behaviour? If you have known me at all, give up this suspicion. That my body touched Rāvana's was not because of my desire, but because I was helpless when he lifted me. I can control my mind and heart, which have never deviated from you. But I cannot control anybody else touching me. After all these years of being together, if you have not known even this much about me, then it is better for me to just die.'

Seetā wasn't finished yet, 'When Hanumāna came to look for me, why didn't you let me know then that you were giving up on me? I would have given up my life then and there. What was the need for you to take the trouble of coming here and putting your friends through so much trouble? Don't you know that I am no ordinary woman? I am the daughter of the earth and still you cast allegations on me like this?'[57]

Words were pouring out of Seetā's heart. Rāma, her Rāma, had doubted her character as if he had never known her. She was not going to take these false allegations lying down. She was going to earn her self-respect and her reputation back. 'Lakshmana, light a pyre. This is the only medicine for my agony. My husband has given me up. He doesn't approve of my virtue. Hence, I will now enter the fire,' she instructed.[58]

When addressed like this by Seetā, Lakshmana looked at Rāma, his face red with fury. He was angry at Rāma's uncharacteristic treatment of Seetā. But Rāma's expressions and body language suggested Lakshmana should do as Seetā wished. Lakshmana complied. With a heavy heart, he lit the pyre.[59] Seetā went around Rāma once, her hands folded. Rāma kept looking down at the ground. She went before the burning pyre and proclaimed loudly so that everyone could hear, 'If my heart has never moved away from Rāma ever, then let Agni, the witness of this entire world, protect me from all sides. If I am chaste though Rāma thinks I am not, then let Agni, the witness of this entire world, protect me from all sides. If I have never transgressed in my commitment to Rāma, in speech, action and thought, then let Agni, the witness of this entire world, protect me from all sides. If the sun, wind, moon, the directions, day, evening, night and all other devatās know me to be honourable, then let Agni protect me.' Saying so, Seetā, with an unwavering mind, walked right into the blazing fire as the world looked on startled. The women let out a scream as they saw Seetā engulfed by the flames. The gods in heaven came to witness this nerve-wrecking event.[60]

Just then Brahma deva appeared to Rāma, along with other devatās. They reminded Rāma of his divinity. 'You are no ordinary man, O Rāma, you are an avatār of Vishnu. You took birth to kill Rāvana and liberate the innocents from his harassment. Be reminded of your divinity,' he said. As if on cue, Agni deva appeared and walked out of the pyre along with Seetā, who looked as resplendent as before. Agni deva had protected her. That was the testimony to her flawless character and immaculate conduct in Lankā. 'There is not an iota of blemish in her character. She was unmoved despite all the temptations Rāvana offered her,' attested Agni deva.

The expressions on Rāma's face changed. Tears of joy rolled down his cheeks. 'I have never had a doubt about Seetā's character. She is protected by the strength of her own aura. She is like a flame of fire herself, unattainable for Rāvana. Even though I knew this all along, I didn't stop her from proving her virtue. It was important to bring out the truth. Against her wish, she was forced to stay in Rāvana's captivity. But people, not knowing her, would have raised doubts about her character. Hence, a public attestation was necessary to reaffirm their faith in her. Just like splendour can never be separated from the sun, Seetā is inseparable from me. I can never give up on her,' said Rāma. His voice softened and he held Seetā in his arms. Seetā held no grudges. She too had probably known all the time that Rāma did not really doubt her. He wanted the general public to get the proof. Seetā cooperated.

Seetā was committed to Rāma, but she was not subservient to him. She was a princess in her own right, who did not shy away from making her desires known and having her way, be it about accompanying Rāma to the forest or getting him to bring her the unique gem-studded deer or forcing Lakshmana to go look for Rāma on hearing Māreecha's imitation of Rāma's voice. She was not the one to be scared by the dangers of forest life or the threats of Rāvana. She knew that there was one man who would always be with her, come what may. It was this confidence that made her reject Hanumāna's offer to be carried to Kishkindhā on his back. She chose to wait for Rāma to come and claim her with his valour.

Just like Rāma was concerned about the blemish people would wrongly attribute to Seetā for staying in Lankā and wanted to ensure that she was cleared of it, Seetā too knew that if she allowed Hanumāna to take her back, the blemish would be on Rāma, for leaving his wife unprotected in the jungle and for not punishing the man who committed such a heinous crime. She was not going to allow that, even if it meant another month of captivity and mental trauma for her, and a Bhageerathi endeavour for Rāma, entailing crossing a hundred yojanas of the ocean and taking on the mighty king of rākshasas on his home ground.

That history may think of her as unpragmatic was not Seetā's concern; that history may label him harsh and unemotional was not Rāma's concern. What they both cared about was how history would judge their beloved. Possibly, they weren't thinking about history at all at that point. Their concern was the perception of their people. And by their actions, they did set the norms for them.

Seetā was Rāma's Sahadharmachārini—an equal partner in dharma—in the truest sense of the word. Theirs was a match made in heaven.

However, destiny wasn't done adding twists to their story yet. There was more to come!

भूमेर्दुहितरं विद्यां नमामि प्रकृतिं शिवाम् ।
पौलस्त्यैश्वर्यसंहत्रीं भक्ताभीष्टां सरस्वतीम् ॥

ॐ ψ ॐ

10

Kinship in Kishkindhā

Bordering Dandakāranya towards the south was the kingdom of Kishkindhā, ruled by Vāli, the very powerful and intelligent king of the vānara tribe. Vāli was so strong that he could traverse the eastern, western, northern and southern oceans every day at dawn, offering prayers to the sun during sandhyopāsanā,[1] without any trace of fatigue.[2]

It was said that he was mightier than even Rāvana, the king of the rākshasas. Once Rāvana challenged Vāli to a duel. Vāli was doing sandhyopāsanā at the time. Rāvana planned to attack him from behind. But before Rāvana could make his move, even without looking back, Vāli tucked him under his arm and jumped across the four seas, while offering prayers to the sun. Rāvana had to concede that Vāli was stronger than him. Smartly enough, Rāvana patched up with Vāli and they became good friends after that.[3]

Vāli was undoubtedly extremely strong. But he was also short-tempered and reckless. His wife was Tārā, a wise and beautiful lady. With Tārā, he had a son named Angada. Vāli had a younger brother named Sugreeva who resembled him in appearance and was very devoted to him. Sugreeva's wife was Rumā. He loved her deeply.

A tussle with a rākshasa named Māyāvi created a rift between the brothers. A provocation by Māyāvi had led Vāli and Sugreeva to chase him. Māyāvi entered a cave to escape. Vāli followed, ordering Sugreeva to guard the entrance of the cave. Many days passed but Vāli did not return. Then one day, Sugreeva saw a stream of blood flowing out from the cave and heard screams. He assumed Vāli was dead. So he blocked the entrance of the cave and returned to Kishkindhā. Everyone believed Vāli was dead. They crowned Sugreeva as the king of the vānaras. According to the customs of the tribe, the widow of an older brother could be married to the younger brother if she consented. Thus, Sugreeva got the kingdom as well as Tārā.

However, Vāli wasn't dead. He killed Māyāvi and while trying to exit the cave, found the entrance blocked. He got out anyway and came to Kishkindhā to find Sugreeva on the throne. Vāli was fuming as he entered the court of Sugreeva. He blamed Sugreeva for deserting him and usurping the throne on purpose. Sugreeva fell at his feet and offered the crown to Vāli. He tried to explain what had happened and apologised multiple times for his misunderstanding. But Vāli was in no mood to listen. He was thirsting for Sugreeva's blood. To save his life, Sugreeva fled from Kishkindhā along with four ministers. He went around the earth multiple times to escape Vāli and finally found shelter on a mountain named Rishyamukha, close to Kishkindhā. Vāli was prohibited from entering that area by a curse of Rishi Mātanga. Meanwhile, with Sugreeva away, Vāli laid claim on Rumā, Sugreeva's wife, and forcibly took her for himself.[4]

Around this time, when Sugreeva was trying to keep himself safe from Vāli in Rishyamukha, Rāma and Lakshmana encountered Kabandha during their search for Seetā. Kabandha directed the brothers to Rishyamukha to seek help from Sugreeva. In a way, both Sugreeva and Rāma were dealing with similar fates, though the reasons were different. Both were forced to leave their kingdom and their loved ones. Both had been forcibly separated from their wives.

The Friendship

Sugreeva was initially scared when he heard about two young men arriving in Rishyamukha. He was certain it was another plan of Vāli to trick and kill him. But once Hanumāna, one of his ministers and confidantes, confirmed their identities and reasons for coming to Rishyamukha, he relaxed. Rāma and Sugreeva shared their sorrows and bonded over their afflictions. One needed to find and get his wife back from Rāvana, the other needed to get his wife back from Vāli and ward off danger to his life by eliminating Vāli. They agreed to support each other in their respective endeavours. Sugreeva extended his hand in friendship and Rāma happily accepted it and embraced Sugreeva. Hanumāna quickly rubbed two wooden sticks to create fire. Rāma and Sugreeva circumambulated the fire to cement their bond of friendship formally. Sugreeva promised to extend every kind of support to Rāma to look for Seetā and get her back safely. Rāma promised to kill Vāli and end the threat to Sugreeva's life.[5]

The Importance of Agni

Agni or Fire is one of the pancha mahābhutas—the five basic elements of nature. In Vedic culture, Agni is a very important deity. The very first sukta of *Rigveda* is for Agni. The first verse is 'ॐ अग्निमीळे पुरोहितं—Om Agnimeele purohitam'. The seer praises Agni as the priest of the devas, the bestower of wealth and prosperity, one with miraculous powers and one established in truth, among other things.

Agni is considered as the medium that connects the humans to the divine, as the carrier of our prayers and oblations to the gods. It is also considered as the witness of the entire world and has a quality to purify. Hence, most Hindu rituals involve Agni in some form as yajna or ārti. Hindus cremate their dead. Marriages happen with Agni as sākshi or witness. Oaths are taken over Agni. A promise made or oath taken in the presence of Agni is considered as an inviolable commitment.

Hearing about Seetā's abduction, Sugreeva was reminded of an incident that occurred some months ago. They had seen a rākshasa flying away with a woman who seemed to have been forcibly captured. The woman had dropped a piece of the yellow cloth she was wearing along with some ornaments. Sugreeva showed the ornaments to Rāma to check if they were Seetā's. Rāma saw the ornaments and was once again overcome with sorrow. The ornaments were definitely

Seetā's. This corroborated what Jatāyu had told them about Rāvana flying away with Seetā.

But before beginning the search for Seetā, it was important to get Sugreeva crowned the king of Kishkindhā. That would entail killing Vāli. Rāma sounded very confident about achieving the feat. Sugreeva, however, was not sure if Rāma knew enough about him. Vāli was exceptionally powerful. Killing him was not going to be child's play. Sugreeva wanted to educate Rāma about his opponent and, more importantly, test if Rāma was capable enough to rise to the challenge.

'I have no misgivings about your abilities, but I must honestly tell you about Vāli so that you can make an informed decision about your plan of action,' said Sugreeva to Rāma. 'Vāli strides across the four oceans praying to the sun at dawn. He climbs on mountain peaks, picks up huge boulders and throws them high up in the sky, only to catch them back. The big boulders are his toys. He uprooted many huge trees in the forest with his arms, just to prove his strength. Once there lived a mighty rākshasa named Dundubhi who was in the form of a buffalo. He was as gigantic as the peak of Kailāsh, no less. Dundubhi was known to possess the strength of a thousand elephants. To prove his might, Dundubhi went around challenging all who he believed were powerful. But none had the daring to accept his challenge.'

Sugreeva continued the story. 'Then he was told about Vāli's prowess. So Dundubhi came to Vāli and challenged him. Vāli was inebriated at that time. But he still accepted the challenge. He came out of his palace, took the huge buffalo by his horns, swirled him around and with full force flung him on the ground. Vāli repeated the swirling and flinging multiple times till blood gushed out of every part of Dundubhi's body. The rākshasa died without even putting up a fight. Vāli then lifted the corpse of the dead Dundubhi and flung it one yojana away. The blood-soaked corpse fell near Rishi Mātanga's āshram in Rishyamukha. Rishi Mātanga was upset because his sacred space had been polluted by the corpse and the blood. He punished Vāli by prohibiting him from entering this area. Because of that prohibition, I am able to take shelter here with my ministers. Such is Vāli of unmatched strength. How will you be able to kill him?' asked Sugreeva, worry evident in his voice. He also showed Rāma and Lakshmana the skeleton of Dundubhi that was still lying in the area.[6]

'Hmm, what do you want Rāma to do to prove that he can easily kill Vāli?' asked Lakshmana smiling. One should test even one's close friends before trusting their abilities completely, is a precept leaders are told to live by. Sugreeva was a pragmatic leader. He had thought of ways to test Rāma already. 'Vāli can shake these seven sālā trees one after another so vigorously that they shed all their leaves. If Rāma can fell even one of these trees with one arrow, I will have faith that Vāli will be killed by him. And if he can lift and kick the skeleton of Dundubhi two hundred bow-lengths away, I will be fully confident of Vāli's defeat,' he said, while explaining his position. 'I am fortunate to get a friend in you, Rāma, please do not misunderstand. I do not mean this as an insult to you. It is just that I am aware of how indomitable Vāli is. I fear him. And I do not know enough about your strength.'[7]

Rāma did not mind being tested. He understood Sugreeva's concern. 'If you do not trust my abilities yet, I will inspire confidence in you with my actions,' he said. He went near Dundubhi's skeleton. He simply flicked his big toe, and the skeleton was lifted and flung ten yojanas away. It was an unbelievable feat, but Sugreeva realised it was not enough, for Vāli was a formidable match. The skeleton was much lighter than the corpse which had its flesh and blood intact when Vāli threw it. He requested Rāma to pierce the sālā tree, too.[8]

Rāma held his magnificent bow, adjusted his arrow and pulled the string. The sound of the string reverberated through the jungle. The arrow zoomed through, piercing one tree after another. With just one arrow Rāma had pierced seven trees simultaneously. Sugreeva was stunned. He had no more doubts about Rāma's dexterity and prowess.[9]

They now hatched a plan to get Vāli to come out and fight. Sugreeva would challenge Vāli to a duel and Rāma would kill Vāli while hiding behind the trees in the jungle. As per the plan, Sugreeva went to the gates of Kishkindhā and called for Vāli to come out and fight with him. Hearing Sugreeva's voice, Vāli was red with fury. He rushed out screaming for Sugreeva's blood. A gory duel began between the two. Both mauled each other with their blows. Rāma watched the fight from behind the trees in the forest. Both of them appeared the same to him. They had the same build and similar features. Rāma was confused and didn't want to shoot till he was sure his arrow would not kill Sugreeva. A mistake would be a disaster.

While Rāma waited for the opportune moment to identify and kill Vāli, Vāli had significantly injured Sugreeva. Sensing that there was no help forthcoming, Sugreeva ran away from the field to save his life. Mutilated and indignant, he came back to Rishyamukha where Rāma was waiting for him.

'If you had no intentions of helping me, why did you encourage me to challenge Vāli? Look at how he has mangled me,' Sugreeva groaned in agony. 'Do not be so upset,' replied Rāma. The reason I didn't shoot was to avoid hitting you by mistake. You and Vāli look very similar. Your mannerisms are alike. I was confused about who is who. But don't worry. I will do what will give you pleasure soon,' promised Rāma. He asked Lakshmana to give Sugreeva a big mālā—a necklace—made of Gaja Pushpa, a kind of a creeper. Rāma would then be able to easily identify Sugreeva during the fight.[10]

Sugreeva was convinced. He went back to Kishkindhā to challenge Vāli in the early hours of the morning. Vāli got out of his bed, full of wrath, and began rushing out to tramp Sugreeva under his feet. But Tārā was suspicious. She attempted to stop Vāli from acting recklessly and urged him to think before accepting the challenge. 'Don't give in to anger which comes rushing to you like a stream of river. It is very early in the morning. Wait for an appropriate time to respond. Going out now doesn't seem right to me. Think about it. Just yesterday, Sugreeva came calling upon you for a fight but got badly mauled by you and ran away. And he has come back again to challenge you. Isn't it too soon? Something is not right here. The arrogance and the confidence in his voice when he talks of defeating you do not seem trivial either,' she reasoned.

'He is certainly not alone,' she added. 'He has been guaranteed support by some mighty person. Sugreeva is an intelligent man. He is not likely to befriend anyone before he tests the person's strength. I have heard some news through Angada. Sugreeva has been seen with two princes of Ayodhyā, Rāma and Lakshmana. Both the princes look tough and are known to have never lost a battle. I do not approve of you antagonising them. Rather, make peace with Sugreeva, appoint him the crown prince of Kishkindhā as earlier and make the princes of Ayodhyā your allies. After all, Sugreeva is your younger brother, and you should be looking out for him instead of baying for his blood. I do not see anyone else who can be good and dedicated like a brother as Sugreeva is to you. Hence, give up hostility and call him by your side. If you believe that I love you dearly and I am saying all this for your benefit, then please consider my words. Enmity with Rāma is not in our favour,' appealed Tārā.[11]

Vāli, as if wanting to welcome death, ignored Tārā's wise counsel. 'There is no way I will allow an opponent roaring like that, desiring to fight, to walk away without punishment. I will fight and teach him a lesson right away. And why will Rāma do anything to me? I have no enmity with him at all. I will destroy Sugreeva's arrogance, but I will not kill him,' he said and went out of the palace, much to Tārā's dismay.

The Killing of Vāli

Vāli saw Sugreeva standing in front of him and was overcome with excessive anger. An intense combat began between the two brothers, each wrestling the other with vengeance. At one point, Vāli overpowered Sugreeva. Sugreeva seemed too weak to retaliate. Rāma was standing at a distance and observing the fight intently. When he saw Sugreeva failing, he swiftly mounted an arrow on his bow, took an aim at Vāli and shot it. The momentum of the arrow and the reverberations of the string of the bow rattled everything around. Rāma's aim was unfailing. The arrow cut through Vāli's chest with such a force that the towering vānara instantly collapsed to the ground with a thud. Blood gushed out of his body, colouring the earth around red.[12]

Vāli was in immense pain. His end was near, but his magnificent aura and his fighting spirit were intact. He was angry, upset and confused, all at once. How and from where did the arrow come and hit him like that? It was unfair and underhand to hit someone engaged in a combat with another opponent. Who had done such a treacherous act? He was to learn about it soon.

As soon as he fell, Rāma, Lakshmana and other ministers of Sugreeva gathered at the place where the vānara brothers had been fighting and where Vāli lay grievously injured now, waiting for answers and his death. They stood respectfully before Vāli. Despite his vices driven by extreme ego and anger, Vāli was a person of unmatched strength and valour. He was unassailable in most combats. For that, he deserved reverence, no less.

Seeing Rāma and Lakshmana, Vāli guessed who the perpetrators were. Addressing them, he asked, 'You both are the famous sons of King Dasharatha, aren't you? I was fighting my opponent, not you. But I will die today because of you. What have you achieved by killing me? Tārā had warned me about you. But considering your kingly virtues and the reputation of your family, I ignored her pleadings. I was confident you will not attack me from behind my back when I was engaged in a fight with someone else. Alas, I was wrong. You are only clad in a cloak of dharma. In reality, you are unethical men, deceptive like the unseen flame of fire covered by a sheath of grass.'

'I don't remember having harassed or insulted you ever,' Vāli continued. 'Nor do I remember creating any problem in your city or kingdom. I am a simple forest dweller subsisting on fruits and roots, roaming in these jungles. Why then did you resort to such treachery even though you are born in a reputed royal family to a well-known king and have the wisdom to know what is right and wrong? Land, gold or silver assets are usually a cause of conflict between people. But there is no such conflict between us. Our assets are our forests and fruits. What greed made you commit such a crime? A king has the right to dispense punishment and favour, but he is expected to be responsible for making use of this right and not be capricious about it. By attacking me you have clearly displayed your fickle-mindedness, as I am completely innocent in relation to you.'

Vāli continued his tirade. 'Hunting in the forests is allowed to kings. The objective is to gather valuable resources in the form of animal skin or meat for food. But flesh and skin of us vānaras are of no use to you because our skin is unwearable, and flesh is inedible. What led you to kill me then? My wife, Tārā, was prescient but I didn't listen to her and here I am, lying helplessly, waiting for death. Or is it that you undertook such a vile task to favour Sugreeva so that he can help you to find Seetā? That too, I think was unwise of you. If you had sought my help, I would have simply tied a rope around Rāvana's neck and brought him before you without the need of a war.'

Vāli added, 'I am not upset that I am going to die soon. One who is born is bound to die at some point. Nor am I upset that Sugreeva will get the throne of Kishkindhā after I am dead. But what bothers me is that you have killed me unrighteously.' Vāli's breath was becoming heavier with every word.[13]

Vāli deserved an answer and Rāma obliged, explaining in detail why his action was aligned with dharma, not otherwise. He said, 'Vāli, you talk like one who understands dharma, but you don't. You should know that this whole region including the forests and mountains is under allegiance to the kings of Kosala. They hold the right and responsibility to dispense justice in this region. Bharata is the king of Kosala currently and I am his representative in this region. Wherever we see dharma being undermined, it behoves us to step in to restore it and punish the unrighteous ones. Giving in to your sensual indulgences and baser instincts, you had gone astray from the path of your Rāja Dharma. The wise people in the region have always criticised you for this.'[14]

'An elder brother is like a father and a guru to the younger brother, who is akin to his son and student,' Rāma continued. 'Given the stature, it is important for an elder brother to have a nuanced understanding of dharma about what is doable and what is not. You forcibly took away your younger brother's wife, your own daughter-in-law, to satisfy your desires. By this one act, you failed in upholding your dharma. In fact, you committed an unforgivable crime that necessitated punishing you. Anyone who commits a crime that sets the wrong precedence and leads to perversion in society must be necessarily punished.'[15]

'In a civilised society,' Rāma added, 'a man who looks at his daughter, daughter-in-law, sister or younger brother's wife with lust must be punished. I cannot condone such depravity. Punishment of such act is death.' Rāma's stand was unequivocal.[16]

'Moreover, Sugreeva is like Lakshmana to me,' Rāma continued, 'a younger brother who came to seek my support to get his wife and kingdom back. I promised to get him justice. There was no way that I wouldn't have fulfilled my promise.'

'If you, being a king,' Rāma went on, 'would have behaved like a king, you would have done what I did. Let me tell you the edict that the scriptures have for kings in this regard. If a criminal gets punished by the king for his wrongdoing, and the person accepts the punishment, then he doesn't accrue the bad karma associated with that crime any longer. He is cleansed of that sin. However, if the king doesn't punish the wrongdoer, the bad karma of that action accrues to the king, who eventually must suffer the consequences of it. In the past, an ascetic had committed such a grave crime as yours. My ancestor Mandhātā had given him as severe a punishment as prescribed by the scriptures. Hence, accept your death as a punishment and harbour no ill will. It will cleanse you of your grave misdeeds.'[17]

And finally, in reply to Vāli's comparison of his killing with hunting 'non-useful' animals, Rāma said, 'And if you believe that you are like any other wild animal in the forest and my killing of you is like hunting, then you shouldn't be upset with me at all. Hunting is allowed to kings and there is no prohibition on who can be hunted. In hunting, there are no rules stopping the hunter from killing his prey from behind or by using tricks. Thus, from that perspective too, what I did was right.'[18]

Karma and Punishment

The edict regarding importance of punishment for a crime to cleanse the doer of the bad karma is also found in *Manusmriti*.[19]

The thief becomes absolved from the theft, either through punishment or through acquittal. By not punishing the thief, the king imbibes the guilt of the thief (3.10).

Men who, having committed crimes, have been punished by kings, become freed from guilt, and go to heaven, just like well-behaved good men (3.18).

–Translation by Gangānāth Jhā

The same injunction is found in other Dharmashāstras as well, such as *Bodhāyana Sutras*, *Yājnavalkya Smriti*, etc.

Vāli was trumped by his own arguments. He realised his folly. There were no more questions clouding his mind. But he was a smart person. He wanted to ensure that his only son, Angada, was taken care of after his death. He had also understood that Rāma held no malice towards him personally and was firmly established in dharma. The only way to secure his son's future was by surrendering his care to Rāma. He knew that Sugreeva, being indebted to Rāma, would follow Rāma's instructions. Vāli performed his last duty as a father. 'Rāma, I have one request to make of you. I do not grieve for myself or Tārā, but I am worried about my son. Angada has excellent virtues. He has been brought up with a lot of love and care until now. Seeing me dead, he will be devastated. I urge you to take him under your care and protect him. Please look out for both Sugreeva and Angada and advise them on what should be done and what should not be done. Take care of them, like you care for Lakshmana. Please look after Tārā as well. Ensure Sugreeva doesn't treat her as a criminal because of me,' he requested.[20] Rāma assured him that Tārā and Angada would be cared for like before.

Because of immense loss of blood, Vāli had become very weak. He fainted but opened his eyes again after some time. By then, Tārā and Angada had also come by his side. This time Vāli addressed Sugreeva. 'Sugreeva, after I am gone, do not harbour any animosity against me. It seems to me that some past karmas made us antagonistic towards each other despite being born as brothers. Accept this kingdom of Kishkindhā. I hereby renege my claim on the kingdom and all its wealth. But please take care of my son who is dearer to me than my own life. Angada is as valiant and strong as you are. He will always be at the forefront in the wars you fight and the tasks you undertake. Also, do not disregard Tārā. She is a very erudite woman with strong, intuitive power. If she gives any advice, follow it without hesitation,' he advised.[21]

Vāli also had a message for Angada. 'Son, understand the exigencies of place and time. Whatever you get, happiness and sorrow, as destined, endure it. Cultivate forgiveness in your heart and obey your Uncle Sugreeva. Never align with his enemies. Remain loyal to him and follow his orders. Don't get over-attached to anything, nor become indifferent. Develop a sense of equanimity towards everything you do.' These were Vāli's last words. He passed away soon after. Even in his last moments, he knew exactly what the most pragmatic approach was for his son to adopt.[22]

Tārā was devastated. She wished to give up her life on Vāli's funeral pyre. Hanumāna consoled her and reminded her of her responsibilities towards Angada. Rāma suggested that Sugreeva should be coronated without delay and Angada should be declared as the crown prince of Kishkindhā.

There is a popular story about this incident. Vāli is said to have a boon through which, in face-to-face combat, he obtained half the strength of his opponent and became stronger, leaving the opponent weaker by half. This boon, it is said, was the reason for Rāma attacking Vāli from behind.

This story is not found in Vālmiki Rāmāyana.

Tārā Saves the Day for Sugreeva

The monsoons had already arrived by the time the coronation of Sugreeva took place. Monsoon was a time of relaxing and rebuilding. All those who were travelling returned to their homes. No military expeditions were undertaken at that time. So Rāma decided to wait for autumn to start the search for Seetā again. He and Lakshmana stayed in a cave in the Prasavana mountains while Sugreeva settled in Kishkindhā. Time went by rather slowly for Rāma. Sleep had deserted him. He was reminded of Seetā in every waking moment. Pangs of separation from his beloved were becoming more and more intense.

When the rains stopped and the skies cleared, the onset of autumn was evident. But Sugreeva was nowhere to be found. Rāma and Lakshmana started getting uneasy but decided to give him some more time.

Back in Kishkindhā, Sugreeva was revelling in luxuries he had been deprived of for so long while trying to save his life from Vāli. He was in a state of intoxication all the time, surrounded by women who happily did his bidding. He lost sense of time. The day-to-day administration of Kishkindhā was being managed by his ministers.

But Hanumāna hadn't forgotten the promise that Sugreeva had made to Rāma. Having observed the change in season, Hanumāna reminded Sugreeva about it. Sugreeva, still in a state of drunkenness, ordered all the vānaras from across Bhāratavarsha to gather in Kishkindhā in two weeks, and went back to his revelry. Hanumāna arranged for the orders to be sent out.

All this while, Rāma and Lakshmana received no communication from Sugreeva. Rāma was forgiving and kind, but he had a strong sense of duty. He held himself and others accountable for what was committed. If Sugreeva had forgotten, he needed to be reminded. If Sugreeva believed he could get away after getting his work done and not reciprocate, he was underestimating Rāma and needed to be put in place.

Rāma sent Lakshmana to Kishkindhā to remind Sugreeva of his duties. Rāma's message to Sugreeva was concise and clear, without mincing words, 'The road by which Vāli has gone hasn't closed yet. With just one arrow I felled him. Now if you renege on your responsibility, you will meet the same fate, rest assured.' At the same time, Rāma clearly instructed Lakshmana to only threaten Sugreeva, not kill him. Sugreeva was a friend, after all, who only needed some prodding.[23]

Lakshmana went to Kishkindhā carrying Rāma's warning. His body language and expression were enough to convey his anger. The vānaras who saw him enter were initially combative, but Lakshmana's ire scared them. Lakshmana saw Angada and ordered him to inform Sugreeva of his arrival. Angada did as he was told. Sugreeva, though drowsy and drunk, was surprised on hearing about Lakshmana's anger. 'Making friends is easy but maintaining friendships is not. I am forever indebted to Rāma for doing what he has done for me. I think someone is instigating them against me,' surmised Sugreeva before his ministers.

The wise Hanumāna judged the situation correctly. 'Although you haven't forgotten Rāma's favour and friendship,' he said, 'in your revelry, you lost track of time. Autumn is underway. You haven't informed Rāma and Lakshmana about how you plan to help them look for Seetā. I do not see any other reason for their ire. It is best for you to seek pardon from Lakshmana and expedite the search operation. It will not be wise to anger Rāma and Lakshmana.' Hanumāna, added, 'A minister must always give advice which is in the interest of the king. Hence I have said all this without fear.'[24]

By then, walking through the wide and well-laid streets of Kishkindhā, Lakshmana had entered Sugreeva's palace. The luxuries of the palace and Sugreeva's revelry were a stark contrast to Rāma's pain and this angered Lakshmana even more. On seeing Lakshmana, Sugreeva, his eyes still bloodshot, stumbled towards him with folded hands. Lakshmana was seething. 'Sugreeva, only a king who has controlled his senses, is grateful, truthful and patient, is respected by his citizens—not the one who, giving in to vices, forgets the favours done to him by his friends. An ungrateful man who gets his work done but reneges on his promises deserves to be killed.' Saying thus, Lakshmana repeated the warning given by Rāma in as many words.[25]

Sugreeva couldn't say a word but Tārā, who was standing close to him, responded, politely but assertively, 'Lakshmana, Sugreeva doesn't deserve to hear such harsh words from a friend like you. He is not a cheat nor ungrateful, neither untrue nor cruel. He hasn't for a moment forgotten that it is through Rāma that he has obtained this kingdom and all its luxuries, along with Rumā and me. All these years he suffered hardships due to Vāli's anger. Now, after so long, when he tasted luxuries and pleasure again, he lost track of time. Sensual pleasure sometimes has this impact on people who are otherwise great and virtuous. Haven't we heard the story of Rishi Vishvāmitra and the nymph, wherein lust made the rishi forget about his tapasyā? If it can happen to a rishi, what can we say to Sugreeva, who was deprived of these pleasures for so many years?'

Building Sugreeva's case, Tārā continued, 'A wise person like you shouldn't react out of anger. It is my firm belief that if required, Sugreeva will give up everyone and everything just to honour his promise to Rāma. I have heard that Lankā has innumerable mighty rākshasas. You won't be able to defeat them and bring Seetā out safely without help. You will certainly need Sugreeva's assistance to make that happen. In fact, he has already called vānaras from across the region to assemble in Kishkindhā, only for the sake of Rāma. Now he is just waiting for them to reach here so that the expedition can begin. Hence, give up your fury and rest assured the work will be done.'[26]

Very smartly and concisely, Tārā not only explained Sugreeva's lapse but also politely suggested to Lakshmana that Sugreeva was an important ally for the fulfilment of their objective.

After Lakshmana had calmed down, Sugreeva apologised for his indiscretion and reaffirmed his gratefulness as well as loyalty to Rāma.

The vānara contingents arrived soon after and the search for Seetā began.

The Search

Trying to save his life from Vāli, Sugreeva had travelled across the earth in every direction. That had helped him gather a lot of information about the geographies and people of different regions. His knowledge of world geography was one reason why Kabandha had directed Rāma to Sugreeva. Who better than an expert in geography to guide a search operation? Once all the vānaras had gathered, Sugreeva asked Rāma to decide the course of action, 'Our teams are well versed in undertaking such operations. Even so, we are all here to follow your commands. Please give orders as you consider appropriate, and we will follow them.'

Rāma was an astute administrator. He could read people well and gauge their capabilities. He knew how to delegate tasks, inspire ownership and get work done. Hugging Sugreeva, Rāma smiled and replied, 'Our objective is to determine where Rāvana lives, where he has taken Seetā and whether Seetā is alive. Once that is known, we will plan our next steps together. For now, you are the expert and best suited to give relevant instructions for the search operations. Neither I nor Lakshmana has the knowledge that you have in this regard. You are my well-wisher just like Lakshmana, and you understand our objective very well. Hence, please give orders as you deem fit.'[27]

Sugreeva then took over and divided the contingent into four groups to look for Seetā, one for each of the four directions. He appointed Vinata to lead the contingent to the east, Sushena to the west, and Shatabali to the north. As Rāvana was seen taking Seetā towards the south and Lankā was known to be in the south as well, he sent Angada, Hanumāna, Jāmbavana, Nala and Neela, some of his most trusted ministers, in the southern direction. Sugreeva gave all the groups detailed instructions about the major landmarks they would find and the characteristics of people they would see in those regions. He gave them a month's time to come back with their information.

Given the probability of finding Seetā southwards, Sugreeva had some additional instructions for Hanumāna. 'Endowed with brain, brawn and bravery, you are also an expert in management and polity and have a deep understanding of time and place. I do not see anyone else more capable than you in accomplishing our task. Hence, think through thoroughly and do what is needed to be done to find Seetā,' he told him. Observing the trust Sugreeva had placed in Hanumāna, and his own experience with him thus far, Rāma too felt hopeful that Hanumāna would come back with the happy news. Therefore, he gave Hanumāna the ring he wore on his finger that had his insignia. 'This ring will convince Seetā that you have been sent by me and she will place trust in you without fear,' he said.[28]

The three groups from the north, west and east returned after a month but had nothing to report. The group that went south hadn't even reached the seashore in a month. They initially got lost in the labyrinth of a cave but were shown out safely by a saintly woman, Swayamprabhā. She guided them to the shore. The path ahead was still unclear. A vast ocean lay before the vānaras, but where were they to go and how? Angada decided to fast unto death. He thought returning to Kishkindhā would mean death anyway, as his Uncle Sugreeva would punish him with death for failing to find Seetā.

But a chance meeting with Sampāti changed their course of action. Sampāti was Jatāyu's elder brother. Sampāti was pained on hearing about Jatāyu's death at the hands of Rāvana and pledged to help the vānaras to the best of his ability. He had an eagle's vision. He could see Seetā in Rāvana's Lankā situated a hundred yojanas across the ocean. The challenge now was to reach Lankā. Who could possibly leap across a hundred yojanas and come back safe?

Angada had the strength, but he was the crown prince. It was not a good idea to send him. The mantle fell on the shoulders of Hanumāna. Though unsure to begin with, Hanumāna successfully reached Lankā, found Seetā, created havoc in Lankā and returned safely to Kishkindhā to inform everyone about Seetā's whereabouts. Rāma was elated. He hugged Hanumāna tightly. His heart finally found some peace.

The task at hand was even more challenging. How were all of them going to cross the ocean to reach Lankā? Hanumāna, Angada, Neela and Sugreeva were the only ones who could leap across, but it was an impossible feat for the others. With the answer to that question still unclear, they decided to reach the seashore first and think about the solution after that. The entire contingent of vānaras along with Rāma, Lakshmana and Sugreeva arrived at the coastline.

After Hanumāna had given a taste of his powers to the people of Lankā, Rāvana had begun to keep a close eye on the activities of Rāma and Lakshmana. Though publicly he said he was confident that they could never reach Lankā, he knew that the act of Hanumāna was out of the ordinary. Hanumāna had informed him about the alliance between Sugreeva and Rāma. Rāvana had very good relations with Vāli. After the initial drubbing that Rāvana had received at Vāli's hands, Rāvana had patched up and the two had become close like brothers. Rāvana wished to exploit that relationship to create a rift between the Sugreeva and Rāma. He sent his messenger Shuka to Sugreeva with a message.

The message said, 'Sugreeva, you are born in the respectable family of Riksharāja and are yourself a very powerful king. I have always considered you my brother. We have no animosity whatsoever between us. Even if we may not have actively helped each other in the past, we have done nothing to harass each other either. I have abducted Rāma's wife, which is his problem and of no concern to you. There is no chance that you can cross the ocean and come to Lankā, anyway. It is better for you and your people to return to Kishkindhā.'

Sugreeva was unconvinced. He had deep gratitude for what Rāma had done for him. He was also aware of Rāma's strength and ire. Sugreeva was not going to switch sides. He responded firmly to Shuka's message. 'Rāvana, neither are you my friend, nor are you dear to me, nor have you done anything that I must be grateful for. Being an enemy of Rāma, you are worthy of being killed by me. I will certainly come to Lankā with my army and destroy you and your kingdom. You don't seem to realise that you have called upon your destruction by cowardly kidnapping Seetā when she was alone in her āshram. Rāma is invincible. You don't seem to understand that he will end your life soon,' he said, reiterating his commitment to Rāma's cause.[29]

Before Shuka could leave, Angada caught hold of him. 'He is not a messenger but a spy who has come here to assess our strength and sow seeds of disharmony among us,' conjectured Angada. Sugreeva agreed and ordered his imprisonment. Shuka was allowed to go on Rāma's advice, only after they reached Lankā and organised their army. Shuka's release was strategic. Rāma knew Shuka would tell Rāvana everything he had learnt about the vānara army. His observations couldn't harm the vānaras anymore as they were already in Lankā, but it would help rattle Rāvana's self-confidence.

Nala Setu

The vānara army camped by the shore for a few days. The challenge of crossing the ocean remained. Then help came totally unexpected, in the form of Vibhishana, Rāvana's younger brother, who defected to Rāma's side. He suggested that Rāma should meditate on the deity of the ocean, Varun deva, and seek help. Accordingly, for three days and three nights, Rāma meditated on Varun deva, but to no avail.

Time was running out but Varun deva showed no signs of being appeased. His obstinacy angered Rāma. He threatened to dry the ocean of all its waters for such audacious stubbornness, only to be held back by Lakshmana. Varun deva finally emerged and provided a solution to their dilemma. 'Make a setu—a bridge—over me. This vānara Nala who is with you has the grace of Vishvakarmā. Entrust him with the task. He is capable of building a bridge that will allow all of you to get to Lankā,' he said.[30]

On hearing Varun deva's words, Nala spoke, 'What Varun deva has stated about me is true. I am born of Vishvakarmā. He gave a boon to my mother that the son born through them would be like him in capabilities and skills. As I was not asked about this before, it was not right for me to boast. But I believe I will be able to construct a bridge across the ocean.' Saying this, Nala got to work right away. He gave clear instructions for the material he wanted and how to procure it. The vānara army enthusiastically started bringing material from the forest in the form of boulders, rocks and trunks of all types of trees, including Sāla, Arjuna, Ashoka, mango and bamboo. They uprooted trees of coconut, neem and Bakul and also brought various shrubs and reeds.

Boulders as big as mountains were thrown into the sea. From the shrubs and the barks of trees, strong ropes were made to keep the rocks in alignment. The material collected from the forest was used to bind the stones and tree trunks together. Long reeds were used to fasten parts of the bridge together.

On the first day, 14 yojanas of the bridge was constructed, followed by 20 yojanas, 21 yojanas, 22 yojanas and 23 yojanas on consecutive days. In five days, a hundred yojanas long and ten yojanas wide bridge was built by the vānaras. Nala had made the impossible possible. His bridge was comparable in style and strength to what Vishvakarmā would have built himself. Huge, well-constructed and held tightly together, the bridge looked like a long, beautiful line cutting through the ocean.[31]

Using the bridge, the army, along with Rāma, Lakshmana and Sugreeva, crossed the ocean and set foot on the glorious city of Lankā. Till then, Rāvana had assumed he was invincible. Hanumāna's exploits had shaken him but even then, even in his wildest dream, he had not imagined that a bridge could be constructed over the ocean, allowing thousands and thousands of vānaras to descend on Lankā.

Nala Setu: A Civil Engineering Marvel

In some re-tellings, the construction of the bridge is presented more allegorically. They say that the vānaras threw stones inscribed with Rāma's name in the ocean. The stones simply floated on the ocean, making a bridge, using which the contingent crossed over to Lankā. The allusion is made to the power of Rāma nāma. Such narrations must be understood as the expression of the poet's bhakti in Shri Rāma.

In Vālmiki Rāmāyana, the event is described in detail, not as magic that defies science but as a civil engineering construction project par excellence.

The War

Before formally sounding the war conches, Rāma wanted to give Rāvana one last chance to return Seetā and avert the war. He sent Angada to Rāvana's court to convey the message. But peace was not to be. Rāvana tried to capture Angada but the latter was brave and agile. He escaped through the ceiling of Rāvana's palace.

Sugreeva took charge of the war strategy with Vibhishana's input and arranged the army so that they could counter the attacks from all the four gates of Lankā. The rākshasa army had weapons of all kinds. The vānaras fought with their bare hands and sheer might, using tree trunks and rocks for weapons. Still, they were more than a match for the rākshasas. Many commanders of Rāvana received a good thrashing at their hands.

There were times when the rākshasas overpowered the vānaras, especially when Kumbhakarna entered the fight. He was a colossal cannibal—huge in size and cannibalistic in nature. His entry itself sent shudders in the vānara army. Innumerable vānaras were trampled by him. Innumerable vānaras were mutilated and even more were eaten by him. The earth was drenched in the blood of the vānaras due to Kumbhakarna's assault.

The vānaras got so terrified of Kumbhakarna that many began to run away from the battlefield. It was Angada's leadership and motivation that brought them back and gave them the strength to fight. Angada coaxed them by igniting their pride. He reminded them of their family honour and how being called cowards would bring a bad name to their families. He lured them with dreams of victory if they lived and of heaven if they died fighting bravely. His encouragement worked. The vānaras returned, determined to fight till their last breath.[32]

It was impossible to match Kumbhakarna in physical strength. Following Lakshmana's suggestion, the vānaras decided to use their numerical strength to counter him. Many vānaras climbed on him and started biting him with their teeth and scratching him with their nails. Angada and Sugreeva lead the attack on the ground. Kumbhakarna was irritated but remained unfazed by the vānara assault.

At one point, Kumbhakarna hit Sugreeva so hard that the latter fainted. To the shock of the vānaras, Kumbhakarna lifted Sugreeva on his head and headed back to the city. But Sugreeva regained his consciousness soon. Using his nails and teeth, he began biting Kumbhakarna's ears and ripped the rākshasa's chest, causing blood to flow. Kumbhakarna's grip loosened. Sugreeva immediately leaped out and escaped to his camp.

This was the second time Sugreeva's life had been endangered. The first time he got into trouble was during a tussle with Rāvana. This happened even before the war had begun. Rāma, Lakshmana, Vibhishana, Sugreeva and other vānaras were standing on the peak of the Suvela mountain in Lankā to view the city and its fortifications. They spotted Rāvana standing on the terrace of his palace, far away. Seeing him made Sugreeva so furious that he leaped across to Rāvana's terrace and challenged him to a duel. Both began hitting each other. But before it got too ugly, Sugreeva exhausted Rāvana and returned to Rāma.

Rāma was not too pleased with this reckless act of Sugreeva. 'What you have done is not befitting of kings. It was a rash act. Even though I have full faith in your strength, if something untoward had happened to you, I had made up my mind to finish the task in Lankā and give up my life. Bharata can continue to rule Ayodhyā,' admonished Rāma lovingly.[33]

Over the course of the war, the vānaras were very successful in taking down many commanders of Rāvana. Some renowned rākshasas killed by Sugreeva's army have been included in the accompanying table.

Sugreeva	• Praghasa • Kumbha (Kumbhakarna's son) • Virupāksha (2) • Mahodar (2)
Angada	• Vajradanta • Narāntaka • Kampan • Prajaghna • Mahapārshva

Hanumāna	• Jambumāli • Dhumrarākshasa • Akampan • Devāntak • Trishirā • Nikumbha (Kumbhakarna's son)
Neela	• Prahasta • Mahodar (1)
Nala	• Pratapan
Dvivida	• Ashniprabha • Shonitāksha
Sushena	• Vidyunmāli
Maind	• Vajramushthi • Yupāksha
Vibhishana	• Shatrughna
Lakshmana	• Virupāksha (1) • Atikāya • Indrajeet
Rāma	• Agniketu • Rashmiketu • Suptaghna • Yajnakopa • Makarāksha • Kumbhakarna • Rāvana

Note: The list is not exhaustive. The numbers in brackets are used to differentiate rākshasas with the same name.

Not only did the vānaras fight valiantly, but on occasions, they also saved the lives of Rāma and Lakshmana. Twice during the war, the princes of Ayodhyā were rendered unconscious, once by the nāgapāsh[34] and then by the Brahmāstra of Indrajeet. The first time, the princes were saved by the divine intervention of a garuda[35] who came unexpectedly and helped relieve them of the snake poison. The second time, to respect the Brahmāstra, Rāma strategically decided not to resist but accept it. That helped because the weapon didn't kill them but made them unconscious. The way to recover from Brahmāstra induced unconsciousness was to administer some medicinal herbs found in the Himālayas. Jāmbavana informed where the medicines could be found and Sushena gave details of the herbs to be brought. Hanumāna brought them all the way from Himālayas—he couldn't identify the plants, so he brought the entire boulder itself—and Sushena administered the medicines, thus helping the princes of Ayodhyā get back on their feet, ready to fight once again.

Life-Saving Herbs

Sushena instructed Hanumāna to get not one but four herbs[36] for administering to Rāma and Lakshmana; every herb had a specific purpose. We can find a mention of these medications in Ayurveda as well, though it is difficult to ascertain if the herbs are the same. The medications mentioned by Sushena were:

- Vishalya karani: A herb that is applied on open wounds caused by arrows to control bleeding. There is a herb called Ayapan in some Indian languages which is used in the healing of such wounds. Its medicinal name is *Eupatorium triplinerve*.[37]
- Sāvarnya karani: A herb that helps restore the colour of the skin when a wound causes discolouration of the skin. There are many herbs mentioned in Ayurveda texts that help restore skin colour. They are called 'varnya' herbs. 'Varna' means colour.[38]

- Sanjeeva karani: A herb that helps revive someone from a state of unconsciousness or near death. Often called Mrita-Sanjeevani, this herb has piqued the interest of researchers for long and there have been a lot of efforts made to identify such a herb that has life restorative properties. There have been a couple of herbs that have been zeroed down by researchers that seem to match the properties of Sanjeevani.[39]
- Sandhāni: The word 'sandhi' means 'to join'. Sandhāni is a herb or herb extract that helps join broken bones. There have been several herbs mentioned in Ayurveda, which help in the recovery of fractured bones. Some of these are used even today.[40]

The war ended with the killing of Rāvana at the hands of Rāma. Rāma had a reason to fight Rāvana as the rākshasa had abducted his wife. But the vānaras had none. Even then, they did everything in their capacity to help Rāma get Seetā back. So many vānaras risked their lives for Rāma. So many died for Rāma.

And Rāma did whatever he could to ensure their happiness. After the war, when Indra wished to grant a boon to Rāma, he requested that the dead vānaras be brought back to life so that they could unite with their families. Though a difficult ask, Indra resurrected the vānaras who had died fighting Rāvana's forces.[41] Later, when Vibhishana wanted to give expensive gifts to Rāma for crowning him the king of Lankā, Rāma refused anything for himself. Instead, he requested Vibhishana to gift the vānaras with the jewels and wealth. They deserved the gifts and gratifications rather than him, he said.

After the war, the vānaras, along with Sugreeva and Vibhishana, accompanied Rāma, Lakshmana and Seetā to Ayodhyā. They made a stop in Vatsa desh to see Rishi Bharadwāja. The rishi wanted to grant a boon to Rāma. This time, too, Rāma did not ask anything for himself but requested that the trees and shrubs en route to Ayodhyā blossom with sweet fruits for the sake of the vānaras.

Rāma, Seetā and Lakshmana had left Ayodhyā alone. But they came back with friends like Sugreeva, Hanumāna, Angada, and Jāmbavana. What began as a relationship of reciprocation soon became a bond of brotherhood, strengthened by mutual respect, empathy and devotion.

The association of vānaras with Rāma had been brief but it was only through their support that the itihāsa of Bhāratavarsha got charted. It was through their efforts that Rāma could kill the formidable Rāvana and defeat his huge forces, despite not having a sophisticated army.

Rishi Vālmiki tells us that the birth of the vānara warriors was meant to help Rāma fulfil his task of establishing dharma and eliminating adharma in the society, which had become a playground of Rāvana's whims and fancies. Rāma was the avatār of Vishnu. No one else could have taken Rāvana head-on. The vānaras were no ordinary beings either. They were incarnations of various devas who had taken birth on Brahma deva's commands to support Vishnu's quest.

Neither Rāma nor Sugreeva knew beforehand that their paths were to cross. With the benefit of hindsight and Rishi Vālmiki's narration, we can now claim that the kinship in Kishkindhā was pre-ordained. But isn't that true for life in general? When one is on the path of dharma, help comes from unforeseen and unexpected sources. What we need is humility, some patience and detachment to accept both joy and sorrow that life brings, while continuing to do what we must. More often it is through sorrow that the path of life is illuminated. We need to trust life to bring to us what we need to remain steadfast on the path of dharma to realise the goal of our life.

Sugreeva's Atlas

Sugreeva had travelled the world multiple times over while trying to escape from Vāli. That had made him an expert in world geography. His knowledge is amply evident in the directions he gave to his troops which went in the four directions to look for Seetā. The descriptions of regions, places, people and details mentioned by Sugreeva have been the subject of research for many itihāsa aficionados because there are many resemblances to landmarks seen even today.

Among the many interesting descriptions, one is of Yawadwipa, which is present-day Java in Indonesia. Interestingly, during my travels in Indonesia, I found that people in Java still relate to this ancient civilisational memory, considering themselves to be descendants of some of Sugreeva's men who stayed back in Yawadwipa and did not return to Kishkindhā after the search operation for Seetā concluded. The verse mentioned in Kishkindhā Kānda regarding Yawadwipa is:

रत्नवन्तं यवद्वीपं सप्तराज्योपशोभितम् ।
सुवर्णरूप्यकं चैव सुवर्णाकरमण्डितम् ।।

Sugreeva tells his troops going east that they will reach Yawadwipa—a land of gold, silver, precious gems, a land with many gold mines, administered by seven kingdoms.[42]

To be noted here is that one of the kingdoms in the vicinity, the present-day island of Sumatra, was called Suvarnadwipa in ancient times—the island of gold. The region was known to be rich in gold and silver.

There are many such fascinating details reinforcing the fact that our ancestors knew the world beyond Jambudwipa and knew it well.[43]

ॐ ψ ॐ

11

Vāyuputra

When Sugreeva heard that two young, warrior-like men with majestic personalities, wielding huge bows were seen in the precincts of Rishyamukha, he panicked and started pacing up and down. 'These two young men, dressed in barks, have been sent by Vāli to kill me deceitfully,' he inferred. His ministers agreed. Together they began jumping from one peak to another, nervously thinking about how to escape the two men.

Among Sugreeva's ministers was Hanumāna. He was the only one amidst the vānaras present there who did not panic. 'Give up this agitation. We have no fear of Vāli here,' he said, addressing Sugreeva and added, 'As a king, you must not lose your wits because of Vāli. Think objectively before arriving at any conclusion.' Sugreeva had his reasons to fear the two men. 'Just look at them. Look at their broad shoulders and their strong weapons. How will they not inspire fear? Vāli is very smart. He knows he can't come here to kill me. That is why he must have sent his friends to perform the task for him. But you are right, we must first find out more about these two,' he replied and sent Hanumāna to get more information about the two young men, 'Take them in confidence by praising them, enquire their reason for coming here, observe their body language and make a careful assessment of their intention,' he instructed.[1]

First Meeting, First Impressions

Hanumāna disguised himself as a sage and went to meet the princes. He greeted them and enquired about them using laudatory words, 'Are you royal sages or avatār of some devatās? Why have you come here? Your presence seems to embellish this bank of river Pampā. Your golden aura and that look of courage are arousing fear in the hearts of the wild animals and the forest dwellers here. Who are you two young men upsetting the beings of the jungle with your arrival? Both of you seem valiant, powerful, handsome and seem to have the focus of a lion. Your arms resemble the trunks of an elephant. You are illumined by your own splendour. This mountain has begun to appear resplendent as it reflects your aura. Both of you deserve to rule kingdoms. Broad-chested and lion-shouldered, you are worthy of being adorned by precious ornaments. But I see that you have worn no jewellery. Who are you and why have you come here?' Hanumāna kept showering praises on Rāma and Lakshmana, hoping they would be flattered and say something in reply.[2]

But the princes of Ayodhyā looked on intently at Hanumāna without saying anything. 'I have been speaking to you, why don't you respond?' asked Hanumāna finally, after failing to extract any answer from the two. But the princes still didn't say a word.

Hanumāna figured these were no ordinary men. He changed his tactics and decided to introduce himself honestly upfront and watch their expression. 'There is a vānara chief, Sugreeva by name; he is a virtuous man. I am Hanumāna, his minister. I have been sent here by Sugreeva. He desires friendship with you.' After this, Hanumāna stood there saying nothing. He had made his offer. The ball was now in the court of these two young men.[3]

Rāma hadn't said a word until then. While Hanumāna spoke, Rāma had keenly observed him—his words, his body language and his mannerisms. Rāma was both pleased and impressed. He was pleased to know that the person they had come looking for, Sugreeva, had himself approached them through his minister, Hanumāna. He was impressed with the wit, erudition, articulation and intelligence of Hanumāna. Sharing his observations in detail with Lakshmana, Rāma concluded with a smile, 'One who has people with Hanumāna's qualities as his envoy and minister, will surely have all his tasks accomplished.' Taking this as Rāma's approval, Lakshmana responded to Hanumāna, 'We are aware of the virtues of Sugreeva. We have come all the way to meet him. Your proposal is acceptable to us.' Hanumāna was delighted to hear this. He took Rāma and Lakshmana to meet Sugreeva and the other vānaras.[4]

Rāma and Sugreeva opened their hearts to each other spontaneously. Each agreed to help the other. The first step of their friendship was to punish Vāli and crown Sugreeva as the king of the vānaras, which Rāma accomplished successfully. The next was to look for Seetā. The arrival of the monsoon delayed this task. Meanwhile, giving in to sensual pleasures, Sugreeva lost track of time. It was Hanumāna who reminded him of his promise to Rāma and his duty towards fulfilling it. That Sugreeva didn't mind being told bluntly about his lapse is a testimony to both his own humility and the trust he put in Hanumāna's discretion.

That Hanumāna was not an ordinary person was clear to Rāma in that first meeting itself. Some of Rāma's impressions of Hanumāna which he shared with Lakshmana were:[5]

No one who is not learned in *Rigveda*, *Yajurveda* and *Samaveda* can speak like how Hanumāna had spoken.

His speech was concise, clear, without delay, without tremor and was spoken in a medium tone.

He spoke so much, but not one word was amiss. He sounded like one who is well learned in vyakarana (grammar).

His speech was refined and coherent. He spoke words that were auspicious and pleasing to the heart.

There was no flaw noticeable on his face or eyes or his forehead or anywhere else.

He is so well spoken that his words will enchant even an enemy who is ready to attack him with his sword raised.

From Rāma's observations, it is amply clear that Hanumāna was extremely erudite and well-spoken. Not only were his words timely and contextual, but his tone was also pleasant to the listener and his speech was sophisticated as that of a pandit who had mastered the vyakarana and the Vedas.

The Angada Dilemma

Tārā was devastated when she was informed of Vāli's death at the hands of Rāma. She was ready to give up her own life after his. Hanumāna consoled her and reminded her of her motherly responsibilities towards her only son, Angada. Eventually, she reconciled to the situation and even accepted Sugreeva as her husband for the sake of her son.

Vāli had only one worry on his death bed—the well-being of his and Tārā's son, Angada. Angada was in many ways like Vāli in strength and acumen. He also had his mother's wisdom. Vāli advised Angada to obey his Uncle Sugreeva, never to align with his enemies, to remain loyal to him and to follow his orders. It was wise advice. Having witnessed Rāma's feat in felling Vāli with just one arrow, the vānaras were in awe of Rāma. If Rāma backed Sugreeva, the vānaras would follow suit and align behind Sugreeva also. Vāli understood that well. He realised that it was in Angada's interest to seek refuge in Rāma and stay in Sugreeva's good books.

Sugreeva didn't seem to harbour any ill-will against Angada either. To show his commitment towards Angada, he accepted Rāma's suggestion and made Angada the crown prince of Kishkindhā. Angada too had taken his father's advice seriously. He had shown no anger or bitterness overtly in front of Sugreeva or others, until one day....

Sugreeva had sent his best team towards the south to look for Seetā. The team included Hanumāna, Neela, Nala and Jāmbavana. Angada was asked to lead the team. A few days into the expedition, while trying to find water to drink, the team lost their way in a cave known as Riksha. Here they met a saintly woman called Swayamprabhā who protected the cave. Swayamprabhā ensured the vānaras had a comfortable stay in the cave with lots of fruits and drinks.

The vānaras lived in the cave and feasted for days together until one day they realised that they had been in the cave for over a month. Swayamprabhā helped them reach the northern shore of the sea. However, the one-month time stipulated by Sugreeva had already passed, and the vānaras remained clueless about Seetā's existence as well as the location of Lankā. As the vānaras stared at the wide expanse of the sea not knowing what to do next, a sense of despair began to set over the team.

Being the leader of the team, Angada was especially stressed. He had failed his uncle. Rather, he believed he had been set up for failure intentionally. As a sense of helplessness engulfed him, he addressed his team, declaring that he was going to fast unto death. 'As you all can see, it is already autumn. The time given to us by Sugreeva to find Seetā has lapsed. Hence, it is better for us to fast unto death here than go back and face punishment by Sugreeva. Sugreeva has been always harsh, and now he is our king. There is no way he will forgive us if we return empty-handed. In fact, when he learns that we haven't found Seetā, he will kill us. Instead of meeting undeserved death at Sugreeva's hands, making our near and dear ones suffer, giving up our lives by fasting here is a much better option.'

The wounds in Angada's heart manifested in his words. As he now believed his end was near, he didn't hold back his emotions. 'Sugreeva has long held the desire to kill me and get me out of his way. My failure will give him that opportunity. He didn't confer upon me the position of crown prince out of any goodwill. It was Rāma who got me coronated. Sugreeva has always seen me as an enemy,' he said.[6]

The other vānaras were upset hearing these words from Angada. In a way, they feared Sugreeva too, so they agreed with Angada and expressed the intent to fast unto death with him. Among them was a vānara named Tār. He had another suggestion. 'Why be so sad and die here unnecessarily? We can go back and live in that Riksha cave. There is enough food for our survival there. No one can harm us there, not Sugreeva, not Rāma,' Tār said. Angada liked the idea. The vānaras loved it. 'We should leave immediately, this will save our lives,' they chorused in one voice.[7]

The turn of events made Hanumāna uncomfortable. The narrative of Angada and the idea floated by Tār could have dangerous implications for Sugreeva's kingship and the unity of the vānaras. If not nipped in the bud, the idea had the potential to instigate the vānaras to lay a siege on Kishkindhā at a later point.

Hanumāna was aware that Angada had a very sharp intellect, with eightfold cognitive abilities. He was a master of the four essential strengths required of an administrator and had all the fourteen qualities expected of a leader. He was full of valour and strength. His popularity and stature were steadily on the rise, like the waxing moon of the bright fortnight. Angada had great faith in Tār's advice. Tār was an intelligent but shrewd vānara who seemed to be provoking Angada to rebel. Hanumāna decided to create a rift between Angada, Tār and the other vānaras who were supporting them.

By way of some smart manoeuvring and cajoling, Hanumāna made many of the other vānaras change their mind about deserting Sugreeva. Once he had the majority on his side, Hanumāna decided to make Angada aware of the consequences of any misadventure he may be envisaging. 'You are as capable and full of energy as your father on the battlefield. And you have the potential to hold together vānaras and reign over them, just like your father did. But you forget one thing. The vānaras tend to have very wavering minds. They won't be able to tolerate staying away from their kith and kin for too long. When that happens, it will be impossible for you to get them to obey you.'

He then added, 'And while you may be able to get some vānaras on your side, you will not be able to win over us—myself, Jāmbavana, Suhotra and Neela—or convince us to leave Sugreeva, not by money, not by threats. Do remember, Sugreeva is much stronger than you are. The one who is weak cannot ever live peacefully by antagonising the stronger person. It is always wise for the weaker side to patch up with one who is undoubtedly stronger. And if you truly believe that you are going to be secure in that cave, then you are gravely mistaken. Lakshmana's arrows can cut through mountains. You will not be able to escape his ire if you do not finish the task they have assigned to you.'

Once the stern message was conveyed, Hanumāna toned down his speech. To inspire trust and confidence in Angada towards Sugreeva, Hanumāna added, 'However, if you remain loyal to Sugreeva, you are sure to succeed him to the throne of Kishkindhā. Sugreeva will himself give the kingdom to you at the appropriate time. Your uncle is a man of virtue and truth. He is genuinely fond of you and doesn't harbour any resentment towards you. He cannot and will not kill you. He also dearly cares for your mother and tries to behave in a way that would please her. Neither does he have any progeny apart from you. Therefore, hold no grudges and come to him.'[8]

Angada understood the purport of Hanumāna's counsel. But his own belief of Sugreeva's qualities wasn't aligned with Hanumāna's assessment. For once, Angada gave vent to the reasons for his discontent before Hanumāna: 'I do not quite agree with all the virtues you mention about Sugreeva. What kind of a virtuous man would close the mouth of a cave in which his brother had gone to fight an opponent? How can a man who takes on his elder brother's wife as his own even while his elder brother is alive be called virtuous?[9] Sugreeva had even forgotten the promise he made to Rāma, the very person because of whom he got the kingdom of Kishkindhā. A person who forgets the favours done to him; how can he be trusted? Sugreeva hasn't undertaken this mission for Seetā's search out of any concern for righteousness.

He has sent us on this expedition fearing the sharp arrows of Lakshmana. How can an ungrateful and vicious person like him ever accept me as his son?'

Saying this, Angada's voice was overcome with sadness. He continued, 'I had secretly planned to live away from Sugreeva. But now that has been exposed. I am already guilty for not being able to find Seetā and now with you all against me, I have become weak and vulnerable like an orphan. In such a situation, I will certainly be killed if I go back to Kishkindhā. Or there is a possibility that Sugreeva may even imprison me for life. Rather than live life in painful imprisonment, I am better off fasting unto death right here by the coast. I request you all to return and leave me alone here. Please do take care of my dear mother. She will be devastated hearing about my death.'[10]

The other vānaras began to shed tears hearing the sad words of Angada. They decided to follow his lead and fast unto death with him. Hanumāna didn't oppose them. His quick thinking and vision had averted a major crisis in the Kishkindhā's royal household by stopping the rebel group from going to live in the cave. Angada's concerns, even though misplaced, were, in a way, understandable. Hanumāna let Angada grieve, to allow time to take its course. Sometimes it is important to vent and grieve. Reconciliation can happen only after acceptance of reality.

Time did show the way. It was here by the coast that they met Sampāti, Jatāyu's elder brother, who informed them about Seetā in Lankā, an island situated a hundred yojanas towards the south, across the ocean.

A Leader's Qualities

The eightfold cognitive abilities, four tactics and fourteen leadership qualities that Hanumāna acknowledges in Angada are:[11]

A. Eight aspects of cognitive abilities:

शुश्रूषा श्रवणञ्चैव ग्रहणं धारणं तथा ।
ऊहापोहार्थविज्ञानं तत्त्वज्ञानं च धीगुणाः ॥ [12]

- शुश्रूषा—desire to hear attentively
- श्रवण—act of listening
- ग्रहण—grasping or receptiveness
- धारणा—retentiveness
- ऊह—deliberation
- अपोह—removal of doubt
- अर्थ विज्ञान—comprehension of meaning
- तत्त्वज्ञान—thorough knowledge, both physical as well as metaphysical

B. The fourteen qualities expected in a leader:

- देशकालज्ञाता—understanding of place and time
- दार्ढ्य—firmness or resoluteness
- सर्वक्लेशसहिष्णुता—endurance for all kinds of troubles
- सर्वविज्ञानिता—all-round understanding
- दाक्ष्य—skill in implementation
- ऊर्जा—vigour
- संवृतमंत्रता—maintaining confidentiality
- अविसंवादिता—free of contradictions
- शौर्य—courage
- शक्तिज्ञत्व—recognising strengths and weaknesses of self and opponents

- कृतज्ञता—gratitude
- शरणागतवात्सल्य—compassion to those who seek refuge
- अमर्षित्व—rightful anger
- अचापलम्—steadfast, not fickle-minded

C. The four tactics/strengths (different sources mention these in two different sets):

- साम—convince through persuasion
- दान[13]—convince by exploiting a need or greed
- दंड—convince by (threat of) punishment
- भेद—convince by sowing dissension (strategy of divide and rule)

Or

- बहुबल—physical strength
- मनोबल—mental strength
- उपायबल—strength of resources and strategy
- बन्धुबल—strength of alliances or partnerships

The Leap to Lankā

Sampāti's information elated the vānaras. There was a possibility now that they could go back to Kishkindhā without fearing Sugreeva's fury. But how were they to cross a hundred yojanas over the sea? Once again, the vānaras were despondent. The new information had raised Angada's spirits too. He stepped in to cheer up his people. 'Do not give in to despair. Dejection destroys vigour just like a snake that bites a child who goes near it. This is the time to show your valour. A dispirited man cannot achieve success,' he said. Trying to jolt his people into action, he asked every vānara how far he could leap and stay afloat. But except Angada, no one had the potential to cross a hundred yojanas and come back.

Angada, being the leader, couldn't be sent. 'Without a leader, the team would be lost. Hence, to keep the team together and engaged, the leader must be protected,' said Jāmbavana while assuring Angada that there was one other person who was intelligent and powerful enough to accomplish the task.

Hanumāna had kept quiet all this while. Addressing him, Jāmbavana said, 'Why are you sitting here without saying anything, Hanumāna? You are equal to Sugreeva in valour, and in wisdom, you are comparable to Rāma and Lakshmana. You outshine everyone in strength, intelligence, vitality and strength of character.[14] Why aren't you taking up this task?' Hanumāna looked unsure.

Jāmbavana then said, 'You possibly are not aware of your own potential. Let me remind you of an incident from your childhood. While your father is Kesari, being the husband of your mother, your biological father is Vāyu deva. Once, enamoured by your mother's beauty, Vāyu deva approached her. He promised your mother that the son born through their union would be as strong, agile, resplendent and capable of leaping across long distances, like his own self. That is why she agreed to have you.'

Jāmbavana continued: 'One day, when you were still a child, you saw the sun rising in the sky. Thinking that it was a large, yellow fruit, you leaped almost three hundred yojanas towards the sky to pluck the sun. It was some feat. We were all flabbergasted. After going high up in the sky, you fell on a mountain peak and fractured your jaw. Since then, you have been called Hanumāna.[15] Being the son of Vāyu deva, you are equivalent to him in strength, speed and energy. Therefore, get up, leap to Lankā and cross the ocean. Don't you see how dejected all the vānaras are? Why are you ignoring them? Stand up and take the stride.'[16]

Jāmbavana's words had a deep impact on Hanumāna. A new life and a new vision appeared to sprout in him. His confidence soared as if a hidden valve of infinite potential had been unlocked in his mind. With the realisation of his strengths came their physical manifestation. To everyone's amazement, Hanumāna began stretching and expanding his body till he became gigantic. He slipped into a state of trance and began speaking to the vānaras assembled there who were watching this miracle unfold, 'Vāyu deva is infinite in strength and moves with infinite speed. He can break the biggest mountains and uproot the largest trees if he wishes. I am the son of that Vāyu deva. Like him, I can leap and stay afloat across long distances. As I leap across, I will raise the water from the oceans with my strong arms and bathe the entire earth, along with the mountains, forests and plains. With the force of my thighs and calves, as I push up the ocean water, huge alligators living in it would be thrown up to the earth.'

Hanumāna's assertions energised the entire group. Jāmbavana blessed him and others wished him success as he got ready to take the leap to Lankā.

The journey to Lankā was not all smooth. A few yojanas over the sea, Hanumāna's flight was obstructed by Surasā, the mother of the nāgas, disguised as a demoness. The devas had requested Surasā to test Hanumāna's grit and wit, it is said. Surasā insisted that Hanumāna was her god-ordained food and wouldn't let him go. Hanumāna tried to convince her about the urgency of his task. Surasā intended to test him, hence she said, 'I have a boon that one who comes in my area cannot go ahead without entering my mouth. You will have to do that—you have no choice.'

Hanumāna agreed. He expanded his body, making Surasā expand her mouth too so that he could enter. Suddenly, Hanumāna shrank his body and became tiny. He quickly entered Surasā's mouth and came out before she could close her wide-open mouth. Thus, Hanumāna outwitted the devas and continued to proceed to Lankā.[17]

Next, Hanumāna got pulled into the mouth of a vortex.[18] This wasn't as benign as the previous encounter with Surasā. Sugreeva had warned him of this phenomenon in the southern ocean. But Hanumāna wasn't daunted. He was full of his newfound energy and determined to get to Lankā. Exploding the vortex with his momentum, he forced his way out. While there were several more challenges, there was also help that came unexpectedly. A huge mountain called Mainak emerged out of the ocean only to allow Hanumāna to take some respite on its peak. Hanumāna was grateful for Mainak's thoughtful gesture but politely declined to take a break as he could not afford to lose any more time.[19]

Finally, Hanumāna landed in Lankā, crossing a hundred yojanas over the ocean.

> *Sometimes all a person needs is a mentor who can remind him of his dormant potential and jolt him to action.*

Hanumāna set his foot on the shores of Lankā and took in its grandeur. The city was perched on a mountain top and was protected on four sides by huge walls guarded by giant rākshasas. Seeing its fortifications, both natural—due to its location, surrounded by ocean—and man-made—security arrangements done by Rāvana—his heart sank. 'How will the other vānaras, Rāma and Lakshmana get here? Except for Sugreeva, Angada, Neela and I, no one has the capability to leap across the ocean. And even if Rāma manages to get here somehow, how will we capture the city? It looks invincible. If its prosperity and military strength are real, then even the policy of sāma, dāna, danda and bheda will be of no use.' Then he stopped himself, 'This is not the time for negativity. My task is to figure out whether Seetā is alive or dead. All other considerations can wait.'

He took a deep breath and focused on the task at hand. 'With this size and body, I will raise an alarm. I must assume a tiny form that doesn't catch the eye of these powerful guards of Rāvana. I should wait for the sun to set before entering the city. I will have to carry out the search for Seetā very surreptitiously and only in the dark. Otherwise, if I am caught, Rāma's entire effort will be a colossal waste,' he thought to himself.

When light gave way to darkness, Hanumāna entered the city. Keenly observing its architecture, its fortification and its people, he jumped from one building to another, peeping through doors and windows to see if he could find a lady resembling Seetā. He had never seen Seetā except for the fleeting glimpse he had when Rāvana was carrying her away. Hanumāna let his intuition guide him. He then saw a majestic looking multi-storeyed building. From its stature and build, it could only belong to the king or someone very important. He became even more alert and careful as he explored the various chambers of the palace.

The palace was Rāvana's. Hanumāna was astonished upon seeing the inside of the palace. It was elegant and sumptuous. It seemed to gratify every one of the five senses of the resident. For a moment, Hanumāna went into a state of reverie as his eyes fell on a line of golden lamps flickering simultaneously, spreading a golden hue in the room. He observed that the room was full of women. Possibly, these are the wives and mistresses of Rāvana, he thought. It seemed like an evening of revelry had just concluded. The women were all decked up in beautiful garments and ornaments but looked drunk and tired. Some of them had passed out on the floor, some others had bent over and fallen asleep on the musical instruments which they had been playing. Some had their hands on the bodies of other women sleeping next to them while some others used their hands as pillows. Some had dozed off unaware of their dishevelled garments.

Some of these women had been lustfully abducted by Rāvana, some had given in to him out of their own greed. But now all of them seemed to consider him as their master and were devoted to him, or so it appeared to Hanumāna as he observed their faces and expressions. No woman looked as if she was forcibly kept there against her wishes. 'Seetā couldn't be among them,' he concluded and continued his search.[20] A little further inside the room, he saw a platform on which stood a grand bed. On that, he saw a man sleeping and women fanning him from all sides. His aura could be felt even from a distance. He exuded grandeur and power even in his sleep. It could only be Rāvana, inferred Hanumāna. A little further he saw another bed on which slept a woman of divine beauty. Her face had an unmatched glow. For a moment, Hanumāna thought he had found Seetā, but he dismissed that thought, 'How can Seetā sleep so peacefully and comfortably in Rāvana's chamber?' From what he had heard of Seetā and judged from Rāma's love for her, she was completely committed to Rāma. It was impossible for a woman like her to accept Rāvana. He was absolutely correct. The woman sleeping on the bed was Mandodari, Rāvana's chief queen.[21]

Looking at these women fast asleep, Hanumāna was gripped by a sense of guilt. 'Isn't watching someone's women unrighteous? Am I engaging in a sinful act?' he questioned himself. 'Never have I eyed other women in this manner, sneaking into their private quarters.' Another chain of thoughts emerged in his mind as if his own brain was responding to his query. 'While I am definitely looking at Rāvana's wives in this manner, I feel no lust nor desire for them. That is not my intention either. This mind is the cause of the activity of all sensual desires. But my mind isn't affected by seeing these women. It continues to remain steadfast in my goal. Moreover, this is the only option I have. Where would I look for a woman if not among women?' he reasoned, shaking off the guilt.[22]

However, he failed to find Seetā in the city. He was beginning to lose hope. 'What if I don't find Seetā at all? What if she is already dead? If I don't find her, my efforts will be completely futile. The vānaras are waiting for me with a lot of expectations. How will I face them? We have already crossed the stipulated time; how will I return to Sugreeva and tell him I failed? How will Rāma react when he learns his beloved could not be found? He will surely give up his life. Lakshmana would not survive without Rāma. Kaushalyā would be devastated. Oh, what a tragedy that would bring upon everyone. I think it will be better for me to fast unto death or jump into a blazing pyre than go back to give such bad news,' thought Hanumāna, his mind constructing scenarios of failure.[23]

Then Hanumāna made a conscious effort to slip out of all the negativity. 'Depression discourages enterprise while enthusiasm and hope inspire action, develop endurance and help to succeed. Hence, I will not give up hope and continue to look for Seetā in places I haven't explored yet,' decided Hanumāna, determined to stabilise his distressed mind.[24] An idea struck him—he could himself kill Rāvana or abduct him and take him to Kishkindhā for Rāma to punish. Once again, he pushed out such diverting thoughts and focussed on his key task—to locate Seetā.[25]

His search took him to Ashokavātikā where he finally spotted Seetā and witnessed a verbal tussle between Rāvana and Seetā. The king of Lankā initially pleaded and then threatened Seetā to accept him and Seetā consistently rejected his advances. Hanumāna was moved to see Seetā's dedication towards Rāma. He had already been a witness to Rāma's longing for Seetā. They were meant for each other, he was convinced. After Rāvana had left, Hanumāna approached Seetā and had a long conversation with her. He offered to take her back to Kishkindhā right then, to which Seetā did not agree, with good reasons. Taking her message for Rāma and her chudāmani, he bid Seetā goodbye after consoling her and assuring her that Rāma would come soon to rescue her.

Hanumāna's Eight Siddhis

Hanumāna is shown to expand and shrink in size at will in Vālmiki Rāmāyana. He is the only one who has such extraordinary capabilities.

According to Patanjali's *Yoga Sutras*, through intense practise of yoga, it is possible to achieve a state wherein one gains complete control over the five senses and raises the consciousness to a level where one transcends the five senses to seek inputs and inspirations from the universe. The third chapter of Patanjali's *Yoga Sutra*, 'Vibhuti Pada', calls such a state sanyama, which ignites intuitive wisdom in a yogi and grants supra-natural powers called siddhis.

There are eight types of siddhis—अष्टसिद्धि (ashta siddhi)[26]—generally spoken of which such a realised yogi achieves at will. These are:

अणिमा महिमा चैव लघिमा गरिमा तथा।
प्राप्तिः प्राकाम्यमीशित्वं वशित्वं चाष्ट सिद्धयः॥

- अणिमा—ability to reduce one's physical body
- महिमा—ability to expanding one's body
- लघिमा—ability to reduce one's weight and become weightless
- गरिमा—ability to become infinitely heavy or dense
- प्राप्तिः—ability to travel anywhere instantaneously
- प्राकाम्यम्—ability to fulfil any desire
- ईशित्वम्—ability to control one's will and nature
- वशित्वम्—ability to control the minds of others

- Hanumāna possesses all the eight siddhis. Goswāmi Tulsidās refers to Hanumāna as 'अष्ट सिद्धि, नौ निधि के दाता—one who grants eight siddhis and nine treasures'—implying Hanumāna is the master of the eight siddhis and nine nidhis and grants them to anyone he wants. A person wanting to acquire them would need to pray to Hanumāna with the right intent and a clean heart.

Encounter with Rāvana

By confirming Seetā's whereabouts, Hanumāna had achieved the task assigned to him. But Hanumāna was not just a minor follower who would do only as much as he was told. He was a man of wisdom. There was a reason he was called buddhimatām varishtham—the greatest among those with intelligence. As he bid farewell to Seetā, his mind fired up. 'I have done the work assigned to me but the overall purpose of getting Seetā back is yet to be accomplished. I can claim to complete the task only if I can return to give Sugreeva a good assessment of the strength and size of Rāvana's army and commanders. That will allow us to compare our strengths and weaknesses versus Rāvana's and help to decide our plan of action,' he reasoned. The possibility of a war with Rāvana was very real. The information about Lankā's war preparedness would come in handy in the war.

Besides, Hanumāna had a keen desire to meet Rāvana face-to-face before heading back. An idea struck him, one that would allow him to meet Rāvana, gauge the strength of his forces and give the people of Lankā a peek into his own powers.[27] 'This garden around here is beautiful and attractive. If I ravage the garden, Rāvana will become furious. He will come along with his army to capture me. There is no way he can defeat me in a confrontation. I will destroy his army and give him a taste of my powers before returning to Kishkindhā,' he thought.

Hanumāna began uprooting the trees and shrubs, crushing the hillocks and destroying the water ponds.

In no time, he lay waste to the entire garden. The birds and animals began to make terrified noises. Their screams, coupled with the breaking of trees and crushing of boulders, created a huge commotion, alerting the guards. They came running to see who the culprit was. Hanumāna intended to alert the rākshasas and scare them. When they came near, he expanded his body, assuming a mammoth form.

The rākshasa women guarding Seetā were startled to see such a massive creature. They remembered seeing something similar-looking but smaller, talking to Seetā, and asked her about him. Seetā feigned ignorance. She did not wish to endanger Hanumāna. 'How am I to know him? I have never seen him before. I was also scared when I saw him today. To me, he appeared like a powerful rākshasa,' she said. The guards rushed to inform Rāvana about the ravaging of his garden by a weird-looking, gigantic vānara. 'Possibly, he is sent by Indra or Kuber or Rāma,' they speculated. Rāvana was obviously angry. He sent a division of his army to imprison the offender.

As Rāvana's soldiers attempted to corner Hanumāna and catch him, the son of Vāyu roared loudly, 'Victory be to Rāma and Lakshmana. Victory be to Sugreeva. I am the son of Vāyu deva and the servant of Rāma. I am Hanumāna, the nemesis of my enemies. Having ravaged Lankā, see how I escape from here.' His declaration was loud and clear. It was done with the obvious intent of disclosing his identity to Rāvana. It was important to disturb the self-assumed notion of invincibility of the king of Lankā.

Hanumāna was more than a match for the soldiers who had come to capture him. They all died at his hands. Before Rāvana could send another battalion, Hanumāna rampaged and set on fire the sacred area of worship of Lankā. With the instructions to capture or kill Hanumāna, Rāvana sent many of his trusted commanders, along with their armies. One by one all of them succumbed to Hanumāna's offensive. Rāvana couldn't deny that the vānara was extraordinary. 'I have met powerful vānaras such as Vāli and Sugreeva earlier. But no one has been as forceful, smart and splendid as this one. It appears to me that one of my enemies has unleashed this creature to destroy Lankā. He cannot be a forest-dwelling vānara. Do not underestimate his might and capture him as soon as possible,' he ordered.[28]

In the skirmish that followed, among other rākshasas, Rāvana's son Aksha was also killed by Hanumāna. Shocked at the news of his son's death, Rāvana sent his most celebrated and intrepid commander, his son Indrajeet, to attack Hanumāna. A gruelling combat ensued. Finally, Indrajeet used the powerful and divine weapon given to him by Brahma deva. The weapon had the power to tie down the opponent. Hanumāna was aware that the weapon would do nothing to him as he was blessed by Brahma deva. But to show his reverence to Brahma deva, he let himself be entangled by the weapon. The other reason was his desire to meet Rāvana face-to-face. 'If I am captured alive, Indrajeet will take me to the royal court of Lankā where I can speak to Rāvana directly,' he thought to himself. His assumption was correct. Indrajeet indeed took Hanumāna to Rāvana's court.[29]

As Hanumāna was dragged to the assembly hall, he looked around and saw the pomp of Rāvana's court. He had seen Rāvana thrice earlier—the first time he had only caught a glimpse of his in Rishyamukha when they had spotted a rākshasa carrying away Seetā, not knowing then that the rākshasa was Rāvana or that the lady was Seetā; the second time was the previous night when Rāvana was asleep in his chambers, surrounded by women; and then again, a few hours later in Ashokavātikā, when Rāvana was still groggy from the revelry of the previous night.

In the court, Hanumāna saw Rāvana in his full glory. Dressed in silken clothes, bedecked in jewel-studded gold ornaments, Rāvana's might shone through his personality. The king of rākshasas emanated an aura of opulence and brilliance. Hanumāna observed him, enraptured. 'If only Rāvana's adharma wasn't so potent, he could have enjoyed the lordship of this world and even the world of devas,' he thought sadly.[30]

Rāvana was startled seeing Hanumāna. 'Can this creature be Nandi, the attendant of Shiva who had cursed me once earlier at Kailāsh? Or is he the mighty demon Bānāsura?' he wondered. At the same time, he was furious. Standing before him was the man who had killed his son Aksha. He ordered Prahasta, his minister, to enquire from Hanumāna about his identity and purpose for coming to Lankā. Prahasta obeyed and asked, rather politely in the beginning, 'Don't be afraid. Let us know who you are honestly. If you inform us who sent you here, you will be set free. Tell us, has Indra sent you here, or has Kuber? Is Yama your master or have you come on behalf of Vishnu, who always desires victory over us? We don't believe you are a vānara. Even though your form is like them, your power transcends theirs. Tell us everything truthfully if you seek freedom.'

Hanumāna was waiting for this opportunity. 'I have not been sent by Indra, nor by Kuber, nor by Vishnu. I am indeed a vānara born in the vānara tribe and have come here to meet the king of the rākshasas. I ravaged the garden hoping to get the opportunity to see him in person. Your rākshasas attacked me and I had to kill them in self-defence. Frankly, no weapon is powerful enough to tie me down. I let myself be tied only because I wanted to be brought before Rāvana. I have come to Lankā as an emissary of Sugreeva, for the cause of Rāma. Knowing this, I request you to give me a chance to convey to you the message from Sugreeva,' he said.[31]

Hanumāna proceeded to narrate the story of Rāma, Lakshmana and Seetā in the court of Lankā. He spoke about their exile, Seetā's abduction, the friendship of Rāma and Sugreeva and their commitment to helping each other. To ensure Rāvana understood whom he had chosen to antagonise, Hanumāna reminded him of Vāli, the mighty vānara by whom Rāvana had been subjugated years ago. 'Sugreeva promised Rāma to help locate Seetā and Rāma promised to win back the kingdom of vānaras for Sugreeva. To fulfil his promise, Rāma killed Vāli and established Sugreeva on the throne of Kishkindhā. You knew Vāli, didn't you? Rāma killed him with just one arrow.'

Informing Rāvana about Sugreeva's search expedition for Seetā and his own feat of crossing a hundred yojanas of the ocean to reach Lankā, Hanumāna advised him to let Seetā go free and not seek to enrage Rāma further for his own good and for the good of his people. 'I have done my job by locating Seetā. The future course will be charted by Rāma. I have met Seetā and taken note of her grief. There is no way you can ever have her. You have accumulated a lot of luxury and success due to your good deeds in the past. But it seems the good deeds have run their course and it is time for you to bear the fruits of your adharma. Do remember, Rāma and Sugreeva are neither gods nor demons. They are human beings. The boon conferred by Brahma deva on you doesn't protect you from them.'[32]

Rāvana was enraged even more by Hanumāna's audacity and ordered his soldiers to kill him. Vibhishana intervened, 'Hanumāna has declared himself to be an emissary, hence it is not appropriate to kill him. Such an act is not undertaken by learned men. Do not act in haste and anger, reconsider your decision.'

'But he is an enemy who destroyed our garden and killed our men. It is not inappropriate to kill an enemy,' protested Rāvana.

'No question about his being an enemy, that he surely is. But he is also a messenger. You must not do what is not ordained by the scriptures. You must not kill him. However, you can punish him. There are many options suggested for punishing a messenger like injuring one of his body parts, shaving his hair or whipping him. There is little to gain by killing this vānara. He is bound by his masters. Those who really deserve death are his masters and that can happen only if you fight a war with them. With him dead, there is no way you will get a chance to fight and punish those who have sent him here,' said Vibhishana, trying to coax the king of Lankā into changing his mind.[33]

The idea appealed to Rāvana. He ordered his men to set Hanumāna's tail[34] on fire and parade him around in Lankā. The soldiers obeyed enthusiastically. They tied Hanumāna tightly with ropes once again, set fire to his tail and began to drag him around the lanes of Lankā. Hanumāna's brain was fast at work. 'While I can escape from here without much effort, how can I turn this situation into an opportunity to collect information on Lankā and wreck more havoc before leaving? I have only seen Lankā at night, now I have a chance to see it during the day. Let me utilise the opportunity.' Thinking thus, he let the soldiers parade him around for some time, as the citizens of Lankā came to gape at the enemy of their state. When they were close to the city entrance, Hanumāna swiftly broke his bondages and jumped high, to settle on the tall entry gate.[35]

He expanded his body to acquire his colossal form once again and began leaping from building to building, setting them on fire with his burning tail. In no time a large part of Lankā was up in flames. The whole city was in chaos, with people running helter-skelter, trying to save themselves. The only major building he left unburnt was Vibhishana's palace. Hanumāna then leaped into the waters of the ocean to douse his burning tail. He was about to leave when he remembered Seetā. Was Seetā safe or had the fire engulfed her too, he wondered, panic-stricken. He returned to Ashokavātikā to check and heaved a sigh of relief on seeing Seetā untouched by fire. Bidding her farewell one last time, Hanumāna leapt off to return to the northern shore of the island, having successfully accomplished the assignment entrusted to him.[36]

Did the fire not have any impact on Hanumāna? Hanumāna had the same question. 'How is it that the fire feels to me as cold as the snow,' he wondered.[37] Rishi Vālmiki tells us that multiple things worked to protect Hanumāna from the pain of the burns.

- When the rākshasa women informed Seetā about Hanumāna's tail being set on fire, she immediately began meditating on Agni deva, requesting him to be cool towards Hanumāna, using the power of her chastity and her tapasyā.[38]
- Vāyu deva being his biological father blew in a way that cooled the fire.

Hanumāna attributes the miracle to Seetā's kindness, his father's favour and Rāma's grace. He was there to accomplish a noble task, not for himself but for Rāma.[39]

There was one other factor, possibly the most potent. When his tail was being set on fire, Hanumāna did not cower; rather he told himself, 'पीडां कुर्वन्तु रक्षांसि न मे अस्ति मनसः श्रमः—Let the rākshasa torture me as they please, there is no anguish in my mind.'[40]

It was this willpower of Hanumāna coupled with, rather due to, his yogic siddhis—the ashta siddhis—that helped him bear the pain of the burns without any overt manifestation. Yogis are known to live in extreme conditions without any pain, where an ordinary human being would struggle to survive. Such mental strength, along with grace and noble wishes, is an enduring combination.

Hanumāna's successful return infused energy and enthusiasm in his team. Angada wanted to attack Lankā and free Seetā right away, without returning to Kishkindhā. Jāmbavana advised against it. 'It is important to know what Rāma has in mind before we venture to do anything else at this moment,' he advised. The team returned to Kishkindhā.

'I have met Seetā. Pining for you every moment and observing intense vows, she awaits in Lankā,' said Hanumāna bowing to Rāma. Everyone was overjoyed. Sugreeva's confidence in Hanumāna's abilities had been vindicated once again. Rāma looked at Hanumāna with enhanced respect.[41] 'I see no one on this earth except you who could have achieved this feat. No one else could have even imagined doing it. You have immensely gratified Sugreeva and protected my family's dharma. I have nothing valuable to gift you right now. All I have to offer is my heartfelt embrace,' Rāma lauded Hanumāna, giving him a tight, affectionate hug.[42]

As the group began to prepare for their journey to Lankā and the impending war, Rāma asked Hanumāna detailed questions about the fortification of the city. Hanumāna had all the answers. He had made the effort to collect the information through his adventures in Lankā—some adventures he had initiated, some had come his way as troubles which he turned into opportunities. Hanumāna's clarity of thought and goal-oriented focus were unparalleled.

Soon the war started. Lankā had already witnessed what a remarkable warrior Hanumāna was. His performance in the war was no different. He killed many formidable commanders of Rāvana. He was instrumental in bringing Rāma and Lakshmana to consciousness on two occasions by bringing a boulder of medicinal herbs from the Himālayas. The first was when the two were hit by Indrajeet's Brahmāstra. And second, when in a combat with Rāvana, Lakshmana had fainted.

Then again, during Rāma's first face-off with Rāvana, Hanumāna lifted Rāma on his shoulders to give him some elevation to fight as Rāvana was fighting from a chariot. He did the same with Lakshmana during the latter's encounter with Indrajeet.

Hanumāna met Rāma much later in life, only in their thirteenth year of vanvās. He quickly became Rāma's trusted lieutenant because of his qualities and trustworthiness. There is not a single instance in the Rāmāyana where an assignment given to Hanumāna was not done—or not done well. For any task that needed courage or strength or sensitive handling, Hanumāna became Rāma's obvious choice, as is evident from the following episode:

Finally, the war ended. Rāma, Seetā and Lakshmana were all set to return to Ayodhyā but there was one task pending that Rāma needed to get done. When the Pushpak landed in Rishi Bharadwāja's āshram, Rāma called Hanumāna and asked him to go and inform Bharata of their arrival and narrate to him the incidents of Dandakāranya and Lankā. But informing was not the real reason; Rāma had something else in mind.

'Observe Bharata's expressions keenly as he hears the news from you, study his body language and his eyes. Figure out how he feels about me and my return,' Rāma explained the importance of the task to Hanumāna. 'Having acquired the kingdom of one's ancestors replete with food, wealth and prosperity, any person's mind will be tempted to retain it for himself. If it appears to you that Bharata desires to rule the kingdom of Ikshvākus all by himself, then so be it. I will give up my claim on the kingdom. May he rule the earth as he pleases.'[43]

But Bharata hadn't changed his mind. He was genuinely and eagerly waiting for Rāma to return. Nonetheless, the event shows how much Rāma trusted Hanumāna. This was a very personal but important task. The smallest error could ruin the relations between the brothers forever. Such work could be entrusted only to someone intelligent, perceptive, empathetic and loyal. There were many with Rāma who were loyal but none as intelligent and perceptive as the son of Vāyu.

Rishi Vālmiki tells us that there are four qualities important for success in life:

- धृति—strong willpower that keeps one firm in one's resolve

- दृष्टि—vision or wisdom to see long term consequences
- मति—intellect for objective reasoning
- दाक्ष्य—skill/capability in implementation

Hanumāna had all the four qualities,[44] coupled with a sense of devotion and responsibility towards his people, be it Sugreeva or be it Rāma. He never shied away from giving the right advice to Sugreeva or reminding Sugreeva of his duties when needed. Sugreeva knew Hanumāna's worth and took his advice seriously.

Rāma assessed Hanumāna perfectly in their first meeting itself. He told Lakshmana, 'One who has a person like Hanumāna working for him, all his tasks are bound to succeed.' Hanumāna always lived up to his reputation.

In popular narrations and depictions, Hanumāna is always shown carrying a gadā or a mace. But Vālmiki Rāmāyana has no mention of him carrying any mace. No vānara is shown to carry a mace or any other weapon for that matter. In the war too, they fight with their hands using their sheer might or use tree trunks and boulders as weapons.

मनोजवम् मारुततुल्यवेगम् जितेन्द्रियम् बुद्धिमताम् वरिष्ठम् ।
वातात्मजम् वानरयूथमुख्यम् श्रीरामदूतम् शरणम् प्रपद्ये ॥

ॐ ψ ॐ

12

The Trap of Lust

Rāvana was born to Rishi Vishrava and Kaikasi. Kuber was his elder stepbrother. Kuber was an ideal son and a great leader. He turned around the fortunes of Lankā, transforming a deserted land into a bustling and prosperous city that came to be known as the golden city. Kaikasi was very fond of her stepson Kuber. She wanted her own children to follow his lead. Rāvana took his mother's prodding as a challenge and resolved to acquire immense strength. He did intense tapasyā, pleased Brahma deva and got a boon of near immortality—no one could kill him except humans. When devas, dānavas, gandharvas couldn't kill him, what chance did mortal humans have?

Rāvana was intelligent, powerful and had tremendous vitality. Even then, instead of establishing another city like Lankā through hard work and intelligence, he chose the easier way out—usurping Lankā from Kuber. Kuber handed over Lankā to Rāvana without a fight on his father's advice and established his residence in Kailāsh.

Having taken over the reins of Lankā, Rāvana went on a journey to prove his supremacy over other kings in Bhāratavarsha. He subjugated innumerable kings. Some like Vāli and Arjun, the king of Māhishmati, overpowered him. King Arjun not only defeated

Rāvana but also imprisoned him. Arjun freed him only because Rishi Pulastya, Rāvana's grandfather, personally intervened. But Rāvana was smart. Whenever he lost, he immediately extended a hand of friendship and patched up with the king. When he won, he left a trail of destruction.[1]

As his power consolidated, he increasingly became an insufferable tyrant. Many rishis and innocent people fell prey to his reign of terror. Kuber tried to drill sense into him by sending a word of caution about his adharmic and oppressive ways through his messenger. In response, a power-drunk Rāvana attacked his brother in Kailāsh and took away his Pushpak. While on one hand, Rāvana broke every edict of dharma, on the other hand, he also conducted many yajnas and gave charity generously. His own people were, therefore, happy with him.[2]

To be able to wield unbounded power, a person needs colossal strength and a powerful personality. Rāvana possessed both in ample amounts, without a doubt. No wonder Hanumāna was awestruck when he saw Rāvana in his full glory in his court at Lankā. Hanumāna's immediate reaction was one of wonder as well as regret.

अहो रूपमहो धैर्यमहो सत्त्वमहो द्युतिः।
अहो राक्षसराजस्य सर्वलक्षणयुक्तता ।।
यद्यधर्मो न बलवान् स्यादयं राक्षसेश्वरः ।
स्यादयं सुरलोकस्य सशक्रस्यापि रक्षिता ।।

Oh, what beauty, what daring, what vigour,
what splendour, what amazing traits this king of
rākshasas is endowed with! If only his adharma was

not so huge, he would have become the protector of
all the worlds including of deities like Indra.[3]

Dashagreeva Becomes Rāvana

When Hanumāna was captured and brought to his court, Rāvana wondered if the person in front of him was Nandi, Shiva's attendant. There was a good reason for this doubt. In the past, when Rāvana was roaming in and around Kailāsh after having defeated Kuber, he had an interesting run-in with Nandi that eventually got him the name the world was going to remember him with.[4]

Rāvana wasn't always known as Rāvana. He was born Dashagreeva.

Exhilarated by the victory against Kuber, Dashagreeva and his men began roaming in the beautiful jungles and peaks of the Kailāsh in his newly acquired Pushpak vimān. Suddenly, on reaching a particular spot, the vimān halted and wouldn't move further. Dashagreeva got off the vimān to look around, trying to understand the problem. A stout, short, dark and not-so-pleasant looking being came by and stopped next to him. 'You are forbidden from entering this space. It is the kridāsthala—playground—of Bhagvān Shankar. No one is allowed here,' he proclaimed. This being was Nandi.

Dashagreeva was red with rage. He asked arrogantly, 'को अयं शङ्कर—Shankar, who?' Shrugging off the warning, he proceeded towards the mountain. Nandi tried to stop him once again. This time the king of Lankā not only disregarded him but also made fun of his vānara-like looks. Infuriated, Nandi pronounced a curse on him, 'As you have laughed at me scornfully because I resemble a vānara, there will be born extremely powerful vānaras who will be responsible for crushing your arrogance, rest assured.' It was this curse that Rāvana was reminded of on seeing Hanumāna in his court.

At that time, however, Dashagreeva did not give any thought to Nandi's words and carried on his foolish talk. 'By what authority does Shankar enjoy this place? Does he not know that great fear befalls him (through me)? Wait and watch how I uproot this mountain of yours that dared to halt my vimān.' Saying so, the king of Lankā haughtily put his hands beneath the mighty Kailāsh and attempted to lift and displace it.

Bhagvān Shankar, who was witnessing all this, simply smiled. He playfully pressed his toe just a little bit harder on the ground. The weight of Shiva's toe crushed Dashagreeva's strong arms. The mighty king of the rākshasas cried in pain. So loud was his scream that the earth began to shake. The noise frightened all the beings of the three worlds and they began to scream, making a dreadful noise.[5]

Rāvana repeatedly tried to free his trapped arms. His efforts were futile. When nothing worked, some of his wiser ministers made a suggestion, 'It seems to us that the only way you stand any chance of setting yourself free is by appealing to Bhagvān Shankar himself.' In desperation, Dashagreeva began singing paeans to please Shiva. It is said he sang and sang for many days till his ego was completely humbled. Eventually, the ever-benign Shiva was pleased and set his arms free.

Because his scream—राव (rāva)—made the whole world scream, Shiva gave him the name Rāvana.

Rāvana's humbling of ego was only short-lived and Shiva-specific. His unrighteous ways continued unabated.

There is another popular story that states that Rāvana tried to move Kailāsh because he wanted Shiva to be with him in Lankā. It is also said that Rāvana's appeals to please Shiva are compiled into what we call the 'Shiva Tāndava Stotram'. However, Vālmiki Rāmāyana makes no mention of these.

Rāvana becomes a Shiva bhakta not out of any inherent dedication, but out of desperation.

The ever-merciful Shiva accepts bhakti in whichever manner it comes!

Multiple Transgressions

Rāvana's obsession with power manifested perversely in his unquenched lust for women. He kidnapped and raped numerous women. Resigning to their fate, most eventually gave in to the might and power of the king of rākshasas. Hanumāna had seen some of these women in Rāvana's palace when he went looking for Seetā.

Shurpanakhā knew her brother's weakness for beautiful women. Hence, to get him to inflict pain on Rāma and Lakshmana, she used the ploy of describing Seetā's beauty to him rather than making a case for revenge for her own disfigurement. Her elaborate description of Seetā created an intense desire in Rāvaṇa to possess Seetā even though there was no dearth of beautiful women for him in Lankā.

When lust strikes, it topples every sense of discrimination in a person.

Rāvana was so enslaved by lust that Māreecha's wise counsel, pleadings and description of the hazards of potential consequences of Seetā's abduction, fell on deaf ears. Arm-twisting Māreecha into complying with his instructions, Rāvana abducted Seetā from Janasthāna and brought her to Lankā.

Rāvana had not taken any of his ministers into confidence before embarking on this misadventure of Seetā's abduction. He mentioned it to them only after Hanumāna's exploits which, even though Rāvana didn't overtly show it, got him worried. He wanted to bring his ministers on board to decide a plan of action if Rāma were to come to Lankā.

Seetā's abduction did not come as a shock to any of Rāvana's ministers. This trait of his was not news for the people of Lankā either. Most ministers, to stay in his good books, even encouraged his ways. To prove their loyalty, some even boasted that Rāvana had nothing to fear as the rākshasas could easily defeat the prince of Ayodhyā and his army.[6]

Kumbhakarna did rebuke Rāvana for performing such a rash act without consulting anyone. But despite his reservations, he promised to kill Rāma to please his brother.[7]

One thing which surprised all the ministers was Rāvana's willingness to wait for Seetā's acquiescence. One of his ministers, Mahāpārshva, gave a voice to that view, 'Only a fool doesn't drink the honey he has acquired from a forest full of wild animals. You are the master. Enjoy Seetā as you wish. Like a dog, attack her again and again and amuse yourself. Once you have had your way, you will have nothing to fear. We will decide the right course of action when the time comes. We have illustrious warriors like Kumbhakarna and Indrajeet on our side, what is there to worry about?'

Looking approvingly at Mahāpārshva, Rāvana disclosed one of his closely guarded secrets. 'Some years ago, I had seen an extremely attractive lady, as resplendent as a flame of fire. Her name was Punjiksthalā. I was infatuated. Pulling her clothes off forcibly, I enjoyed her fully and let her go. She complained to Brahma deva about my actions. Angrily he cast a curse on me, "From today, if you force yourself on any woman against her wish, your head will explode into a hundred pieces." This curse is why I am not forcing myself on Seetā.'[8]

Rāvana told his ministers only about this one curse through Punjiksthalā, probably because it was given by Brahma deva and consequently the most potent. But there were many other women who wished him death due to the pain he had inflicted by molesting them. Usually, he kidnapped women and brought them to

Lankā, where they were forced to spend the rest of their lives in his service. But some were more fortunate; they managed to escape after he had his way with them.[9]

One such woman was Vedavati. After receiving a drubbing at the hands of Rāma in their first combat, Rāvana was reminded of her. 'It seems that Vedavati, who had cursed me earlier for molesting her, has taken birth as Seetā,' he said in a moment of weakness.[10]

Vedavati

Vedavati was a young tapasvini dwelling in a forest on the foothills of the Himalayas. One day, while roaming around the area, Rāvana's eyes fell on her. Seeing this beautiful lady in the full bloom of her youth, Rāvana was overcome with an intense desire. He tried to tempt her with sweet, flattering words. When that didn't work, he forcibly pulled her hair and began molesting her. Vedavati was not the one to give in. With all her might, she pulled herself free. She was burning with anger at being violated. Right in front of Rāvana, she set herself on fire after pronouncing a curse on him that she will take birth again as his nemesis.[11]

Rambhā

There was another curse on Rāvana, that of Nalakuber and Rambhā. Rambhā was a nymph married to Nalakuber, the son of Kuber. By that relation, she was Rāvana's daughter-in-law. Once, during his Himalayan escapades, when he was camping in a garden, he noticed Rambhā pass by. Her beauty was unparalleled. Rāvana was aware of who she was. Still, he began to woo her, boasting about his strengths.

Rambhā was shocked at Rāvana's overtures. She reminded him of his relationship with her and pleaded with him not to speak in that manner. 'I am your daughter-in-law. You should be protecting me if other men cast a lustful eye on me,' she implored. But Rāvana's lust was so overpowering that he refused to recognise the sanctity of their relations. He violated her to his heart's content. Rambha was embarrassed and in tears. She told her husband, Nalakuber, about the incident. He was mad with rage. Rāvana was way too powerful by then for anyone to challenge him in a fight. Hence, both Rambhā and Nalakuber pronounced a curse on Rāvana that if he dared to force himself on another woman, his head would split into pieces.[12]

Rāvana was afraid of forcing himself on Seetā because the thoughts of these curses were playing on his mind—it was not because he cared for 'consent'. Before Brahma deva's curse, he had never waited for any woman's consent. A lot many women had fallen prey to his unbounded lust.

The story of Punjiksthalā is mentioned in the Yuddha Kānda, so is the reference to Vedavati's and Rambhā's curses.

Beyond Redemption

While Rāvana had a sycophantic group of courtiers who supported him in everything he said and did, it was not as if he did not have any wise counsel. Māreecha had already warned him of dire consequences when Rāvana had sought his help for Seetā's abduction.

Kumbhakarna had reproached him for his brash act of abducting Seetā's but had eventually expressed solidarity in the fight against Rāma. Vibhishana, too, never approved of Rāvana's lustful ways. He had tried to stop him earlier as well but to no avail.

Rāvana had escaped, apparently with impunity, in spite of his transgressions for far too long. The men whose wives and daughters he had violated were too weak to retaliate. Most had already lost their lives at his hands. Unlike them, Rāma was not weak. He also had supporters who were not meek either. The people of Lankā had witnessed Hanumāna's prowess. They had also heard of Rāma's annihilation of Khara and Dushana in Janasthāna. It was not a trivial feat. Vibhishana had sensed that it would be unwise to underestimate an opponent like Rāma.

He appealed to Rāvana to liberate Seetā and send her to Rāma with respect. 'Don't be so eager for war. A decision to attack should be taken when the opponent is either unaware or weak or is busy fending off attacks by other opponents. Rāma is not unaware, he would be looking forward enthusiastically to fighting a war with you. Nor is he weak. We have seen his strength in Janasthāna and Hanumāna's strength right here in Lankā. Besides, we have no enmity with Rāma. Hence there is no justification for abducting his wife. His fight with Khara, Dushana and their forces in Janasthāna was only in self-defence. It is therefore wise to let Seetā go rather than calling upon the destruction of Lankā,' Vibhishana advised.[13]

He beseeched Rāvana's council of ministers too, reminding them of their duty towards the king, and told them, 'Our king has been overcome by lust and is not able to think clearly. By your ready acquiescence, you are behaving more like his enemy in the disguise of a friend, calling for the destruction of our community. Until now, it is through Rāvana that all your desires have been fulfilled. Behave like his true well-wishers and show him the correct path. Measure the pros and cons of an action before supporting it. If preventing Rāvana from going astray requires you to admonish him, you must do so.'[14]

Even before Rāvana could respond, Indrajeet jumped in, accusing his uncle of cowardice. 'Why are you trying to scare us like a coward? Any rākshasa of ours can kill those two humans. And do you not know of my achievements? I have brought even Indra to his knees,' he sneered at Vibhishana. Then he addressed Rāvana, 'In our family, only this uncle seems to be devoid of any kind of courage and vitality.'[15]

Puffed up at his son's ready approval, Rāvana further insulted Vibhishana, 'I am very aware of the nature of kinsmen. They cannot digest the success of one of their own but are happy to celebrate his troubles. You are jealous of my prosperity and authority. You are not my well-wisher, but a disgrace to our community.[16] Had someone else spoken like you have, he would have been dead by now.'[17]

This humiliation was far too much for Vibhishana to take. He told Rāvana, 'Your mind has become completely deluded. You have lost your way. To the person who is so driven towards his own destruction, beneficial words do not make sense. It is indeed easy to find people who will always say pleasing words to flatter you. But it is very difficult to find speakers, who will say the right thing, even if unpleasant, and listeners who can take the feedback.[18] It seems to me that you are beyond redemption. Your end is near. Whatever I said was only because I care for your well-being. But you don't seem to like that. So be it. Protect yourself and Lankā. I will leave. May you be happy without me.'[19]

Vibhishana left. No one tried to stop him.

After Vibhishana went away, Rāvana was alerted about Rāma's prowess by others as well. Rāvana had revelled in the fact that there was no way Rāma and Lakshmana could reach Lankā. His belief was probably justified until the bridge across the ocean had not been built. But the bridge did get built and Rāma reached Lankā. Rāvana's spies Shuka and Sāran informed him of the might and preparedness of the vānaras in detail. Their voice had an undertone of fear. 'There is no way we will be able to contain the army of Sugreeva and the power of Rāma and Lakshmana. We have nothing to gain by opposing them. It is better for us that you let Seetā go,' they said.[20]

Rāvana dismissed their concern angrily. 'It appears to me that you have been intimidated by the vānaras due to which you have become so scared that you are asking me to return Seetā. Can you name any opponent who has defeated me in battle till now? Even if the devas, dānavas and gandharvas come together to fight me in a battle, I will not let go of Seetā,' he thundered.[21] He even mocked Shuka and Sāran for praising the enemy and threw them out, calling them ungrateful. But at the same time, he sent some other trusted spies to assess the planning and preparations in the vānara camp. They too came back with similar observations but without offering any advice on what their king should do.[22]

When the vānara army reached the Lankān shores and war seemed imminent, Rāvana's mother Kaikasi and some of his elder ministers who still had the courage to give Rāvana unbiased opinions, advised him to avoid a confrontation with Rāma by letting Seetā go.[23]

Malyavān, Rāvana's maternal grand-uncle, also made an attempt at advising him against war, explaining the concept of political pragmatism. 'Only that king survives and prospers who knows when to ally and when to wage a battle. When an opponent is equal in strength or stronger, it is better to make an alliance with him. Hence, allying with Rāma is a better strategy for us,' he advised.[24]

As expected, Rāvana paid no heed.

Instead, he tried to trick Seetā into believing Rāma was dead to get her to yield. The opposing army was knocking at the door but Rāvana's priority was to somehow attain Seetā. Seetā didn't yield—she was never going to. That his lust would push his people, his citizens, into an ocean of misery didn't occur to Rāvana.

Clash of the Titans

Angada came as a messenger to formally propose peace through freeing Seetā, or war. Rāvana's behaviour was predictable. He ordered Angada's capture, but he escaped. War conches were blown. In the first few days, except for Indrajeet, all the commanders sent by Rāvana were killed on the battlefield. After losing one of his dear ministers, Prahasta, in the war, the king of Lankā decided to enter the battlefield himself to lead the army of rākshasas.

Rāma had seen Rāvana once, standing atop his terrace in Lankā. But he was too far away to make an impression. Hence, when Rāvana came to the battlefield, Rāma did not immediately recognise him. But he was impressed by the lustrous aura of the incoming warrior. He asked Vibhishana about the new commander of the rākshasa army. Vibhishana gave an elaborate introduction.

Rāma looked on, amazed. 'Oh, what effulgence the king of rākshasas radiates. Such physique, such vitality is rare to find even in devas. Good that he has finally come before me. Today I will direct on him the anger that has been swelling in me since the time he kidnapped Seetā,' he announced, half impressed, half angry.[25]

Rāvana was a formidable warrior on the battlefield. That day he fought with Lakshmana, Sugreeva, Neela, Hanumāna and other vānara commanders. His attack left Sugreeva and Neela unconscious. With Hanumāna, he had a hand-to-hand combat, both matching each other in strength. Rāvana quickly moved on to challenge Lakshmana. Lakshmana was waiting for his turn to take on the king of Lankā. A fierce battle of arrows ensued. Then Rāvana used a brutal shakti weapon that struck Lakshmana's chest, sending burning sensations down his body. Lakshmana collapsed on the ground unconscious, but still alive. Hanumāna saw Lakshmana fall. He angrily rushed towards Rāvana and dealt a huge blow on Rāvana's chest with his fist. The force was such that blood spilled out of Rāvana's mouth, eyes and ears, and he fell unconscious in his chariot. Hanumāna then lifted Lakshmana and brought him to a safe place, close to Rāma.

Soon Lakshmana and Rāvana both regained consciousness. They stood up, ready to fight once again. This time Rāma challenged Rāvana. As Rāvana was on a chariot, Hanumāna lifted Rāma on his shoulders to enable him to fight better. Rather than respond to Rāma's challenge, Rāvana aimed his arrows at Hanumāna and severely injured him. This made Rāma furious. He showered back-to-back arrows on Rāvana and completely disarmed him. In no time Rāma killed Rāvana's horses and the sārthi[26] and even broke his chariot. Rāvana stood there shocked, completely exposed, not knowing what had hit him.

Rāma halted his attack. Looking sternly at Rāvana he said, 'You have shown great energy on the battlefield today, combating some of my best commanders. I see that you are completely exhausted at this point. Hence, I will not kill you. Go back to your city now. You will see my prowess when you are back on another chariot, having rested and replenished your weapons.'

Embarrassed, Rāvana didn't say a word. He quickly turned around and headed back to his palace.[27]

The defeat crushed Rāvana's pride and confidence. But he was too invested in the war by then to do anything to stop it. He sent Kumbhakarna to the battlefield. Rāvana was confident that Kumbhakarna, his ace warrior, would win the war for him. That was not to be. After Kumbhakarna created havoc both on the vānara and the rākshasa side, he was eventually slain by Rāma.

The news of Kumbhakarna's death shook Rāvana. His sorrow reminded him of Vibhishana's wise words of caution. If only he had listened! But there was no stopping the war now. The sons and brothers of the rākshasas who were killed in the war wanted revenge. They were determined to fight it out. They fought well. Sugreeva's army led by Rāma and Lakshmana, however, was much stronger. One by one, Rāvana's men met their death. Rāvana's final hope was Indrajeet, his son, who had vanquished even the mighty Indra and had never tasted defeat ever before. But Indrajeet too succumbed. Lakshmana killed him after a long fight.

With Indrajeet gone, Rāvana had lost everything. His lust for Seetā then turned into extreme anger. He wanted her dead. He even went to Ashokavātikā to kill her, only to be held back by Supārshva, one of his ministers.[28] Eventually, Rāvana left Seetā alone and returned to his palace.

The war had to go on. Rāvana then sent some other of his surviving rākshasa warriors to the battlefield. Rāma eliminated them all with his unparalleled skills.

Lankā was now in ruins. Every household had lost someone or the other in the battle. The women were mourning. No one blamed Rāma. They knew he was there to rescue his wife. They were angry at Shurpanakhā. She was the root cause of this tragedy. 'How audacious of an old woman like her to lay eyes on the young princes of Ayodhyā. She is the one who pushed Khara, Dushana and then Rāvana into this war. It is because of Shurpanakhā's instigation that Rāvana abducted Seetā and antagonised Rāma. Vibhishana did give worthy advice to Rāvana, but our king disparaged even him. Only if Rāvana had acted as Vibhishana had suggested, our Lankā wouldn't have turned into a cremation ground,' thus wailed the women of Lankā.[29]

It was too late to make any amends. Rāvana decided to go all in—throw all of whatever and whoever was remaining into the battle. He entered the battlefield again, aggressively taking down anyone who came in his way. He was looking for Rāma. Lakshmana tried to stop him but Rāvana continued to head towards Rāma. Once again Rāma and Rāvana came to face each other. Both knew this was the final battle between them.

A huge battle took place, with both displaying exceptional talents, each matching the other in might, skill and execution. The thunderous sounds created by the pulling of bowstrings struck terror in the heart of all the creatures around. Sometimes their blazing arrows would meet halfway and split, falling asunder; at other times they would strike and injure their target.

The intensity of the fight went up a notch with every strike. Both started using the powerful Agneyāstra, Raudrāstra and other celestial weapons on each other. Lakshmana stepped in to give Rāma some respite and led the fight against the mighty rākshasa king. Rāvana shot a very powerful shakti at Lakshmana, once again making him fall unconscious. Seeing his brother severely injured and unconscious, Rāma was filled with rage. He channelled his rage into his arrows and shot a volley against Rāvana. Unable to stand the force, Rāvana escaped, giving Rāma some time to tend to Lakshmana.[30]

By the time Lakshmana regained consciousness, Rāvana was back, too. The fight began once again. Rāvana attacked from his chariot while Rāma fought from the ground. It was an unfair match, tipped against Rāma. Then something very interesting took place. A sārthi named Mātāli came over to offer his chariot to Rāma. 'Indra has sent this chariot for you along with this armour and these weapons. Mount this chariot, Rāma, and kill Rāvana; I will be your sārthi,' Mātāli said.[31]

When the intention is aligned with dharma and determination to act prevails, when the time is right, divine intervention invariably takes place!

After circumambulating and bowing to the chariot, Rāma mounted it and began his assault on Rāvana. Rāvana matched Rāma's attack. An electrifying battle followed. One after the other, they showered their most potent weapons on each other. Each was equally capable of countering the other's weapons and laying them waste. It was not as if they weren't hurt.

Every limb of theirs had been hit by arrows. Blood oozed out of their wounds. But their spirits were undaunted and they kept going. Their fight was not limited to weapons alone. Both hurled verbal assaults on each other as well. At one point, Rāvana's sārthi observed that his master had become visibly weak and slow. Rāvana was losing his grip over his bow and struggling to attack or even contain Rāma. The sārthi, therefore, slowly pulled the chariot away from the battlefield, much to Rāvana's indignation.[32]

'What have you done you fool! Do think I am a coward and have become devoid of energy, vigour and weapons? How did you even think of belittling me like this and driving me out of the battlefield? You have destroyed the fame that I had rightfully earned with my heroism. You have behaved like my enemy. Turn around and take me back to the battlefield immediately,' Rāvana screamed at his sārthi.

The sārthi maintained his composure and explained his actions politely, 'Neither was I scared, nor had I lost my discrimination. Neither did I intend to belittle you, nor have I forgotten all that you have done for me. I did this because I thought it was in your best interests, even if you may not approve of it. I observed that you were showing signs of exhaustion and were not able to contain the attack properly. My horses were also extremely tired and were losing their balance. The situation on the battlefield appeared unfavourable for you.'

The sārthi continued, 'A sārthi must be capable of determining the need of the time and place. He must be able to study the body language of his master as well as that of the opponent. He must have complete knowledge of the terrain of the land where he is driving the chariot. He should always remain alert and be astute enough to assess where and how to move the chariot on the battlefield, and when to exit if the situation so arises.'

He added, 'I left the field just to allow you and these horses to get some rest. My decision was not based on any whim, but it was because I care for your well-being.' Rāvana had calmed down by then. Satisfied with the sārthi's response, Rāvana asked him to get back to the field where Rāma awaited him.[33]

Rāma too was exhausted after the battle with Rāvana. With Rāvana gone, he got some respite. It was during this break that Rishi Agastya came to see him and gave him the powerful Āditya Hridaya Stotra,[34] a prayer eulogising Surya deva.

'One who recites this stotra revering Surya deva doesn't perish even when faced with grave danger or severe affliction. With your mind focused, meditate on the sun and chant this stotra thrice for victory in this war,' said the rishi. Rāma obeyed. The mantra had its impact. Rāma felt rejuvenated and invigorated, ready to face Rāvana again.[35]

When Rāvana returned to the battlefield, Rāma spoke to Mātāli. 'O Mātāli, without giving in to fear or doubt, with a stable mind and vision, controlling the reins well, manoeuvre the chariot quickly. Not that I need to teach you your job—you are the sārthi of Indra himself. As I prepare myself for the battle, I am only reminding you of your role, not trying to teach you anything,' he said. Mātāli was impressed with Rāma's steadfastness. He moved the chariot to place it past Rāvana's. The wheels raised a storm of dust as the chariot sped by, inciting the rākshasa king.

The battle between Rāma and Rāvana began once again. It was so fierce and so marvellous that both the vānara and the rākshasa army stopped fighting and stood in their tracks to witness the combat between the titans play out. It was as if the whole world, including the devas and the gandharvas, stood still, just to watch this exceptional face-off between Rāma and Rāvana.

To describe the battle between Rāma and Rāvana, Rishi Vālmiki uses a very interesting figure of speech called the अनन्वय अलंकार—ananvaya alankār—in which the object compared and the object with which the comparison is made are one and the same. It is used where the object or phenomenon is such that it has no parallel. Rishi Vālmiki says:

गगनं गगनाकारं सागरः सागरोपमः |
रामरावणयोर्युद्धं रामरावणयोरिव ||

Like the sky is its own cognate and the ocean its own simile, the battle of Rāma and Rāvana was akin to the battle of Rāma and Rāvana only.[36]

Nothing can describe the vastness of the sky as the sky itself. There is no other object that can fully explain the boundlessness of the ocean as the ocean itself. Likewise, the battle between Rāma and Rāvana had no precedence. It was one of its kind.

Finally, Rāma decided it was time to put an end to the battle. He aimed his arrow at Rāvana's neck. Rāvana's head got cut from his body and fell to the ground. To everyone's amazement, another head appeared in its place. Rāvana was undoubtedly adept at using powers of illusion. Rāma cut his head off once again. Once again, a new head appeared. This happened over a hundred times. Rāvana roared with laughter. He mocked Rāma's helplessness as they continued their duel.[37]

Rāma wondered how to succeed against Rāvana when Mātāli offered some useful advice—as a good sārthi should. 'You are being too defensive. You have the shakti of Brahma deva. Use that fail-safe shakti on Rāvana. He is a suitable opponent on whom it should be used.'

Rāma remembered the arrow—the shakti of Brahma deva—that Rishi Agastya had given him when he had visited his āshram with Seetā and Lakshmana. He took it out and aimed at Rāvana. The arrow pierced through Rāvana's chest. The mighty king of Lankā collapsed dead, instantaneously.[38]

The war was over. Rāma and the vānaras had defeated the great king of Lankā decisively on his home ground.

When Rāvana's women heard about his death, they came rushing out of their palaces to see their husband one last time. Mandodari, his chief queen, came too. She was still mourning over her eldest son Indrajeet's death and here lay the only man she had ever loved. Holding her husband's dead body, she cried and lamented like someone who had lost all reasons to live. Her lamentations were laced with regret, for she had seen all this coming.

'Previously, having won over your senses,' she said, 'you achieved victory over the three worlds. Possibly, the senses remembered that and decided to avenge your control on them. By deluding you completely, they won over you. After I heard of Rāma's activities in Janasthāna, I was convinced he was no ordinary man. How many times I tried to discourage you from seeking animosity with him! But you paid no heed. It was clear to me that your desire for Seetā would destroy your prosperity, your loved ones and your life. What surprised me is how did the fire of Seetā's focussed devotion to Rāma not burn you instantly when you kidnapped her?'

Mandodari continued in the same vein. 'That a sinner has to face the results of his karma is beyond any doubt. You have received what you deserved. You had so many women in the palace who were more beautiful than Seetā. Seetā was no match to me, neither in beauty nor in skill nor family of birth. But you were so blinded in your lust for her that you refused to see or understand. Every living creature eventually must die, he only needs a trigger. Seetā came in your life as that trigger of your death,' sobbed Mandodari.[39]

With the way the war had progressed, no one was surprised at the outcome. Rāvana had been warned by all his well-wishers. But then, who is more blind than the one who refuses to see, who is more deaf than the one who refuses to hear? The sheath of conceit and the smoke of lust had clouded every sense of his, making him tread the path of injustice. Neither Brahma deva's boon nor the prosperity of Lankā, neither the best of rituals nor an all-conquering son like Indrajeet, neither any amount of bravery nor any kind of smart wit, can save a person who has completely surrendered the reigns of his thoughts and mind to the impulses of desire and ego.

Shurpanakhā possibly wished to manipulate Rāvana by exploiting his lustful ways. Little did she know she was pushing Rāvana into the hands of death—or did she? He was responsible for the death of her husband, after all.

In the Srimad Bhagavad Geetā, Krishna talks about how obsession due to lust, anger, greed and pride leads to one's downfall. It matters little how courageous or intelligent a person is otherwise. Krishna says:

ध्यायतो विषयान्पुंसः सङ्गस्तेषूपजायते।
सङ्गात् संजायते कामः कामात्क्रोधोऽभिजायते।।
क्रोधाद्भवति संमोहः संमोहात्स्मृतिविभ्रमः।
स्मृतिभ्रंशाद् बुद्धिनाशो बुद्धिनाशात्प्रणश्यति।।

When a person dwells on objects (excessively), there arises attachment for them. From attachment grows intense desire (to own it); from such desire springs anger (when the desire is not fulfilled). From anger follows delusion; delusion leads to failure of memory; failure of memory causes the loss of intellect (wisdom) and the person is destroyed.

For Duryodhana and Karna, it was intense jealousy. For Rāvana, it was his unquenched lust and overblown ego.[40]

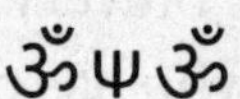

13

The Difficulty of Being Good

'Whatever I said was only because I care for your well-being. But you don't seem to like that. So be it. Protect yourself and Lankā. I will leave. May you be happy without me,' Vibhishana had said before leaving Lankā, when Rāvana accused him of jealousy and ill-will. Vibhishana's crime was his open disagreement with his elder brother on the issue of Seetā's abduction. It was not the first time that he had disagreed with Rāvana. He had let his displeasure known when Rāvana, befuddled with lust, seized unwilling women and brought them to Lankā. There were times when Vibhishana succeeded in tactfully persuading Rāvana to do the right thing, as he had done by stopping him from killing Hanumāna. But more often than not, Rāvana's obduracy prevailed and Vibhishana submitted.

But this time it was different. Vibhishana desperately tried to dissuade Rāvana from holding on to Seetā and starting a war with Rāma. It was as if he had a premonition of the devastation that Rāvana's lechery and arrogance was going to bring to Lankā. Rāvana did not like warnings. He was so irritated that he insulted his well-meaning younger brother, calling him all kinds of names.

The Deliberations

Shrouded in an assumed sense of invincibility, few in Lankā bothered about the tussle between the brothers of the royal family and even fewer cared about Vibhishana leaving Lankā.

Vibhishana left but he chose not to remain a bystander. Along with four trusted men, he went across to the other side of the ocean where Rāma and the vānara army were trying to find a way to reach Lankā.[1] When the tall and sturdy Vibhishana and his men entered the camp, carrying their weapons and looking for Rāma, Sugreeva was alarmed. 'Beware, it seems these rākshasas have come to kill us,' he said, alerting his commanders. The vānaras immediately got ready to retaliate.

Vibhishana guessed the reason for the sudden commotion in the vānara camp. To allay their fear, he halted and addressed Sugreeva to let him know the reason for his unannounced arrival, 'I am Vibhishana, the younger brother of Rāvana. My brother abducted Seetā from Janasthāna, killed Jatāyu and has now imprisoned her in Lankā. I earnestly appealed to him to return Seetā respectfully to Rāma. But like a person rushing towards death refuses to take medicine, Rāvana ignored my warnings. Instead, he humiliated me as if I were a slave. Hence, leaving behind my wives and children, I have come to seek refuge in Rāma. Please convey my message to him.'

Sugreeva, still wary, rushed to inform Rāma and Lakshmana of this questionable visitor. 'A few men who were earlier in Rāvana's army have arrived suddenly, saying they want to be on our side. I do not trust them at all. I believe they will wait for us to drop our vigilance and then attack us, just like an owl who assaults the unsuspecting crows. Possibly, they are spies sent by Rāvana to foment trouble in our army. One can include soldiers of friends, of other warrior tribes and even paid mercenaries in one's army, but never those who have served in the enemy's army earlier. This man who has come with four others says he is Rāvana's brother Vibhishana and seeks refuge. I am sure Rāvana must have sent him purposefully to destroy us. We must not trust him at all. He is as good as our enemy, Rāvana. Therefore, we must punish him with death.'

Rāma heard Sugreeva patiently and gave a lot of thought to what he said. Then he addressed the other vānaras, 'You just heard the astute observations of Sugreeva about Vibhishana. It is important to hear the views and suggestions of one's friends and well-wishers when a situation of doubt arises. Hence, I would like to know your opinion on this. What should we do?'

Asked thus, the vānara chiefs felt gratified and began sharing their opinions. Angada spoke first. 'As Vibhishana comes from the enemy camp, we cannot instantly place trust in him. Some people are experts in concealing their true intentions. We must keep an eye on him and think about what we can gain from him. If he has qualities that help us, then we can accept him. However, if he shows traits detrimental to us, we should keep him away.'

Sharabh, another vānara chief, spoke next. 'We could appoint a spy to study Vibhishana's actions and motivations and test him. Depending on what we find, we can decide what to do with him,' he advised.

'Rāvana has chosen to antagonise us, and he is very cunning. Vibhishana comes to us from Rāvana's camp. The place and timing of his arrival seem dubious. Hence, we must remain circumspect with respect to him,' said Jāmbavana thoughtfully.

Maind put his diplomatic intellect to use, 'We must use tact to figure out Vibhishana's true intentions. We must make relevant enquiries of him using sweet words to gain his trust and make him divulge the truth. Only after that can we decide whether to include him in our team or not.'

Then Hanumāna arose to speak. 'Before I begin, I want to state that I do not intend to belittle anyone. Whatever I am about to say is my opinion and not a criticism of what people here have said. I do not think we are in the position to test Vibhishana. His motivations can be known only after we accept him and assign some work to him. But testing him beforehand seems inappropriate to me. Spying on him is not possible in the current situation as he is already here.'

Pausing for a moment, Hanumāna continued, 'I believe the timing of his coming here is not so dubious. He has clearly expressed the reason for leaving the immoral Rāvana and coming to the side of the righteous Rāma. When else would it have been a better time to take this call? If we attempt to make too many awkward enquiries of him, there is a chance he will feel disrespected and we may lose an important ally. And while it is extremely difficult to know what is in a person's mind, a smart person can find that out by closely observing the other person's tone and expressions. The face always reflects the intentions. I do not observe any such flaws in his tone and body language.'

Hanumāna was the only one among the vānaras who had seen Vibhishana earlier. It was Vibhishana's intervention that had dissuaded Rāvana from killing Hanumāna in Lankā. Therefore, Vibhishana's claim of disagreement with Rāvana did not seem doubtful to him. 'I think Vibhishana has taken this decision to come over to our side after weighing in all the pros and cons. He is aware of Rāma's extraordinary feats and believes Rāvana's defeat is imminent. He may have come to our side, desirous of the kingdom of Lankā after the fall of Rāvana,' said Hanumāna.[2]

Pondering deeply over all that was said, Rāma expressed his opinion, 'Vibhishana has come to me as a friend, seeking refuge. Therefore, even if it appears inappropriate, we must accept him. Great men do not proscribe giving shelter to the one who comes seeking.'

Hearing this Sugreeva spoke again, respectfully disagreeing, 'It doesn't matter how he has come to us. How can we trust a man who gives up on his own brother in times of calamity? If he cannot stand by his brother in need, which other relations will he not betray?'

Rāma smiled. It was a fair point but possibly not applicable to Vibhishana, he believed. 'You make a sharp observation Sugreeva. However, we need to consider other aspects as well before proclaiming that he has betrayed his brother. Kings are wary of two kinds of threats, external—from other kingdoms—and internal—from their own people. Sometimes, even a valid criticism from his kinsmen is seen as a threat by the king. Given Vibhishana's overt disapproval of Rāvana's ways, even though done with the best of intentions and with the welfare of Lankā in mind, Rāvana may have started viewing Vibhishana as his enemy. In such a situation, having lost the trust of the king, Vibhishana's worry about the threat to his life and his subsequent abandonment of Rāvana cannot be called betrayal.'

Displaying sharp insights and acumen in understanding human psychology, Rāma added, 'Moreover, he seems to desire the kingdom of Lankā. If we accept him and promise to crown him the king of Lankā, he will not abandon us. Rather, he will become happy and prove to be an asset to us in this war. This situation also tells me that the rākshasas do not trust one another, a factor that can work to our advantage. It's rare to find a brother like Bharata or a friend like you.'

Sugreeva was not completely convinced but Rāma had made up his mind to accept Vibhishana. It was the right thing to do morally and strategically, he believed.[3]

The Induction

On getting affirmation from Rāma, Vibhishana came to see him and fell at his feet. 'Having faced severe humiliation from my brother Rāvana, I have given up my family, Lankā and my friends and have come to seek refuge in you. My possessions, my life and my happiness are all subject to your will,' he said earnestly. Rāma welcomed him with compassion. He understood Vibhishana's struggle. But he was also pragmatic. He knew there was an important war to be fought for which Vibhishana's information as an insider would be immensely helpful.

'Tell me about the strengths and weaknesses of the rākshasa forces in detail,' asked Rāma, wasting no time. Vibhishana's answer, body language, tone and tenor would also help to evaluate his intentions. Vibhishana did not hesitate. He explained the security arrangements of Lankā, giving details of the strength of Rāvana's armies. He also gave an elaborate description of Rāvana and his key commanders. Lankā was definitely a force to reckon with.

Rāma listened to Vibhishana's words intently and declared, 'Let it be heard loud and clear. However strong Rāvana and his ministers are, I will kill all of them and crown you the king of Lankā. I promise that. I will not return to Ayodhyā unless I kill Rāvana along with his kinsmen.'

Vibhishana also let his resolve known. 'I will support you to my full capacity to kill the rākshasa army and capture Lankā,' he promised. Rāma embraced him. With the vānaras as witnesses, Rāma declared Vibhishana as the king of Lankā.[4]

Vibhishana's candid, unambiguous declaration helped to alleviate the doubt that many vānaras had harboured in their minds about him even after Rāma's decision to welcome him.

The War

Before the war began, Rāvana sent his spies to foment trouble in the vānara camp. Vibhishana's presence foiled their attempt.[5] Vibhishana was determined to ensure Rāma's success. On reaching Lankā, he arranged for his companions Anal, Panas, Sampāti and Pramati, to enter the city, infiltrate Rāvana's army and get updates on the most recent happenings in the city and the war preparations. He informed Rāma and Sugreeva about the commanders guarding the gates of Lankā and the size of the army deployed with each of them. Based on this, Rāma deployed his vānara commanders on the four gates to match the strength of the rākshasas.[6]

Once the war began, Vibhishana served as a source of intelligence about the rākshasas and their war strategies. He was also a pillar of strength for Rāma and Sugreeva. Every time a new commander came to lead the rākshasa army, Vibhishana would diligently give a detailed background about him to Rāma to help him make a plan to counter him.

When Indrajeet made Rāma and Lakshmana unconscious by using a nāgapāsh on them, the vānaras and Sugreeva were disheartened. Frightened and tormented by Indrajeet and shocked at seeing Rāma and Lakshmana lying like dead men on the ground, they didn't know what to do. How were they to fight if the princes of Ayodhyā were dead? Sugreeva was almost in tears.

Vibhishana was the only one who held himself together. He comforted Sugreeva and said, 'Don't be scared and don't lose hope. Battles tend to be uncertain and such things happen. This is not the time to grieve. Rather, you should be commanding the forces in Rāma's absence and ensure they don't fall apart. Rāma and Lakshmana aren't dead, they have only become unconscious. Look at Rāma's body. It retains its lustre. The princes will rise soon and lead us. Till then, motivate your army so that they remain enthused to fight.'[7]

Inspired by these words, Sugreeva got into action. He rallied his soldiers and instructed them to watch out for a potential rākshasa attack. Some commanders were assigned the task of protecting Rāma and Lakshmana from all sides. A garuda's intervention brought them back to consciousness, relieving them from the effect of the snakes.

Vibhishana's insights played a very important role in holding Rāma together in the second half of the war. To confound the vānaras and shock Rāma, Indrajeet used his powers of illusion once again. He showed an illusion to the vānaras in which they saw him killing Seetā. This had the desired impact. The vānaras rushed to inform Rāma. The news shook Rāma to the core. In the meanwhile, Indrajeet had planned to conduct a ritual in the Nikumbhilā temple to gain even stronger powers of illusion, making him invincible in the war.

When Vibhishana saw Rāma and the vānaras in a state of agitation and anguish and learnt the reason for it, he knew instantly what must have transpired. 'There is no way Indrajeet can kill Seetā. Rāvana will never permit that. This was Indrajeet's deception to buy time and complete the ritual that will make him practically unassailable. We must kill him before he finishes his rituals,' Vibhishana informed them, with a sense of urgency.[8] Following his advice, Rāma sent Lakshmana to challenge Indrajeet and in the battle that followed, Indrajeet was eventually killed.

In addition to all this, Vibhishana and his four men actively participated in the war, killing warriors of the rākshasa army.[9]

The Allegations

Rāvana was the reason why Vibhishana left Lankā. As the war progressed, Rāvana came to realise the wisdom and foresight of Vibhishana's words. But the realisation fell short of making him correct his course. Both Rāvana and Indrajeet were upset about Vibhishana allying with Rāma. The anger came to the fore when they saw Vibhishana on the battlefield, fighting alongside Rāma.

Indrajeet had never particularly respected his uncle Vibhishana. He had called him a coward when Vibhishana had suggested making peace with Rāma. That same uncle was responsible for foiling his yajna at Nikumbhilā temple. Except for him, the rest of his opponents had bought into his hoax of killing Seetā. When Indrajeet saw Vibhishana inciting Lakshmana to fight, he flared up and snapped at him, 'You are born on this land. You have grown up here. You are the brother of the king of this land. And being my uncle, you are like a father to me. Why then are you being hostile to us? Clearly, you have no love for your brethren, neither do you have any sense of belonging to the community in which you grew up, nor do you understand your responsibilities and duties. You are but a stigma on the rākshasa clan.'

'Giving up interests of your clan, you have accepted the slavery of the enemy,' continued Indrajeet. 'What can be more reprehensible than this? A kinsman without any qualities so to speak of, is way better than one who may be very smart but doesn't want to belong to one's own community. A traitor who aids the opponent in the destruction of his own people is, without doubt, destroyed by the same opponent once the purpose is achieved. Only a heartless man like you could have brought Lakshmana to this place to kill his brother's son.'[10]

Vibhishana had heard many aspersions being cast by Indrajeet on him even earlier. He was not going to take his words lying down. 'What are you bragging about? Give up this unworthy condescension,' Vibhishana retorted. 'Do you not know my virtues and character? Even though I have been born in the community of rākshasas, my nature was never similar to theirs. I have striven to live by values of noble human beings. Unrighteousness has never appealed to my conscience. Even then, just because natures don't match, how can an elder brother disown his younger brother like Rāvana did to me?'

'It is anyway better to give up a person who has gone astray from the path of dharma and be happy. One must cast away a person who indulges in violating the wives of other men or in stealing the wealth of others, just like one would cast away a house on fire. Three vices are said to destroy a person—stealing other men's wealth, eyeing other men's wives and being excessively suspicious of one's well-wishers. Adding to these, my elder brother is marred by arrogance, unrighteousness and tyranny. His vices have overshadowed his otherwise lofty qualities. Hence, I left him. His end is near. And so is yours. You are arrogant and rude, and also naïve. You'll face the consequences of all your insults to me today,' said Vibhishana sternly.[11]

The battle between Lakshmana and Indrajeet began. It was a fight of equals. Vibhishana had orchestrated this fight, in a way. There were times when he came close to fighting with Indrajeet himself. But he became emotional and tears clouded his eyes. To the vānaras standing near him, he said, 'He is my brother's son and thus mine too. While it is not right for me to kill my nephew, I will do that if needed to help Rāma achieve his purpose. But these tears don't seem to stop. So Lakshmana alone will have to defeat him.'[12] Indrajeet had no such compunctions. He attacked and injured Vibhishana before being challenged once again by Lakshmana.[13] Eventually, Indrajeet met his end at Lakshmana's hands, as Vibhishana had desired and predicted.

Vibhishana and Rāvana came face-to-face on the battlefield in the last days of the war. When Rāvana was fighting Rāma and Lakshmana, Vibhishana intervened and killed the horses of his chariot. That was when Rāvana's eyes fell on Vibhishana. He did not indulge in any war of words. Rāvana channelised all his pent-up anger into his weapons. He shot an extremely powerful weapon at his younger brother. The ever-vigilant Lakshmana countered the weapon with his own, saving Vibhishana. Rāvana then used a deadlier weapon to try to kill Vibhishana. Once again, thanks to Lakshmana's intervention, Vibhishana was saved.[14]

Soon after that Rāvana was slain by Rāma.

The events occurred as Vibhishana had forewarned. Rāvana's arrogance and lust led to the complete destruction of Lankā. Nevertheless, when Rāvana lay dead on the ground, Vibhishana broke down. He was upset with his brother, but he had no hatred for him. It was not as if Rāvana did not have any virtues. He had many. He was a generous and brave man. He had done intense tapasyā. He had conducted numerous yajnas and given huge charities. He had been a great friend to those he cared for and had taken good care of the people of Lankā. It was just that, as Vibhishana told Indrajeet, Rāvana's vices overshadowed his virtues.

Vibhishana wanted to give a respectable cremation to Rāvana. He sought Rāma's permission. Rāma encouraged him to do everything in the best possible manner, as ordained by the scriptures. 'Enmity ends with death. Our goal has been achieved. Now Rāvana is as dear to me as he is to you. Please make all the necessary provisions and cremate him as he rightly deserves,' said Rāma.[15]

The mighty Rāvana's body was consigned to the flames following all rituals, in front of his wives and surviving citizens.

Vibhishana was then formally crowned the king of Lankā.

When Vibhishana went over to Rāma, he had no doubts that he was doing the right thing. When he helped Rāma fight the war, providing all kinds of intelligence and support, he was in no doubt about his objective, which was to ensure Rāma won against Rāvana. While he felt bad having to cause his nephew's death, he was clear it had to be done. For his stand, Vibhishana was branded a traitor by his nephew. Many others in Lankā may have also felt the same way. The fact, of course, remains that Vibhishana defected to the opposite side and helped the destruction of Lankā to take place.

Vibhishana understood clearly that dharma was on Rāma's side. Rāvana, on the other hand, had become an epitome of adharma. The choice for Vibhishana was whether to continue to support adharma or stand solidly by dharma. He chose the latter.

When Brahma deva offered to grant boons to Rāvana and Vibhishana following their intense tapasyā in their younger days, Rāvana sought immortality. But Vibhishana had a unique wish. He made a request of Brahma deva:

परमापद्गतस्यापि धर्मे मम मतिर्भवेत्

'Even in the worst of calamities, let my mind be always established in dharma.'

'You'll never go astray from the path of dharma,' Brahma deva said. It was this insistence on dharma that directed Vibhishana towards Rāma.[16]

Loyalty and Dharma

Vibhishana's choice wasn't an easy one. It was between doing the right thing versus standing behind his brother in trouble. It was between being loyal to the family though it was on the side of adharma or choosing to be disloyal but being on the side of dharma. His actions are often described colloquially as घर का भेदी लंका ढाए—*ghar ka bhedi Lankā dhāy*—which translates to 'the spy from inside the house lead to the destruction of Lankā'.

Vibhishana played an instrumental role in Rāma's victory and Rāvana's destruction by sharing insider information about Lankā's and busting the war strategies of Indrajeet and other rākshasas. The criticism isn't misplaced.

Was it right for Vibhishana to abandon his brother in trouble, notwithstanding that the problems were caused by his brother and his unrighteous behaviour?

There is one other thing for which Vibhishana's intent itself is questioned—his willingness to be crowned the king of Lankā even before the war began.

Vibhishana had foreseen Rāvana was heading towards destruction and pushing Lankā towards devastation. In such a situation, was it really such a bad idea to want to take the reigns of the kingdom in his own hands once the war ended? Vibhishana belonged to the royal family after all.

Even if one were to consider tactically, it made sense for Vibhishana to accept Rāma's proposal to be crowned the king of Lankā. Most vānaras were already suspicious of him. Vibhishana's refusal would have only made them more doubtful of his intentions.

Vibhishana had never proactively misguided Rāvana nor had he colluded with Rāma to destabilise Rāvana until he was insulted by Rāvana himself and asked to leave. Vibhishana had tried his best to persuade his elder brother multiple times to act righteously in the interest of Lankā, in vain.

Vidur had once told Dhritarashtra to give up Duryodhana for the sake of dharma. He said:

त्यजेदेकं कुलस्यार्थे ग्रामस्यार्थे कुलं त्यजेत् ।
ग्रामं जनपदस्यार्थे आत्मार्थे पृथिवीं त्यजेत् ।।

Give up a son if it saves the family. Give up the family if it saves the village. Give up the village to save the larger state. But to protect one's ātmā, one's virtues and value systems, be ready to give up this earth as well.

Vibhishana lived by this advice.

ॐ ψ ॐ

14

Soumitri

Lakshmana was not happy at Rāma's deference to his father's order of exile, giving in to Kaikeyi's egregious demands. As a kshatriya, he believed, Rāma should fight for his rightful claim to the throne. People in Ayodhyā had given their consent to Rāma's coronation. Lakshmana had even suggested that for dharma, they should imprison Dasharatha, if such a need arose. But Rāma was determined to obey his father. Nothing could change his decision. Seetā too decided to accompany Rāma to the forest.

Lakshmana and Rāma were inseparable from their childhood days. Lakshmana was always beside Rāma. He couldn't have left his side in this situation. He insisted on going with him. Rāma tried to dissuade him, but Lakshmana was firm. 'Let me come as your attendant, I will be obliged,' he pleaded earnestly and added, 'I will walk ahead of you with my bow, making the way. I will gather fruits and tubers for our food. When you and Seetā sleep, I will stay awake and guard you.' Rāma was pleased. 'Seek permission from all your near and dear ones and join me,' he said.

The vanvās, for the most part, was a dream for Seetā. Rāma was with her all the time. Rāma indulged her in every way possible. But Lakshmana had a clear purpose laid out for him during the time, one that he had committed himself to voluntarily—to serve Rāma and Seetā. He would stay awake when Rāma and Seetā were asleep to protect them from the unknown dangers of the forest. He would build āshrams for them to stay in whenever they arrived in a new place. He would build boats with his hands when they had to cross rivers. He would ensure they had food to eat and that Rāma always had all the material he needed for his regular yajnas.

Lakshmana stood by Rāma, tackling every danger that came their way in the forest, either fighting, as he did with Virādh and Kabandha, or protecting Seetā from rākshasas when a need arose, as he did when Khara and Dushana attacked them in Panchavati.

But more importantly, he played a role in Rāma's life that no one else could. Lakshmana was the only one apart from Seetā before whom Rāma would bare his emotions. Lakshmana always knew exactly what Rāma needed to hear and when. He held Rāma together in his weakest moments.

Rāma was stoic when all of them left Ayodhyā. People of Ayodhyā were not. The city was in tears seeing their favourite prince leave. The news was as much a shock for them as it was for Dasharatha. Some followed their chariot, determined to accompany their prince in vanvās. The love of the people of his kingdom had moved Rāma.

The first evening after leaving Ayodhyā, they stopped by the banks of Tamasā. Rāma was mentally preparing himself for fourteen years away from his motherland, but he was worried about his parents. He shared his thoughts with Lakshmana, 'I hope our father and my mother do not become blind crying after us, unable to deal with the separation, though I am certain Bharata will console them and take care of them. Thinking about Bharata gives me some solace. He is a person of strong character.'

Then, looking approvingly he added, 'Lakshmana, I am glad you have come. You have helped me achieve my purpose by coming along, or else I would have had to get help to protect Seetā in the jungle.'[1]

Driven by Sumantra, crossing Vedashruti, Gomati and Syandikā rivers, they reached the outskirts of Shringaverpur, the city ruled by Rāma's friend, Guha. Determined not to enter any city for the next fourteen years, Rāma refused Guha's hospitality. Instead, he requested Guha to take care of the horses pulling their chariot. Later that evening, Rāma and Seetā chose to sleep on the ground, on a sheet of dry grass.

Lakshmana did not sleep that night. He and Guha stayed awake to protect Rāma and Seetā. Guha requested Lakshmana to get some rest. He had asked his men to prepare a comfortable bed for him. 'I and my people are used to the forest life. We will stay awake and protect Rāma,' he said.

'With you here Nishādarāj, we have no fear,' Lakshmana replied. 'However, when Rāma and Seetā are sleeping on the floor like this, how can I use any kind of luxury? Just look how this brother of mine, who otherwise is unassailable even by devas and asuras, sleeps peacefully on a sheer sheet of dry grass.'

Overwhelmed at seeing his brother dressed in valkal and sleeping on the ground, he continued. 'It took innumerable prayers and immense effort on the part of my father to obtain a son like Rāma. There is no way he will be able to survive this separation from Rāma. Neither he nor Kaushalyā Mā or my own mother will be able to bear this shock of separation. Will we be able to return to Ayodhyā and meet our parents ever again?' he wondered, with a touch of melancholy in his voice. Lakshmana's pain brought tears to Guha's eyes. Both of them sat talking all through the night.[2]

It was after Shringaverpur that the real vanvās for Rāma, Lakshmana and Seetā began. Rāma convinced Sumantra to return to Ayodhyā from Shringaverpur and sent messages for everyone with him. His messages were conciliatory. To his mother, he asked not to give up on his father and have no ill-will against Kaikeyi. To Bharata, he requested to take care of his mother like his own and be kind to their father.

Lakshmana made no such concessions. Sumantra told Dasharatha and Kaushalyā on reaching Ayodhyā that Lakshmana was fuming. Lakshmana had asked, 'For what crime has Rāma been exiled? Whatever be the reason for banishing Rāma, either Kaikeyi's greed or the king's eagerness to fulfil the boons given to her or even destiny's ordain, the decision itself is not justifiable in any way. Hence, I am unable to conjure up any emotion of affection towards my father, the king. Rāma is my everything—my friend, my brother and my father.'[3]

After Sumantra returned to Ayodhyā, the three of them ventured into the dense, uninhabited forest.

Their first day was spent exploring the area. Rāma and Lakshmana even hunted a few wild animals. As the day segued into dusk, the three of them settled down under a tree. Having done their sandhyopāsanā, Rāma and Lakshmana got talking.

Rāma had no doubts about accepting the vanvās. It was the right thing to do. But Kaikeyi's ill-will behind the demand and his father's capitulation to his favourite wife were not lost on him. On this first night away from any janapada, the memories of the day of the coronation came rushing back to Rāma. 'Tonight, our father will be sleeping terribly pained, grieving my departure. But Kaikeyi must be sleeping happy and contented. The king is indulgent towards her and is completely under her sway. He is also quite old and frail now. I hope Kaikeyi doesn't take his life for the sake of the kingdom once Bharata returns to Ayodhyā,' Rāma confided his fear in Lakshmana.[4]

Rāma continued to lament, 'Observing this situation that has befallen us, I have come to believe kāma is a lot more powerful than artha or dharma. Else who will abandon an obedient son like me because he is infatuated by a woman, as our father has? One who is so overpowered by lust that he completely neglects all the aspects of artha and dharma, will certainly call upon his doom, just like our father has. It appears to me that Kaikeyi has come to Ayodhyā to take the king's life, exile me and usurp the kingdom for Bharata. I fear that revelling in her good fortune, Kaikeyi may harm our mothers Kaushalyā and Sumitrā.' Overcome with anxiety for his mothers, he urged Lakshmana to return to Ayodhyā immediately.

The thoughts about his mothers led to a surge of bittersweet emotions in Rāma's heart. 'Shame on me!' he exclaimed, fighting back tears. 'My mother nourished me,' he continued, 'and took care of me with so much love all these years. Now when it is my turn to takc care of her, I have left her all alone. May a noblewoman never give birth to a son like me who brings so much grief to her. I think my mother's pet bird gives her more love than I have been able to. How unfortunate is my mother to beget a son like me!'

Rāma continued, 'It is not that I am not capable of fighting to get what I want. If I wish, I can single-handedly win over Ayodhyā and all other kingdoms on the face of the earth. But I do not wish to challenge my fate, nor do I want to do anything unrighteous. That is why I refused the coronation and accepted vanvās.' While speaking, tears were flowing freely down his cheeks. Having poured his heart out, Rāma became silent, like a serene, waveless ocean.[5]

Lakshmana had opposed Rāma's acceptance of vanvās. He was very angry with his father and had minced no words about it. He had let his disapproval of his father's stance show even in the message he sent through Sumantra. Yet, when he saw Rāma's uncharacteristic mental agony, he didn't add his own to it. Worrying about the parents, Rāma had asked him to reconsider his decision and return to Ayodhyā. But Lakshmana was determined not to leave Rāma's side, come what may.

He reminded Rāma of what he meant to him and Seetā. 'Undoubtedly, without you, Ayodhyā has lost all its sheen, like a night without a moon. But it doesn't suit you to mourn like this. Your agony is causing immense pain to both Seetā and me. Neither of us can survive a second without you, just like a fish cannot live without water. Without you, I do not desire to see Shatrughna or even my own mother. I do not even desire the heavens without you,' he said earnestly.

Lakshmana's sweet words touched Rāma's heart. He decided to let Lakshmana stay with him for the entire period of vanvās.[6] Never again did Rāma suggest to Lakshmana to return to Ayodhyā. For Lakshmana, even the thought of that was non-existent anyway. Rāma was rarely flustered. But whenever he was, he had Lakshmana as his pillar of support, standing strong.

To the otherwise calm and composed Rāma, nothing troubled more than any threat to Seetā and nothing caused him more distress than separation from Seetā, even if it was momentary.

Their life in Dandakāranya had begun on one such note. A rākshasa name Virādh, enamoured by Seetā's beauty, attempted to take her away. Rāma was distraught and his immediate reaction was to blame Kaikeyi for the situation. Lakshmana stepped in and encouraged him to fight, 'You yourself are the protector of all beings, no less than the mighty Indra himself. And I am here by your side. Wait and watch how I slay this rākshasa, channelising all my anger towards him. Let the earth be drenched by his blood today.' All Rāma needed to hear were some words of support. He got ready along with Lakshmana to kill Virādh.

The episode of the exquisite deer was one that tested Lakshmana's patience. Seetā's accusations were too much for him to handle. He went to look for Rāma as she demanded. Rāma wasn't happy about Lakshmana's decision to leave Seetā alone in the āshram. Rāma reasoned that Seetā was distressed hearing Māreecha's imitation of his voice, but Lakshmana should have known better. Lakshmana did not argue. He knew it was not the time for talking about how Seetā had wrongly accused him. That subject was never brought up again. The priority was to ensure Seetā's welfare.

Rāma's agony knew no bounds on learning about Seetā's abduction. Anything and everything would remind him of her. Her memory would leave him anguished and in pain. The fragrance in the air, the flowing stream, the rustling of leaves, the songs of birds—all of them made him miss Seetā. The only person who kept him sane during this time was Lakshmana. With immense patience, he would hear Rāma express his agony and then console him with words of love, courage and resolve, as the situation demanded. His words were comforting. They helped pull Rāma out of his misery and move him to action.

On one such occasion, Rāma was pining for Seetā so much that he did not wish to live anymore without her. To cheer him up, Lakshmana reminded Rāma of the importance of zeal and perseverance to achieve one's goals. He said, 'O prince, give up such pitiable thoughts and maintain composure. Without making efforts, we will not be able to regain what we have lost. In perseverance lies great strength. For the one who is willing to put in the effort, nothing is unattainable. Perseverant men will not be disheartened when they commit themselves to a task. We will definitely get Seetā back through our incessant efforts.'[7]

Rāma rarely lost his cool apart on a few occasions when he was fighting the war. 'But when he did become angry, even the devas would be afraid,' Nārada Muni had said. Once Rāma became furious when, despite their earnest pleas, Varun deva refused to budge and show them the way to Lankā. Even after three nights of waiting upon Varun deva, when he did not show up, Rāma's eyes began to turn red. He turned to Lakshmana and said in a tone manifestly angry, 'This is the arrogance of the lord of the ocean to not show up despite our genuine prayers. It is true that forgiveness, straightforwardness and sweet words have no impact on those who are without any virtue.'

He added, 'There is no glory or victory to be gained through such pleadings. Now you wait and watch how my arrow makes the ocean completely dry and shatters to pieces the large crocodiles and other animals residing in the ocean. Once I dry the ocean our army can cross over to Lankā on foot. Varun deva has taken me for granted. He probably thinks I am incapable of such action. Now he will see for himself what I can do.' Rāma roared and shot an arrow, causing shock waves in the ocean and striking dread in the hearts of the creatures in the ocean as well as on land.

Lakshmana rushed to calm Rāma down before he brought about any major destruction. 'Not any more, not any more,' he said as he held Rāma's bow. 'Do not give in to rage, we can have our task accomplished even without causing the destruction of the ocean. Think calmly of another noble alternative,' Lakshmana pleaded. Rāma steadied himself. He did not shoot the second arrow that he had readied on his bow but continued to threaten Varun deva with dire consequences till Varun deva finally appeared and apologised profusely.

However, as the arrow was already out of the quiver and ready to be shot, it couldn't be put back or wasted. Hence, on Varun deva's request, Rāma shot it towards the north, targeting a place called Drumakulya, creating a famous desert called 'Maru'.[8]

Thus, Lakshmana saved not just Varun deva from complete annihilation but also secured the welfare of future generations through the continuation of the oceans.[9]

It was not that Rāma couldn't manage his emotions. But even the strongest of people have their weak moments which manifest usually in front of those they value and trust. Lakshmana was that person for Rāma—no one else came close, apart from Seetā.

How well Lakshmana understood Rāma and how subtly and effectively he could use his words to have an impact on him was evident in Lankā when Indrajeet's illusion convinced everyone that he had killed Seetā.

Rāma was despondent. The hope of reuniting with Seetā had kept him going all these months. He had left no stone unturned in the quest to find the love of his life, coming all the way to Lankā, only to be told that Seetā had been mercilessly slain by Indrajeet. Rāma was beyond any consolation. He was slipping into bouts of unconsciousness.

No words of solace can console a man who has just heard of the death of his beloved in the most unjust manner. Lakshmana understood that well. He did not offer any such comfort to Rāma. Instead, he gave vent to the most natural thoughts that arise in a man's heart in such a tragic situation. He said, 'It seems to me that all the virtues that you have steadfastly held all these years are quite useless. They have been unable to protect you from these adversities. Dharma is non-existent, as I see. If that were not the case, Rāvana should have been in hell by now for all his unrighteous acts, and someone like you, who has never gone astray from dharma, wouldn't have been subjected to this misery. There appears to be no connection between virtue and vice and their consequences. Or is it that even virtue, when faced with might, surrenders to power? I think it is better to not practise such powerless and ineffective virtues. Better to resort to raw might instead of this subservient virtue.'

Lakshmana continued his diatribe, 'If we believe that abiding by truth is dharma, then we have failed on that front too. Our father Dasharatha falsified his promise of your coronation to the people of Ayodhyā. Weren't you bound by that truth too?[10] I believe dharma was compromised that day when you chose to give up the kingdom and its wealth to follow our father's orders. A man with wealth is respected by everyone. Therefore, your decision to abandon your rightful wealth and kingdom was not quite desirable either. Even dharma can be achieved only when one has means.' Lakshmana was trying to provoke Rāma.

'You came to the forest giving up the kingdom to keep our father's word. And here this rākshasa abducted your wife and inflicted colossal pain on you. How can you take it lying down? I will surely not. I will get rid of this grief thrust on us by Indrajeet by my might. You must also take control of yourself and get ready to face the challenge. See yourself for what you really are.'[11]

Soon after that Vibhishana came and informed them of Indrajeet's trickery, bringing relief to Rāma, Lakshmana and the vānaras.

Lakshmana was an able partner of Rāma in every adventure of his since they were young boys. He was an outstanding warrior in his own right as well. In Lankā, he left the enemy floundering on multiple occasions. He slew many a mighty rākshasa, including Virupāksha and Atikāya. But his greatest feat was reserved for Indrajeet.

Vibhishana had divulged Indrajeet's plan of completing the yajna, which had the potential of making him invincible, at Nikumbhilā temple. Lakshmana had to kill Indrajeet before he could finish the yajna. Indrajeet was no ordinary warrior. This son of Rāvana was born Meghanād. He was popularly known by his sobriquet Indrajeet, the vanquisher of Indra, because he had defeated and captured Indra in a war with the devas. He had freed Indra only at Brahma deva's request.

The war between Indrajeet and Lakshmana was not for the faint-hearted. They were both courageous warriors, full of energy, and fearless. They were matched well in power and energy. They fought like two mighty lions on the battlefield. Their bodies were severely injured by each other's arrows, but they continued to duel, each trying to overpower the other with weapons and skills. Their bleeding bodies shone like Palāsh trees in full blossom.[12]

The crescendo of the sounds created by the strings of their bows and the booms of the celestial weapons kept increasing with each passing moment. They fought non-stop for three days and three nights. Finally, Lakshmana killed Indrajeet using the Aindrāstra, severing his head from his neck. Hanumāna and Vibhishana also had a role to play in the battle, but the attack was led and sustained by Lakshmana.

Rāma was joyous and proud of Lakshmana's achievement. He hugged Lakshmana tightly and even made him sit on his lap.

The defeat of Indrajeet was a breakthrough in the war with Rāvana. He was Rāvana's trump card, one who was to secure a decisive victory for him. Indrajeet had managed to torment the vānaras on multiple occasions before in the war and had even caused Rāma and Lakshmana to become unconscious twice. His death announced, loud and clear, that Rāvana's end was near.

Sometime later, after Rāma's coronation, a few rishis came to see him in Ayodhyā. They got talking about the war when one rishi mentioned that the fight between Lakshmana and Indrajeet was one of the highlights of the battle because Indrajeet was the strongest and the most skilled warrior in Rāvana's army, probably better than Rāvana himself. Everyone agreed.[13]

Lakshmana's reverence of Rāma was reciprocated in equal measure by Rāma's affection for him. Lakshmana and Seetā meant more to Rāma than even his own life.

Injuries are unavoidable on the battlefield. They are often worn as a badge of honour. There was one instance when Rāvana's shakti had pierced through Lakshmana's chest, making him unconscious. Seeing his dear brother in such a state made Rāma extremely agitated. He channelised his agitation into an unbearable force with the arrows he shot at Rāvana, making him leave the battlefield.

After Rāvana was pulled away by his sārthi, Rāma returned to find Lakshmana still unconscious. He couldn't hold back his tears anymore. 'What will I do with this life, all its pleasures, this victory or even the kingdom of Ayodhyā if Lakshmana were to die here like this? How will I ever find another brother like Lakshmana? He walked behind me as I left Ayodhyā for vanvās. Now I will follow him to the world of Yama. Every time I was overcome with grief in the forest, he was the one to hold me together. And now look at him, he doesn't even talk to me,' he lamented as the vānaras looked on helplessly.

Once again, Hanumāna came to the rescue. He brought herbs from the Himālayas and using them, Sushena resurrected Lakshmana.

On returning to Ayodhyā, Rāma decided to declare Lakshmana as the crown prince of Ayodhyā. But Lakshmana refused the position. Titles and authority weren't for him. His purpose in life was to serve Rāma. A title would come in the way of his service. He didn't want that. He happily let Bharata become the crown prince.

Before leaving for vanvās, Lakshmana sought blessings from his mother Sumitrā. Sumitrā didn't lament, and neither did she plead with Lakshmana not to go. Rather, she was proud of the decision her son had made of accompanying his elder brother voluntarily. She gave Lakshmana an important advice that day. 'See your father in Rāma, see me in Seetā and think of the forest itself as Ayodhyā. Serve them earnestly, as a son should,' she had said.[14]

This son of Sumitrā lived true to his mother's advice, every moment of his life.

> In some popular depictions of the Rāmāyana, Lakshmana is shown to be an angry young man who is ready to unleash his anger at the slightest provocation.

In Vālmiki Rāmāyana, as we see, Lakshmana is a lot more mature and composed. In fact, whenever Rāma lost his cool, Lakshmana was the one to calm him down.

There is a well-known story often narrated about Lakshmana's wife, Urmilā. It is said she made a promise to Lakshmana that she will sleep through the fourteen years of vanvās, accepting his share of sleep as well, so that Lakshmana could stay awake and serve Rāma and Seetā every single moment he was with them in the forest. This story does not appear in Vālmiki Rāmāyana. In Vālmiki Rāmāyana, there is no mention of Urmilā's life during the fourteen years of Rāma's vanvās.

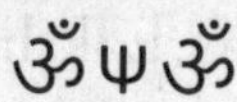

15

Rāmo Vigrahavān Dharma

Img. 3 Shri Rāma imagined as per the description in Vālmiki Rāmāyana. Art by Hitarth Bhatt

What was Rāma like? What was it about Rāma that everyone—young and old, women and men—showered their love on him? His citizens, his gurus, his friends like Nishādarāj Guha, the rishis he met during vanvās and the vānaras he met later in life, all came to adore him, nay, even lay down their lives willingly for him. What was Rāma's appeal to such a diverse set of people?

The narration of the Rāmāyana begins with a conversation between Rishi Vālmiki and Devarishi Nārada. Rishi Vālmiki wanted to know if there was anyone in their times who possessed all the sixteen qualities desirable in a man but rarely found together—virtue, valour, dharma, gratitude, fortitude, firm determination, strong character, good looks, predisposition to the well-being of all creatures, resplendence, erudition, capability, control on anger, justified anger when needed, composure and non-jealousy.

Nārada Muni knew one person who fitted the requirement perfectly—Rāma, the celebrated king of Kosala desh. He then proceeded to give an even more elaborate account of Rāma, describing his personality, his physique and his qualities. The description, tabulated here, is vivid enough to allow the reader to picturise Rāma.

Attributes of Rāma

Physical attributes:

विपुलांस—broad-shouldered	सुललाट—large and beautiful forehead
महाबाहु—strong-armed	समविभक्ताङ्ग—well-proportioned limbs
कम्बुग्रीव—conch-shaped neck	स्निग्धवर्ण—radiant complexion

महाहनु—prominent and strong cheeks	प्रतापवान्—mighty and powerful
महोरस्क—broad-chested	पीनवक्षा—strong, well-developed chest
महेष्वास—armed with a great bow (having a body strong enough to carry a bow)	विशालाक्ष—large, expansive eyes
गूढजत्रु—fleshy collar bones	लक्ष्मीवान्—lustrous body and personality
आजानुबाहु—long-armed, with arms reaching the knees	शुभलक्षण—having auspicious features
सुशिर—well-proportioned head	प्रियदर्शन—pleasant looking

Rishi Vālmiki refers to Rāma as श्याम, one who is dark-complexioned.

Personality attributes:

नियतात्मा—steady-natured	धर्मज्ञ—understands nuances of dharma
महावीर्य—valiant and powerful	आर्य—man of virtue
द्युति—dignified	सत्यसन्ध—true to his words
धृतिमान्—steadfast	ज्ञानसम्पन्न—omniscient
वशी—in control of his senses	शुचि—pure and devout
बुद्धिमान्—intelligent	वश्य—obedient to elders
नीतिमान्—learned in statecraft	प्रजानाम् हिते रतः—committed to the welfare of people
वाग्मी—proficient in speech	स्वस्य धर्मस्य रक्षित—protector of his dharma
समाधिमान्—attentive and focused	स्वजनस्य रक्षित—protector of his subjects and allies

स्मृतिमान्—highly retentive memory	सर्वलोकप्रिय—beloved of all
धनुर्वेदे निष्ठितः—skilled in archery and warfare	अदीनात्मा—undaunted and cheerful
सर्वशास्त्रार्थतत्त्वज्ञः—learned in scriptures	सर्वदा अभिगत—always approachable
प्रतिभानवान्—endowed with presence of mind	सर्वसमः एव—equitably disposed towards all

'Rāma is profound and calm as the ocean and steadfast as the Himalayas. He is as powerful as Vishnu, as good looking as the moon, as fiery as death when angry, as forgiving as the earth, as generous as Kuber and as truthful as Dharma[1] himself,' said Nārada, summing up Rāma's qualities.[2]

Rāma, the Warrior

Rāma, as we are told in Vālmiki Rāmāyana, is exceptionally strong and an extraordinary warrior. His strength is abundantly evident in the epic. He was not even sixteen when he guarded the yajna of Vishvāmitra and got rid of the menace of Māreecha and Subāhu, and Tātaka before them. Immediately after that, he lifted the bow of Shiva in Mithilā, which even 5,000 young men found difficult to drag. When Parashurāma heard of this parākram of Rāma, he wasn't amused. He viewed Rāma's breaking of Shiva's bow as an affront to the devas. As the entourage of the newly-married couples headed to Ayodhyā, Parashurāma stopped them and challenged Rāma to string Vishnu's bow. 'If you have it in you, string this bow of Vishnu,' he roared.

Parashurāma was a veteran and greatly feared figure. He had rendered the earth devoid of warriors twenty-one times, it was believed. When he came to meet Rāma, the latter was only a young boy, recently married, returning home with his new bride. But in addition to having physical strength, he was intuitively wise and endowed with the power of excellent speech.

Parashurāma's anger was coming from a position of arrogance and condescension. Rāma had to make Parashurāma understand that his feat of lifting and breaking the Shiva Dhanush wasn't a stroke of luck. Nor was it an attempt at challenging the authority of any deva. He put forth his position politely but forcefully, mincing no words, 'I am aware of your achievements and respect your exploits. But do not treat me as a weakling. I am endowed with all qualities of a warrior. Watch me perform my feat right in front of you.' Saying this, he took the mighty dhanush from Parashurāma's hands, strung the bow and placed his arrow on the bow, ready to shoot.

It was an incredible act. The great Parashurāma had met his match.[3]

Rāma's exemplary skills in warfare were exhibited during their stay in Dandakāranya as well. They spent more than eleven years in the region during which Rāma and Lakshmana killed innumerable, menace-creating rākshasas to safeguard the rishis and the forest dwellers. In the battle with Khara and Dushana in Panchavati, Rāma single-handedly killed 14,000 rākshasa warriors in one day.

His strength was evident in the feats he performed to convince Sugreeva that he was more than capable of killing Vāli, and he eventually killed Vāli with only a single arrow.

Throughout the war in Lankā, including the last major battle with Rāvana, which Rishi Vālmiki calls 'रामरावणयोर्युद्धं रामरावणयोरिव—one without a parallel', Rāma showed his domination every time he stepped on the battlefield. Besides Rāvana, Kumbhakarna and Makarāksha also fell to his arrows.

Kumbhakarna was an unrestrained force of nature. All of Rāma's major commanders tried in vain to fight and subdue him. Kumbhakarna was on a rampage, devouring the vānaras he captured, licking their blood off his lips. Even Sugreeva barely escaped being captured by him. Rāma was angry seeing this devastation caused by Kumbhakarna. He gave his bow a loud twang, announcing his intention of taking the colossal giant head-on.

Kumbhakarna was so strong that even the powerful arrow which Rāma used to kill Vāli was ineffective on him. The giant rākshasa seemed to just suck in the arrows shot by Rāma into his body, completely unaffected, even as he continued to wield his blood-smeared mudgar, chasing away the vānaras. Subsequently, Rāma brought out a potent weapon called Vyāvaya. This had the desired effect—it severed Kumbhakarna's arm that was holding the mudgar. But the rākshasa still didn't give up. He uprooted a tree with his other hand and continued his attack. Using another powerful arrow, Rāma chopped off his other arm too. Then with two back-to-back arrows, he chopped Kumbhakarna's lower limbs. His next arrow severed Kumbhakarna's head. The momentum was such that the head travelled all the way to the ocean and fell there.[4]

Makarāksha was another powerful rākshasa commander of Rāvana. He had a strong desire for vengeance as Rāma had killed his father, Khara. He challenged Rāma to a duel. 'Since the day you killed my father in Dandaka, I have been roaming the forests, burning with the desire to kill you. I will devour you like a lion devours his prey. Pick up whichever weapon you have learnt. I will fight you with that,' he said.

Rāma laughed at him. 'Why are you bragging?' he asked. You cannot fight a battle with words alone. Do not forget, that day in Dandaka I killed not just your father Khara and uncle Dushana, but 14,000 rākshasas as well, single-handedly. And today, I will satisfy the jackals and the vultures with your flesh.'

A fierce battle ensued. The twangs of their bows resounded through the battleground like repeated rolls of thunder. Makarāksha was quite a warrior. He matched Rāma's pace in shooting arrows. Together, they shot so many arrows that, Rishi Vālmiki tells us, the entire earth seemed to be covered with a veil of their arrows. Rāma started getting angry. He aimed at Makarāksha's bow and broke it. Then in quick succession, he killed Makarāksha's chariot horses and broke his chariot, grounding the rākshasa. The fight continued as Makarāksha employed other weapons and techniques to get back into the battle. But he couldn't and subsequently fell to Rāma's Pātakāstra, the weapon of fire, his heart torn apart.[5]

The sheer magic of Rāma's dexterity was once again on full display in all its majesty the day after Indrajeet's death. Rāvana sent some of his commanders to the battlefield with instructions to gherao Rāma specifically, and kill him. The commanders marched into the battlefield with their armies. A furious battle waged between them and the vānaras. Seeing the vānara side taking a toll, Rāma jumped in with his illustrious bow and began showering a volley of arrows at the rākshasas. He entered among his opponents and began to burn them with his fiery arrows, like the sun which appears in the sky and slashes the sheath of clouds.

The force of Rāma's arrows was so strong and his actions so swift that the rākshasas could see themselves getting hit and injured but couldn't spot where Rāma was, just like a strong gush of wind that uproots huge trees but remains unseen. Like a man deluded by sensual pleasures cannot identify the ātmā seated in the body, the rākshasa army couldn't see Rāma. All they could see was the devastation he was inflicting on them on the battlefield.

The soldiers spoke among themselves, befuddled. 'O there you see Rāma, destroying the army of elephants. O no, he is over there, laying waste the fleet of chariots with his sharp arrows. O no, Rāma is somewhere here, killing our soldiers and their horses,' they exclaimed, trying to make sense of the situation. They were so confused that they even began attacking and killing warriors from their own side.

Sometimes they could see where Rāma was, at other times, they felt as if they were seeing thousands of Rāmas raining their ire on them. So swift were Rāma's manoeuvres, that while he was unseen, the outer edge of his golden bow seemed like a swiftly rotating band of fire. To the rākshasas falling to Rāma's assault, it appeared no less than a kāla chakra—the wheel of destruction.

That day, within a span of about three hours, Rāma destroyed 10,000 chariots, 18,000 elephants, 14,000 horses and horse warriors, and 200,000 rākshasa soldiers.[6]

Such was the valour and prowess of Rāma.

Shri Krishna makes a reference to Rāma's extraordinary warfare skills in the Srimad Bhagavad Geetā. In 'Vibhuti Yoga' in the tenth chapter, Krishna exhorts Arjuna to see divinity in what is most excellent and glorious. To explain 'most excellent and glorious', he gives many examples of things and people which are the 'best among the best'. In one of the verses, Krishna talks about Rāma. He says, 'रामः शस्त्रभृतामहम्'—among the warriors wielding weapons, I am Rāma. Rāma was indeed one of the best warriors to have ever walked on earth.[7]

Rāma, the Son

Dasharatha's heart lived in Rāma. Kaushalyā's joy was Rāma. Kaikeyi was excessively fond of Rāma, as were all the men and women in the kingdom.

Dasharatha had once told Kaikeyi about his eldest son, 'Rāma wins everyone over by his virtues. He soothes the poor and needy by offering timely help and charity. He wins the hearts of elders and teachers through his devotion and service. And the enemy, he conquers by the strength of his bow.'[8]

When Kaikeyi told Rāma of vanvās, he wasn't perturbed—not overtly at least. It took him no time to decide his path of action, which was to accept the commands of his father and stepmother. Any other decision would have been incorrect. His father's words were for him to obey. Rāma knew his father couldn't possibly have lived happily if his promise to Kaikeyi was falsified.

While Rāma had immense reverence for his father and mothers, he was not blind to the complexities and layers of their personalities. He was an astute judge of people after all, as the citizens of Ayodhyā had rightly observed. It wasn't lost on him that his father, who was otherwise a great king and much loved, had a weakness for Kaikeyi. Dasharatha's desire for her had led him to ignore his other wives. Though his heart was filled with pain, Dasharatha couldn't bring himself to deny Kaikeyi's unjustified demands, despite the fact that the decision of coronation was according to the family tradition of anointing the eldest son. Besides, it also had the backing of the people of Ayodhyā. Rāma had shared his thoughts about his father with Lakshmana during the early days of their vanvās.

Nonetheless, that did not diminish the stature of his father, or his stepmother, in his eyes. He revered them as an ideal son should. Rather, Rāma said that Kaikeyi's ill-will towards him was uncharacteristic of her. Whatever may be her equation with Dasharatha's other wives, she had always loved Rāma like her own son. The way the situation had shaped indicated the work of destiny at play. Rāma chose to willingly surrender to the larger design of nature. This action of his was just another instance of his profound understanding of context, time and place and how to use them all together to take his decisions.

That is why Rāma requested Bharata also that he should not hold any grudge against Kaikeyi. After the victory in Lankā, when his father came down from the heavens to bless him, Rāma asked him as well to forgive Kaikeyi.

There was only one regret that Rāma had having accepted the vanvās—not being able to fulfil his duties towards his mother, Kaushalyā.

But he ensured he did whatever he could for his mother. When giving away his wealth before leaving Ayodhyā to the people in his service and patronage, Rāma did not miss giving gifts to people in Kaushalyā's service and patronage too. He wanted to ensure they took care of her in his absence. At every opportunity Rāma made it a point to remind Bharata to take care of Kaushalyā like his own mother.

Putra is the word used for a son in Sanskrit. It means one who saves his father from falling into hell named put[9]. Rāma not only saved his father but also brought lasting glory to his entire lineage.

Rāma, the Husband

The war in Lankā had ended with Rāvana's death and Rāma's victory. This was the moment both Rāma and Seetā were waiting for. But the way the events unfolded when they met after months of separation was a tragic irony. Rāma's words casting doubts on her chastity were so stinging that Seetā herself asked for a pyre to be lit. It was beneath her dignity to argue about the accusations using mere words. She left it to Agni deva to prove to all what her true character was.

This incident leaves a bitter taste among many readers of Vālmiki Rāmāyana who do not take kindly to Rāma's words. But to judge either Rāma or Seetā based on any one event will be unfair to the bond they shared.

Every second of their separation had been torture for both Rāma and Seetā. How many times had Rāma expressed to Seetā that she meant more to him than his own life! How many times had he exclaimed that without Seetā even heaven would give him no joy!

To accompany Rāma to the forest was Seetā's decision. She earnestly made her case to go along with Rāma. Living without Seetā wasn't something Rāma preferred, either. But he didn't wish to force it upon Seetā. As he confessed to her, it was important for him to know what her opinion on the matter was. Life in the forest was not going to be easy. Seetā had to know that and desire that. It would have been unfair on his part to push her into it if she wasn't ready. At the same time, he was delighted when Seetā insisted on accompanying him.

Rāma's love for Seetā was very deep. He couldn't bear seeing her in the smallest pain. He shot a Brahmāstra on a mere crow for hurting her. He killed Virādh for attempting to kidnap her. He commanded Lakshmana to punish Shurpanakhā because she tried to harm Seetā. The consequence of this was an attack by 14,000 rākshasas led by Khara and Dushana. Rāma tackled and killed them, all by himself.

Rāma went to catch the deer only because it would make Seetā happy. Since her abduction, Rāma's mind was never at peace. He missed her more and more, every passing day. Hanumāna was correct when he told Seetā that sleep had evaded Rāma all those months because his mind was busy thinking about her. Rāma missed her sorely. He missed her sleeping by his side using his muscular arm as her pillow. Every memory of her caused him to break down. He cried like a child. He threatened to devastate the world if Seetā was not found.

For her, he achieved the impossible—he crossed a hundred yojanas across the ocean, entered Lankā and killed the mighty Rāvana in his own home ground with just an army of vānaras. And yet, when they met, here he was, telling Seetā she was free to go wherever she wished, only to provoke her for agni parikshā. This wasn't a mere whim. It was extremely important for him to ensure no one casted aspersions on Seetā about her conduct as Rāvana's captive. That was Seetā's concern too—that no one should think lowly of Rāma because of her. Hence, she stayed in Lankā till Rāma came for her and did not leave with Hanumāna although that would have set her free earlier.

For both Rāma and Seetā, the reputation of the other mattered more than their own pain. Seetā understood well—that he did everything due to his concern for her reputation. That is why when Rāma said in all sincerity that he did not have even an iota of doubt about her character but had to ensure everyone else understood that unequivocally, she trusted him completely and accepted him unconditionally like she always had.

In a society where polygamy was not only allowed but also preferred, especially for kings, Rāma chose monogamy. That underlines his love for Seetā and the depth of the bond they shared.

Rāma, the King

In Ayodhyā Kānda, Rishi Vālmiki enumerates the personality traits of Rāma. These were the qualities of Rāma that made Dasharatha think about him as a suitable heir to the throne after him. Some of the adjectives the rishi uses are as follows:[10]

उत्तरोत्तरयुक्तीनां वक्ता वाचस्पतिर्यथा—Eloquent strategist and speaker like Brihaspati	अमोघक्रोधहर्षः—One who knew how to impactfully use (display of) anger and pleasure
देशकालवित्—One who understood the context of place and time	त्यागसंयमकालवित्—One who understood when to let go and when to show restraint
पुरुषसारज्ञः—One who could gauge the potential of people	स्वदोषपरदोषवित्—One who was well aware of flaws of self and others

पुरुषान्तरकोविदः—A good negotiator with different parties	प्रग्रहानुग्रहयोर्यथान्यायं विचक्षणः—One who was perceptive enough to judiciously protect and punish, as required
संवृताकारः गुप्तमन्त्रः—One who did not let his emotions show and could keep his thoughts and decisions to himself	आयकर्मण्युपायज्ञ स्सन्दृष्टव्ययकर्मवित्— One who knew the right means of raising revenue and spending money in the prescribed manner
वैहारिकाणां शिल्पानां विज्ञाता—One who understood art as well as modes of entertainment	धर्मकामार्थतत्त्वज्ञः—One who had deep understanding of interplay of dharma, kāma and artha

When Dasharatha called his assembly to deliberate the suitability of Rāma to ascend the throne of Ayodhyā after him, he asked his ministers to share why they believed, if they believed, that Rāma could do justice to the position. Among other things, the ministers, in support of Rāma, used some very interesting phrases to describe Rāma's qualities that made him suitable for the high position. The broader message is captured in the chapter 'A Twist of Fate'. The adjectives are as follows:[11]

विजितेन्द्रियः—One who has achieved control over his senses and desires	मृदुः—Soft-spoken
स्थिरचित्तः—One with a steady mind	विनिर्वृत्तो धर्मश्चापि श्रिया सह—One who knows how to blend both dharma and artha effectively for the best impact

नाविजित्य निवर्तते—One who doesn't return without a victory (always victorious)	पौरान् स्वजनवन्नित्यं कुशलं परिपृच्छति—He asks about the well-being of the citizens and their family
व्यसनेषु मनुष्याणां भृशं भवति दुःखितः—He becomes concerned when someone is in a problem	उत्सवेषु च सर्वेषु पितेव परितुष्यति—Participates and shares their (of citizens) joy in happy occasions as a father does
स्मितपूर्वाभिभाषी—One who always smiles as he speaks	वृद्धसेवी—One who serves elders
प्रजापालनतत्त्वज्ञः—One who understands how to govern	न रागोपहतेन्द्रियः—One who is not afflicted by rage
नाऽस्य क्रोधः प्रसादश्च निरर्थोऽस्ति—His anger and favour are not without a purpose	हन्त्येव नियमाद्वध्यान्—He rightfully kills (punishes) those who deserve to be slain

As an astute judge of people, Rāma made an accurate assessment of Hanumāna in their first meeting itself. The same trait helped him develop a deep bond of friendship with Sugreeva, even though Vāli could have been a more powerful ally. Even when Sugreeva wanted to put him through a test to assess whether he was capable of killing Vāli, Rāma happily went along. He understood the context and the need of the situation, as well as Sugreeva's concerns—it was an indication of Sugreeva's prudence.

His strategic thinking was evident in his decision of inducting Vibhishana to their side and immediately crowning him the king of Lankā.

Rāma's anger also had a strategic intent. He knew where to show anger and how to channelise it. He used anger as his source of strength to rout the enemy on the battlefield. His anger was cause-oriented and ended once the objective was achieved. This applied even to an enemy like Rāvana. That is why, once the war was over, he encouraged Vibhishana to give Rāvana the cremation according to his status as a king.

Individual instances apart, the culmination of Rāma's acumen as a king was in the establishment of Rāma Rājya.

It was not that Rāma was devoid of human emotions. It was not that he wasn't overcome with longing, sorrow, anger, grief, love or pain. Nor was he averse to expressing his emotions. Quite the contrary, he experienced all these emotions deeply and opened his heart fully. Rishi Vālmiki has spared no words to describe the delicate emotions of romance that Rāma and Seetā shared, both in Ayodhyā and during vanvās. When the entourage was returning to Ayodhyā from Lankā in Vibhishana's Pushpak vimān, Rāma made Seetā sit in his lap. Seetā blushed but happily complied. Throughout the journey, he pointed out to her the different places he had been to look for her when she was in Lankā. Similarly, the emotions that Rāma experienced during his separation from Seetā, as the rishi has described, were so intense that they can move the toughest of us into tears.

But there was one thing that stood him apart—the play of emotions did not overpower him and make him take rash or impulsive actions. He never lost sight of the role he was expected to play at that point in time. Objectivity was never sacrificed at the altar of impulses. The bigger picture was never lost sight of for short-term gratifications.

With Rāma, every emotion had a purpose. His emotions made him more empathetic and more accepting of others.

He could have chosen to rebel and not agree to vanvās. Probably, people in Ayodhyā would have stood by him given their love for him. He could have rejected the unfair demands of Kaikeyi. But he didn't.

He could have returned to Ayodhyā after Dasharatha's death. Bharata, Rishi Vashishtha, Rishi Jābāli, people of Ayodhyā—all of them wanted him to return. But Rāma didn't. Not because of some rigid stubbornness but because he was acutely aware that it would be setting the wrong precedence for the citizens by compromising the sanctity of relations, contracts and commitments.

Even in vanvās, Rāma never forgot his role as a representative of the royal family that had the allegiance of all the janapadas of Bhāratavarsha. He was aware that it was his dharma to safeguard the people dwelling in the forests. Hence, he readily agreed to protect the rishis and forest dwellers from the menace of the rākshasas, despite Seetā's initial misgivings.

After Vibhishana was made the king, he wanted to offer gifts to Rāma. Rāma declined them. He requested Vibhishana to give the jewels and gems to the vānaras who had put their life at stake for his victory. They deserved the gifts more than him. Their actions were selfless, done only to help him.

His profound understanding of dharma and social constructs made him answer Vāli's stinging criticism with conviction and a sense of responsibility. As much as he was generous and kind, he was not averse to punishing those who deserved to be punished.

People of Ayodhyā rightly called him देशकालवित्—one who understood the context of place and time. Nārada called him धर्मज्ञ—one who understands the nuances of dharma. But the phrase used by Māreecha defines Rāma's personality in totality. Māreecha, while describing Rāma to Rāvana, had said 'रामो विग्रहवान् धर्मः—Rāma is the embodiment of dharma'. Not only did Rāma understand dharma but he also embodied dharma. It pervaded his entire being.

चरितं रघुनाथस्य शतकोटिप्रविस्तरम् ।
एकैकमक्षरं पुंसां महापातकनाशनम् ॥

ॐ ψ ॐ

16

Rāma's Rājya

Rāma received his first practical lesson in Rāja Dharma from Rishi Vishvāmitra, en route to Siddhāshram. Rishi Vishvāmitra had said:

नृशंसमनृशंसं वा प्रजारक्षणकारणात्।
पातकं वा सदोषं वा कर्तव्यं रक्षता सता।
राज्यभारनियुक्तानामेष धर्मस्सनातनः।।

A just king should not shirk from performing any action, even action which appears cruel or apparently criminal and objectionable if that contributes to प्रजारक्षण—welfare and protection of his people. This, indeed, is the eternal dharma of those who are appointed to bear the burden of ruling a kingdom.[1]

Rāma remained true to this lesson all his life—social welfare before self—even if it came at the cost of personal sacrifices. This was the premise of Rāma Rājya.

A brief description of Rāma Rājya comes twice in the Rāmāyana. The first instance is in Bāla Kānda, and is narrated by Nārada Muni; the second time it appears is towards the end of the book, in Yuddha Kānda, after Rāma's coronation.

Nārada Muni tells us, 'The people in Rāma's kingdom were joyous, content, healthy and righteous. There was no fear of hunger or robbery. The state itself was prosperous, overflowing with grains and food.'[2]

Rishi Vālmiki confirms that in Rāma's kingdom, people were happy, virtuous, healthy and without any grief. They lived a contented life, engaged in their affairs in a righteous manner. All people practised their professions, fulfilling their responsibilities dutifully. With their minds focused on Rāma, the communities co-existed peacefully, without any strife.[3] In Rāma's reign, there were neither floods nor famines. People lived their full lives.

What does it take to create such an affluent, righteous and contented nation-state which is in complete harmony with nature and its surroundings?

Rishi Chanakya states in a mantra in *Arthashāstra*:

सुखस्य मूलं धर्मः | धर्मस्य मूलम् अर्थः |
अर्थस्य मूलं राज्यम् ||

A happy society rests on dharma. Upholding dharma rests on wealth. Wealth creation depends on governance (state).

Such a happy, prosperous, virtuous, just, inclusive and peaceful society can only exist when the state has some necessary characteristics. These are:

- The state has governance systems tuned to the needs and aspirations of its people.
- The state provides enough wealth creation opportunities to everyone.
- There is a correct balance between rights and responsibilities, regulations and individual freedom, that allows everyone to not just survive but grow and thrive while maintaining order in the society.
- There are effective and timely justice dispensation mechanisms.
- The administration is focused on the welfare of every part of the society equally, without exploiting any segment.
- The state preserves its natural resources and respects the laws of nature. In such a state nature, too, remains bountiful.

In essence, Rāma Rājya was a perfect, well-governed state owing to Rāma's administrative acumen and keen understanding of dharma.

When Bharata came to Chitrakoot to request him to return to Ayodhyā, Rāma, unaware of the latest developments, began asking Bharata about the affairs of the kingdom by way of questions, covering a range of topics.[4] An account of the conversation between Rāma and Bharata is summarised here. It gives a good insight into how Rāma would have managed the affairs of the state during his reign.

Minister Appointment, Decision-Making and Project Management

- Apt counsel by trustworthy experts and well-learned ministers is pivotal to a king's success. Hence, the appointment of able ministers with the right skills-set for the right kind of jobs is a very important task for the king.
- Some qualities to look for in the ministers and officers are—those who the king can get along with, are courageous, have the expertise (in their fields), have self-control, come from good families, are perceptive, are incorruptible and are full of integrity.
- Governance related decisions should not be taken in isolation, nor should they be discussed with everybody. Such decisions should typically involve 3–4 persons who understand the topic and can maintain confidentiality.
- Decisions and discussions of national interest taken by the king along with his group of ministers should not be made public intentionally or unintentionally, without consent.
- While appointing ambassadors for other kingdoms, the king must ensure the person's loyalty lies fully with his kingdom. The messenger should be erudite and articulate; he should have been born in the same kingdom as the king.
- Before initiating projects, a king must determine tasks that are low hanging fruits and can yield big results with limited effort. Once such tasks

are determined, the king must get them started immediately and not procrastinate.

- Allocation of work must be done after proper consideration of the capabilities and merit of the people.

Justice Delivery

- Well-learned ministers should consider every case of disbursement of justice for all citizens in distress, dispassionately and objectively, irrespective of whether the citizen is rich or poor.
- An honest person must not be punished out of malice or impatience before a proper inquiry is undertaken to prove the crime. The tears that fall from the eyes of the falsely accused destroy the children and wealth of the ruler who rules according to his whims and fancies.
- A person caught for theft or wrongdoing, whose guilt is proven by evidence, should not be set free out of greed for money (bribe).
- Punishment must be commensurate with the crime, not so aggressive that it agitates the citizens.
- A learned person involved in fomenting trouble, a person engaged in corrupting the officers and employees of the state, a brave man overpowered by lust and luxury (so much that he can conspire against the state), must be slain. A king who does not kill them is himself killed in due course.

Administration, Citizen Welfare and Security

- Trade and enterprise are the cornerstone of a kingdom's prosperity. All those engaged in economic activities and resource generation (farming, animal husbandry, etc.) must be taken care of.
- Expenditures must be commensurate with (that is, lower than) income.
- Taxes should be appropriate and not a burden on the people. If the taxes are excruciating, the citizens scorn at the king like women scorn at a lustful lover (typically, scriptures prescribe tax at one-sixth of the produce of the citizens).
- The king's fort should always be well-stocked with ammunition, food, water and requisite tools required for any kind of work.
- Never underestimate any enemies, especially those who were defeated once and have returned to fight again.
- A well-established network of spies who operate within the kingdom as well as outside is critical for the kingdom's security.
- Appropriate wages should be paid to the army and other employees, and on time. Wages if not paid on time can make the workers hostile and corrupt, leading to a great calamity for the employer.
- Soldiers who are courageous, powerful, skilled in warfare and have proven heroic exploits must be felicitated and honoured.
- Patronage should only be given to the deserving, not the underserving.

- Women's safety and happiness are the king's responsibility. But not just men, one must not trust even women blindly and be careful about disclosing secrets to them (to avoid the possibility of honey traps and leakage of state secrets).

Discipline and Accessibility

- A king must have discipline in waking up and sleeping. Waking up every day on time (before sunrise) is important, so is not indulging in excessive sleep or at the wrong hours.
- The last part of the night (the time before sunrise) should be spent thinking about administration and statecraft, and planning for the day.
- A king must be accessible to his people. He must present himself every day on the royal pathway before the people at a given time during the first half of the day.
- While a king must be approachable to his people, he should also be careful about not letting his employees get too close so they take him for granted. The dignity of the position must be maintained.
- A king must allocate adequate time for attending to all the three expedients of life, that is, dharma—religious practices, artha—administration and resource generation for material prosperity, and kāma—sensual pleasure and entertainment. All three are important and a king must know to balance them for his and his kingdom's happiness.

Fourteen Areas to Watch Out for the King

- Gratification of the five senses
- Planning alone regarding the affairs of the kingdom
- Consultation with people who are not proficient
- Failure to implement decisions
- Inability to keep the counsel secret
- Opening many battlefronts at once
- Omission of auspicious practices
- Non-belief in the wisdom of the Vedas
- Not keeping the company of the wise
- Falsehood
- Anger
- Inattention
- Procrastination
- Indolence

Many of the administrative do's and don'ts mentioned here are seen in the Mahābhārata as well as in Chanakya's *Arthashāstra*. For example:

- Vidura tells Dhritarāshtra that there are two ways in which resources are wasted—not giving to the deserving and giving to the undeserving.
- Bhishma tells Yudhishthira that a king who wishes to enjoy power must not destroy the wealth of his citizens, and all dues owed by the king to the citizens must be repaid on time.
- Chanakya emphasises a king's ability to give 'yathārtha danda', which literally means 'commensurate punishment', not too aggressive nor too lax, just right enough for the gravity of the crime, to punish the guilty and deter the rest.

Rāma's discourse with Bharata is a testimony of his deep understanding of Nitishāshtras and Dharmashāstras, which talk extensively about how a king should govern.

But understanding itself is not enough to establish a happy society. The understanding must translate into right decision-making and action. Rāma could make that happen.

What was it about Rāma that other leaders struggle to achieve?

The last part of Rishi Chānakya's mantra gives an insight into this question as well. He says:

राज्स्य मूलं इन्द्रियजय।

Good governance depends on control of the senses and mind (of the leader).

How well a state is governed eventually depends on its leadership (in this case, the king). Crystal clear objectivity, absence of any kind of bias, detached thought process, understanding of context and dharma, long term vision, are important aspects of leadership. These can come only when one's mind and senses are firmly under control, not otherwise.

Rāma had achieved that control. He has been described as vashi, niyatātmā, vijitendriya and so on, which imply a person who is steady-minded and has won over his senses and desires.

Rāma Rājya can happen only when the leader has the qualities and acumen of Rāma.

ॐ ψ ॐ

Part 3

Epilogue

17

A Short Note on the Approach to Understanding Itihāsa

There are two events in Uttara Kānda on which many scholars, seekers and readers have divergent and strong opinions. Some consider Rāma's actions in these situations unfair. Some others consider Uttara Kānda as a later-day interpolation and reject the authenticity of the two events.

As the events are popular, often discussed, and found both in the Baroda Critical Edition of Vālmiki Rāmāyana as well as Gita Press's Vālmiki Rāmāyana, I have included them here in the Epilogue.

Our itihāsas are case studies for us to learn from and implement in our own lives as relevant. Most importantly, the stories from the lives of our ancestors underscore the fact that dharma sankatas are a reality of life. Even Rāma and Krishna had to deal with such ethical dilemmas. Often, alternatives available to resolve the sankatas may seem sub-optimal. But decisions, we still must make. How we navigate our dharma sankatas will depend on our strength of character as well as our mind, value system and viveka buddhi.

The objective of the study of itihāsas, dharma shāstras and education in general, is just that—to help develop our discrimination faculty, character and value system. Hence, while judgement comes naturally to us when reading itihāsa, instead of outrightly dismissing that which seemingly contradicts our beliefs, we must seek to understand whether there is something we can learn from the events that would help us deal with our own dharma sankatas better, keeping in mind our current realities and contexts.

The first step to that would be to ask the right questions about the motivations for the decisions made, the contexts in which they were made and the scope of responsibility of the person making the decisions in relation to the society he or she was a part of. The last part is especially crucial—what could be the right action for an administrator or an official may not necessarily be so for a subject or a common person. Likewise, what seems like an undesirable act for a subject may be important for an administrator to undertake. For example, it may be important for an administrator to employ violence, if the situation so demands, to ensure peace and security in the society but that doesn't mean an individual has the right to use violence at will to resolve conflicts. That latter would push the society into anarchy and chaos.

The next step would be to understand what alternatives were available to the individual and the possible implications of not making the decision that was taken. Such an approach is more likely to help us form a more balanced and objective view of the events. Even then, we may not get a binary right or wrong answer because we play multiple roles in our lives and being true to one role may often mean compromising on another. Such is the nature of dharma sankatas.

Let's consider the two events.

18

Shambuka Vadha

It was said that during the reign of Rāma, nothing untoward ever happened in the kingdom. This was due to the dharmic and just rule of Rāma that encouraged the citizens to lead equally righteous lives as their king. No one died without having lived their full life. There were no young widows, nor parents who had to see the death of their children.

Then one day, an event took place. A father came crying to Rāma's court, carrying the body of his seemingly dead son. No reason for the death could be ascertained.

The sorrowful father blamed Rāma for his son's death. 'It seems that some unworthy act has been done by the king or he has allowed unjust activities to foster in the kingdom that has caused this. My son was otherwise perfectly healthy,' the father wailed.

Rāma was overcome with grief. He called upon his gurus to deliberate what could be the reason for such an unprecedented event. Nārada gave his opinion, 'It seems like someone is indulging in certain acts in your kingdom that he is not qualified to perform. You must investigate if someone in your kingdom has undertaken rituals and tapasyā he is not supposed to, leading to such an unnatural event.'

Rāma decided to tour his kingdom to find out if someone was indulging in such acts. Somewhere in the southern direction, by a lake, he saw a man engaged in an aggressive penance, hanging upside down. Rāma was astonished. He accosted the person and enquired his identity and the reason for such intense practice.

Still hanging upside down, the man said, 'I am Shambuka. I have undertaken this tapasyā because I wish to achieve deity-hood in this body itself. I wish to conquer the heavens with the strength I gain through this tapasyā.' As soon as Shambuka uttered these words, Rāma took out his sword and severed Shambuka's head.

In the palace, the boy who was thought to be dead opened his eyes and sat up. The aberration had been corrected; natural order had been restored.[1]

This incident is often narrated to brand the Rāmāyana as a casteist text because Shambuka was born in a shudra family. The premise of the argument is that Rāma killed a Shambuka, a shudra, just for doing tapasyā.

But that would be an incorrect conclusion.

Shambuka was punished not because he was just doing tapasyā, but because of the purpose of his tapasyā. His objective was to break the laws of nature—to achieve deity-hood in the human body was unnatural and not possible for any human, no matter what his caste. In Rāma's rājya, nature was bountiful because people lived in harmony with nature. When the balance is disturbed, unnatural consequences are bound to happen. Shambuka was guilty of attempting to disrupt this harmony leading to an unnatural consequence (the death of the child). It was Rāma's duty to punish the guilty and restore nature's balance.

Trishanku, one of Rāma's ancestors, had a similar desire, to enter heaven in his human body. He urged his guru, Rishi Vashishtha, to perform rituals that would make it happen. The rishi refused outright because it entailed challenging the laws of nature. Trishanku then approached the rishi's sons. They too refused to grant such an outrageous request even though Trishanku was the king.

The misinterpretation of the Shambuka incident occurs because of the error of viewing the episode only through the lens of identity. Without the imposition of the identity lens, there is nothing negative in the incident.

The question to be asked here is—what was the motivation for Rāma's action? Would he have behaved differently if a non-shudra had performed an intense ritual that would have caused harm to some innocent citizen? The answer is a resounding 'No'!

Rāma's past actions show he would have been unbiased. Rāma killed Rāvana, even though Rāvana was the son of a brāhmin. He killed Tātakā, a woman, although scriptures prohibit the killing of women. There is a respectful mention of two non-brāhmin, non-kshatriya tapasvis in the Rāmāyana—Shravan and Shabari. Shravan was the son of a vaishya father and a shudra mother. Shabari was a shudra. No one stopped either of them from engaging in tapasyā.

The sustainability of a society depends on protecting nature and its laws. It behoves an administrator to punish those who act in a way that harms the sustainability of society. It behoves an administrator to do all that must be done to protect innocent subjects. Rāma understood his responsibilities extremely well.

For him, there was no grievance too trivial, no citizen unworthy. He did everything he could to ensure every person was justly treated and those who deserved to be punished were rightfully punished. Rāma had explained to Vāli in Kishkindhā that it was a king's moral duty to protect the innocent and punish the guilty, whoever the person may be. Dharma must prevail, irrespective of the position of the culprit.

Shambuka's crime was not his birth but his attempt to transgress the laws of nature.

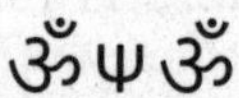

19

Forsaken

'I so wish to visit the charming forests and āshrams again,' said Seetā, as she rested her head on Rāma's lap. 'So it will be,' said Rāma loving stroking her forehead. The years since Rāma's coronation had passed by swiftly. While life had been comfortable, Rāma had become busy with the affairs of the kingdom. Seetā missed their time in the forest when he was only hers. There was not a moment in those thirteen years before the fated Lankā tragedy that the two were separated. Nevertheless, the present days were also among their happiest. Seetā was pregnant. Rāma couldn't stop pampering her. When Seetā pined for the forests and made the wish, she didn't know that her desire was to come true soon, but in the most unexpected manner.

A few days later, Rāma was entertaining some artists and storytellers in his court. He also used these men as his eyes and ears to learn of the happenings, talks and gossip in the kingdom. One of them was a man named Bhadra. 'Tell me Bhadra, what are the talks among the citizens about me, Seetā, Lakshmana, Bharata and other members of the royal family? A king should always know what's been spoken of. Tell me without hesitation. I will continue to do what the people think is good and give up what they think is not desirable.'

'The citizens often discuss your Lankā exploits. They are in awe of them,' said Bhadra and abruptly stopped short of saying what he was about to say next. Rāma noticed his unease and convinced him to speak out whatever he had heard. 'The citizens have been gossiping about you and Seetā,' said Bhadra, 'and they say, "Rāvana carried her in his lap and took her to Lankā. There she stayed for so many months among the rākshasas in the beautiful Ashokavātikā, which is known to be the place for Rāvana's indulgences. Does Rāma not feel any aversion when touching Seetā? Because Rāma has put up with such lapses of Seetā, we are having to tolerate those of our wives too. As citizens, we have no choice but to follow the precedent set by our king." This is what I heard.' Bhadra was uncomfortable, unable to hide his embarrassment.

Rāma was shocked. He couldn't believe his ears. He looked at the other men present there. 'Is that true? Have you all heard something like that too?' he asked. 'Yes Mahārāja, we have heard these talks among the citizens as well,' they said with their eyes downcast, unable to look at Rāma directly. Shaken, Rāma took their leave and called for his brothers. Something had to be done to handle the situation. A king's conduct must be beyond reproach. The final award of justice rests with the king. Hence, he needs to ensure that every citizen trusts him completely, without even a speck of doubt about the king's character or intentions.

The brothers came and were surprised to see Rāma's countenance. He was in a state of extreme grief. Tears had swelled up in his eyes. He told them about the falsehood spread widely about him and

Seetā among the people of Ayodhyā. 'Though I had no doubt about Seetā's chastity, I knew people may raise questions about her character. Hence, I provoked Seetā in Lankā. And Seetā proved herself by undergoing the agni parikshā. But now such talks have been doing rounds among the people,' he said and stopped. A whirlwind of emotions was rising in his heart.

He composed himself and spoke again, 'I should not do anything that makes the citizens look down upon me or lose trust in me. I can't bear losing my reputation. Hence, I have decided to leave Seetā. There has been no bigger pain than this that I ever had to deal with before.' He ordered Lakshmana to drive Seetā to the outskirts of the kingdom and leave her in the forest beyond the banks of Gangā. 'Seetā wished to spend time in the forests and āshrams. May her wish be fulfilled now,' he choked as he spoke, unable to control his tears any longer.

The next morning, Lakshmana took Seetā in the chariot. Seetā was under the impression that she was going to visit a few āshrams and would return to Ayodhyā in a few days. She couldn't understand why Lakshmana looked so grim and sombre. Only on reaching the banks of Gangā did Lakshmana disclose Rāma's decision to her. 'I would have preferred death to saying what I am about to say. Please do not be upset with me because I am helpless in this. There are a lot of unworthy things being said about you in Ayodhyā. This has agitated Rāma's mind so much that he has decided to leave you. I know your character is without blemish. But Rāma has taken the defamation to heart. May you live comfortably in this sacred land of the rishis, in their āshrams as was your wish,' said Lakshmana, with a heavy heart.

Seetā was dumbstruck. She couldn't speak for a few minutes. Tears rolled down her eyes like streams of water. Then she spoke as a sahadharmachārini would: 'Lakshmana, you have only done your duty, as you must. Ideally, I should have given up my life in such a situation, but I am carrying Rāma's child. It is not right for me to do so now. But do convey my message to Rāma. "Rāma, I know that you are fully confident of my chastity and the purity of my character. You also know that I have only loved you and I have always done only what is favourable for you. The criticism you are facing in the kingdom is due to me. It is my responsibility to do whatever will cleanse you of such censure. Therefore, you continue to live in a way that you never lose your fame or reputation among the people, and I will live like a committed wife should, doing whatever is agreeable to you."' Lakshmana took the message and left. He was sobbing loudly by then. Seetā stood still, looking at the chariot moving away. Then she sat down and began crying even more profusely as if the dam of restraint had been broken by the force of grief.[1]

Some young students of Rishi Vālmiki saw Seetā in that state and informed their guru about it. Rishi Vālmiki brought Seetā to his āshram. This became her home for the rest of her life. She gave birth to twins—Lava and Kusha—in Rishi Vālmiki's āshram. The rishi took the boys as his disciples and taught them all that a prince should know. Lava and Kusha were the first recipients of the Rāmāyana from the rishi. They were singing the Rāmāyana on the streets of Ayodhyā when Rāma spotted them and invited them to sing it in the palace.

When the people of Ayodhyā saw Lava–Kusha, they were astonished by their resemblance with Rāma. Over the course of the rendition of the Rāmāyana in the palace by the boys, the mystery behind their resemblance was revealed. They were Rāma's sons, born through Seetā in Rishi Vālmiki's āshram.

Rāma was delighted but restrained in his expression of joy. He sent a messenger to Rishi Vālmiki to invite him to the palace along with Seetā. 'I do not doubt Seetā at all. I had to forsake her because of the widespread slander about her in the kingdom. If she proclaims her chastity before the people of Ayodhyā, I will accept her back,' his message said. The next day, Rishi Vālmiki came to the palace, with Seetā following him. Before the who's who of Ayodhyā, the rishi proclaimed, 'There has never been a thought of another man in Seetā's mind apart from Rāma.'

Rāma was very happy with Rishi Vālmiki's public endorsement. 'I trust Seetā fully. I am also aware that these two boys are mine. Seetā had already proven herself in Lankā. Now you too have asserted the same. May I be forgiven for letting her go out of fear of public criticism? But I will be happier if she can herself affirm this in front of the people of Ayodhyā, removing vestiges of any doubt in their minds,' he said.

All eyes fell on Seetā. Dressed in saffron like a tapasviṇi, Seetā folded her hands and lowered her eyes, her sight fixed on the ground. She spoke loudly enough for everyone to hear, 'If I have never thought of any man except for Rāma, Mother Earth, I urge you to take me in your lap. If I have worshipped only Rāma with my mind, speech and action, Mother Earth, find me space within you.'

As if on cue, tremors shook Ayodhyā and the earth split wide open where Seetā stood, taking her in as she had desired. The crevice that had opened closed immediately. Seetā was gone forever.

Rāma, the king, her husband, had asked her to testify her character publicly once again. She, being a citizen, a wife and the queen, couldn't have violated the order. Seetā affirmed her chastity openly, that was her duty. But returning to the palace and to Rāma, or not, was not a call of duty—that was a choice she had to make. She chose not to return.

The king had fulfilled his duty towards the citizens. But what about the husband? He put her through this humiliation twice, knowing fully well she was without even a touch of taint.

Seetā didn't complain when Rāma questioned her chastity in Lankā. She understood his issues. She voluntarily took the agni parikshā. She did not even complain when Lakshmana told her that she was forsaken. Dejected and hurt she surely was. But even in her sorrow, she didn't harbour any grudge against Rāma. She understood that the king and queen have to be beyond reproach. Instead, she immersed herself in bringing up her sons. They were princes of Ayodhyā, the future of the Ikshvākus.

Seetā had fulfilled her role as a wife, a queen and a mother to the fullest. Beyond that, she was a woman in her own right. She had protected her dignity in the direst of circumstances in Lankā. She chose, once again, not to bargain her honour for the luxuries of the palace or even Rāma's acceptance. Seetā was the daughter of the earth, and it was on earth that she found her final vindication.[2]

Seetā's character shines dazzlingly bright in this episode. It is impossible not to feel her pain. It is impossible not to be upset with Rāma for the treatment he meted out to her. She deserved better, especially from the man she loved so deeply and sincerely.

Why did Rāma behave so heartlessly when he knew the criticism of Seetā was unfounded? Lakshmana asked the same question, probably rhetorically, to Sumantra who was driving the chariot on the way back, after leaving Seetā in the forest. Sumantra consoled Lakshmana saying that this was all destined. He told Lakshmana about a prediction made by Rishi Durvāsā to Dasharatha about Rāma.

Rishi Durvāsā had told Dasharatha about the curse that Rishi Bhrigu had pronounced on Vishnu for killing his wife. 'Rishi Bhrigu's wife had sheltered the daityas who were a constant source of harassment to the devas. This had angered Vishnu. He slew her for the offence. The rishi put a curse on him for that. "You too will have to suffer the pain of separation from your beloved wife as I am suffering," the rishi had said. To end the menace of Rāvana and establish dharma on earth, Vishnu has been born in human avatār as Rāma. But in this birth, he had to live the curse of Rishi Bhrigu too. The separation of Rāma and Seetā was fated,' concluded Sumantra.[3]

But that doesn't absolve Rāma from taking the decision he took. Our mind boggles at the enormity of his actions because we know he loved Seetā more than his own self. While some people are quick to call him a misogynist, none of his actions suggests he was one. In fact, his entire life had been shaped by the decisions of the women in his life. Kaikeyi got him exiled, Shurpanakhā unleashed Rāvana on him, and eventually, Seetā not only insisted on the never-before-seen deer but also insulted Lakshmana in the worst possible way to make him leave her alone and go to look for Rāma. This gave the opportunity that Rāvana was waiting for to carry her away. In a way, the women led him to achieve the purpose that he was destined for.

Why, then, did Rāma behave the way he did?

Some questions will need to be answered putting ourselves in Rāma's shoes to understand the 'why'.

- When the role of a husband conflicts with the role of a king, which one should take precedence?
- What could have been an alternate approach to handle the issue he faced? What could be the possible short-term and long-term implications of these alternate approaches?
- What kind of behaviour do we expect from our leaders in such situations where their personal and social responsibilities are in conflict?

In most ancient civilisations, the king and queen were expected to be beyond suspicion as people looked up to them. They were expected to set standards of social morality. The king can inspire unquestioned trust from the citizens, who look to him for justice, only when his own life choices are beyond question. The status accorded to the king was akin to God on earth, and so were the expectations from him.

The public censure of Seetā was widespread. If Rāma had insisted on holding on to her, it would be realistic to believe that people would have labelled him lustful like his father. It takes time and effort to build a reputation and just one thoughtless action can break it into smithereens.

The thing about dharma sankata or ethical dilemma is that a choice has to be made among apparently sub-optimal outcomes. The wisdom of the person lies in choosing the least problematic sub-optimal option. Such is life and such is the lesson of the Rāmāyana—public respect, public reverence and public trust demand personal sacrifices. Nor did Rāma have the luxury of giving up the kingdom. To protect and govern the kingdom was his duty, his swadharma. He chose to sacrifice his personal life at the altar of his kingly duties. He chose to be an ideal king at the cost of his duties as a husband.

Is this not what we expect of our leaders too—to put society before self? It is easy to judge Rāma, but not so easy to be Rāma. That requires immense strength of character, absolute clarity of priorities and the ability to withstand emotional pain.

Rāma knew Seetā would understand. She did. Not once did she complain about being forsaken. She understood how painful the situation was for him. In that pain, they were equal partners.

Seetā drew a line when the demands on her crossed the boundary of self-respect and entered the area of humiliation. Rāma had forsaken her to protect his honour; she eventually forsook everyone and everything to protect hers. He never strayed away from his dharma, nor did she!

May Rāma's strength and Seetā's resilience,
May Rāma's valour and Seetā's fortitude,
May Rāma's wisdom and Seetā's commitment,
Forever inspire us!
Jai Siya Ram!

ॐ ψ ॐ

Img. 4 Rāma Sintā (Seetā) in Bali, Indonesia. Photo courtesy: author

NOTES

INTRODUCTION

1 Bāla Kānda 1.2.36.

SUMMARY STORYLINE

1 Resolve to undertake the fire ritual in the prescribed way.

THE DIVINE INSPIRATION

1 Bāla Kānda 1.1.2–1.1.4. कोन्वस्मिन्साम्प्रतं लोके गुणवान्कश्च वीर्यवान्।धर्मज्ञश्च कृतज्ञश्च सत्यवाक्यो दृढव्रत: । चारित्रेण च को युक्तस्सर्वभूतेषु को हित: । विद्वान्क: कस्समर्थश्च कश्चैकप्रियदर्शन: ||1.1.3|| आत्मवान्को जितक्रोधो द्‍तिमान्कोऽनसूयक: । कस्य बिभ्यति देवाश्च जातरोषस्य संयुगे ||1.1.4||

2 Bāla Kānda 1.2.15.

3 The phrase used is वेदोपबृंहणार्थाय meaning that which is meant to reinforce the message of the Vedas. This is mentioned in Bāla Kānda 1.4.6.

4 Bāla Kānda 1.3.8.

5 Uttara Kānda 7.96.19.

6 Skanda Purāna Vaishākhamāsam Mahātmya.

7 'Sankshipta Jeevani' in Vālmiki Rāmāyana, Gita Press, p. 4.

BLOODLINES

1 Three of the four purushārthas of Hindu life are righteousness, enterprise and pleasure. The fourth purushārtha is moksha—liberation from the cycle of birth and death and from the cycle of desire and pain. Translations of the terms are only directional as the terms are a lot more profound. Simply put, they stand for value and actions important for a fruitful and fulfilling life.

2 Bāla Kānda 1.5.1–1.5.4.

3 Bāla Kānda 1.70, Ayodhyā Kānda 2.110.
4 Bāla Kānda 1.66.12–1.66.15.
5 Bāla Kānda 1.71.
6 Tapasyā—physical and mental effort undertaken to achieve a prescribed goal. It involves strict control on sensory organs and single-pointed focus. Typically, the word is translated as 'penance' in English.
7 Uttara Kānda 7.2-7.8.
8 Uttara Kānda 7.9.
9 Brahma deva is considered the grandfather of all beings given his 'Creator' status among the Trideva—Brahmā, Vishnu, Mahesh. In Rāvana's case, Brahma was his great-grandfather by relation as well. Rishi Pulastya, Rāvana's grandfather, was Brahmā's son.
10 Uttara Kānda 7.10.
11 Uttara Kānda sarga 7.12.
12 Uttara Kānda 7.23.17–7.23.18.
13 https://www.ncbi.nlm.nih.gov/pmc/articles/PMC4366788/, https://www.myind.net/Home/viewArticle/kumbhakarna-kleine-levin-syndrome-a-new-theory-about-the-ramayana.
14 Bāla Kānda 1.17.20–1.17.23: The shlokas translate to, 'The devatās, rishis, gandharvas, garudas, yakshas, kimpurushas, siddhas, vidyadharas, uragas and other forest dwellers happily procreated with apsarās, vidhyadaris, nagas and gandharvas, and gave birth to gigantic vānaras who wandered in the forest.' The YouTube channel *21 Notes*, which creates educational videos on Vālmiki Rāmāyana, proposes that the animal names (monkeys, bears, langurs, etc.) have been given due to the way the forest dwelling tribes dressed and presented themselves. Such ways of dressing are still found among the forest dwelling tribes in Amazon, parts of Africa and other places. The epic talks about Hanumāna being learned in Vedas, Vāli performing Sandhyopāsanā and Rāma addressing Sugreeva as his brother, clearly indicating vānaras are not monkeys as we understand today but a tribe of people who also followed many aspects of Vedic civilisation.
15 Kishkindhā is believed to be the present-day Hampi area.

16 Dandaka forest region extended from south of Vindhyas to the south Indian peninsula.
17 Kishkindhā Kānda 4.66.10–4.66.20.
18 *Skānda Purāna* translated by G.V. Tagare.

CITIES AND CITY LIFE IN THE RĀMĀYANA

1 The word used is महापुरी.
2 One yojana is equivalent to about 8 miles or 13 kilometres.
3 Bāla Kānda 1.5–1.7.
4 Kishkindhā Kānda 4.33,1-4.33.17.
5 Uttara Kānda 7.11.
6 Sundara Kānda 5.2–5.4.

VISHVĀMITRA'S QUEST

1 Yajna vedi is an altar in which the yajna (fire ritual) is conducted.
2 Bāla Kānda 1.18–1.21.
3 Bāla Kānda 1.22.
4 Present-day Bihar region, around the districts of Bhagalpur and Munger. In the Mahābhārata, Karna's foster parents—Adhirath and Rādhā—came from Angadesh. Duryodhana conferred the title of this janapada on Karna.
5 Bāla Kānda 1.23.2.
6 The word used is 'चातुर्वर्ण्यहितार्थाय'—for the welfare of people belonging to all four varnas.
7 It was believed that the power of the rākshasas became more potent at night.
8 Bāla Kānda 1.23–1.27.
9 In the Hindu world view, Vishnu takes ten births, or Dashāvatār, to establish dharma on earth. Nine avatārs have already taken place; the tenth one, the Kalki avatār, is yet to happen. Vāmana avatār is the fifth one, in which Vishnu is born as a dwarf child of Rishi Kashyap and his wife Aditi.
10 Mānavāstra, Agneyāstra, Vayavyāstra are different kinds of arrows and missiles that were used in warfare.
11 Bāla Kānda 1.30.
12 Purohit is a priest who conducts ceremonial rituals.
13 Bāla Kānda 1.66.13–1.66.24.

THE MAKING OF VISHVĀMITRA

1 Vāchaspatyam—ऋषति ज्ञानेन संसारपारं ऋषी गतौ.
2 सर्वजन हिताय, सर्वजन सुखाय.
3 Shabda Kalpadruma—ब्रह्म वेदं परब्रह्म वा ऋषति वेत्ति इति.
4 One akshauhini army comprises 21,870 chariots, 65,610 horses, 21,870 elephants and 1,09,350 soldiers on foot.
5 Bāla Kānda 1.52. The imagery of Shabalā is beautifully explained in *21 Notes*, a YouTube channel presenting the stories of Vālmiki Rāmāyana. Shabalā is seen as the chief administrative officer of Rishi Vashishtha's āshram. Her efficiency and resourcefulness impressed Kaushik, who felt that someone as good as Shabalā should belong to the royal palace. The appearance of warriors from her 'moo' is explained as the people dwelling in forest around the āshram who shared a symbiotic dependency on the āshram. These people assembled at Shabalā's call to protect the āshram.
6 Bāla Kānda 1.53.
7 Bāla Kānda 1.58–1.60.
8 Bāla Kānda 1.63.
9 Bāla Kānda 1.64.
10 Bāla Kānda 1.65.

AHALYĀ

1 Uttara Kānda 7.30.22–7.30.23.
2 Surashreshtha—the best among Suras. Suras are deities in the Hindu pantheon.
3 While the word used for Gautama's punishment to both Indra and Ahalyā is 'shaptvān', that is, 'cursed', a distinction is made here—curse for Indra and atonement for Ahalyā. The reason is apparent in Gautam's words itself. Unlike Indra, who has been cursed with impotency, Gautama doesn't proclaim any lifelong affliction on Ahalyā; rather, he tells her the way to make amends for the folly in a manner that will help her achieve mastery on her own self.
4 Bāla Kānda 1.48.11–1.48.33.
5 Bāla Kānda 1.49.11. The word used is देवरूपिणी—one who is in the form of the divine.

6 Ahalyā, Draupadi, Kunti, Tārā and Mandodari are the five illustrious women of Indian epics. In some variants, Seetā is included instead of Kunti.

THE DESCENT OF GANGĀ

1 'Lectures on Rāmāyana' by Professor B. Mahadevan on YouTube channel, *Practical Vedanta IIMB*; stories of the Rāmāyana on YouTube channel *21 Notes*.

A TWIST OF FATE

1 Gandharvas were considered experts in all forms of arts, especially music and dance. Gāndharva shreshtha implies the best among Gandharvas. Rāma was that proficient in music and art.
2 Ayodhyā Kānda 2.1.
3 This line is the author's inference. The text doesn't say anything more than Dasharatha being in a hurry for not inviting Kekaya and Mithilā.
4 Ayodhyā Kānda 2.2.
5 According to Hindu astrology, there are twenty-seven prominent stars in constellations around the earth's elliptical orbit. These stars or groups of stars are called nakshatras. Their positions are considered to decide auspicious time to perform any major activity. The moon goes around the earth in 27.5 days, spending roughly a day in every nakshatra. Pushya is one such nakshatra which falls in the Karka or Cancer constellation. When the moon appears in conjunction with Pushya, it is said to be the time of that nakshatra.
6 Ayodhyā Kānda 2.3.38–2.3.45.
7 Ayodhyā Kānda 2.4.
8 Ayodhyā Kānda 2.7.
9 Ayodhyā Kānda 2.8.5–2.8.7, 2.8.22–2.8.39.
10 A special room in palaces where a queen would stay to show her disapproval or anger. Without having to say it aloud, the presence in the room was enough to convey the mood of the person. Krodhāgār literally means anger-house.
11 Ayodhyā Kānda 2.9.1–2.9.33.
12 Ayodhyā Kānda 2.10.23.

13 Ayodhyā Kānda 2.10.29–2.10.34.
14 Ayodhyā Kānda 2.12.99—Kaikeyi doesn't use these exact words when she first makes her demand. Rather, she elaborates her request. But the intent is the same.
15 Ayodhyā Kānda 2.11.1–2.11.28.
16 Ayodhyā Kānda 2.12.7–2.12.16.
17 Ayodhyā Kānda 2.12.42–2.12.49.
18 Ayodhyā Kānda 2.18.
19 Ayodhyā Kānda 2.19.14–2.19.16.
20 Ayodhyā Kānda 2.19.
21 Ayodhyā Kānda 2.20.
22 Ayodhyā Kānda 2.21.2–2.21.6, 2.21.12–2.21.13.
23 Ayodhyā Kānda 2.21.21–2.21.22, 2.21.25–2.21.27.
24 Ayodhyā Kānda 2.21.34–2.21.50.
25 Ayodhyā Kānda 2.22.8–2.22.24.
26 Ayodhyā Kānda 2.31.11–2.31.14.
27 Ayodhyā Kānda 2.31.21–2.31.23.
28 Ayodhyā Kānda 2.34.24–2.34.37.
29 Ayodhyā Kānda 2.37.6–2.37.16.
30 Ayodhyā Kānda 2.37.23–2.37.24.
31 Ayodhyā Kānda 2.32.15–2.32.28.
32 Ayodhyā Kānda 2.52.61–2.52.62.
33 Ayodhyā Kānda 2.74.6–2.74.7.
34 Ayodhyā Kānda 2.103.30, 2.104.13–2.104.15.
35 Ayodhyā Kānda 2.106.
36 Ayodhyā Kānda 2.108.
37 Ayodhyā Kānda 2.109, 2.110.1–2.110.2.
38 Ayodhyā Kānda 2.112.23–2.112.25.

SAHADHARMACHĀRINI

1 A valiant act, very difficult to achieve.
2 Ayodhyā Kānda 2.26.5–2.26.8.
3 Ayodhyā Kānda 2.26.19–2.26.26.
4 Ayodhyā Kānda 2.27.
5 Ayodhyā Kānda 2.28.
6 Ayodhyā Kānda 2.30.3–2.30.4.
7 Ayodhyā Kānda 2.60.8–2.60.12.
8 A set of daily rituals which are expected to be performed by Hindus. These include, snana (bathing), sandhyāvandanam and agnihotram, among others.

9 Ayodhyā Kānda 2.94.
10 Aranya Kānda 3.2.18–3.2.19.
11 Aranya Kānda 3.6.11–3.6.14.
12 Aranya Kānda 3.9.
13 Aranya Kānda 3.10.3–3.10.6, 3.10.20.
14 Aranya Kānda 3.11.24–3.11.26.
15 Aranya Kānda 3.13.3–3.13.4.
16 Aranya Kānda 3.17.24–3.17.28.
17 Aranya Kānda 3.18.2–3.18.3.
18 Aranya Kānda 3.18.9–3.18.10.
19 Aranya Kānda 3.18.14–3.18.21.
20 Aranya Kānda 3.34.15–3.34.25.
21 Aranya Kānda 3.33.
22 Aranya Kānda 3.37.
23 Aranya Kānda 3.37.13.
24 In common tales, Māreech is a said to take the form of a golden deer but in Vālmiki Rāmāyana, he takes the form of a unique multi-coloured deer.
25 Aranya Kānda 3.43.
26 Aranya Kānda 3.45.5–3.45.8.
27 Aranya Kānda 3.45.22–3.45.34.
28 Aranya Kānda 3.47.33–3.47.42.
29 Aranya Kānda 3.49.17.
30 Aranya Kānda 3.56.24–3.56.25.
31 Aranya Kānda 3.58.2–3.58.11, 3.59.2.
32 Aranya Kānda 3.59.22–3.59.24.
33 Aranya Kānda 3.60.10–3.60.11.
34 Aranya Kānda 3.62.14–3.62.15, 3.63.5–3.63.6.
35 Aranya Kānda 3.64.71–3.64.72.
36 Aranya Kānda 3.65.4–3.65.16.
37 Aranya Kānda 3.66.5–3.66.10.
38 Sundara Kānda 5.15.23–5.15.27.
39 Sundara Kānda 5.15.32–5.15.34, the shloka is ताम् स्मृतीम् इव संदिग्धाम् ऋद्धिम् निपतिताम् इव, विहताम् इव च श्रद्धाम् आशाम् प्रतिहताम् इव, स उपसर्गाम् यथा सिद्धिम् बुद्धिम् सकलुषाम्, अभूतेन अपवादेन कीर्तिम् निपतिताम् इव ।।
40 Sundara Kānda 5.15.52.
41 Sundara Kānda 5.20.
42 Sundara Kānda 5.21.

43 Sundara Kānda 5.22.8–5.22.9.
44 Sundara Kānda 5.24.8–5.24.10.
45 Sundara Kānda 5.24.18–5.24.19.
46 Sundara Kānda 5.35.46–5.35.49.
47 Sundara Kānda 5.37.46–5.37.47, 5.37.48–5.37.52, 5.37.57, 5.37.62–5.37.63.
48 Sundara Kānda 5.38.11–5.38.40.
49 Sundara Kānda 5.65.25.
50 Sundara Kānda 5.66.10–5.66.11.
51 Yuddha Kānda 6.112.24–6.112.26.
52 Yuddha Kānda 6.113.
53 Yuddha Kānda 6.113.49.
54 Yuddha Kānda 6.114.5–6.114.7.
55 Yuddha Kānda 6. 114.18, 6.114.32–6.114.35.
56 Yuddha Kānda 6.115.2–6.115.6, 6.115.15–6.115.24.
57 Yuddha Kānda 6.116.3–6.116.15.
58 Yuddha Kānda 6.116.18–6.116.19.
59 Yuddha Kānda 6.116.20–6.116.21.
60 Yuddha Kānda 6.116.25–6.116.30, 6.116.33–6.116.34.

KINSHIP IN KISHKINDHĀ

1 Sandhyopāsanā—sandhyā upāsanā—ritual prayer prescribed by scriptures for people of Sanātana Dharma, offered at dawn, dusk and noon, to the Sun—Savitr.
2 Kishkindhā Kānda 4.11.
3 Uttara Kānda 7.34.
4 Kishkindhā Kānda 4.8.9–4.8.10.
5 Kishkindhā Kānda 4.5.11–4.5.15.
6 Kishkindhā Kānda 4.11.22–4.11.68.
7 Kishkindhā Kānda 4.11.69–4.11.81.
8 Kishkindhā Kānda 4.11.83–4.11.90.
9 Kishkindhā Kānda 4.12.1–4.12.5.
10 Kishkindhā Kānda 4.12.21–4.12.42.
11 Kishkindhā Kānda 4.15.3–4.15.30.
12 Kishkindhā Kānda 4.16.
13 Kishkindhā Kānda 4.17.
14 Kishkindhā Kānda 4.18.4–4.18.12.
15 Kishkindhā Kānda 4.18.13–4.18.21.
16 Kishkindhā Kānda 4.18.22.

17 Kishkindhā Kānda 4.18.25–4.18.33.

18 Kishkindhā Kānda 4.18.37–4.18.40. A point to be noted here is that Rāma has called Sugreeva as his brother. Later, Bharata hugs Hanumāna, calling him his brother. We are told about Vāli performing Sandhyopāsanā, and about Hanumāna being learned in the scriptures. All these facts must be kept in mind while reading this explanation of Rāma. He categorically states the crime of Vāli that necessitated punishment. Such rules of civilisation are valid only for a society of humans, not animals. Neither does Rāma call Vāli an animal by himself. This argument of hunting is in response to Vāli's, where he positions himself as an animal while questioning his killing.

19 The reference to *Manusmriti* verses is mentioned as a note in Srimad Vālmiki Rāmāyana, Volume 1, published by Gita Press, page 797.

20 Kishkindhā Kānda 4.18.50–4.18.56.

21 Kishkindhā Kānda 4.22.3–4.22.14.

22 Kishkindhā Kānda 4.22.20–4.22.24.

23 Kishkindhā Kānda 4.30.81–4.30.82, 4.31.1–4.31.7.

24 Kishkindhā Kānda 4.32.1–4.32.22.

25 Kishkindhā Kānda 4.34.

26 Kishkindhā Kānda 4.35.

27 Kishkindhā Kānda 4.40.9–4.40.15

28 Kishkindhā Kānda 4.44.6–4.44.13.

29 Yuddha Kānda 6.20.9–6.20.28.

30 Yuddha Kānda 6.22.44–6.22.46.

31 Yuddha Kānda 6.22.52–6.22.74.

32 Yuddha Kānda 6.66.20–6.66.25.

33 Yuddha Kānda 6.41.4–6.41.7.

34 'Nāgapāsh' literally means a weapon which binds the opponent with snakes. This could also allude to weapons or arrows which may have been dipped in snake poison and when hit, the poison spreads in the opponent's body.

35 Garuda is a bird of the eagle family and is supposed to be a nemesis of snakes. Here it could also refer to people who had an antidote to snake poison. In the Hindu belief system, Garuda is the vāhan of Vishnu. As Rāma is considered a Vishnu avatār, the arrival of Garuda has a

special significance here. The Garuda is believed to have to come to save his master in need.

36 Yuddha Kānda 6.101.31–6.101.32.

37 https://www.planetayurveda.com/library/ayapan-eupatorium-triplinerve/.

38 https://www.ncbi.nlm.nih.gov/pmc/articles/PMC4623628/.

39 https://pubmed.ncbi.nlm.nih.gov/16184012/; https://pubmed.ncbi.nlm.nih.gov/30087785/.

40 https://www.ncbi.nlm.nih.gov/pmc/articles/PMC5512407/.

41 Yuddha Kānda 6.120.5–6.120.13.

42 Kishkindhā Kānda 4.40.30.

43 Interested readers must check out the talks of Shri Nilesh Nilkantha Oak on *Sugreeva's Atlas*. There are other blogs such as https://vediccafe.blogspot.com/ which also discuss Sarga 40–43 of Kishkindhā Kānda in detail.

VĀYUPUTRA

1 Kishkindhā Kānda 4.2.1–4.2.27.

2 Kishkindhā Kānda 4.3.1–4.3.18.

3 Kishkindhā Kānda 4.3.19–4.3.24.

4 Kishkindhā Kānda 4.3.36–4.3.39.

5 Kishkindhā Kānda 4.3.28–4.3.34.

6 Kishkindhā Kānda 4.53.8–4.53.19.

7 Kishkindhā Kānda 4.53.25–4.53.27.

8 Kishkindhā Kānda 4.54.

9 By this, Angada is referring to the time when Vāli was thought to be dead in the tussle with Māyāvi in a cave, whose mouth was blocked by Sugreeva assuming Māyāvi had killed Vāli. Everyone believed Sugreeva and crowned him the king. As per the norms of the community, Vāli's widow Tārā accepted Sugreeva as her husband. But as it was found later, Vāli was alive and Māyāvi was the one who was killed. Angada is suggesting that Sugreeva was intentionally lying about Vāli to obtain his wife and kingdom.

10 Kishkindhā Kānda 4.55.

11 This note is given in Vālmiki Rāmāyana published by Gita Press, Gorakhpur, page 820.

12 Vachaspatyam, Shabda Kalpadruma give *Kāmāndakiya* 4.22 as the source of this verse.
13 More often, the word spoken of is दाम. The original Sanskrit word is as indeed दान. The meaning conveyed through in both cases is the same.
14 The words used are bala, buddhi, teja, sattva.
15 'Hanu' is a Sanskrit word which means 'jaw'. Hanumāna is one who has a disfigured jaw. It could also mean one with a prominent jaw.
16 Kishkindhā Kānda 4.66.
17 Sundara Kānda 5.1.152–5.1.168.
18 Sundara Kānda 5.1.184-198. The text mentions this episode in the form of a giant-sized demoness Simhikā. The description of the event says that the demoness captured Hanumāna's shadow. The pull was so strong that he just couldn't move. This appears to the author to be some place akin to the much talked about Bermuda Triangle, an area with probably a very strong magnetic field or something like a vortex in the sea that pulls into it everything in its vicinity.
19 Sundara Kānda 5.1.131.
20 Sundara Kānda 5.9.29–5.9.73.
21 Sundara Kānda 5.10.
22 Sundara Kānda 5.11.37–5.11.44.
23 Sundara Kānda 5.12.5–5.12.9, 5.13.1–5.13.48.
24 Sundara Kānda 5.12.10–5.12.11.
25 Sundara Kānda 5.13.49–5.13.51.
26 The ashta siddhis are mentioned in many Hindu scriptures including *Shiva Purāna*, *Yoga Vashishtha* and *Skanda Purāna*, among others.
27 Sundara Kānda 5.41.5–5.41.9.
28 Sundara Kānda 5.46.8–5.46.13.
29 Sundara Kānda 5.42–5.48.
30 Sundara Kānda 5.49.14–5.49.18.
31 Sundara Kānda 5.50, 5.51.2–5.51.3.
32 Sundara Kānda 5.51.1–5.51.29.
33 Sundara Kānda 5.52.
34 The word used is लाङ्ल which, in addition to tail, also means penis or male organ—शेफ. Vachaspatyam gives both meanings of langula.

35 Sundara Kānda 5.53.
36 Sundara Kānda 5.52.
37 Sundara Kānda 5.53.34–5.53.35.
38 Sundara Kānda 5.53.26–5.53.31.
39 Sundara Kānda 5.53.38.
40 Sundara Kānda 5.53.16.
41 Sundara Kānda 5.64.42–5.64.43.
42 Yuddha Kānda 6.1.2–6.1.14.
43 Yuddha Kānda 6.125.12–6.125.18.
44 Sundara Kānda 5.1.201.

THE TRAP OF LUST

1 Uttara Kānda 7.14–7.34.
2 Uttara Kānda 7.15.
3 Sundara Kānda 5.49.17–5.49.18.
4 Uttara Kānda 7.16.
5 The phrase used was 'rāvitam bhayam āgatam', meaning 'screamed overcome with fear'.
6 Yuddha Kānda 6.6–6.7.
7 Yuddha Kānda 6.12.28–6.12.35.
8 Yuddha Kānda 6.13.10–6.13.15.
9 Uttara Kānda 7.24.1–7.24.20.
10 Yuddha Kānda 6.60.10.
11 Uttara Kānda 7.17.
12 Uttara Kānda 6.26–6.26.27.
13 Yuddha Kānda 6.9.
14 Yuddha Kānda 6.14.17–6.14.25.
15 Yuddha Kānda 6.15.1–6.15.5.
16 The word used is कुलपांसन—kulapāsana; kula—community, pāsana—disgrace.
17 Yuddha Kānda 6.16.3–6.16.17.
18 This is a very famous and oft repeated shloka—सुलभा पुरुषा राजन सततं प्रियवादिन: । अप्रियस्य च पथ्यसय वक्ता श्रोता च दुर्लभ: ।।
19 Yuddha Kānda 6.16.19–6.16.26.
20 Yuddha Kānda 6.25.28–6.25.33.
21 Yuddha Kānda 6.26.1–6.26.4.
22 Yuddha Kānda 6.29.8–6.29.14, 6.29.20, 6.30.
23 Yuddha Kānda 6.34.20–6.34.23.
24 Yuddha Kānda 6.35.6–6.35.10.

25 Yuddha Kānda 6.59.26–6.59.31.
26 Charioteer.
27 Yuddha Kānda 6.59.
28 Yuddha Kānda 6.92.20, 6.92.64–6.92.65.
29 Yuddha Kānda 6.94.
30 Yuddha Kānda 6.100.
31 Yuddha Kānda 6.102.15–6.102.17.
32 Yuddha Kānda 6.103.28–6.103.31.
33 Yuddha Kānda 6.104.
34 Even today, this strota is recited in Hindu homes exactly as Rishi Agastya had taught Rāma. It occurs in Yuddha Kānda Sarga 105. A strota is a hymn of praise, or a prayer.
35 Yuddha Kānda 6.105.
36 Yuddha Kānda 6.107.51–6.107.52.
37 Yuddha Kānda 6.107.
38 Yuddha Kānda 6.108.
39 Yuddha Kānda 6.111.15–6.111.29.
40 Srimad Bhagavad Geetā 2.62–2.63.

THE DIFFICULTY OF BEING GOOD

1 How did Rāvana, Vibhishana and other rākshasas cross the ocean when Rāma and others couldn't? There is no clear-cut answer to this in the literature of the period. Today we can only make guesses about it.
It seems that the rākshasa tribe either had the physical power or technology that allowed them to cross the ocean, which the others didn't. The technology development could have been indigenous as Lankā was an island and the people would have felt the need to travel to other places. We are told about Kuber having the Pushpak vimān, which shows that technology may have preceded Rāvana's rule in Lankā.
2 Yuddha Kānda 6.17.
3 Yuddha Kānda 6.18.
4 Yuddha Kānda 6.19.1–6.19.27.
5 Yuddha Kānda 6.25.13—6.25.14.
6 Yuddha Kānda 6.37.6–6.37.24.
7 Yuddha Kānda 6.46.30–6.46.44.
8 Yuddha Kānda 6.84.10–6.84.19.

9 Yuddha Kānda 6.89.1–6.89.7.
10 Yuddha Kānda 6.87.11–6.87.17.
11 Yuddha Kānda 6.87.18–6.87.27.
12 Yuddha Kānda 6.89.17–6.89.18.
13 Yuddha Kānda 6.88.49–6.88.50.
14 Yuddha Kānda 6.100.17–6.100.27.
15 Yuddha Kānda 6.109.22–6.109.25.
16 Uttara Kānda 7.10.30–7.10.34.

SOUMITRI

1 Ayodhyā Kānda 2.46.4–2.46.9.
2 Ayodhyā Kānda 2.51.
3 Ayodhyā Kānda 2.58.17–2.58.31.
4 Ayodhyā Kānda 2.53.6-2.53.8.
5 Ayodhyā Kānda 2.53.9–2.53.27.
6 Some commentators are of the opinion that Rāma's lament was meant to test Lakshmana's resolve about continuing the vanvās. The last line does seem to indicate that. On the other hand, Rāma has lamented more than once in varying degrees, especially after Seetā's abduction. Possibly, Rāma wanted to assess Lakshmana's resolve, as he had done with Bharata also before returning to Ayodhyā after completing vanvās. But his concern for his mother seems very genuine too.
7 Kishkindhā Kānda 4.1.120–4.1.122; the word used is 'utsāha'. The word has a range of meanings including zeal, perseverance, fortitude, firmness, enthusiasm, joy and happiness, among others. In the context which Lakshmana uses it, perseverance seems more apt as he is encouraging Rāma to not lose hope and continue to act.
8 This seems to be a reference to present-day Mārwār region in Rajasthan. Mārwār is called Māru Pradesh.
9 Yuddha Kānda 6.21.13–6.21.35.
10 An implication stated here is that had Rāma abided by the truth, none of these miseries would have befallen him.
11 Yuddha Kānda 6.83.14–6.83.44.
12 Flowers of Palāsh are red in colour. The bloodied bodies of Lakshmana and Indrajeet are given the analogy of flowering Palāsh trees.
13 Uttara Kānda 1.28.

14 Ayodhyā Kānda 2.40.9.

RĀMO VIGRAHAVĀN DHARMA

1 Here Dharma implies Yama. Yama is considered the deity of death and Dharma. He is responsible for ensuring justice based on one's karma, post death.
2 Bāla Kānda 1.1.17–1.1.18.
3 Bāla Kānda 1.78.
4 Yuddha Kānda 6.67.
5 Yuddha Kānda 6.79.
6 Yuddha Kānda 6.93.
7 Srimad Bhagavad Geetā 10.31.
8 Ayodhyā Kānda 2.12.29—सत्येन लोकान् जयति दीनान् दानेन राघवः| गुरून् शुश्रूषया वीरो धनुशा युधि शात्रवान् ||
9 It is a type of hell reserved for those who don't have children per certain Puranas. In general, it is to be understood as a worthy child who delivers his/her parents from falling into undesirable conditions.
10 Ayodhyā Kānda 2.1.
11 Ayodhyā Kānda 2.2.

RĀMA'S RĀJYA

1 Bāla Kānda 1.25.16–1.25.18.
2 Bāla Kānda 1.1.90–1.1.93. प्रहृष्टमुदितो लोकस्तुष्टः पुष्टः सुधार्मिकः | निरामयो ह्यरोगश्च दुर्भिक्षभयवर्जितः | न चापि क्षुद्भयं तत्र न तस्करभयं तथा| नगराणि च राष्ट्राणि धनधान्ययुतानि च ||
3 Yuddha Kānda 6.128. सर्वं मुदितमेवासीत्सर्वो धर्मपरो अभवत् | स्वकर्मसु प्रवर्तन्ते तुष्ठाः स्वैरेव कर्मभिः | निरामया विशोकाश्च रामे राज्यं प्रशासति ||
4 Ayodhyā Kānda 2.100.

SHAMBUKA VADHA

1 Uttara Kānda 7.73–7.76.

FORSAKEN

1 Uttara Kānda 7.43–7.49.
2 Uttara Kānda 7.95–7.97.
3 Uttara Kānda 7.50–7.51.

ALSO FROM THE AUTHOR

Mahabharata Unravelled

LESSER-KNOWN FACETS OF A WELL-KNOWN HISTORY

AMI GANATRA

BLOOMSBURY

ISBN – 9789354351273 Price – 599

Paperback Pages – 406